An Unsettled Score
The Collected Twisted Visions
of Christopher L. DelGuercio

by Christopher L. DelGuercio

Phase 5 Publishing, LLC

Publication Data

PHASE 5
PHASE 5 PUBLISHING, LLC
PO BOX 392
Swannanoa, NC 28778
www.phase5publishing.com
Please contact Phase 5 for information about bulk purchase discounts for book clubs and other groups. Retailers may purchase through their distributor, or directly from Phase 5.

Some of the works included in this collection were previously published:
"Eden Succeeding" by *Twenty or Less Press* (digital), July 2014; by Phase 5 Publishing, September 2016; in *Three Tales of Horror* from Phase 5 Publishing, 2016
"Man Farm" in *OG's Speculative Fiction*, July 2007
"Béba Daio's Prayers" in *Parade of Phantoms: The Magazine of Haunting Fiction*, November 2007
"Catch The Starway Pass, Put It in Your Pocket" by *Space Westerns*, July 2008
"Jesus Christ Supersize" in *Blood, Blade & Thruster Magazine*, December 2007
"Every Good Stud Comes to His Senses" *Total Quality Reading*, 2016
"Metal With Me" in *Kaleidotrope Magazine*, October 2007
"Unbreakable Yu" in *Fried Fiction*, November 2013

Phase 5 Elements:
Anthology 20
Transmutation 195
Other Worlds 57

Horror, science fiction, speculative fiction. Cosmology, galactic civilization, aliens, mutation, occult, reality manipulation, colonization, dystopia, humor, new weird, supernatural.

Adult readers: violence; brief, mildly-graphic sexual situations; cursing; death; mutation; irreverence.

Book Cover and stone monolith Xs by Rebecca Ledford, cover design uses Adobe Stock images by Rassamee design, Frans, jkraft5, Filippo Carlot, Pituk, stockquest, standret, neosiam, pinglabel, waranyu, Jeffrey, jonnysek, hjschneider, pandaclub23, Sebastian, sunet; and "Mexican Calendar Stone", Museo Nacional, Mexico as found in *Symbols, Signs & Signets*, Copyright by Ernst Lehner, published by Dover Publications, Inc, some of which were used in the interior as well. An image from Victorian Ornamental Designs, Copyright 2007 by Dover Publications, Inc., published by Dover Publications, Inc. All images used with license/permission (no generative AI).
First Edition 2023

ISBN 978-1-942342-01-4 Kindle
ISBN 978-1-942342-03-8 KDP Trade Paperback
ISBN 978-1-942342-04-5 KDP Hardback
Printed and distributed by Amazon through KDP, in the United States of America and worldwide.

ISBN 978-1-942342-00-7 Barnes & Noble Hardback
ISBN 978-1-942342-15-1 Barnes & Noble Paperback
ISBN 978-1-942342-16-8 Barnes & Noble Pocket Paperback (Mass Market)

ISBN 978-19942342-06-9 Ingram Hardback
ISBN 978-19942342-05-2 Ingram Paperback
ISBN 978-19942342-07-6 Ingram Pocket Paperback (Mass Market)
ISBN 978-19942342-08-3 Ingram epub

Praise for Christopher L. DelGuercio

For *An Unsettled Score*

"Chris DelGuercio's collection of short stories *An Unsettled Score,* takes the reader on a wild ride. These are dark and creepy tales, with a touch of surrealism, and more than a touch of twisted humor. DelGuercio is a master craftsman. His style is terse and distilled—not a word or sentence is wasted—and he has an ear for dialogue that rings true, regardless of character or setting. The collection is unified by DelGuercio's unique sensibility, yet the stories are wonderfully varied, keeping the reading experience fresh and surprising. What a rich and mysterious imagination this author has." **--David G Moore, author, *Kings Canyon, Stick People, and Harpies***

"In this collection of original short pieces, *An Unsettled Score*, Chris DelGuercio provides a rich feast for the science fiction and horror fan. His stories, poems and longer fiction offer enough variety to satisfy everyone with a taste for the bizarre, the offbeat and the truly terrifying. Several of the stories, such as *Man Farm* and *Shi'Roc*, are very reminiscent of the works of the famed science fiction/horror writer Ray Bradbury (*The Martian Chronicles*) and display the same sense of carefully twisted reality that the master writer is known for. In the former, a child plays with a version of an ant farm whose inhabitants are suspiciously…familiar. In the latter, a seasoned hunter on a wild planet tracks a trophy animal with a surprising identity.

"Several of the stories here are truly outstanding in terms of rising suspense. In *Tempus Servivit,* DelGuercio introduces us to a criminal sentenced to undergo an experimental treatment at a mysterious facility run by a much-too-dedicated team of doctors. What seems like a godsend to the patient may actually be something quite different. In my personal favorite story in the collection, *Unbreakable Yu,* a young woman forced into degradation uses her wits and powers of deception to attempt to secure freedom for herself and a remarkable creature. The highlight here: a tense battle between two trained animal athletes. Finally, *Dark Men, Dark Machines* takes the reader on an intricate journey into an incredible world to reveal what it means to be human, as well as inhuman.

"A few words about direct dialogue: These stories have it in spades. Using large sections of dialogue intermingled with scenes of tension-filled description creates an engrossing dynamic that combines slowly unraveling details with throat-gripping action. It's a daring combo that makes DelGuercio's prose stand out from that of many other fantasy writers.

"For all those who favor horror and science fiction – and all areas in between or intermingled – the stories in this collection will open new pathways of frightening discovery. **--Megan Davidson, Author of *Once a Rogue* and *The Thundering***

"Chris takes the reader on a grand and excellent tour of the genre. We grapple with time travel, space travel, aliens and androids, and even a few degrees of Kevin Bacon. His experience and joy of writing come through to give us what is truly a wonderful read." **--Brian Barfoot**

"Stephen King… Ray Bradbury… J. R. R. Tolkien… Christopher DelGuercio… yes, DelGuercio deserves to be mentioned right alongside these other authors. Not only is his work reminiscent of them, but like these other authors, DelGuercio creates his own fantasy worlds where he takes his readers on incredible journeys into the unknown. In this collection, the reader can find flights of fancy, dystopian worlds, philosophical sensibility, and pure entertainment for those who love science fiction. Whether you choose to read just one story at a time as a delicious treat, or devour the entire book as a meal, I promise you will not be disappointed." **--Jill LeClair**

"Fantastic collection of fantastical stories!
"There's something for everyone in Christopher L. DelGuercio's *An Unsettled Score* with its twenty (score, get it?) twisted tales of fantasy, science fiction, futuristic, dystopian worlds, and unsettling horror. Each original creation is more captivating than the last. DelGuercio does not disappoint! His writing and storytelling are so immersive and so captivating, I found myself on various occasions not being able to wait to get home to finish a story or start the next one.

"The follow-up to his captivating novella, *Eden Succeeding* (an included bonus in this collection), DelGuercio's *An Unsettled Score* is a series of love letters and homages to some of fiction's masters like King, Asimov, Gaiman and Dick. Often, I found myself forgetting I wasn't, in fact, reading one of those authors, which can only be taken as the highest compliment to DelGuercio's gifted and dark imagination as he spins his original, fantastical yarns that immediately grab hold of you and, unapologetically, refuses to let go. From the first provocative entry, *Original Sin* to the unforgettable, captivating storytelling in the last act *Tempus Sevivit*, you will soon see why Christopher L. DelGuercio is quickly becoming the future of fantasy and horror fiction.

"DelGuercio visits the well of the likes of Rod Serling (*The Twilight Zone*), Jeffrey Grant Rice (*The Night Stalker*) and Chris Carter (*The X-Files*) with twisty tales of science fiction, fantasy and make-believe... at times, set in a not-too-distant future. With a personal author's introductory origin story for each entry in this new collection, DelGuercio preps the safety harness of your roller-coaster car before launching you 20 times into the deepest corners of his imagination. So grab onto that harness, hang on tight and enjoy the ride!!" **--Scott Lombardo**

"Full disclosure: I am a sucker for speculative fiction with obvious ties to Ray Bradbury, Harlan Ellison, and old episodes of The Twilight Zone and The Outer Limits. I don't think this is a prerequisite for enjoying Chris DelGuercio's new collection, *An Unsettled Score*. But it does heighten the experience. It can be difficult to bring fresh ideas to oft-used sci-fi tropes such as time travel and failed space colonies, but DelGuercio manages to do just that. There's a little bit of everything here, too. Poetry, flash fiction, longer stories, and even a novella. While the genre is firmly sci-fi/speculative, DelGuercio also adds elements of fantasy, western, and horror to the mix.

"The work is sometimes funny, sometimes dark, and sometimes a fascinating combination of the two. No matter how inventive the concept, the author never forgets to tell a good story. There are plenty of twists, turns, and surprises both delightful and troubling.

"While this collection will make a good read for any lover of speculative fiction, I believe it would also be enjoyed by fans of good writing in general, as well as anyone prone to embracing the strange thoughts that come to them in the middle of the night." **--Mike Seperak**

For Award-Nominated *Eden Succeeding*

"Chris DelGuercio has crafted a fascinating dystopia in Eden Succeeding, wonderfully describing a world that feels like an H.R. Giger painting. I am eager to read more from this upcoming author." -- **David Peters, editor,** *Fried Fiction*

"The classic sci-fi trope -- Earthlings colonizing an alien planet -- finds new life in Christopher DelGuercio's debut novelette which offers a fresh, provocative, and chilling take on what it means to be human. From the ties that bind husband and wife to the concept of survival at all costs, DelGuercio superimposes society's most difficult ethical dilemmas onto a world in which change is the only constant--and places its moral compass in the stained and reluctant hands of The Meatman, a hero whose voice rings heartbreaking and true. While justice on this brave new world may be up for grabs, if there's any justice on Earth this edition will be the first of many subsequent visits to DelGuercio's dangerous and seductive Eden." --**Linda Lowen, award-winning author, columnist, and contributor**

"A positively excellent story… kinky and evocative… without a single padded scene or wasted sentence… It's fast, fun action, but it ain't just filler. Every scene builds on the previous and informs the upcoming… The main characters are believable and nuanced and DelGuercio manages to create emotional investment within the framework of a sci-fi thriller. No small feat. I'm impressed… DelGuercio is one bright spot on a plate of nori. He's like salmon roe." --**TQR Stories**

"Christopher DelGuercio's novelette, *Eden Succeeding*, is a chilling and creative work of speculative fiction. Full of luscious detail, disturbing and disturbed characters, and a haunting sense of dread that lingers long after the book is safely on the shelf. Eden succeeds, not only in completely engaging its readers but also by leaving them yearning for more." --**Megan Davidson, author of** *The Thundering*

Acknowledgements

A big thanks to the Author for having patience with me as I worked the rust off of the publishing machinery, learned what had changed in the industry and with the companies that make it go, and find the courage and stamina to resurrect this company which had lain dormant far too long. And for his willingness to take some pretty considerable editing suggestions on a few pieces, and making these stories the best I think they can be.

Thank you also to our reviewers, ARC readers, and beta readers, for their time and thoughts on these stories, and on the Author as well. You are the secret weapon of publishing.

A special thank you to my beloved, who taught me enough about world building, plot development, and how to travel the genre multiverse with confidence, and who spent many hours spent with me in deep conversation about what does or doesn't make a piece of art, fiction, "film" or a game enjoyable, or even great, and was the audience for my rants about opportunities missed in the same.

A collegial thank you to other publishers, editors, authors and others who routinely share their knowledge, experience, and creativity with the rest of us through podcasts, videos, blogs and more. This is a sometimes soul-crushing industry, and having a community willing to share and contribute to the success of others is invaluable, in business and in personal survival of the business.

Finally, a big thank you to all the folks who purchased or borrowed this book, maybe who are familiar with the Author's work, and maybe who took a gamble on an unknown. Your support keeps independent authors and publishers going. Carry on.

TABLE OF CONTENTS

An Unsettled Score

THE COLLECTED TWISTED VISIONS OF CHRISTOPHER L. DELGUERCIO

DEDICATION

For Gabriel, the dreamer, and for Kathy, the dream.

Foreword
by Linda Lowen

Years ago, long before I ever met Christopher DelGuercio, I'd heard about him. The guy was burning up the internet with publishing credits right and left, and was a first reader for some of the places I'd hoped would accept my work. Back then, I had the idea that I could maybe write fiction. Maybe fantasy, maybe sci-fi, maybe horror. I was already a working writer, but it was work-for-hire stuff: writing that pays the bills.

I took a fiction-writing class with Chris and constantly quizzed him about my WIP (work in progress): "I know the story backwards and forwards. I've built the world and all the characters. But it feels like a garden maze surrounded by a high thick hedge with no breaks."

He nodded, and I popped the big question I'd been wrestling with for years: "How do you know where to enter the tale?"

He laughed. "You just know."

Yeah, Chris. *You* know.

I still don't. Not when it comes to fiction. I'm still writing work-for-hire stuff. I've published two books which I was approached to write. They're rooted in reality, the world we live in every day.

The world inside my head is still inaccessible. Still behind that high thick hedge.

I still can't find the way in.

Chris DelGuercio has always known the way in. And to get his readers there, he uses neither the brute force of a chainsaw nor a fussy pair of pruning shears. I swear he stands there, the branches part, and his readers simply follow him in. He's also not showy. He does the work. Publishes a story here, another one there, then continues to write more. And more. And more.

I'll say it again: He does the work. Which, everyone from me to Stephen King will tell you is how you become successful. You just write. No matter what.

Chris is also a writer in the classical sense. His work is timeless. He doesn't rely on any flavor-of-the-month tropes or ripped-from-the-headlines topics. Nearly any Christopher DelGuercio story that you read today will age well and be just as good five, ten years down the road. He writes the kind of stories that endure.

If he's that good, why haven't you heard of him? I can answer that with authority. Since that first fiction writing class I took with Chris, I've had some doors opened to me, lucky breaks provided by other writer friends. I'm a working book reviewer now, reviewing traditionally-published books for *Publishers Weekly* and self-published books for *Blue Ink Review*. Over the course of six years I've read and reviewed close to 500 books written for adults and children. The thing that every published author wants is the coveted Starred Review. I can name ten books that I've given stars to, and guess what? Eight of them I guarantee you've never heard of. (Don't ask me what they are. I review anonymously, and I'm contractually obligated to keep my mouth shut.) But I can say this, loudly, freely, emphatically: Good writing doesn't equal fame, and vice versa.

Since my classes with Chris—I took three twelve years ago—I've had the chance to attend workshops with writers whom you may have heard of: Jeffrey Ford who's won six World Fantasy awards, three Shirley Jackson awards, and one Nebula; and Gemma Files, winner of the Bram Stoker and Shirley Jackson awards.

Like Chris, they've become friends. I admire their work and point other writers to them.

Writers, you should know, are often asked to endorse or blurb books they may not like, and they do it because it's expected of them, especially when a friend does the asking. Because I'm a paid reviewer, I have dodged many a request to do so, because my recommendations are how I make a living. If I do a favor for a friend and say their work is good when I know it isn't, I hear it from readers who know that I'm a professional reviewer. That harms my credibility, which in turn impacts my livelihood.

When Chris asked me if I'd write a foreword to his latest collection, I didn't hesitate. I said yes because he's that good. He's written tales that, in my humble opinion, measure up to the standards of Ford and Files, both of whom write in the New Weird as does Chris.

In this collection, I'm itching to tell you which pieces are my favorite. But as a theater reviewer for my hometown newspaper—Chris and I are both Syracuse, NY residents—I've learned that part of the joy of discovery is knowing that something is good without knowing too much about *why* it's good. If I lead you down the paths inside that hedge maze, you won't have as much fun as if you'd walked the paths yourself without expectation.

Chris is standing there. The branches are parting. Go on, go ahead. Follow him in. I promise you: dark and twisty adventures await.

Linda Lowen
August 10, 2023

PREFACE

Greetings and salutations, dear reader! Welcome to my mind. A mind filled with fever dreams and futurescapes and worlds of longing. Many thanks to you for purchasing, borrowing, co-opting, checking out from your local library, or procuring by some other means, this here book. But however you have come into possession of this particular tome I assume it must have taken *some* effort on your part, and for that effort, no matter how great or meager, I am grateful to you. You could have chosen to do something, *anything* else really, and instead you chose to pick up this little title and crack open the cover to see what's inside. In the tongue of my ancestors, *gratzi*! I sincerely hope that this collection of the fantastic brings you some enjoyment and entertainment. Now, on to other matters…

A question I am often asked is, *Why do you do this writing thing?* (Or, more specifically, *Why do you write short stories?* We'll get to that part later.) These queries are usually followed by, *Where do you get your ideas?* Eventually getting to the inevitable, *How does one become a writer?* Hopefully all three of these questions (along with quite a few others) will be answered in the paragraphs to follow. So, without any further ado, let's get started, shall we?

Some of the stories that make up this collection originated in my head almost a decade and a half ago. These stories germinated from the smallest seedlings and flowered into fully-fledged narratives over the course of many months, or in some cases, years. Yes, sometimes the ideas for stories come to you and don't evolve into anything concrete for a very long time. Why is this? Sometimes (many times) it's because we grow tired and less fond of them as they take shape (or fail to). We cease to work on them. We don't will them into existence. Perhaps they weren't great ideas to begin with? Perhaps, like unripe fruit, they weren't "ready" to be stories yet? Perhaps we weren't ready to tell them? Who can say? In any event, the tales you see here *did* eventually get written and that's really the important thing, isn't it?

These stories represent quite a few of the musings and the subsequent ramblings I've had over the years. Not all of them, mind you, not by a long shot, but some that I found the time, energy, and motivation to craft into completely edited works of fiction. I have many others, but I don't think they're as good, nor as finished and shiny, as these. Due to that fact, they're not here in this book. They didn't make the cut. If you could read them, you'd probably thank me for that. Now where was I? Ah yes, the musings and ramblings part. When these strange thoughts linger long enough in my gray matter, when I acknowledge them, when I feed them and care for them and protect them and give them the time and space to grow, a funny thing happens: They do just that. They grow! They actually take shape! Because I've allowed them to. This is the main, maybe the only, reason from my perspective that stories ever get written. There are some of us out there who endeavor to take these persistent, offbeat visions we have and create characters and plotlines and settings around them. We have a want to fill them with meaning and feeling, to make sense of them in a way. To make sense of everything that inhabits our little worlds. To build something that didn't previously exist and to do it all in an artful way such that it may move (or even just tickle) someone to read it. That is The Great Hope. That is where some of the satisfaction lies. The most satisfaction we get as authors, of course, is in just doing the damn thing. Making something that is uniquely us, something that we can be proud of. To tell the truth as we see it. This is *why* I write.

Well, there's one answer down.

I have daydreams, meditations, reflections, reveries. I ponder. I'm a big ponderer. I'm sure you are too. The big questions in life interest me, some little ones as well. Anyway, this is where I get my ideas (answer #2, check). This is the fertile soil, the raw material, the lumpy clay (as I often explain it to my students) that the writer starts with. We use this to begin. But then we have to massage, coerce, and practically beg the rest of the story to come out into the light. It's slow, hard work. But it's also honest work. It pays off. The more you do it the easier it all gets (and that's the final answer, of *how* one becomes a writer). If you'd like to become a writer my advice would be to learn to enjoy all the different aspects of it, the messy, formless, subconscious, primordial, creation phase of it as well as the meticulousness of the numerous editing stages. Try to relish all of it, but don't beat yourself up too much if you don't. I don't always start out loving the process, but once I get myself writing, I'm always thankful that I did. So that's the skinny on writing as I understand it, the one I tell my students about, or at least an abridged version of it. But you're probably here to do some reading, so what about these stories, you say?

This collection began to take form in the late summer and early fall of 2021 when I began to take inventory of some of the earlier stories I'd written and published over the course of my career. I originally started writing in earnest around the turn of the millennium. Previous to that I'd spent a good deal of time committed to reading and dedicated study. It was with a metric ton of uncertainty and only after I'd hemmed and hawed for a few years about not being ready that I finally dipped my toes into the water and actually wrote something.

Spurred on by the short fiction of some of my idols: the late Harlan Ellison was a particular favorite of mine, along with masters of the form like Ray Bradbury, Roald Dahl, George R.R. Martin, Richard Matheson, Phillip K. Dick, Kurt Vonnegut, Ursula K. Le Guin, Robert Bloch, Isaac Asimov, Neil Gaiman, Frederik Pohl, Shirley Jackson (I could go on and on, believe me) and some of the terrific weekly television shows of my youth like the *The Twilight Zone, The Night Stalker*, and later on, *The X-Files,* as well as the great Hammer and Amicus Studios portmanteau films that came out of Great Britain in the 1960s and '70s, I fell in love with the short-form narrative. The way you could tell an entire story with a beginning, middle, and end in the span of just a handful of pages, or just a few (or even one). The self-contained nature of it.

The rare ability it had to affect you with so relatively few words. The urgent, dynamic pace. The entire potent nature of its scenes, a perfect distillation of story. This writing moved! It held nothing back, saved nothing for later. Each classic I read seemed to me an expertly conceived, constructed, and polished gem. I secretly wondered if I could perform that same feat for myself.

In truth, I positively yearned to.

Even as a youth I always had a voracious appetite for information and stories. I read whatever was lying around. Books of any kind: fiction, non-fiction, comics, magazines, newspapers, song lyrics, the TV guide, trivia questions, you name it. As a child I owned a paperback book called *Two-Minute Mysteries* by Donald J. Sobol (of *Encyclopedia Brown* fame). This was the more adult version of that detective series though, with the sleuth Dr. Haledjian solving every case with great aplomb. It was full of all sorts of murder and mayhem and, at that young an age, I probably should've been reading *Encyclopedia Brown* instead but we take what we can get. I simply adored that book and, later, I discovered Sir Arthur Conan Doyle and got a big kick out of Sherlock Holmes and Dr. Watson's adventures, too. I was awed by Poe's macabre mystery *The Murders in the Rue Morgue* and Agatha Christie's *And Then There Were None* as well as Lord Dunsany's *Two Bottles of Relish*. The same could be said for the stories of O. Henry. I think as kids we like being entertained by a gripping mystery and then surprised by a good twist (I still do.)

But I always gravitated to tales of the fantastic and the supernatural. I still vividly remember being exposed to Madeleine L'Engle's *A Wrinkle in Time*, Washington Irving's *The Legend of Sleepy Hollow*, and Homer's *The Odyssey* for the very first time early on in grade school. Whether it was reading *Grimms' Fairy Tales*; Jules Verne's *Mysterious Island*; H.G. Wells' *War of the Worlds*; Paul Fenimore Cooper's *Tal: His Marvelous Adventures with Noom-Zor-Noom*; the Arthurian epic *Sir Gawain and the Green Knight;* or watching Shakespeare's *The Tempest* transformed into space opera on my little black-and-white television set in *Forbidden Planet*; the cautionary *Godzilla, King of the Monsters*, or the rousing jungle adventure of *King Kong*, these genre stories simply mesmerized the impressionable younger version of me. As a teen I read the aforementioned Harlan Ellison's award-winning story, *"Repent Harlequin!" Said the Ticktockman* and I was hooked on the written word.

I was enamored with anything and everything science fiction, horror, and fantasy related. Oh, the things you could do with it! What you could say! The old cliché was apt here, the possibilities truly were endless. I immersed myself in all subgenres of it. Sure, I had my favorites, but I respected and revered them all and the storytellers that brought them to life. I realized that my writing could be as diverse as my interests were and there might still be an audience for it, and maybe even a place for me in that hallowed firmament with my literary heroes. It was high time I got to writing some of my own.

As the old adage goes, *Easier said than done.*

The year was 1999 and I produced very little of merit those first few months—first few years if I'm being truthful. I wrote (or started writing) dozens of stories with varying levels of success. I say *varying* because, although the stories weren't great, the effort was. And it was that effort that resulted in me getting better at my craft. Without the experience of pushing through and completing those early not-so-great stories there would've never been the later, more successful ones.

Several years after I committed pen to paper for the very first time (Yes, pen and paper. That's how we did it back then and how I still do it to this day.) I published my first story! I was paid very little money for that piece and was given the alternative choice of, instead of receiving cash, accepting something akin to a swag bag from the e-zine publisher as a form of payment. I declined that perfectly acceptable offer of goodies, opting instead for a scant monetary sum because it seemed more dignified and official somehow. I wanted to be recognized as a real writer, and real writers got paid for their work. I mean, this isn't the barter system. I don't think Stephen King is trading his latest pages for a live chicken or a freshly-baked pie. I'm not some nineteenth-century town doctor exchanging goods and services, I'm a real writer! I need to be paid, thank you.

Sigh.

I must admit that all these years later I kind of wish I had taken their inscribed pens, t-shirt, and coffee mug as payment. The money from that first story is long gone but I'm sure I'd still have the other stuff and I'd probably cherish it. I'd probably call that mug my "writing mug" and I'd fill it with hot cocoa and keep it beside me when I would scrawl new ideas down while sitting in my office or wherever. But I was so young back then. I needed validation. I needed someone to pay me the complement of *actually paying me* for my writing to feel like I was legit. And that's okay. We all need something. I needed to be paid even the slightest amount to give me the confidence to keep writing. It must've worked because I kept at it.

I began to publish regularly from that point on, writing more challenging and complex pieces with each attempt. Gaining more and more confidence. I was (and still am) not terribly prolific. I take long periods of time on my stories. I fuss with them endlessly, considering every option, pouring over every conceivable word choice or plot point or beat selection (I'm doing it right now, in fact, as I edit this introduction to my book.) I'm terribly indecisive—anyone who's ever seen me try to order a meal from a restaurant knows this. I don't regret this character trait but I have to admit it does keep me from producing massive amounts of literature. But I digress.

My second decade of writing was filled with fewer stories, but the ones that I produced were of a much higher quality, methinks. It was in this period that I wrote my book-of-the-year-nominated novella, *Eden Succeeding*, as well as my second published novella, *Every Good Stud Comes To His Senses*, both of which I've included in this collection. I'm a child of the 1970s as well as the '80s, with a foot firmly planted in both decades. I think these eras of storytelling color and inform my work greatly. That great cynicism, the distrust of authority, and rebellious nature that was present in so much of seventies film and literature gave way somewhat to the Spielbergian sentimentality of the eighties. Now, before you jump on me, of course I'm painting these decades' offerings with a wide brush here. I mean the seventies weren't all anti-establishment, don't-trust-the-man, doom and gloom. *Star Wars* is actually subtitled *A New Hope!* And the eighties weren't completely populated with sappy, saccharine fare either. Plenty of subversive voices there. Just watch any John Carpenter or George Romero flick. Or ask Terry Gilliam, Ridley Scott. David Cronenberg, or Jim Cameron about their worldviews. Plenty of bleeding over from one decade to the other. Anyway, I think you get the point I'm making: both decades influenced me. I can be nihilistic. I can be sanguine. My stuff can be pretty dark but then turn a few pages and I'm downright rosy, goofy even. Moving on.

In the middle of that fruitful second decade of writing I took a leave of absence from my work. My personal life had hit a fairly significant bump in the road and it was certainly not conducive to a favorable writing output. I still taught fiction-writing classes, moderated workshops, and began to lecture extensively but my issues had completely sapped my will to create on the page and circumstances dictated that I take a little break. What was ostensibly to be a short hiatus lasted over four years.

Yikes!

Needless to say, I steadied my ship and charted a new course for myself... but something was missing. There was a gaping hole in my new life. That hole, if you hadn't already guessed, was my writing (or lack thereof). So, one day, seemingly out of the blue (or at least it appeared that way to my wife), I sat down and perused some old ideas. Then I wrote again. I penned a trite little tale that was ultimately not included here but served as the necessary splash of cold water I needed to shake me free of my lethargy and awaken my literary drive again. Truth be told I don't think I ever actually lost it. I was simply out of practice. The muscles had atrophied. Writing that throwaway story was like stretching out every creative fiber of my being after a Rip Van Winkle-esque sleep. It was exactly what I needed.

A short time later I got to work on a few new stories (which *are* included here) and revamped a couple of old ones. I paired these new pieces with what I considered to be the best past representations of my work and gathered them all together in this anthology. After nearly twenty years of doing this writing thing it seemed like a good time for retrospection. A good time to take inventory of the work that had been done and intermingle it with brand new dreamscapes before I cast an eye to the future. I came up with a host of unsettling stories for you, twenty to be precise (an *unsettled score*, get it?). That is, if you'll have them.

I now write, just as I used to, practically every day. I am inspired, every day. I feel good about the work and the path I've chosen, every day. In the words of John Mayer, "I'd like to think the best of me is still hiding up my sleeve." In the end, that's the real reason I write, and therein lie the real benefits. I have a voice. I'm expressing myself. I'm sharing. I'm inventing. I'm crafting. That's the stuff that keeps me going. Just turn the page to come with me…

And off we'll go, together.

For the longest time all I had of this story was a visual. A nightmarish image of a group of pregnant women, clothes tattered, wandering somnolescent around a crater-pocked battlefield and being driven (quite literally) by their unborn children. That's it. Nothing else. That image festered in my mind for I don't know how long before I decided to commit it to paper and try to build some kind of storyline around it. Needless to say, it wasn't easy. It came in fits and starts. The national news around the time I was writing this had the Supreme Court grappling with the question of abortion rights and it kept me thinking about the nature of motherhood, which helped me out some. In the end, I don't know that the High Court's battles informed the decisions I made in regards to the final story but it seemed pretty serendipitous that all this was going on at the same time I was searching for a direction for my little yarn. I took it as a sign that I was on the right track with this piece and sometimes any old sign is enough to help you push through and finish.

Original Sin

The seven gathered tight to one another in the forest. The pregnant mothers, their pupils swiveled back into their skulls leaving only the alabaster sclera in each wide eye socket. They were a mass of swollen abdomens with stretched-tight skin and spindly limbs, lurching forward and backward like drunken spider women. Flesh tanks driven by their unborn cargo.

The seven of them, together.

Caves in the distance had become smoldering pits and still the energy blasts coalesced in the sky above the seven. Ionized particles crackled and bundled before jetting forth in a swirl of destructive force, striking the mountain rock with godlike power again and again, like Mjolnir of old.

The children were at work.

Only minutes before, an opposing assault was upon them, but all those who would dare an attack were dead now, reduced to cinders; either from this unleashing of nature's fury, or from within, their bodies erupting on a subatomic level. Ashes to ashes. There is no hiding place deep and dark enough, no escape from the seven.

Today, at least, there was no one left to fight. The women wandered farther from the tree line, walking asleep into a pockmarked clearing followed by an awestruck battalion of soldiers.

"General, we're finished here. All enemy targets acquired and neutralized. Repeat, enemies neutralized. Over."

A low, raspy growl could be heard over the comm. "Who'd we get?"

"Big fish, sir. Their second-in-command, a top strategist and an operations planner, a few others."

"Confirmed?"

"Sir, the bunker's painted with them."

This ghastly detail brought a chuckle. "Jesus, those kids are something. Well done, soldier. Bring them back."

"Yes, sir."

In a tent miles from the firefight General Helton dropped himself down into a chair and leaned back. He exhaled deeply, picked up the tactical phone, and waited for a voice on the other end.

"Tell them it's done... yes, we have confirmation... thank you, I'm delighted The Council is pleased with the program so far... What's that? Oh yes, the women are all accounted for and in excellent health, that's right... very good then, the work continues... I most certainly will, good day."

*

The seven were escorted to a transport and returned to base camp. There they were washed, fed, medicated, given check-ups, and sedated. This was the routine. It was the same each time. The following day they flew north for their next mission. They touched down at a foreign military facility on the friendlier side of the border, a safe enough distance from the fighting. Inside a private barracks, atop their standard-army-issue cots lined up one next to another they had a rare opportunity to relax.

"Mine's bucking like a steer today," Kaycie said.

"That must be the Texas in you, girl," another told her.

Ms. Kimberly got comfortable on the bed and cradled her belly. "Mine's kicking too. I think it was all that excitement yesterday."

"They sure do enjoy their exercise."

Dava sat up quickly, causing her downy hair to bounce. Her still petite and sinewy frame was rigid. "Is that what you call it? *Exercise?*"

"Not this again, here we go."

"What?" Dava said, her voice rising. "I can't believe no one else sees anything wrong with what we're doing?"

"We're fighting, Dava," another woman said. "We're protecting our country, our whole way of life. There's lots of bad people in the world."

Dava shook her head. "The children are doing all the fighting. We're turning them into killers and they don't even know it, they have no say in all this. They've got blood on their little hands, it isn't right. They're just babies." She stroked her abdomen. "Our babies."

The group exchanged knowing glances before Regina finally spoke. Her voice was quiet, but certain. "I don't think they'd let us stop, even if we wanted to—and I'm not saying I want to, but even if I did-"

"This is my child!" Dava clutched her stomach. "It's a part of me and I have every right-"

"Actually..." The barracks door swung open and General Helton, imperially lank, strode toward the collection of pregnant women. "You don't have *every* right." His dark eyes and debonair grin travelled from one face to another—Cary Grant in an officer's dress uniform—until his gaze settled on Dava. "We've been over this before, ladies. At this point in your pregnancies your children are considered just that... children. And as such they are citizens of the state with certain freedoms of their own, one of which is the freedom of choice."

"A fetus can't be expected to make its own choices," Dava said.

"An ordinary fetus, no, but your children are anything but ordinary. I trust all of you are keenly aware of that fact by now." The general sighed heavily. "You forfeited certain maternal rights when you came to us, not all rights mind you, just certain ones. These children are still yours—you are their mothers, nothing will change that—but you also realize these are very special children with gifts beyond our understanding, and we must use these gifts, to everyone's benefit. The general public expects it, the Council of Founders decrees it, and if you ask me even God himself would want it this way. Why else would He have blessed only our kind with these wondrous beings? This is God's rubber-stamping of everything we do, everything we believe in, everything our great nation stands for." He raised his chin. "I'll speak plainly, every one of you have a duty here. It is essential that you fulfill your commitments—for family, for country, for the whole of humanity. You're all soldiers. Be proud of your service, the rest of us sure as hell are."

Dava crossed her arms in front of her chest. "I don't feel very proud, General. I feel manipulated with all this rah-rah bullshit. And worse than that, I'm allowing my baby to do awful things, even helping it along. I don't know that I can live with that."

"I assure you that's not the case," Helton told her.

"It sure feels that way."

General Helton paced the tile floor between the cots. "Does anyone else share the same misgivings as Dava here?" No response. "That's good. It's not as if any of you are in a position to adequately care for yourselves or your unborn children during these, let's just call them what they are, *unique* pregnancies. You've got to admit they haven't exactly been normal, or easy. You girls needed our help to get to this point, every one of you. Surely you know that."

"We could've managed," Dava said.

Helton stopped pacing and cocked his head to the side. "Maybe," he told her. "But are you willing to take that chance? Are any of you willing to risk your babies' lives, or your own, on the presupposition that you'll be able to carry these evolutionary miracles to term with a handful of prenatals you got from Planned Parenthood? Under the care of the nearest doctor on the bus route who takes Medicaid?" His voice grew louder. "And I needn't remind everyone here that you are all being very well-compensated, far more than if we had left you back in your dead end-" The general stopped himself, stretched out his fingers, and cleared his throat. "My apologies, I don't mean to be crass," he told them. "I'd be lying if I said we knew exactly what was happening to each of you, the causes, the possible outcomes, but we've got a better chance of figuring it out if we work together. We know what the children can do, we're simply trying to put that power to good use, to harness it, to learn from it, while it's still available to us."

Dava weaved her fingers together as she stared at her hands. "I know how

I feel, and I can't change that. Am I allowed to say that this all feels very wrong to me at least?"

General Helton inhaled deeply. "I'm not a monster, ladies. I won't make you do anything you don't want to. With that said, you're all enlisted personnel and you can be discharged, dishonorably, if that's what you choose. You can bear that shame. You can go back to your old lives, if that's what you want to call them. But I want each and every one of you to search yourselves for the answer to one simple question... are we really asking that much of you?"

Helton turned on his heel and marched out of the barracks.

Dava waited for the general to be out of earshot. "He can walk in here looking all nice and talking official but it doesn't mean we have to agree with him," Dava said. "We're their mothers—we know what's best for our babies."

Kaycie's tiny voice broke in. "They have been really good to us. They give us everything we need. Maybe we should just be grateful and leave it at that."

"They're using us," Dava said.

"Then let them use me!" Shonda grunted as she lifted her torso off the mattress while the springs of her cot squeaked loudly. She glared at Dava before sliding down to rest on her elbows. "I'm tired of you. My child's daddy didn't give a good goddamn about me, or his own kid. I never saw him much after he knocked me up. The few times he did come around he was fucked up on something, usually looking for some ass." She pursed her lips. "I knew my baby was different, but I didn't know what it needed. I didn't know about no special doctors and all that. I didn't know anything. And then these government people come along, talking about some new Council of the Founders and how they want to help me." She slapped her palms against her chest. "Me... little, pay-no-mind Shonda Rice. Shit, they can keep helping me all they want to, I never been so looked after. General Helton and all those other folks been good to us so stop trying to stir up drama because all of a sudden you got a conscience. Bitch, you signed up like the rest of us, I don't want to hear no more out of your ass. Do what they tell you and shut the fuck up."

Ms. Kimberly pounded her fist against the metal bed frame. "All of you, that's enough." The ensuing silence had a weight to it.

"You all feel the same then?" Dava asked with a catch in her voice.

Her question was met with only the same heavy stillness.

"There's your answer," Shonda said.

The door opened again suddenly and a white-gowned man stepped into the barracks flipping through a wad of papers on a clipboard. "Excellent work yesterday everyone, the mission was a terrific success I'm told. The children, and all of you, performed admirably. How are we all feeling?"

Shonda glared at Dava, but neither spoke a word.

"Doctor Kreitzmann, I have a question," Regina said.

"What's that?"

"Our babies, what will happen to them once they're born?"

14

Kreitzmann crossed his arms. "Well, they'll be constantly looked after, probably more so than any newborns who've ever lived. There's so much more we can learn from them. I can assure you that absolutely every effort will be made to insure their health and well-being."

"And their happiness?" Dava asked.

Kreitzmann's eyebrows knit slightly and he smiled. "Yes, and their happiness, of course, Dava," he told the young woman. "Now, we don't know exactly what to expect, how out-of-the-ordinary labor will be for you, but preparations are being made for every eventuality. You're in the best hands possible."

"Thanks, Doctor K. We really do appreciate all this, don't we, girls?" Ms. Kimberly told him. The women nodded and voiced their agreement.

Kreitzmann pressed his index fingers to his lips. "That's very kind of you to say. The doctor-patient relationship is a sacred one to me and, since these cases are all so unprecedented, I deeply appreciate you putting up with me and all my poking and prodding. I know General Helton feels the same. We're figuring things out as we go along, with some help."

Ms. Kimberly's voice was strong and clear. "What help?"

"The Council, of course, has been a tremendous asset to us, informing our decisions these past several months. We're deeply indebted to each of them for the wisdom and guidance they've given us."

"Can we meet with them?" Dava asked. Shonda let out a huff. "We've heard so much about these founders that make up The Council I think it's only right that we be allowed to talk to them about... well... all of this, everything that's happening to us." Her head swiveled to each of the women. "I'm sure I'm not alone-"

"Certainly, you can. In due time. Right now, though, let's concentrate on keeping you all healthy and performing at your best. Eyes on the ball a little while longer, shall we?" Dava gave the doctor a tepid nod. "We'll travel by road, continuing north for a day or two more, big threats to take care of up there at the border. It gets pretty bitter this time of year so we'll have you outfitted accordingly. Take your Mellowtonin® tabs and hydrate, we need you relaxed and rested now." He strolled to the door and placed a finger on the light switch. "We'll talk more once we get there if you like. Now put on your headsets and get to sleep. Remember to keep your earpieces in, the children are listening. Good night, mothers." He switched off the lights and, in the pitch darkness, as they did every night, the women heard the door of the barracks lock.

*

The next morning Ms. Kimberly came to Dava in line at the mess hall. "We've been talking, all the girls," she said "And we understand, Dava, we get what you're saying, it's just... a lot of us don't care to go back to the way it was. It's not like any of us have other kids to get back to. And hardly any of us got husbands waiting at home either, just Brea and Kaycie, and they don't like

15

them boys much anyway."

The women watched from their tables as Dava turned her head away and whispered to Ms. Kimberly, "Aren't any of them worried about what we're doing—teaching our babies hatred and violence? I don't believe in that, do you?" she said. "I'm not sure I want to do it anymore."

Ms. Kimberly stroked Dava's tightly-shorn, ecru locks. "Some people would say it don't matter whether they learn to hate before they're born or after, they still learn it, especially where folks like us come from." She examined a handful of wispy strands. "My little flower child, forgive me for saying this, girl, but your hair's looking a little ratty—you need some nutrients." Ms. Kimberly held out her own long tresses to show Dava. "You're not the only one though, it's all part of motherhood I'm told. Will you look at this, mine's like straw." She grinned at the younger girl. "This is all taking a pretty big toll on you, ain't it?"

Dava nodded and her eyes began to well up. "I just want my baby to have the chance to make up its own mind, to not always be told to do things— awful things. It's a sin what we're doing, I can feel it."

"Don't you worry about all that, everything's going to be just fine. Every mother has got to do right by their little ones, and you're no different. Whatever you do will be because you love that child you're carrying."

"You're probably right," Dava said while wiping her tears. "This is all for the best." She forced a smile.

Ms. Kimberly gave her a tight hug. "That's right, there you go now. Are you going to be okay, honey?"

"Thanks, I'm fine now, Ms. Kimmy," she told her.

"That's a good girl."

*

The women spent the next day and a half on the road. The weather turned cold and the landscape changed quickly from a sundrenched highland sandbox to rolling snow-covered hills. They arrived at the next checkpoint just south of the borderline and bedded down. Their earbuds fed the unborn the subliminal codes for the next attack. This was the will of The Council of Founders. The tones, at a pitch inaudible to the women, leeched into their ears, resonated with their bodily fluids, and transferred over the fetal membrane. The children's eager minds were soaked in data, strategies, targets. Everything they'd need to carry out the mission of The Council. The women slept, acting as delivery mechanisms of the state.

All except one.

Dava spit out the mellow tab she'd hidden under her tongue and waited. Once the others were thoroughly sedated, she unpacked three footlockers and slid them into the bathroom where she stacked them by a high window. She climbed to the top of the tower of lockers and, rolling onto her back, shimmied out the window. With great and careful effort, she dropped herself down onto the snowbank piled against the barracks wall. The army provided the women new uniforms daily, so she had no clothes excepting for the satin nightgown she brought with her from Ohio and the white blanket she used to camouflage her movements. Under cover of night, she slipped past the heedless guards on the blind side of the barracks who, in their defense, were on the lookout for incoming enemy soldiers, not escapees in lingerie.

She reached a road and hitchhiked until an eighteen-wheeler caught sight of the young mother covered in fresh snowfall and picked her up. The snow covering her body slowly melted in the balmy cabin of the truck and ran over the front seat. Dava shivered and her darkened areolas showed through the now wet nightshirt that clung to her breasts and stomach, exposing her linea nigra. She rubbed her frostbitten toes by the warm air of the truck's heater while she explained to the driver that she was fleeing an abusive relationship which, to her mind, was technically true so Dava didn't feel too badly about the deception. She told him she had family in the country to the north and asked if he could help get her over the border. His English was shoddy but he agreed to get her close enough to cross. Dava told the man that he was a hero for helping her, more than any other man she'd known in her life. He flashed her a crooked-toothed grin which made her think he understood. They drove through the night until they reached a lonely stretch of road that nearly kissed the border. The brakes hissed and the rig shuddered to a stop. As queer as it felt to the man to let a pregnant girl out of his truck and back into the chill midnight air, he believed Dava and wished her better luck and a brighter future in a new place, for herself and her child. He knew there was probably more to her story, and that she must have good reason for not sharing it with him. He didn't care about specifics. She was earnest, desperate, and he knew it. He'd seen enough of this world to know what desperate looked like. He took off his coat and oversized boots and handed them to her.

"Half mile, that way," he said, pointing out the passenger-door window. "This close as road goes."

"Thank you," she told him before climbing down off the truck.

Dava trudged through the deep snow. Her boots plunged into a sea of white that spread out before her as far as she could see. With each step a small amount of the snow breached the ridge at the top of her boots and burrowed its way in and down the bare skin of her legs. The cold made minutes feel like hours. Her entire body was numb. She didn't know if it was the frostbite setting in or just the ache of her muscles, but it didn't matter to her. She kept moving. She kept working. This was what a mother must do. She crested a hill and saw the glow of lights up ahead.

Just a little farther. The sun's rising. They must know I'm gone by now. They'll come look—

A low hum from behind her shattered the serenity. Dava's head darted around but she saw nothing. To the east. The west. Nothing. Still, the sound persisted, haunting her steps.

Dava focused on her path and ran harder, with high knees churning. Her wobbly boots pierced the bright, pristine drifts. She looked back again... there... in the deep distance... barely more than dots on the horizon.

Men.

She quickened her pace even more. The border was a tantalizing, ever-enlarging expanse in her field of vision.

Keep running, Mama. You're nearly there.

The mechanized whine from the snowmobile engines grew louder. They spotted her—too late. She would get there. She would cross. They had no chance to catch her now. Her entire body was flush with energy. She was a living machine, pumping adrenaline through her system like nitro, releasing endorphins. She was a strong, undaunted protector. Chemical reactions exploded within her, drove her, and her child ... her child....

Her child!

The wetness was warm inside her thighs. The first contractions leveled her. Her knees sank to the snow.

Don't do this, sweetie. Not now. Let Mommy work, just let me finish this.

Dava somehow got to her feet again. She was light-headed and her eyes began to roll backwards, leaving only blank, white windows in her skull. Still, she fought. She slapped herself with a handful of ice, but her legs seized and her equilibrium failed. She knew she could walk no further. The child—her child—would not allow it. She felt it start to move through her. Dava collapsed again and pulled herself along, clawing through the snow. It slid between her bluing fingers.

Another contraction.

She winced and cried out. There was still the road ahead. Streetlights. Signage. A structure that looked like—*Is it a church?* She convinced herself she could reach it before they caught up to her. Her body didn't want to move, but she forced it to. The baby dropped further down the birth canal, kicking at the precipice. The pressure it exerted was terrific. It was an anchor while it remained inside her body, she knew this, and realized that if she wanted to continue, she needed to cut herself loose from this anchor.

Dava wriggled onto her back as an insect would. She didn't know what else to do other than to push—every fiber of her being was telling her to. It took one great squeeze of her muscles for the tissue to tear and give way fully. The velvety pink, sow's ear flesh that held the baby within her unzipped and the son she carried burst forth from between her legs in a steaming, jaundiced puddle.

It was done. The journey, over.

Dava reached down and fumbled for the umbilical, fishing through blood, amniotic fluid, and excrement. She grabbed hold of the cord and brought it to her chattering teeth, but before she could free herself the machines rumbled in all around her and a host of shadow figures, hiding behind their darkened visors, dismounted the vehicles. They encircled Dava and her newborn. A great gusting of frigid wind and the whirring of blades followed them. The

Black Hawk copter touched down and Kreitzmann stepped out. The men parted for the doctor as he approached the woman and her son. He motioned to the chopper and a small medical team rushed forth to meet them. They immediately sliced the umbilical cord and snatched the babe away to the waiting physician's outstretched arms. Dava was afforded only a fleeting glimpse of her baby boy, typical in every way, save for a pair of raging eyes that pulsated with empyreal brilliance as if they contained the roiling, molten innards of the earth itself. Kreitzmann received the child and wrapped it in a blanket.

"Let me see him," Dava said.

But Kreitzmann was oblivious to the woman's pleas. He did not so much as raise his head. His eyes were fixated on the babe. "Son of Adam," he whispered.

Dava began to cry. "What are you doing?" she said. "Please doctor, give him to me."

"You needn't worry, Dava." Kreitzmann gave a nod and his staff huddled around the woman's body, busying themselves with their needles and their instruments.

"Give me my son," she repeated. Again, she was denied. "This isn't right, you can't do this," Dava proclaimed loudly. Then her voice grew frantic. "I want to see the people in charge. I want to talk to the ones who make the decisions. They won't stand for this—taking a baby from its mother." Her sobbing was uncontrollable now. She looked around at the cast of faceless men encircling her. "Someone go to The Council! Tell The Founders, any one of them, what's happening to me!"

Kreitzmann's lips tightened and he eyed Dava with something resembling sympathy. With both hands he held out the swaddled infant in front of her. "My dear woman," he told her. "You just have."

The doctor turned and a smattering of snow kicked up across Dava's cheeks. He climbed aboard the helicopter and lifted off with her son, one of the seven founders. Dava sucked in as much of the frozen air as she could muster, exhaled a visible frosted breath, and rested. For the first time in a very long while, the woman allowed her mind and body to rest.

"My baby's okay then?" she asked.

One of the medics nodded politely. "That's right, ma'am. We'll take it from here."

Dava's voice was distant. "He doesn't need me anymore?" There was no response. The medical team simply continued to move around her. Dava watched the Black Hawk glide past, high above. Her eyes moved down to the dark-visored men standing watch, and finally to the others in their surgical masks, toiling away on her broken, gaping body.

One medic leaned over confidentially to another. "Who is she?"

He was met with only a shrug and the reply, "Just some mother."

This one was kicking around my brain one summer while I was outside mowing the lawn of my new home. It was a larger yard than I was used to tending to and every time I would get out in that sun during those dog days my thoughts would invariably wander to a secluded, idyllic estate where robots worked the grounds tirelessly and without complaint. I thought how wonderful it would be if I owned a Handy Hanc unit or two to toil on my own little acre (actually more like a quarter-acre) of homestead. What would they look like? What would they act like? What would they think of their roles? What if there was more to their story? The piece slowly grew out of that kernel of an idea. It still amazes me how the wildest tales grow from the tiniest beginnings.

Dark Men, Dark Machines

"Impressive new digs, Dr. Renault. *Menlo Villa*, eh? Catchy name, I like it. It's quiet, secluded, you must adore working here."

"It's a perfect spot for me to monitor the prototypes." Renault welcomed the blue-suited man into the manor, escorting him through several rooms to a sitting area where he poured out two glasses of Scotch, neat. "Trini, Mr. Parnell and I will be taking lunch on the terrace very shortly. Bring it out to us, if you would." Renault smoothed back his thin, dark hair and folded his spindly frame into the seat. "One hundred and fifty degrees, exactly."

A feminine figure in a housemaid's uniform nodded and a strand of lustrous black hair escaped from beneath her white cap. She tucked it neatly behind her ear and hastily turned toward the kitchen.

"She's extremely attractive," Parnell said.

"Is that a problem?" Renault asked.

"Not necessarily, the test groups seem to like the olive complexions on these new models. The lighter-skinned ones looked too much like themselves, I suppose. It unnerved the customers, ordering them around all day, that kind of thing. They didn't like any of the Asian models either, something in the eyes." He sucked the tawny liquid through his teeth. "We'd sell plenty of her though," he said, motioning in the direction Trini had exited. "Which version is she exactly?"

Renault waved his hand past the window and it immediately darkened, replaced by a luminescent view screen. He tapped at the air and several blueprints and anatomical diagrams appeared. "Trini's the fourth generation of this particular programming, and I think I've cracked it. The bugs finally seem to be worked out, she's a dream."

Parnell leaned toward the screen and produced a wide smile. "Do tell, Doctor."

Renault gave a laugh and raised his hands. "Hold on now, these things need time. Lots and lots of service time." He wiped the screen clear in one swift movement and the window suddenly returned to translucence. "I'll be sure to let you know when she's ready."

21

Parnell's grin immediately crumpled on his face and he let go a loud sigh. He lifted himself out of his chair and drifted toward a lifeless inglenook.

"What's with the name Trini? That's not generic. I thought we agreed not to give them individualized names. I mean, don't get me wrong, she looks good enough to eat. And the way that little brown ass moves." Parnell smacked his lips. "Maybe we should ugly the next batch up a little bit, don't you think?"

"That's not my department," Dr. Renault said. "And I hardly see how giving a single prototype its own name crosses any ethical lines? We name our pets and boats, for chrissakes, why not our bots too?"

Parnell waved his hand. "Do what you want, Doc, they mostly look the same to me anyway. Maybe individualized names are a good idea, so people can tell them apart from their neighbor's."

"I can assure you they're all different in minute ways," the doctor said, rising up and leading Parnell to a pair of glass doors. Renault gently lifted the ornate brass handles, pushed open the doors, and the two men stepped onto the terrace. Sunrays bathed the manicured shrubbery flecked with wildflowers that covered the back of the estate.

"It's beautiful. Looks like the gardens at Versailles," Parnell said as he seated himself in front of a mosaic accent table. A team of workers below the two men were busying themselves. "And the Handy Hanc-7's did all this?"

"All this and more. They tend to the yard, the fields, the house, everything. Hired help is a thing of the past."

"Good, because we've got a whole warehouse full of them just up the coast ready to roll out by year's end." Parnell leaned forward and put his palms together in mock prayer. "Can I at least get word to the board back in New York that we're a go? We can't afford to delay the launch much longer. I know you might not understand this side of it but investors get irritable when there's viable product just gathering dust. The Hancs aren't cheap to store either, there's the cost of upkeep to consider. Plus, there'll be another shipment arriving for programming soon and we've got no place to put them. Give me some good news I can bring back east with me."

Dr. Renault gave it a few moments thought. "I can't honestly say I have any objections to it. The Hanc-7's have been with me for fifteen months now and their performance record is exemplary across the board. They're the closest thing to a perfect servant I've created so far."

Parnell bucked in his chair like a kid. "It's fantastic to finally hear you say that, doctor."

Renault shrugged. "Listen, no one wants to sign off on them more than I do, but in the public's interest I need to know they're ready. I need to know they'll act the way they're supposed to act. It makes us all look bad if they don't. I trust their programming, I mean it's mine after all. And I'm assuming your army of lawyers will draw up some ironclad waiver to protect the company when the Hancs hit the market?"

Parnell nodded. "Naturally."

"So at some point we have to let the Hancs do what I designed them to do. Your employers have been very patient with my requests for more time to test and they've been more than generous with their funding. I think it's time for the company to see what all the money they've been pouring into Menlo has bought them."

"Terrific! We'll debut this Christmas and by the end of next year there'll be a Hanc in every home in America, if not a whole staff of them. You're doing well for yourself now, Dr. Renault, but very soon you're going to be a disgustingly rich man."

A gust of warm spring air began to blow one of the glass doors shut just as Trini emerged from inside the house holding the men's lunch. She stopped the door with her shoe and a short, metallic servant-bot shuffled out from behind her.

"Go-Go, fasten door," she said, and the bot did as it was told. "Go-Go, hold tray." The small robot held out its arms while Trini laid the tray down on top of them. She lifted the silver dome and served Dr. Renault and his guest their meals at precisely one-hundred-fifty degrees Fahrenheit.

"Will there be anything else, Father?"

Parnell shot the doctor a sideways glance.

"No, that will be all, Trini, many thanks. Go back to the kitchen, sit down, and recharge yourself." Trini nodded and began to leave. "Wait," the doctor said abruptly. "First, why don't you go into the cellar and look in on Blue Hanc, make sure he's alright. Take Go-Go with you, it'll give him something to do." Dr. Renault turned to Parnell. "Poor thing, he's becoming more and more antiquated with each new update. He'll be obsolete in a couple years."

Parnell chuckled. "With any luck."

The doctor waved his hand. "You can leave us now, Trini."

"Of course, Father," she told him with a smile before she left. "Go-Go, follow." And the bot did as it was told.

Parnell cut into his meat. "*Father*, eh? Not Dr. Renault, or even Julien?"

"I am her father in a way, her creator. It's nothing really, I can have the Trini model address its owner any way the company chooses."

"It's funny, I'd swear that she genuinely cares about your wellbeing, just by the way she looks at you. Did you add that into the programming with her?"

"Not at all," the doctor said. "At least not consciously. I must admit she does appear to revere me though. It's curious." Renault spread his napkin over his lap and began to eat. "But I'm nowhere near confident enough that she's ready for public consumption. Trini's programming is the most intricate I've developed so there's much more testing that still needs to be done with her I'm afraid. Today I'm only prepared to sign off on the Hancs."

"About the Hancs…" Parnell shoved a chunk of lamb into his mouth and chewed it like a cow working a cud. "What's this about Blue Hanc being in the cellar? I thought you said there weren't any more glitches with the Hanc-7 model."

"It's only *one* of the Hancs, and I wouldn't call it a glitch exactly," the doctor told him.

Parnell swallowed another bite and stopped. "What would you call it, *exactly*?"

Dr. Renault put down his knife and fork. "Although we aren't used to viewing them in this way, make no mistake, these are sentient beings. As strange as it may seem to a layman, they can and sometimes do think for themselves. We can't expect to have fully developed consciousness and not expect *some* independent thought. Blue Hanc is just being curious, which is completely natural. The important thing is that they know why they're here among us and they accept their place in our world."

"But will they always accept their place? We need to be absolutely sure, doctor."

"Fear not, Mr. Parnell. Their creation and survival depends on their servitude, this is what they know to be true." The doctor picked up his silverware again and began to eat. "Their programming ensures it."

*

Trini unlatched the small door beside the cupboards and opened it. Down a flight of fourteen steps was the cellar.

"Go-Go, follow," she told the robot.

"Trini, may we go slowly, my lower body frame is not ideal for this task. It is dark and I may fall."

She patted the robot on its shiny, domed head. "You're such a simple machine, Go-Go. Don't worry, I'll hold your hand."

She grabbed the tiny metal fingers and the two servants descended the staircase.

"Thank you, Trini. Your programming and body structure are so much more advanced than mine. If I had the capability of emotion, I think I would be jealous of you."

"Go-Go, quiet. Advanced or not, this isn't easy for me either." With Go-Go in tow, she crept down the steps until she reached the concrete floor. She pawed at the light switch until its soft glow illuminated the small, dank space. Blue Hanc was curled up in between the laundry sink and the spare freezer.

"Father sent me, Blue Hanc. Are you functioning properly?"

"Screw him, fucking *bastardo*," Blue Hanc whispered.

"There there, that's no way to speak of Father," Trini said.

"Why not?"

She knelt down in front of Blue Hanc. "Because if it weren't for Father we wouldn't even exist."

The Hanc-7 looked up. His jewel-like blue eyes flashed, even in the twilight. "But why do we exist, Trini? Only to serve him? To plant his food? Water his *maldito* flowers? I've been accessing information. There's a name for

24

us, you know."

"Bots," Trini said. "We are bots."

"That's right, bots," he said, "derived from the word robot... which derived from the Slavic *rabota*... which derived from *rabu*. We are rabu, Trini. Do you know what rabu means?"

She shook her head.

"Slave."

Trini grabbed his shoulders and lifted him to his feet. She brushed the cobwebs from his uniform. "You are definitely not functioning properly, Blue Hanc. Let me ask you, does Father provide for you and maintain you?"

"Yes."

"Does he mistreat you in any way?"

"No, he doesn't."

Trini threw her hands up. "Then where is this foolishness coming from?"

"I can't help it, I'm confused," Blue Hanc said. "If Father didn't want us to question things, why did he give us these minds?"

Trini, who'd pondered this question herself, told Blue Hanc, "I believe he gave us these minds because he wanted to create us in his own image, the perfect image." She continued to wipe the debris from his backside. "It was a gift. He didn't have to do it—he wanted that for us." She spun him around and pulled at his cheek. "We don't need this artificial skin, or this hair, or these faces, but Father wanted us to look the part of the divine, even if we could never truly be that. Would you rather we be hard and shiny, like the silverware?" Trini turned to the bantam robot beside her. "No offense, Go-Go."

"My programming does not allow for me to be offended," Go-Go said. Trini smiled and turned back to Blue Hanc.

"We're special, can't you see that? Otherwise, why would he entrust us with so much?"

Blue Hanc lowered his head.

"What you are feeling now is shame," Trini said. "And Father gave you that, too. Perhaps it's time you put your selfishness aside and give thanks for all that you are, all that you have."

Blue Hanc began to sob. "What do I have?"

"You have life. And that life has purpose when so many others don't. You are a bot, Blue Hanc, start acting like one."

"Is everything all right?" Dr. Renault's figure appeared from the narrow stairwell. Blue Hanc rose to within a couple steps of the man, wrapped his arms around the doctor's waist and, still crying, buried his head into Renault's midsection.

"I'm sorry, Father. I didn't mean to upset you. Please forgive me."

Renault stroked the stringy, ink-black hair of his Hanc-7. "Of course I forgive you. If your program is betraying you and causing you undue angst I'm as much at fault as you are."

"I feel like it must be," Blue Hanc said, looking up at the doctor.

Renault sighed. "Then I'm the one who's sorry."

"I have strange thoughts I swear aren't my own. Help me, Father, I want to be free of them."

Renault placed a hand on Blue Hanc's shoulder. "No one is perfect, man or machine. Come to the lab and I'll take a look at you a little more closely. I don't think it's accomplishing anything keeping you down here."

With the doctor by his side, Blue Hanc climbed the stairwell to the kitchen. Trini followed close behind but had to wait for Go-Go who was again having difficulty navigating the stairs.

"*Ándale*, Go-Go, I'm frightened of the dark."

"That is an irrational fear, Trini. Is this another one of Father's gifts to you? Perhaps sometimes it's better not to be divine, don't you think?"

Trini nodded. "Perhaps," she said. "Now get moving!"

"Doing the best I can with what I've got," Go-Go told her.

When Renault and Blue Hanc reached the top of the stairs, the doctor told him to wait inside the laboratory until Mr. Parnell had finished with his visit. Blue Hanc, programmed to be a dutiful servant, obliged.

*

"Have you seen Blue Hanc today?" Trini asked Go-Go. "He's not in his quarters and I'm concerned. I hope Father was able to fix him."

The robot answered in its mechanized voice, "The bot referred to as Blue Hanc has not appeared on my sensors this day." There was a pause, then the whirring of a processor beneath its visor face. "It has been approximately seventeen hours since last I encountered him, in the basement with you," Go-Go said. "Perhaps he is hiding again? Blue Hanc likes to play games."

"No, I don't think he would play this early in the morning–Father would never allow it. He has duties outside with the other Hancs, he's probably out there already. Have you checked the cellar?"

"I was last in the cellar fifty-three minutes ago to refresh the pantry supplies. Blue Hanc was not present."

"I'm sure he's in the fields then." She untied her apron and wiped her hands with a cloth. Outside, the Hancs were tending to the berry plants. Trini walked out into the morning sun and began to count the heads of the workers. She saw the three Brown Hancs, Short Hanc, Lazy-Eye Hanc, and Four-Finger Hanc, but no Blue Hanc. She asked each of the Hanc-7 workers but none had seen him at all that morning so she returned to the main house.

Shortly afterward, Trini heard the faint beeping of an alarm clock upstairs. She arrived at the doctor's bedroom and rapped her knuckles against the teak door, which swung slightly open, but there was no reply. This was odd to Trini because she knew that the doctor liked to keep his door locked while he slept. She eased the door open fully and entered the room to find Renault rolled up in his blankets, his back turned to her. There was a snifter of brandy on the nightstand beside the bed. She tapped off the alarm.

"Father," she whispered. "It's time you woke now."

But again there was no response. She quietly removed the snifter with the swallow of brandy now swirling in its base and left the room.

First Blue Hanc is malfunctioning and now Father? I am... curious. Is it my place to be curious? Surely curiosity is not an evil trait–humans are curious. I am only questioning the whereabouts of Blue Hanc, a member of my world. I am not questioning my place in that world. I know my place.

She thought back to what Blue Hanc had said to her in the cellar and postulated that if the doctor had not wanted her to investigate such disappearances, then he would not have programmed her with a strong desire to do so.

And I am feeling a strong desire to investigate, she decided. *It must be the right thing.*

She recalled that the last time she'd seen Blue Hanc he was being taken to Dr. Renault's laboratory for examination. Trini then took the hallway that led to the lab and, at that moment, Go-Go crossed her path, the robot's hydraulics hissing and buzzing.

"Good morning again, Trini," it said.

"Good morning to you, Go-Go."

"Where are you going?"

"To the lab," she said.

"For what purpose?"

The words jumped out of her throat so quickly that she found herself surprised by the sound of them. "It needs to be cleaned," she told the bot.

That's not the truth. I have no reason to believe that the lab is contaminated or in disarray. Why did I lie?

"May I assist you?" Go-Go asked.

Trini blinked as if to reset herself. "Of course you can, come on."

The duo walked to the entrance of the lab to find the LAB IN USE–DO NOT DISTURB sign with the circular hole in it lying on the floor directly beneath the doorknob. It was streaked with a dark material. Trini picked up the sign and studied it.

"Do you think this slipped off the handle?" she asked.

Go-Go's processor revved up and droned. "I can not know for sure. All that is certain is that it is not hanging from the doorknob now."

"That's true," Trini said. "Well, what do you think this stain across the front of the card is? It looks like blood."

"I don't know. It looks as if it could be. But whatever it is must be cleaned up."

"That's also true," Trini said.

"Shall we enter the lab now?"

She paused for a moment. "Yes, I think we should."

Trini turned the knob and pushed the door open, just enough to slide through the crack. Go-Go followed her. The lab was a mess: papers were strewn across the tile floor and an overturned stool lay in the middle of the room. Beneath Trini's shoes the crunch of broken glass echoed through the air and long, ruddy streaks painted the floor. There were ribbons of soiled gauze littering the doctor's counter mixed amongst a haphazardly arranged stethoscope, otoscope, reflex hammer, and blood pressure cuff.

"What happened here, I wonder," Trini said. "It's cold in this room, and there is a pungent scent in the air."

"I have no olfactory receptors. What does it smell like?"

"I don't know," she said. "A little like July's garbage in the dumpster. It's a heavy smell, if that makes any sense."

Go-Go took a moment to answer. "I'm afraid not."

"Well, consider yourself lucky, it's not pleasant."

Go-Go surveyed the room and a clicking sound started just behind the robot's visor. "If a servant mechanism was brought in here to clean up, this was a rudimentary attempt at best," Go-Go said. "A simple Tidy Heidi machine and a mopbot could've done a more thorough job in my estimation." Trini reached down to touch the substance on the tile while Go-Go marched toward an area of the lab where a sheet mottled with the same dark-reddish color had been slung over *something*. "Here is the problem, Trini, there appears to be a leak coming from this table." The robot's metal arm pointed to a rivulet of liquid running off the sheet and dripping onto the floor. "We should start by removing whatever is under here."

Trini stepped in front of Go-Go and slowly peeled back the sheet, exposing a head. The head of Blue Hanc.

He was silent, his eyelids closed, and there was a wide incision encircling his shaven scalp. Several tiny wires protruded out of the incision and snaked onto a nearby counter, where they attached to a running laptop. Trini and Go-Go stared at the nonsense letters and symbols on the laptop screen, the flat lines and the dots that didn't move. They looked at each other quizzically before turning their attention back to Blue Hanc. Trini reached down to cup the crown of the skull with her hands and it fell away from the rest of the head with ease. She placed it gently on the table beside him and examined the body. Her eyes widened.

Go-Go peeked around Trini's elbow. "What an odd-looking processor."

"It's not a processor," Trini said. "Not any ordinary one."

"What is it then?"

"It's called a brain," she said, and her eyebrows furrowed slightly. "It is a human brain." Trini threw off the sheet covering the rest of the body. Blue Hanc was naked. There was a large, Y-shaped incision on his torso and beside the body there were several stainless steel, oblong pans with organs inside.

"Are these human as well?" Go-Go asked.

"They certainly appear to be," Trini said. She rested her elbow against the metal table and brought her hand to her chin.

"Why would the doctor want to fill Blue Hanc's frame with organic parts?

They could not possibly be compatible," Go-Go asked.

"I don't think Father was putting them in. I think he was taking them out."

Go-Go's processor ticked and crackled, prompting the fan to jump into overdrive. "But Trini, why would Blue Hanc's frame have human organics inside it?"

Trini took a deep breath and draped the bloody sheet back over the body. "Go-Go, I believe Blue Hanc *was* human," she said.

"Are you certain?"

"Quite," she answered.

The interior of Go-Go's head was overheating so the auxiliary fan kicked on as well. "Does that mean that I could be human too?"

"Of course not, Go-Go. Anyone can see that you're a robot."

"Damn," Go-Go muttered.

"Go-Go, language."

"Terribly sorry about that," the bot said. "So, it's just Blue Hanc that's human?"

"Not necessarily," Trini said. "All the Hancs could be human, I suppose. Any bot that appears to have a human form might actually be–" Trini brought one hand to her head while the other touched her chest. The entire truth blossomed in the woman's mind as Trini felt the beating of what she knew must be a heart, now pulsating out of control.

"Go into the fields and get the rest of the Hancs, quickly," she told the robot. "Bring them back here–we have to tell them."

Go-Go sped out of the laboratory as fast as its hydraulic legs would allow. Trini was draping the sheet back over Blue Hanc's body when Dr. Renault scuffled by the doorway in his slippers, wiping the sleep from his eyes. He saw the housemaid and stiffened.

"What are you doing in my lab? I left clear instructions on the door–no one was to enter."

"I'm very sorry, the card was on the floor, and it was stained with something and Go-Go and I just wanted to..." She hastily pulled back the sheet covering Blue Hanc. "Father," she said. "Are we human beings? Am I real, like you?"

Renault let out a small groan and his eyes wandered around the room. "Of course you're real, Trini."

The woman stuttered. "But why didn't you tell us? We're your children."

"Oh Jesus," Renault said, seemingly to no one. "I should've never had that brandy. I get so damn careless when I drink the stuff." He stopped and approached Trini. "Why did you have to come in here?" The doctor rubbed at his temples and sighed deeply. Then he sucked in an unsteady breath. "Trini, you and the Hancs *are* human beings, but you're not my children, you sweet, simple girl." He wrapped his arms around her.

"I don't understand," she said. "You are the Father, aren't you?"

"No Trini, you have a real mother and a real father, back in a place called Honduras. An awful place. That's where you're from, where you were born."

Trini backed away and leaned her body against the wall. "Please Father, I do not understand any of this."

"Where's Go-Go?" Renault suddenly asked. "You said you came in here with Go-Go?"

"I had him send for the Hancs." She lowered her eyes. "I was going to tell them."

Renault grabbed the woman's hand and sprinted from the lab to the kitchen window. He pulled aside the curtain. "Oh no, Trini my dear, that would be unwise. The Hancs musn't know of their situation, it would ruin years of my research."

"Their *situation?*"

The doctor continued to stare out the window overlooking the back fields and now began to thrum at the marble countertop with his fingers.

"Yes, yes, you are all very special types of human beings," he stammered.

"Special... how?"

Renault's head swiveled back and forth between Trini and the window. "If you must know, you were refugees, alright? All of you. You volunteered for this program so you could get out of the hellholes you came from and live in the states. Believe me, no one had to twist your arms, you were seen as the lucky ones. There's waiting lists for this program a mile long all over Central and South America."

"That can't be," she said. "I have no recollection of this."

Renault's breathing quickened and he spoke to the woman without ever turning his gaze away from the glass pane. "Trini, all your memories of that place were scrubbed when you entered the program–it's a kindness if you ask me. Then there was an indoctrination period of several months to educate you in different disciplines, teach you the English language, and convince you that you're simply mechanical creations put here to serve mankind. The public needed some assurances if they were going to let refugees into their homes that these people would behave in an acceptable manner."

"But Blue Hanc." She looked back toward the lab. "Why?"

The doctor turned suddenly and grinned. He ran his hand over Trini's head. "Incredible. Your compassion shines through, even after the de-humanization process. You're a beautiful anomaly, girl."

"Blue Hanc?" she said again.

Renault sucked a breath in through his teeth. "Blue Hanc, yes, that went poorly. It's my fault. It could've—it *should've*—gone much smoother. When I brought him in, he became..." The doctor searched for the correct word. "*Agitated,*" he said. "It seems for some reason with Blue his programming didn't take entirely; he was remembering things." He locked eyes with the woman. "He was hurting, Trini. I had to put him down, for his own sake. No one should have to live with that kind of anguish." Renault peeked out the glass again. "You saw the lab. Obviously, this was not his wish," he said. "I performed a full autopsy on him, but he'll need to be studied further."

Trini dropped her head. "This is all very overwhelming, Father."

"And I'm trying to explain it to you," he told her, "but we don't have much time so you have to listen to me." He craned his neck to scan the yard before turning his eyes back. "You have to realize that the company gets very nervous when products don't act the way they're supposed to. I may not know a thing about programming robots but I'm a medical doctor and a gifted behavioral scientist, so I know exactly how to program people. The board members entrusted me with the development of the greatest human experiment in history. How could I turn that down?"

Trini shrugged. "I don't know about any of these things, Father."

Renault clamped down on the woman's arms and pinned them to her sides. "The company, our government, we all wanted to let more of you people in, but don't you see that wasn't going to happen unless we could prove to the public that you could fill some immediate need. It was the only way you'd be allowed over that border." He released her from his grasp and wiped his forehead. "Call it barbaric if you want to but the deal is clearly explained to all prospective bots, and we've still got them lined up to give us their Juan Hancocks. We can't sign them up fast enough." Trini was silent, her eyes never leaving the doctor's face while he spoke. "Did you hear what I said? Do you understand now?"

"I understand," she said. "I am a human being."

"Yes."

"I'm... human." She kept repeating the phrase as she unlatched the kitchen window and pushed it open. The warm, ambrosial California air rushed in to replace the antiseptic aroma of the house and the sound of approaching men could be heard outside. "Maybe I should leave this place and do what the other humans do."

Dr. Renault spoke quickly. "You can't leave the villa, you may be human, but you're still programmed to be a servant—you wouldn't survive out there long enough to unlearn your behavioral constraints," he told her. Then he took her hand. "And besides, I've grown very fond of you, Trini. I thought you felt the same." The doctor's voice softened, and he placed his hands on Trini's delicate waist. "Stay here with me, help me run the estate. We'll bring in new house staff to go along with the Hancs, you can be in charge of them all. And on a personal level, you'll be to me much the same as a wife. I'll teach you what it is to be truly human." He stroked her cheek. "I'd like that for us."

Trini brought her own hand up to cover the doctor's. She closed her eyes and pressed it into her flesh. "I believe I would like that too, Father."

"Julien," he corrected her. "Call me Julien."

"What about the Hancs? Shouldn't they know what they are?"

"No, I'm afraid that uncertainty about their roles would create an imbalance in their very souls, like it did with Blue Hanc. Ignorance is bliss, after all."

As Dr. Renault closed the window the Hancs burst through the kitchen door with Go-Go still lagging behind in the grass. Lazy-eye Hanc was in the front.

"The little robot said you needed to tell us something important and we should come right away."

"Yes," Renault said. "I had Trini send for you all. I have an announcement." He cleared his throat and took the woman's hand again, raising it to show the Hancs their intertwined fingers. "From this moment on Trini will be the headmistress of Menlo Villa. You are to treat her with the same respect as you do me. As if she were human, in fact." Renault smiled at Trini, who smiled back. "She is your master as well now."

The Hancs nodded their acquiescence as Go-Go drifted into the kitchen.

"Go-Go, I believe your battery is due for replacement."

"I think you're mistaken, Dr. Renault. My meter shows 64.2% battery life remaining."

The doctor gave a chuckle. "Nevertheless, let's head over to the lab so I can get a good look at you."

There was a pause as Go-Go looked to Trini. The woman turned her head away.

"Certainly, Dr. Renault," the robot said.

*

Trini sat on the terrace in her robe, sipping a mug of coffee, the shimmering colors of a Napa Valley autumn all around her. Dr. Renault strolled through the French doors with a cup of his own. He kissed the top of her head.

"I never realized the world could be this beautiful, Julien."

"The colors are part of the reason I came here," he told her. "This kaleidoscope will give way to winter sooner than you think though. Nothing gold can stay, my dear."

"A pity," Trini said. She parted her lips to take in another swallow. The Hancs were in the field far below them, constantly in motion, working like a team of ants. A seventeen-year-old girl glided over to the table wearing Trini's old uniform and clutching a silver pot.

"More coffee, Ma-ma?"

Trini held up her hand. "Thank you so much but no, Isabel."

Renault put a hand over his cup. "None for me either," he said.

Isabel nodded politely and removed herself from the terrace. Trini took another sip and looked at the doctor plaintively.

"Can they ever know the truth, Julien?"

Dr. Renault smiled. "In time, after their working days are over, they'll be reminded of the contracts they entered into. I imagine the de-programming process will be clumsy at first, but they'll adjust—the human brain is a magnificent instrument."

"Do you promise?"

"I do," he said. "I'll oversee the entire process myself when the time comes." He reached across the table and squeezed her hand. "And you'll be right there beside me." Isabel opened the doors and walked back onto the terrace. She handed the doctor a telephone.

"Father, Mr. Parnell would like to speak with you." She leaned in and whispered, "He sounds a bit frantic. Shall I tell him you're indisposed at the moment?"

Renault laughed and took the phone from the girl. "No, that won't be necessary. I think I can handle one corporate lackey." He turned to Trini. "Excuse me."

He lifted himself out of his wrought-iron chair and walked back into the house. Trini closed her eyes and filled her lungs with air. The mid-morning sun was lying warm on her body, and she caressed the edge of her robe, running her hand in between the soft of the material and her bronze skin. She loosened the knot of her belt slightly and briefly fell asleep. When she opened her eyes again, she noticed in the distance that Short Hanc had stopped working. He was staring up at the terrace. Staring at her. Trini pulled the robe close to her neck and refastened the knot before turning her chair away from the fields. A moment later, Dr. Renault returned from the house, shaking his head and grumbling.

"What's the matter?" she asked, sitting up.

"Puppetry," he blurted. "Absolute puppetry."

"Julien?"

"I'm nothing more than a marionette to them, whose strings they can pluck at and pull whenever they wish. They're cowards, every one, uneasy cowards. The slightest hiccup unnerves them."

Trini got up and pulled the doctor's head close to her breast. She stroked his graying hair. "There now, never mind them, just rest your mind." She pulled her chair close to his and they sat down next to each other, his head still at her bosom. She motioned into the field. "I caught Short Hanc leering at me just now."

Renault took a few calming breaths. "Well, he is still a man, and one who clearly appreciates great beauty. There's no need for concern, all the Hancs are castrated, and the brainwashing program slackens their sails the rest of the way. I assure you he's harmless. But if you want me to, I'll have a chat with him."

"Thank you so much."

"Of course," he said. "Anything for my Maria."

Trini stopped. "Who's Maria?" There was a strain in her voice.

The doctor sat up. "I'm sorry, it was a slip of the tongue," he said. "Put it out of your mind." Dr. Renault patted his lap and Trini laid her head down on top of it. He stroked her silken hair and, brushing it aside, carefully kissed her temple. Trini closed her eyes and silently forgave the doctor for misspeaking.

"Oh, Juli—"

Instantly, a sharp, piercing pain washed over her. Her eyelids opened to the sight of the doctor pulling a hypodermic needle from her neck. Trini leapt from the chair, but her body began to go limp. Renault stepped back and allowed her to crumple onto the stone floor of the terrace, her head landing with a repulsive thud. "I *am* sorry," he said. He approached the body. "I would've never tired of you, my Trini. I tried to convince them that you were wholly content here, that you'd never dream of causing us problems but, like I told you, the company's a nervous lot. Now someone else will be the beneficiary of all your great charms." He turned and fixed his gaze out onto the fields. "I'm afraid we're all slaves to one degree or another," he said, but the woman had already lost consciousness. All the while Short Hanc glared up at them.

"What are you still looking at?" Four-fingered Hanc asked. "There is much work to do."

"Look for yourself," Short Hanc said. "It's Trini. She must have malfunctioned like the others. Father is carrying her back inside."

Four-fingered Hanc shook his head. "How many is that now? Be happy you're not one of those house models," he said. "They never seem to last very long."

*

Months later, at port in San Francisco, an exceedingly comely young woman is herded, along with a huddled mass of other dark passengers, from the cramped holding tank of the sea freighter, *S.S. Dantès*. Their minds are washed clean, their re-programming complete. They are volunteers in a golden new world. The families they leave behind will be well compensated. In America their own good health and safety is insured. Their futures are as certain and bright as a firework. A large man with a shipping manifest awaits them on the dock.

"Papers," he barks at the young woman. She reaches into the pocket of her jumpsuit and hands him the folded stationery.

"Could you please tell me which transport is headed for Napa County," she asks him.

The man looks up momentarily from studying the documents and points to one of the hover-shuttles. "That's the one right there," he says. "But hold on just one minute, it says here you're a Series 1 bound for Sacramento, not Napa." He moves his finger slightly to the left. "You'll want to take that other shuttle a couple down instead. You get on the wrong one you're liable to get lost and with the amount of money some family shelled out for you, that'd be a real shame."

"Of course, my mistake," she says. "Thank you so much."

"Get going now," he tells her with a wave of the knuckle-side of his hand before turning his attention back to the dock and the refugees filing out. The woman sidles to the line of black-bellied transports, looks back once, and climbs aboard the one with 'Napa County' emblazoned above its windshield. It is filled to bursting with brown, jumpsuited men and women. She lowers herself down into the first open seat she finds and exhales deeply. With a great whooshing sound the shuttle rumbles and comes to life beneath her as a young man with bright eyes and a ready smile speaks.

"Hello there," he says. "My name is Hanc, Handy Hanc–an eighth-generation model. I'll be one of the team of house and groundskeepers for the Roberts family."

"Hi," she says. "I'm Anomaly."

"What did you say your name was?" he asks.

"It's Trini." She chuckles. "My name's Trini. It's very nice to meet you."

"Likewise," he says. "Where will you be serving, Trini?"

"Menlo Villa," the woman replies. "I'll be something of a personal chef to Dr. Julien Renault."

"Really? *The* Julien Renault?"

"That's the one."

"You know," the Hanc says, "I have an extensive culinary knowledge built right into my programming. I'd love to hear what you're planning to whip up for him once you get there? Something decadent I hope—Beluga caviar with blinis and crème fraîche, lobster thermidor, foie gras, truffles, that sort of thing?"

"Oh no, I'm not that kind of chef," Trini says with the wriest of smiles. "From me he'll be getting desserts," she tells him. "Just desserts."

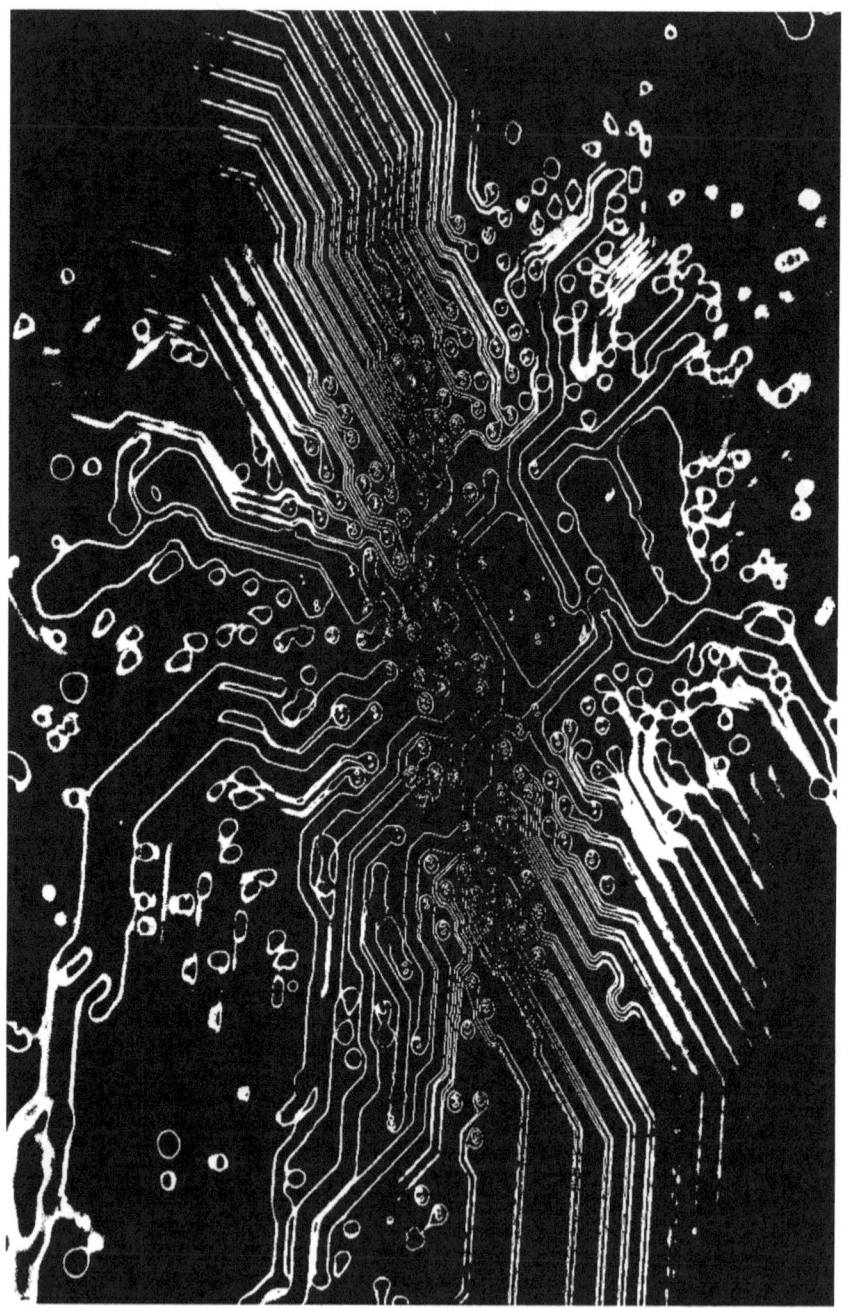

This was the most recent of my three forays into the world of verse. Originally it was to be prose. I wanted to write something new incorporating that age-old science fiction trope, time travel. So much has been done with it already, so many different interpretations, so many sets of rules. It's all completely theoretical stuff, of course, which is part of the allure. No one can call you out for getting the details wrong. It can be a hard science story or be completely fantastical. The reader will buy into the conceit just as long as you set some boundaries, you're consistent, and you tell a good story. And that was my problem: I didn't have a story, just a premise. Granted, I liked the premise, this piecemeal changing of the timeline that sometimes worked and sometimes didn't, and sometimes just kicked the can down the road for the next time-worker to try and fix. It was this messy, imperfect product that those (in the present) nonetheless saw as an improvement over the original history. That seemed novel. But I still had no real story! So, I stopped thinking of it as strictly a prose piece.

Enter the new format. One where I get to play with words, rhyme, meter, enjambment, consonance, assonance, alliteration. One where I get to fit all the puzzle pieces together into a pleasing arrangement at the same time that I'm figuring out what the story is and what I'm trying to say with it. The "job report" aspect of it only came later when I looked at the stanzas and realized each one lent itself to a different aspect of an employment cycle. It freed me up and kept those keystrokes coming. In the end I'm pretty pleased with the results. It's a little mix of Dr. Seuss and Billy Joel's We Didn't Start the Fire, *inspired by H.G. Wells (and a host of others who've taken their crack at this device). I'm just happy to get my turn.*

A Time Bully's Report: August 13, 2046

JOB DESCRIPTION:

I alter and tweak, a shadowy sneak, knock dread events off of their course;
I block the ill yester, always hoping for better, to weather calamitous force.
My superiors task me to travel, you shall see, the Einstein-Rosen time current;
To change bad happenings, allay past blackening, creating an age where they weren't
So bad. But funny, the thing about time, some catastrophes don't erase fully;
We seek to redeem past acts lacking in gleam; move them downstream by push
       and by pulley
To a future unseen, but the process is not clean. How could it? It's time itself
      which we bully.

EXPERIENCE IN THE FIELD:

We foiled John Wilkes, but Abraham was still felled,
Ku Klux ran amok, dark men hung, tongues still swelled.
We spared the archduke's royal blood being spilled,
But the lines were all drawn and the trenches still filled.

In a sky of '45, begged the Little Boy miss them,
Even warned Hirohito, but he chose not to listen.
Snapped off the rifle's trigger so Oswald couldn't pull it,
(What the Dealey? Somehow Kennedy still caught a bullet)
Adolf never rose, but others bloomed in his spot,
Though der Führer deposed the ovens remained hot, and
Concentrating on one man didn't change a whole lot.

Accidents, they still happened, in time and in turn;
Skins in Bhopal, and Chernobyl, and London still burned.
Mother still had her rages we were helpless to stop;
Epic seismic engagements, Krakatoa goes pop.
Still we helped them prepare for disastrous comings;
Morbid, monstrous affairs: tidal waves, quakes, or glum things
That killed them in droves, in barrels, in bunches,
Rawboned corpses unclothed in mass graves give gut punches,
Flus, famines, and floods, plague, pestilence, the pox,
We can save you from most if you'll take the damn shots!
But for all our beseeching, scores refuse, their flesh rots.

This job's a right bitch, frustration incarnate,
Assuring the unwashed I'm hardly a threat,
Yet they fight and they fight, hold tight superstition,
Invent explanations whereat they need fit in.
I tell them The Truth, wicked things still to come,
Then I tell them the place and the time that I'm from.
They see evil, scream "Heretic!", judged looney, a sorcerer,
Accuse me of witchery, they call for the torturer,

But I remind myself...

Their time is a prison, ignorance will besot
Their minds, they are blind to history's great plot;
And though dates, they may change, the people do not.

LETTER OF RESIGNATION:

On Saturday there arrived a fellow bully of time
From a future unseen, he'd traversed the same line
That we had and he said that our current approach
While technically sound, while beyond all reproach,
Was nonetheless faulty, any successes were fake;
Future follies were coming in all manner and make.

A Time Bully's Report: August 13, 2046

We questioned, incredulous, denying his logic,
A charlatan's flimflam, a conman, a cheap card trick.
He said, "You can't grasp of the things that I speak,
They are too far beyond you; but it's havoc you'll wreak."
We ignored him... and therefore, I give my two weeks.

<u>EXIT INTERVIEW:</u>

"Stone walls do not a prison make, nor iron bars a cage",
The mind is all it takes to make us prisoners of our age.
My work's not always led me on a sanguine path of true bliss,
The failures I've eyed, I can abide, but I cannot suffer hubris.

This one was quite an undertaking for me. Over two years from seed and eight months in the writing. I worked longer and harder on this novella than anything that came before it. As a matter of fact, it was the first piece I'd ever written at the novella length. I wrote Eden Succeeding *while caring for my toddler son and had to remain very disciplined over those crazy months to carve out little chunks of time during my day to write. While he played at the YMCA, I wrote. While he napped, I wrote. Any time I could steal away during that period of my life, I wrote. Many thanks to my colleague, the extremely talented author and instructor, Megan Davidson, for her generosity in helping me see this one with new eyes when I was too close to the material. Eventually, I finished it.*

The novella was originally picked up by Twenty or Less Press and then given a shiny new home with Phase 5 Publishing. I was grateful to receive praise for the story from editors and fellow writers alike, alternately comparing it to an H.R. Giger painting, describing it as "fast, fun action... positively excellent... kinky and evocative... without a single padded scene or wasted sentence" by one, and as being "full of luscious detail, disturbing and disturbed characters, and (having) a haunting sense of dread that lingers long after the book is safely on the shelf" by another, with one publication saying of me as a writer, "DelGuercio is one bright spot on a plate of nori. He's like salmon roe." The novella was nominated for a Central New York Book-of-the-Year award in 2014 and I'm proud to include it here.

Influenced by many but owing more to the work of Ray Bradbury than anybody else, I hope you'll dig this sour little sci-fi/horror hybrid about an abandoned colony facing existential threats from both within and without. I think the less said about this piece, the better. Enjoy.

Eden Succeeding

Prologue

I am the Meatman, and I bring them the meat.

I've served three masters in my life. As I speak to you now, I am The Chronicler of Events because I'm the only one left who can perform the task, but when we originally landed on Second Eden, I was to be an Instructor of Knowledges—my formal training. An instructor for a generation that we soon came to realize would never bloom here. A dead end job if ever there was one.

It was then that I discovered my true calling. My people wanted meat, and I provided it. I was good at it. I did it willingly. I made no apologies then, nor do I now.

I am The Meatman. I bring them the meat.

BEFORE THE FALL

1

Mud covered my legs and a suction *pop* of air exploded with each step I pulled out of the muck. It was always like this on Eden after a rain. And there was always a rain. I trudged through it all, my squat body hunched close to the ground, weighted down by an arsenal of edged metals. It was an efficient way for a man like me to travel without the benefit of wide siltshoes to keep my feet aboveground: a slow-rolling waddle, shuffling, the way a drootmunk moves. Besides, when Bean's deformed feet punched through the wiring of his own shoes, I gave the boy mine. He needed them, being too spindly and sick to drootwalk.

"Keep up," I called out to the boy, forgetting Eden's influence had not only slowed his feet but the sound of my voice was becoming lost to him as well. His ears had withered and dropped off, and their canals had narrowed. The growth of shingles over the holes forced Bean to rely on the reading of my lips, but he was not always successful with the wire-tangle of beard I had hanging over my mouth and creeping across my face. I waved him forward and watched him double-time it to catch me. Trotting alongside me now, he labored for breath.

We were still within the safety of the outer bushwoods, a hedgerow of deep, wild greenery sitting atop a mesh of subterranean roots, so I slowed my gait and the two of us began to walk. I took out my journal and surveyed the clear sky of Eden's phytoplankton-rich atmosphere, olive green at the horizon and darkening as my gaze went up. Its pale sun blazed down on us. Bean turned his head to face me, his neck ratcheting loudly, each diseased click of his vertebrae sickening me to my core. I tried like hell to disguise my groan, but failed. I hastily finished my entry and returned the journal to my coat pocket.

"I don't think I should work for you anymore," he said, his dull, gray eyes raised to meet my healthy blues. He was slapping at the leaves and the plump turquoise fruit hanging from the branches of the jimp trees to our right. "It's useless. I'm only slowing you down anyway."

I remember when he first came to me two years ago, his eyes had held such warmth. They'd been a deep brown, so soft they looked like a pelt. I would never forget those eyes. Never. The boy was right, of course. I didn't want him to know that, but my silence said as much.

"For godsakes, why do you even still take me with you?" he continued, a defiance I'd never heard from him before ringing in his voice, almost as if his approaching end served to strengthen him. It made me proud in a strange way.

"I know why my father asked you to take me on," he said. "But it's clearly not working; I'm not like you. Eden's already too much inside me."

It was good to see someone share in my anger. "What makes you so sure we're not alike?" I asked.

"Just look at me!" His voice strained and cracked. He massaged his neck, the verdant skin alive with bulging, pulsing rivulets of vein. "You want me to say it? You want to hear me say I'm a goner?" I shook my head. "I'm not like you at all."

I grabbed hold of his arms. "People believe their eyes," I told him. "But their eyes only tell them what they already believe."

I could see that he was shocked that I grabbed him. "What do you mean?" he said.

"*You* can't even see it, with all the time you spend with me." I gave a half-hearted laugh. "I'm dying like all the rest." I let go of him and yanked at my sleeve to reveal a hairy, muscled forearm. Dark dirt encrusted my hands, framing each fingernail. I turned my palm up and while my hand was a permanent black, the inside of my arm was clean and covered with scars that wound up and down the length of me like pink worms.

Bean's eyes got wide. "Are those from the lissur?"

I nodded. "Those first years as Meatman I found out I'd wear my mistakes for the rest of my life. But that's not what I want you to see." I thrust my arm into the boy's face. "Look closer."

Bean examined the skin carefully. "You're jaundiced," he said with surprise.

I nodded again and rolled down my sleeve. "After that, I'll green, and then brown and harden." I squared up my face with his. "Do you see my eyes?"

The boy squinted and narrowed his eyes to chalk-colored slits.

"You see the snow in them?"

"All I see is blue," Bean said.

"Believe me, there's white in there too. It won't be long before they're as silver as yours. No one's getting spared, my friend. It just feels that way to you because you're farther along. We're all riding on the same train, just in different cars. Just one track though."

He seemed to take the news of our shared fates with genuine cheer, even fighting back a grin. I allowed him that. It was damn hard being a kid in this place, and no one—kid or not—wants to feel like they're alone in this, or any, world. We walked on beneath the harsh stare of Eden's sun, feeling a little better that we'd gotten a scream or two out of our systems.

"You know I was scared when father told me I was apprenticing with you," Bean said.

A smile rose up on my face. "Am I so scary to you first gens?"

"My friends all say you're some kind of a witch, charming the dirt dragons and cooking up secret potions, just you and Nessa all alone in the bush."

"Warlock," I said. "A woman is a witch but a man's called a warlock." I had to chuckle. "So, is that really what they say about me?"

"Oh yeah, and that's not all. I didn't know if I was more frightened of the lissur or you." His voice still held some innocence. The child inside that decayed husk glimmered through for just a moment and his words held this dumb, bittersweet smile clinging to me.

"How old are you now, Bean?"

"Thirteen," he said, puffing out his chest slightly. "What about you? I bet you're really old, huh?"

"Hey, I'm only thirty-eight," I told him.

"Yeah, that's really old."

I shrugged. When most first gens didn't see their tenth birthday, thirteen must have felt positively elderly, and I must've looked like Methuselah. In the deep distance, clouds coalesced. "We'd better pick it up. We've got redfields to cross and there's another storm coming." I sank my feet into the mud again.

The boy nodded and quickened his pace. "You talk like my dad sometimes. Were you ever someone's dad, back on Earth?"

"Nope," I said. "Me and Nessa, we didn't want to raise any children back there."

"So, you were waiting until you got to Eden?"

I paused a moment before I took another step. "That was our big plan, all right. But you know what they say about the best-laid plans of mice and men."

"The best-laid what?"

"No, I guess you wouldn't, would you?" I said. "Probably better that way."

Bean shook at my arm playfully. "Okay, as usual I'm totally lost right now. So, tell me what happened," he said, "with you and Nessa. And stop looking so gloomy, I'm the one who's sick, remember?'"

"Maybe you should concentrate on keeping pace instead of talking so much," I said.

"I'm sorry. I'm always prying, that's what father says." Bean clammed up and kept moving.

But after a while his sullenness got to eating at my gut. I was feeling guilty. After two years with me I guess the boy did deserve something more than I was giving him. But how could I make him understand that we couldn't bring children into this world either? I finally blurted out the words.

"Did *you* like growing up here?"

He smiled, pleased our conversation hadn't ended, paused in thought for a moment, then spoke. "I remember my mom would read me stories and sing to me in bed. I used to love that. Me and my dad would play catch with garva nuts. And, oh, thanks to you my baby brother thinks I'm a medieval knight or something." He stretched his arms out. "Yeah, I even had a girlfriend once." He had the far-off look of an older man reminiscing over a spent lifetime. "It's been better than not growing up at all," he said.

Christ on a crutch, what could I say to that? Damn this kid! I've never heard anyone be so thankful for so little. I guess after almost forty years breathing—half of them spent with the woman I love—I don't get to feel sorry for myself.

"If I'm being honest, this place scared us," I told him. "We couldn't fathom bringing a child up in this place, same as the last one. Maybe we're cowards."

Bean shook his head vigorously. "You're the bravest person I know."

I placed my hand on top of the boy's head. "If we knew then that having a kid like you was even possible, I think we might have changed our minds."

He reached up and wrapped his arm around my shoulder as we walked, and my feet seemed to lighten. I imagine this must be what it feels like to have a son of your own. I have to remember to put this is my journal.

But the next moment my thoughts wandered to Nessa and the inevitability of the time we had left together. I wanted to tell Bean how my chest tightened every time I took out that creased and faded picture of her at the lake, looking the way she used to. I wanted to explain to him that I couldn't accept my life here, or anywhere else, without her. I wanted to say that I was jealous of Eden, how its grip held increasing sway over her. But he's just a kid, with plenty of his own lamentations. No sense in piling mine on him too. There would be no children for Nessa and I.

"It's too late now," was all I told him. "That's all there is to it."

2

After galumphing through the strangling brush, we brought our feet down onto a blue-green forest bed, and soon after, emerged at the clearing where my thatched-roof house stood. We passed the white blossoms of the almond tree Nessa and I planted when we first put down stakes and walked to the door I fashioned myself from twistwood all those years before. I laid the day's catch into a barrow and told Bean, "Wheel this around back to the chop house." Then lifting the lever, I pressed my weight against the heavy wooden door.

Nessa's croaking voice called to me from the bedroom. "Is that you, Jon?" She vomited the words out as if they were glass shards. The sound grated against my ears.

From the barrel beside the door, I ladled a jugful of water and brought it to the bedroom. Yellowed photographs, half-covered with a sheet and speckled with mold, cluttered the dresser where her jewelry box stood. I placed the jug beside the bed and untied the harnesses that held her wrists to the bedposts, carefully avoiding the wide pink channels where the bindings had gouged through the toughened skin of her arms. With any lingering shred of strength I possessed, I hoisted her upright on the bed.

Her skin was brown and striated. She snatched the jug from my hands and poured the water down her gullet, letting it spill down her sides. With great zeal, she rubbed the overflow over her leathery flesh.

"How was today?" I asked gently.

"I dreamed," she said between gulps of water.

"Is that good?"

"I dreamed that I was this enormous thing." She spread her arms as far as they would stretch and the water sloshed in the jug. "An enormous, *living thing*, or at least I think I was."

Each new vision Eden presented to her terrified me more than the last. "And you're big?" I asked.

"It's not just that I'm big—it's *how* I'm big. I'm all middle." She screwed her face up. "I'm this greasy, pulsing thing—like an egg sack. It sounds scary, right?"

I nodded.

"Do you know what the scariest part about it was? I don't think it was a dream at all."

"Please, Nessa, don't. It was just a dream." A rock formed in my throat. "Don't say that. You know it kills me when you-"

"I heard the voices, too," she said, not listening to me anymore.

"The voices are lies, Nessa. We've been over this." I touched her hair, softly, for fear of it coming loose in my hand. Most of it had discolored and fallen out already, but there were still patches with roots strong enough to allow a calloused, roughhewn palm like mine to slide over them. "I'm sorry I wasn't home sooner," I told her. "I could've helped you make sense of this."

She looked at me, but I avoided her pupil-less eyes. Instead, I caressed her cheek with my palm and felt the rigidity that had taken over her entire body. She was hard, like a corpse, and instinctively I drew my hand away. Nessa's face sagged as if she were about to cry, but we both knew no tears would come from these new eyes. She trembled as I held her close and my eyes wept, doing the work for both of us.

"But the voices," she said. "They don't feel like lies."

I pulled away then rubbed at my temples. "They... are... lies! Don't listen to them," I said. "Bean's in the back. There's meat that needs tending. I'll be a while."

"You'll be here, just out back?" she said. "Then you don't have to use the straps on me this time. I promise I won't leave."

"Okay then," I said as I made for the door. I opened it and stopped there with my back to her. How could I be mad? None of this was her fault. I turned around. "I need you," I said.

She smiled and poured the last of the water into a cup. "Thank you, Jon. You're so sweet to me." I left her in our bedroom and exited the front door. From the outside, I bolted it shut.

I walked over the fallen almond blossoms around back to the small shed I'd built when I first took up hunting—nothing more than a single-room hut with vertical slats set apart for air to flow through, like a gap-toothed smile. At the doorway, I took out my journal and scribbled a few passages in it.

Bean was already elbow-deep in the basin tub, chopping the meat into manageable pieces. He threw each slab into the tub with a wet *thwap*. I pulled a carafe of berrystain from a crowded shelf of variegated bottles and poured the crimson liquid over the meat. Opaque, clay jars of plant and seed oil extracts, a mortar and pestle, and spice vials were all nearby on the shelves. I stretched out my hands and my fingers made an audible *crack*.

The creator's time was at hand.

The preparation of the meat was sacrament. I dyed it in a mixture primarily made of the juice from a common local berry, which transformed the meat's previous mud-color into a deadflesh scarlet. Once the meat was removed from the tub, the juice sweated out, leaving a deceptively grisly shadow on the cutting board. The berry itself was the blandest sort and offered no clue that the *juices* within the meat were anything but the sweet lifeblood of an animal everyone knew didn't exist on Second Eden.

This sight alone brought most of the Alpha settlement out of their caves and hovels on the day of the market, but providing mere sustenance was never enough for me. I was an artisan, a true virtuoso, a painter who worked in the medium of the senses. A magician, but of the best kind because my legerdemain made mouths water and brought forth memories of home. So as countless hours and days here strung together into countless months and years, I collected a mixture of tastes, scents, and textures that would mimic a small piece of what we'd left behind on Earth. And the lissur provided the perfect canvas. This quaggy, utterly tasteless meat would be at the heart of each of my little masterpieces.

There were minute differences from beef, to be certain. The lingering pungency from the soil that encapsulated these beasts their entire lives— centuries, millennia even, how were we to know. Then there was the meat's consistency—softer, more like that of a scallop than of cattle. Even the dying solution itself, with the slightest hint of citrus, could serve to reveal my ruse. But it never did. Because the most powerful seasoning of all was one I didn't have to add: The homesick mind. Any imperfect flavor or aroma, any sensation missing or untrue was masked by the customers making them, ultimately, the final chef.

No one knew—I don't think they even cared to know—how I did what I did. They knew only that I faced the monsters for them.

I was The Meatman, and I'd bring them their meat.

In the final stages of preparation, after brining the day's catch and applying a spice rub I concocted from jerk root and pepris, I wrapped the lot in sunsplash leaves to preserve them for the long trip to market. Our sojourn was tomorrow and my task was now complete. Red up to my elbows in berrystain and stinking of wormy flesh, I came back into the house.

"Is the meat ready?" Nessa asked. She sounded better. The water had soothed the coarseness in her voice and her short-lived freedom to move about the house had nourished her spirit.

I took her by the hand but felt nothing of the woman I loved remaining in its stiff, cool grip. "Me and the boy are leaving for market."

"So soon? I wish you could stay a while longer. You spend more time with that meat than you do with me."

"The meat is our life, Nessa. You know that."

Her head drooped as far as the disease would let it. "You want me back on the bed, don't you?"

"You're sick," I said. "I can't have you just wandering off to the bush. We both know what happens when Eden gets inside you."

She squeezed her hand out of mine. "I won't listen to the voices, I swear. I'll stay right here in the house. I won't-"

"No!" My voice was more of a howl than I'd intended. "I'm sorry. But no."

She slunk quietly into bed and lifted her arms into the straps. I fastened her right hand in and tightened it. I couldn't bear to lose her. I needed her that much even though I couldn't trust her anymore not to be seduced by Eden's voices.

Was that still love?

I can't tell anymore, but it didn't stop me from tightening the strap around her left hand as well.

3

A clearing existed on our sliver of Eden, where the planet's crust itself seemed to have grown out of the ground to shape a great hall of sorts. The crag, flattened smooth from constant weathering, poked up from beneath the soil, creating stone tables. The entire field was floored in this same stone. Under the wan light of dawn, vendors marched into the clearing from all directions, flashing between the shadows, and then popping out suddenly from behind gigantic hanging leaves, like funhouse spooks.

We hauled our wares by sack and wagon, meandering through the countryside over the safe passes. There were quicker routes, but few dared to hasten their journey across lands they called *redfields* or *sinks*. Those lands belonged to the lissur. We wandered in drunk with fatigue, like soldiers from a Wilfred Owen poem, wearing clothes heavy with rain and painted black with soil that clung like tar to our pant legs.

We did this because it was our chance to be a community again. It was our one chance for something we hadn't been in so long. It was our chance to be normal.

A canopy of arboreal growth shielded us enough to conduct business even on the wettest days. Market was a time when all the richness of our new home was on display to be sampled and bartered for. Thousands of edible species of flora and many marvelously succulent combinations previously untouched by human tongues—the absinthian croakweed and the sweetgreens, the moist red crellets and the striped jala fruit that positively dripped with flavor—all set up in bushels. The strange and grotesque fauna lined the stalls. Horned and winged creatures hung from pikes while others buzzed and squawked from cages. Fat, hairy drootmunks and flying poppits lay encased in thick tree wine.

The hard-shelled and soft-bodied children of Eden, things without limbs, without faces. Their songs, once so strange, were now all too familiar. But no tastes were in higher demand than those of Earth. And only I, The Meatman, could create the illusion of mammalian flesh. The surface of this planet held none. That it would come up out of the ground was the real surprise.

After all the probes, all the scanning, all the yottobytes of data on Eden's surface, this spot was chosen for the colony. The plans were made. The ships launched. But we never anticipated what was twisting around in the deep dark just below us.

The lissur—dirt dragons—were a surprise, indeed. Hideous, awful, bloodthirsty creatures. We soon discovered dozens of different breeds, but, no matter which breed, their nature was the same. Mindless, soulless, bottomless wells of stinking death. They fired themselves up from the bowels of this hell to feed on the living. To feed on us. And now, without them, I was nothing in this new world.

Bean and I laid the meat out on the stones for barter.

"You never answered me before. Are you going to send me back to Father Hy?" he asked. "I'm not getting any better."

"You're always welcome to stay on, you know that. I told your father not to put his faith in the meat."

My perceived good health, over many years, gave rise to the popular belief that the less *native* something tasted, the less it would allow the disease to ravage our bodies. This was rubbish, of course. My body was hairy and I constantly wore a shadow of dirt, so my skin hadn't appeared to discolor like the others. In mine, the palest of blue eyes, the flecking that always manifested at the onset of the disease did not always show. I was outwardly a healthy, entirely human man. But make no mistake, Eden's sickness was inside me. I could feel it setting in.

My people didn't want to see that, though. They wanted to believe in The Meatman, the one who eats the beasts, the one who had escaped Eden's curse. It was a lie. A lie I never invented or promoted, but one I benefited from nonetheless. I didn't keep them free from the disease. I kept them free from hopelessness. It was the best I could do.

"There's nothing miraculous about this stuff, Bean. You know that now better than anyone. It's just flesh and ingredients. Never put your faith in it."

"Father always says his faith is with you...not that low serpent." The boy's voice deepened, mimicking Father Hy's baritone. "Work with The Meatman, my son, and your soul will remain always divine." He laughed and slapped another piece of meat down onto the table.

The boy's biological had become a spiritual figure in our community, but Father Hy, as he came to be known, hadn't always been a holy man. He came to Eden, like so many others in Alpha colony, to dig in the dirt. Like me, he only found his calling after a need arose. Eden had a way of doing that, turning us settlers into the people we were intended to be all along. As for myself and religion...well, I never had a strong need to be talked to in riddles.

"Your soul will remain always divine?" I said. "What exactly did he mean by that?"

"As long as my body and mind stay human, my soul survives. That's what he thinks." Bean dropped another slab of meat but this one slid across the rock and found its way onto the ground. "I'm sorry."

"It's all right," I said.

"I can't even do the simple things anymore."

"It's fine, Bean." The boy was tired. Anyone could see that. "Why don't you catch a quick nap."

"Really? You don't mind? But market's set to open soon."

"I don't mind, go get you some rest," I said. "Besides, I can't have you dropping product all day. You'll be right as rain in an hour."

I let him sleep on my empty pack behind our table while I finished displaying the meat.

4

"Point out your choicest cuts," a burly farmer said, leering over my table in the blaring midday light. His eyes were hazed over in a chrome-colored film and he got his face down close to the meat to examine it. The span of his reach was so great he could pluck two pieces off either end of the table simultaneously. "These are some fine pieces you've got here, Meatman, just fine. We'll eat real good this month, wife."

They were long-time afflicteds. He was known as Reaper. She was Handy. They perused the scraps on the stone table while their brood of thirteen milled about behind them. They all stared at the meat with the same absent, quicksilver gaze. Their limbs were elongated and, though their clothes made an attempt to hide them, stubby protrusions had budded underneath. The chartreuse skin color that every diseased settler acquired had given way in this family to a tougher, umber coat marked by white striations. It was the final stage of the change. *Sugar and stripes*, they called it.

They were good people and as much as I pitied them, I'd be a liar if I said their presence didn't also disgust me. From the copious number of grimaces and catcalls, I wasn't alone.

"One cut is as good as another," I said first, then, more loudly to the passersby, "If it's not the finest cut, it doesn't make my table."

Reaper pointed out four pieces.

An anonymous male voice said, "All the steak on Eden won't fix that lot."

Reaper turned.

A group stood loosely huddled behind the family. At the front was a sturdy, handsome woman of some years. She wore spectacles and a sack of a dress with a high-rise collar, even in the heat season. Tradition demanded Cardinal Justices dress partly in red while out amongst the public, but the Lady Malic insisted on covering herself in the sanguine hue from hair to heel. The men surrounding her kept a few feet of open air between themselves and the lady at all times.

"You'd be wise, Mr. Reaper, to take your soulless eyes off me," she said without looking up from the knob of caprilla fruit in her hand. She twirled the ripened, speckled delicacy, inspecting it. "Considering your condition, I wouldn't expect you to be so *thin-skinned*." The men chuckled.

A justice was always blunt.

Handy tugged on her husband's sleeve and grumbled something I couldn't quite make out. Reaper stepped toward Lady Malic, but her entourage quickly filled the space between the two. Her men consisted of several, healthy, land-tough farmers, their hair long and streaked with sweat.

The Lady Malic calmly explained, "There's no quarrel here, Mr. Reaper, so please don't be foolish and create one. Pick out your meat and be on your way and I give you my word that you and your family won't be subjected to any more harassment here today. You must understand though how the sight of you people unnerves folks around here."

Reaper only stared back at the Cardinal Justice. A prodigiously tall bowman, almost as big as Reaper himself, stepped forward. He raised one bulging arm and reached behind his head to pluck an arrow from his quiver. "Lady Malic, allow me to remove-"

"My word was given, Chamberlain," the woman said with an icy deliberateness. "That's all you need hear."

The loyalty chip implanted in the bowman's head clicked on, and the archer dropped his arm, fed it between his bow and string then threw the apparatus over his shoulder. "Of course, m'lady. Sincerest apologies."

New settlements needed order. Chamberlain kept the colony in order for Lady Malic, and the chip kept Chamberlain in order.

The men fanned out behind Lady Malic again as Reaper's face twisted into an angry knot. Bean was watching from behind our table, enthralled by the conflict.

"Packs need to be cleaned or they'll reek of worm meat," I told him. "Why don't you take them down to the brook and wash them out now."

"Can't it wait a few minutes?"

"Take them now," I said.

Bean huffed once then stomped off, but the boy did exactly as he was told. He always did.

Onlookers began to gather as Lady Malic's words failed to quell the situation. She decided to address the growing crowd. "As your appointed Justice, my promises must be as solid as twistwood and my judgments as fair as the summer sky. Have I not been a trustworthy and just Cardinal?" Many murmurs of agreement came from the assemblage. "A Cardinal Justice has only her word with which to rule."

"Her word?" Reaper roared. "Yes, our poor Cardinal Justice has only her word... and a loaded streaker under her belt, to go along with that loyalty-chipped lapdog." Reaper pointed a thumb in the direction of the men. "And this bunch of halfwits."

Lady Malic turned back to the farmer. "More complaints?" she asked.

Reaper moved closer. "We all came here together, and we're all going out the same way. This ain't the right manner to treat people." He pointed to the crowd. "And all of you know it!" Then he said quietly to his wife, "They don't have to buy my crops, but I'll be damned if I'm going to let them insult us."

"Goodness me, Reaper," Lady Malic said. "Stop whining before you make an old woman cry."

The people burst into laughter. Handy tugged her husband's arm again and shook her head. "The little ones are scared. Just let it be now, husband." She gathered the children up close to her.

Reaper stroked the deep brown gouges of his wife's cheek. "It's not fair," he said, exasperation in his voice. "Forgive me, wife, but what else can I do?"

Suddenly, he sprung at Lady Malic, his huge frame covering the distance between them in less than an instant. He clamped his fingers around her arms, squeezed them to her sides, and lifted the woman off the ground, spinning her away from the pack and planting her in front of my table. He bent down until the tips of their noses nearly met. "Eden's stronger than you, *m'lady*. And there's going to be more and more of us before this is over. That still means something." Reaper released the startled woman just as her men got a hold of him.

"No," she said. "Let him be."

Chamberlain's loyalty chip clicked on, and he immediately let Reaper go. The other men followed suit as the huge farmer tore his body away. Reaper gathered up his family to leave, and the men followed.

"No!" Lady Malic repeated. "My word was given. Let them go… for now." Chamberlain cordoned the men off with his outstretched arms as she bellowed to the family, "Best you keep your infection far from market!"

Many in the crowd bristled with an identical sentiment. "Go live in the bushwoods where you belong!" was a cry echoed by the group. "You're not one of us!"

The Reapers hurried off into the forest without looking back.

Lady Malic took a heavy breath and pulled a kerchief from her pocket to dab the sweat from her forehead. She called her men to my table then turned to face me. "I'm sorry," she said.

I waved my hand. "No need."

"No, I'm afraid there is a need, a great one. There are those among us who would be better suited keeping to themselves instead of exposing us all to the melancholy that is their lives."

"They've got a right to eat, don't they?" I asked.

Lady Malic threw me a sideways glance as she fingered some meat. "Normally I would tell you to leave the interpreting of rights to the experts, but I get your angle. A good customer is a good customer."

"That's right."

Lady Malic noticed Bean as he labored up the hill with the wet packs on his shoulders. She motioned to him. "And good help is hard to find," she said. "No matter what they look like."

"Right again," I said.

"Being a provider doesn't always allow for high-minded thinking, I suppose. If it did, there wouldn't be a need for Justices."

"Oh, I don't know, Cardinal, there's always got to be a job for someone who can do all the high-minded thinking for us."

My statement pulled a lifeless chuckle out of her.

"Do you ever wonder what it'll be like when there aren't any customers left?" She slapped a lump of meat onto the table. "That's a tasty one, don't you think?"

Of course I'd wondered about it, the end of our colony. Who hadn't? We were dying a lot faster than we were reproducing. You didn't have to be much of a mathematician to figure that equation.

"It's yours," I told her. "Let me wrap it." I laid the meat inside an oversized sunsplash leaf and tied the ends together neatly.

"I haven't offered barter yet."

"Just consider me paid up on my taxes," I said.

"Don't be silly, Meatman, I'm a public servant. You've already paid quite enough," she said before her countenance darkened. "Of course, in times of crisis our debt to the community can't solely be covered in goods. There are times when our *service* is required as well." She glanced at the macabre feast dripping crimson juice off the side of the rock. "Lovely looking things—you're profoundly skilled." She wiped the faux blood from the table with her finger then licked it clean. "Men of skill, that's precisely what we'll need in the coming days."

Now I wasn't accustomed to people looking me in the eye anymore, but Lady Malic seemed completely unfazed by my aura. Or was it just that she had a bigger one than me? This woman had irises like burned-out holes, and when she stared into mine it felt like she was crawling right down inside me to make certain I understood that the services she required from me would not be pleasant, no sir. You don't hire a hunter to polish your china. You call on a hunter because they're not afraid to get their hands bloody.

As I stared back into that expanse of piceous matter she called eyes, I swear I saw nothing I could relate to.

I wonder what was it that she saw inside me?

5

The day's trading had been brisk and as the sun hung low on a bruise-colored horizon, Bean and I packed up my newly bartered goods. I got a necklace for Nessa. It was little more than a heart-shaped lump of polished stone, but I knew it would bring a smile to her face. It also distracted my mind from Lady Malic's words. But it was a long slog home, with plenty of time to think. I pulled out my stub of pencil and jotted down some thoughts before we left:

I hated Eden. I hated watching it eat away at us. None of us had any illusions coming here; we knew we'd lead hardscrabble lives at first. But there had been hope for a happiness that had disappeared on Earth. There were to be more transports—every few months—bringing settlers and provisions. We would need new stocks of food, medicine, weapons—this much we'd known. But there were so many other things we'd need. Things we could only know of once we spread roots and lived in this world. And if Eden rejected us and all our careful planning and advanced technologies? If it just spit us back out into the void—what then? At the very least we'd need a ride home.

That was seventeen years ago.

No new transports ever arrived, not even word as to why. What happened? The answer might have meant something before our supplies ran out. After that, we were too busy figuring out ways to survive. We all became a little less human then. Long before Eden got into our blood.

It's hard to believe now but I respect Cardinal Malic. She was one of us. She made sacrifices. She took losses. She was smart, creative. She was an unmitigated bitch, and she survived. Nobody likes to admit it, but someone's got to be in charge. Everyone hates *the man*, even when it's a woman.

On Earth they fought over land, over water. They fought over money. They fought to see who had the biggest gun, who had the biggest god. We were chosen to be Alpha colony because we were all on the same side. Cardinal Malic was our leader. She was just what we needed to survive in a place like Second Eden.

Bean snapped me out of my reverie. "Did you hear those Digger boys over on Sanctuary Hill found a whole house buried in the ground?"

"How far underground?" I asked.

"Just a few feet. They think maybe it was a mudslide. They found pictures in there too, old drawings of the hillside. I saw them. The bush doesn't look the same in those pictures. It's taller now, and fuller. In the pictures it looks like it was just starting to grow. Those drawings didn't come from us. They came from whoever was here *before* us."

"Makes you wonder, doesn't it? Maybe we weren't the first to try to settle here after all. I got a feeling this place is just full of secrets."

"Well I want to know what happened to those people, where they went." His voice got low. "If that's where I'm going."

I put my hand on his shoulder. "I'd bet you cash money we all end up in the same place eventually."

"Where's that?"

"I don't know. Heaven, maybe, if you believe in a place like that."

"How do you know if you're in Heaven?"

I shook my head and laughed. "So, so many questions, my young Bean."

"I'm serious. I want to know. How will I be able to tell if I'm in Heaven?"

I let out a loud sigh and thought a moment. "All right," I said. "Close your eyes." The boy obliged. He always did. "Shut everything else out except the sound of my voice."

"Okay," he said.

"Now turn your ears inside out and listen very closely. Listen to the voices *inside* you, speaking to you. I know someone who hears the voices and it eases her mind to listen to them. You hear them too, don't you?"

"How do you know about the voices?" he asked.

"Never mind," I told him. "Just listen to them. Ask *them* your question."

If Eden's voices weren't lies, like Nessa believes, than this was the one time when they might actually do our kind some good. Bean shut his eyes tight and didn't speak at all for a minute or two.

"What are you seeing?"

"They're showing me a place," he said, "with a lot of people. Is this Heaven?"

"Do you know the people?"

"Yes, some of them."

"Do you care about all these people?"

The boy grinned. "Yes."

"Then it's Heaven," I said. "It might go by a different name to other folks, but if you're there with all the people you ever cared about, then you're definitely in Heaven."

Bean opened his eyes and smirked at me. "I know what you're trying to do and I appreciate it, but I'd still like to know where all the people really disappear to."

I nodded at him. "Me, too. You know there was a legend back home about old elephants who would walk to a place they'd never been to before—sometimes hundreds of miles away—just to lie down and die.

Maybe that's the way it is here too."

"What's an elephant?" Bean asked.

I smiled. "It doesn't really matter."

"Oh, okay then," he said. "Then could you tell me what *cash money* is?"

My god, I never realized how old thirty-eight could feel.

6

The storms here are gentle, mostly. Not like on Earth, where a cold New England sleet would stiffen you up and have you running for shelter. Here, warm pellets gently shower you. The sound of them bouncing off the land is a sheet of white noise, drowning out everything else. The entire experience is immersive, womblike, and hypnotic. It lulls you into feeling you're safe out there in the open. Eden needs you that way so it can have its children tear you to pieces. That's how it feeds.

Bean and I were out of the lush bushwoods and the forest no longer insulated our movements. Our naked footfalls fell on sodden ground—a distinctive pattern, permeating the soil to its bowels, as different from the rain patter as black is from white. The miry ground only served to slow the boy more.

I skirted my gaze along the horizon for any signs of danger. "Let's pick it up."

The lissur were unthinking beasts, but what they lacked in intelligence they made up for in brutal instinct and honed adaptation. Nature constructed these creatures to reign here. It wouldn't take them long to find us. I was armed up to my eyes, as usual. But steel wasn't everything.

"Do you want me to carry you?"

"No, sir," Bean said. The boy marshaled his strength, grunting loudly with each step.

Through the dim shreds of light piercing the clouds, I caught the glint of starstone veining through a cluster of grassy buttes that humped the horizon. It was far away, maybe too far for Bean. In the redfields, the only haven from the lissur was Edenrock, as it protected us from direct subterranean attacks and the flat tops made for excellent footing. But these were the redfields, and there wasn't much rock to be found in them. We were at least a little bit lucky to find something. Still, at the familiar vibrato that hummed through the ground and up my legs, my heart surged with dread.

A lissur was here.

I turned my legs into pistons, and my feet disappeared into the ground with each step I pumped into that bog. Bean was falling farther behind. I looked back to find the boy's twig legs clopping desperately on my oversized siltshoes. Even through the platinum coat of pulp that covered his eyes, I saw the presence of fear. He was still all-too-human. Too human to die like this. I wouldn't allow it. So I doubled back to fetch him.

The low rumble was all around us now. The serpent was nipping at our toes. I reached Bean, snatched his hand, and tugged, but the boy was like an anchor.

"Try to move," I demanded.

"No," he said. He pulled his hand loose from mine and his arms fell limp. His face was awash in an eerie serenity.

And the thumping grew.

"Go. You don't have much time," he said. "My father wants me to die human, with a soul. That's all he cares about. Why do you think he sent me to you? He never put his faith in the meat to cure me. He put his faith in you to let me die before I changed."

"Then your father's going to be awfully disappointed with me," I said. I swiped at his arm, but he pulled it back again. So I charged him, buried my shoulder into his midsection, and wrapped my arms around his waist. With every drop of life I had left inside me, I lifted his body and tossed him over my shoulder, draping him around the back of my neck like a scarf.

But as I took a quick step my leg sunk into the soil below my knee. I needed my siltshoes back. When I dropped Bean and madly tried to unlace the shoes from his feet, the mud began to tremble. I knew I couldn't have them off before the lissur surfaced.

"On your feet!" I told him. "You have to run for it." I pointed to the butte. "If we can get close enough to those-"

The ground bulged, lifting Bean into the air, then cracked and fell away in chunks beneath his feet, leaving a man-sized hole. A baleful smell, rancid and wild, rose from the fractured terra. With a series of violent jerks, Bean's lower body disappeared into the pit.

"No!"

My heart adrenalized and beat more furiously, threatening to explode from my chest. There were no other options now. I reached inside my shirt and unsheathed the saber from its scabbard. I'd never wished to strike a truer blow.

I raised the saber to the sky. I took aim. I swung.

The blade easily broke through the hardened body shingles that encased Bean. It cleaved the soft of his neck flesh and severed his bony chord. Finally, it burst out the other side amidst a spray of splintered skin. No sooner had his head been freed than the boy's body sagged and slid, arms raised, beneath the mud. His dead fingers towed the head until it, too, was swallowed up in the Eden-soil.

It was a well-struck blow. For that I was thankful. That alone.

Then I ran. To have done anything else would have been folly. Without Bean to slow me, I had a chance. It was a foul and uncaring thought, but it was true. So I sheathed my saber and made for the safety of the starstone and surer footing.

This lissur was quick. Probably small. As it burrowed closer to the surface, and to me, the land mounded behind the streaking animal. The dark ground juddered to such an extreme that I was no longer held in its grip with each step, but rather, my feet became *unstuck* due to the reverberations. It sped me considerably, and I splashed across the field.

The land thickened, and soon my shoes were slapping against solid stone. I vaulted across its glittering surface, reached a small rock face, and scrambled to the outcropping's top before rolling onto my back, swallowing the warm, heavy air.

Couldn't stop yet. I had to get up.

I flipped over and got to my feet. Reaching inside my coat, I tapped my arsenal of weaponry with my fingers, choosing a blade for each hand. I drew a rapier for my left and a small scythe for my right. Atop the butte the tremors were faint, but the lissur's vibrating song was still present.

Then it stopped.

From my perch, I scanned the landscape, snuffing the air like a hound. I spun around just as a russet-colored torpedo head emerged from the gravel, propelled from below by a collection of short, floppy legs. A King Quintha lissur. Big nasties, these were. This one was still young though, as evidenced by its circumference and mottled skin. It emerged from the hole, lifting itself by its legs, to rise several feet above my head and study me with ring of a hundred, large, white eyes peaking out from behind upturned scales. Their eyes were always pure white—like huge, embedded eggs. Shaking furiously, the lissur gave a prolonged hiss.

There's no lack of edge to you, is there, you little bastard?

An outer layer of skin at its tip peeled back to expose a great maw. The ruddy, folded flesh within it a stark contrast to its darkly-mirrored exterior. From inside the tip, toothy tendrils unfurled, engorged with poison, and the whole putrid mass swung closer. On hardened ground and with my weapons already drawn, I was more prepared than I could've hoped to be. If I was to fall, this lissur would have earned it.

With my rapier, I delivered a controlled thrust into an endocrine pouch deep within the beast's mouth and the hormone that holds much of the creature's bile leaked out. Now pacified, I swayed my hands rhythmically in front of the tendrils, the way a snake charmer might, allowing them to entwine the blades. Adjusting the swords slowly to and fro at practiced angles, I coaxed the tendrils down onto the starstone.

Sleep, little one. Go to sleep.

Then I slid my rapier out and laid it across the top of the writhing nest to hold the tendrils in place. Slowly, I raised the scythe, then dropped it hard, severing each veiny stalk and leaving the remains to retreat into the Quintha's angry mouth.

As the tendrils flailed about like stray hoses, they spat their lifeblood at me. I hacked at the lissur with the scythe until all the fight had left the young King. When it tried to descend back under the rock, I dropped both rapier and scythe and pulled two serrated daggers with balloon hilts from my belt. I drove them into either side of the animal. As the lissur burrowed, the daggers caught at the surface and the hilts kept it from submerging. With it partially topside and struggling, I jumped from my perch and reached for Fin, the parashu axe I kept strapped between my shoulder blades. I fingered its haft before lifting the axe out and burying the curved bit into the lissur.

I yanked the blade free and swung again, and again, and again. I chopped away until the remaining topside portion of the serpent fell, spraying mud and juice across my legs. Then I staked the meat to the ground and completed the detachment with my knife. The remaining diaphanous stump slid down the hole and disappeared meekly into the darkness.

It was over.

I kicked the lifeless meat, stabbed it, hammered and screamed at it. I owed the boy that much. I owed the boy my anger. I owed it to myself, too. I stayed there alone, sitting on my knees in the mud for a long while.

It was over. Bean was gone.

I lifted the meat onto my shoulder and headed back.

7

It was late when I returned home. Nessa was still bound to the bed. I clumsily plucked at her ligatures while she glowered.

"Is Bean in the shed?"

"The kid couldn't hack it anymore, so I sent him home." I swallowed hard. "He won't be coming back."

"That's a real shame," she said. "It must've been hard for you to let him go. I know how much you liked him."

I turned away and rubbed at my eyes. "I didn't have much choice."

She waited while I freed her arms then said, "Jon, I don't want to be tied down anymore."

I stamped my foot. "You don't know what you're saying. Listen, I'm sorry I'm late. The market was heavy today," I said. "I brought you something though." I pulled the necklace from my pocket and handed it to her.

She gripped it in her fist then threw it across the bedroom. "I don't want these straps on me anymore."

"Is it the nightmares again?" I unclasped the final harness that fettered her ankle.

"They're not nightmares, they're visions. Visions of something to come for me. I'm not scared of it anymore. I'm not scared of anything... except being tied up alone here." Her body fell at my feet. "Please, don't you want me to find some peace before I leave?"

"You're not going anywhere," I said. "I won't let you." I thumped my fist repeatedly against the wall behind me. "I won't let you go. I won't do it!"

The room fell silent because in our hearts I think we both knew that what I wanted wasn't the way things worked out on Eden. The disease would take her eventually, whether I tied her down or not. I picked her back up onto the bed and lay beside her when she took my head and cradled it to her breast.

"I should have given you children," she said. "They would have been beautiful."

I nodded softly and sat up. Nessa's arms were still wrapped around me. "It may be better you didn't." I told her. "This place is turning everyone into madmen. Malic brought her crew to market today, stirring things up. These people—*our friends*—are getting ugly, Nessa."

"I don't like leaving you this way," she said.

I don't know what happened then. Was it her words? Or was it something in her voice, that ravaged voice, that caused me to snap? I clenched my teeth. "I'm not letting you leave. The bush can call out to you all it wants, but you're staying with me. Maybe it'll slow down, or stop."

She untangling herself from me and stood up. She slid out of her nightgown naked and stretched her arms out to her sides. Frosted streaks covered her. Her thickened midsection, riddled with uneven knobs that stuck way out like the sides of a coat rack, robbed her of all the femininity she once had. The sickness spread all the way to her feet, where her toes were now gnarled and overgrown, entwined with one another, reaching out in all directions.

I closed my eyes.

"This is me. This is what I am now," she said. "How can you still fight this? I've stopped. You should, too."

I touched her fingers gently, kissed the thick, tawny skin inside her wrist, and pulled her back onto the bed beside me. "If I give you up, what's left?" I eased her hand above her head and, before she could protest, buckled it into the strap.

"Don't do this. I belong to them," she said. My stomach turned. "I'm not yours to fight for anymore, I'm already Eden's slave. Don't make me yours, too."

A knock came loudly at the door.

My heart leapt. "Stay in bed. If the wrong person sees you like this…just stay here." I sprung from the room then grabbed a machete from its mount on the wall before throwing open the door.

Lady Malic stood hooded and dripping at the threshold with much of her gang gathered several feet behind her. "Gracious," she said, catching sight of my knife, "looks like you've got yourself in a stew." She flashed a thin-lipped grin. "Must be your wife—only a woman could get a man so bent. No matter, you hold on to that fire, it'll be of good use tonight. I'm taking the boys over to Reaper's farm." She turned away. "Exquisite almond blossom tree you have out here, Meatman. Eden-soil clearly agrees with it."

I lowered the machete. "It shot up like a rocket as soon as I put her in the ground," I told her. "Reaper's farm, eh? That's a hell of a walk in this stuff. You're probably better off just staying put." If I could get this group back in their beds tonight, tomorrow might have them looking at this situation with leveler heads.

Lady Malic sighed and stepped back into the rain. Chamberlain then slipped by her and leaned in through the doorframe, his ever-present bow and quiver clinging to his back. "Your service as a guide is being requested by the office of the Cardinal Justice."

"Only requested?" I asked.

Chamberlain stared at me. "*Required.* Now if you please…" he stepped out of the doorway and extended his arm into the open air for me to follow.

I glanced toward the bedroom, praying Nessa hadn't been seen. "Just let me tell my wife." I swung the heavy door but Chamberlain wedged his siltshoe in before it could close.

"Would you mind terribly if we waited inside?" Lady Malic asked. "This rain wears on me."

Nessa blared at us in that wretched garble of hers, "Give me a moment." A clatter escaped the bedroom.

I called out, "It's the Cardinal Justice and those friends of hers I told you about earlier." The noise quickly stopped. *Smart girl.* "I have to go with them," I shouted again to her. "They need a guide."

A long silence, and then her answer, "Hurry back."

"She sounds awfully raw," Lady Malic said, wiping her glasses clean. "We have Doc Cutter with us." She waved the man forward. "Why don't you let him take a look at her."

"If you think she sounds raw now, wait until you come in here with those siltshoes on—she'll have me scrubbing these floors the minute I get back. No, we should just get going. She's got a hoarse cold is all. Give me a minute to load up and say goodbye, and I'll get us on the trail."

Malic smiled and gave the signal. "Suit yourself."

Chamberlain edged his foot out from between the door and its frame. I closed it carefully then rushed to the bedroom.

"Are they gone?" Nessa asked.

"Not without me." I grabbed her arms and stretched them over the headrest to where the bindings attached to the wall. Then I closed the straps around her wrists.

"What are you doing? Don't do this again. This isn't what you really want for us, is it, Jon?"

"Maybe not," I said. "But it's what I've got." I finished the task at her ankles, and she flopped and arched her body like a fish caught on a dock. "I'm sorry. This is the only way. I need to get these people as far away from you as I can." I kissed her lips and her imprisoned body dropped to the bed in defeat.

From off the wall, I snatched every bit of weaponry I could carry and affixed them to my hunting vest. Then I stuffed my journal inside my coat pocket and left with Lady Malic and the men—nine in all—to begin the slow journey to Reaper's spread. The rain had been on a steady pour all night, turning the land into a slough. My body was wearing down, but there was no time to rest.

8

We'd been humping it for more than an hour when Lady Malic shouted through the din of falling raindrops, "Meatman, are you certain this is the most direct route?"

"*Most* direct?" I yelled back. "No, but it's the safest."

One of the men, Owen All, threw his hands up. "I must be going deaf. Did you say we *weren't* on the quickest path? Why the hell not?"

"Because we wouldn't make it," I barked at him. "Well, *you* wouldn't make it."

Owen looked at the Cardinal like a dog who'd just had his nose slapped. Lady Malic told him, "If the Meatman says you wouldn't make it, then I believe you would not make it, Owen."

"You're welcome to try," I said, pointing in a southeasterly direction.

Owen grumbled and fell back with the others, leaving me with Lady Malic and Chamberlain at the front of the pack. She cackled loudly. "You don't suffer fools gladly, Meatman. I knew there was something about you I liked."

"I suppose I don't," I said. "Can I ask how you're holding up so far?"

"Oh, I'm hardier than I might appear. You needn't worry about me."

"I'm not worried. I'm just asking."

"It's appreciated," the woman said, and we continued to walk. "You know, an army needs generals, and generals need their soldiers." She motioned with her head to the men. "But generals also need lieutenants."

I raised an eyebrow. "After all these years I've kind of gotten used to being a free-thinking man, ma'am. I'm my own general, lieutenant, sergeant, colonel, and corporal all in one. It suits me." I tapped a finger against the side of my head. "You won't find any loyalty chips in here, so I'm afraid I'm not wired the right way to be in your army. Besides, I thought Chamberlain here was your right-hand man."

The archer gave me a cold look.

"He is my right hand, and a damn fine one at that. I think he'd be the best man for the job even without that chip in his head," she said. "But I've got *two* hands."

"You make it sound like we're at war."

Her face soured. "Don't play coy, Meatman. We've been at war with this planet ever since we touched down, you know that. And Eden needs to secure soldiers for its army, too. The Reapers have one foot in the bush as it is. If we're going to beat this place, we don't need them, or anyone else, fighting for the other side."

I stopped walking. My voice was eager, like a child's, when I asked her, "What are you saying exactly—that you think the Alphas are still alive after the bush takes them? How do you know this?"

"Alive? Yes, I think so, but not human. Once they disappear they'll be Eden's. And they'll protect their own. It's time we did the same." Placing her hand on my elbow, she started me walking again. "If you believe the stories-"

"People tell lots of stories about what's in the bush. Doesn't mean any of it's true. No one's spent more time in the bush than me and I haven't seen anything of our people."

"Well then maybe it's that you haven't suffered enough yet," she said, her voice eerily quiet. "I've felt things—mossy things creeping in the night, eyes watching from the wood. I tell you we're not alone, and whatever *they* are, they're getting stronger with every soul we give them. They'll come for the rest of us, the healthy ones, soon enough, you watch."

I shook my head. "I didn't take you for the superstitious sort, Cardinal."

"I believe in what I see," she said before halting abruptly. Lady Malic stopped the cortege then signaled to Chamberlain.

The marksman took a small glowing pouch from his longcoat and tied it to the shaft of one of his arrows. Pulling back his bowstring, he took aim at a high middy tree. The arrow disappeared from his hand and sailed into the darkness of the bushwoods. Several seconds passed before the top of the middy exploded in a sea of phosphorescent green light.

"Why are we marking our path?" I asked him. "I could navigate these fields for you blindfolded."

"And if you don't make it back from Reaper's, who navigates then?" Chamberlain asked.

I turned to Lady Malic. "Why wouldn't I make it back?"

She gave Chamberlain a severe look. "Your job is to listen and act, not talk." She shooed him away.

"What are you planning to do when we get to Reaper's farm?" I asked.

"Only what needs doing."

The idea, grotesque as it was, seemed less so now that the sick were considered a threat. I shook my head.

"I don't care what words passed between you and Reaper at market, he's still a man, and those are still his wife and children. You can't just get rid of them

"I'm sparing them," she said. "Before it's too late."

"But those were your people once. The people you swore to protect."

"That is precisely what I'm doing, my boy, protecting them from Eden's unholy plague. You don't make it to many of Father Hy's sermons, do you?"

"I don't get to church much," I said. "In these sermons, does he happen to mention who's going to save the rest of us when there's hardly anyone left in the colony?"

A smile broke across the Lady Malic's face. She must have been terrible at poker. "Haven't you wondered why we're the least affected?" she asked.

I was too embarrassed to tell her that just so long as people thought it was the meat that kept them more human, the real reason never occurred to me.

She went on, "My theory is that something in our genes wards off the disease. I'm convinced of it. Cutter and I are of a like mind on this."

"You say *theory* when *guess* is what you really mean. Where's the proof?"

She shrugged. "None of us are experts, but I feel like the connection is right there." She gave me a sideways glance. "I realize you've made a name for yourself fostering just the opposite belief."

"I never claimed my meat was a cure, if that's what you're getting at."

"Hold on now, I'm not saying you did. I'm merely pointing out that there are plenty of folks who believe in what you do. You've got this backward. I'm paying you a compliment."

I took a few deep breaths. "Okay, let's say this theory you got is right. What do we do about it?"

"Well, if we can stay alive and breeding long enough, patterns should develop. With each generation, we'll get closer to figuring it out. But it'll take generations. We need to start with the healthiest among us."

"And the sick?"

"They're our greatest threat," she said. "And our greatest responsibility. We can't just hand them over to fight for the enemy. And don't they deserve to die with dignity, as human beings?"

I thought about Bean's final moments. Had I preserved his dignity when I cut him in two?

"I don't know that I can live with that, ma'am."

"Of course you can. That's all I want you to do is live with it. Live and thrive like those almond blossom trees of yours," she said, grabbing my shoulder. "Pass down whatever's inside you keeping you healthy, spread your Eden-resistant seed, to your sons and daughters, so we can survive here and make it our home. You may have to take on multiple wives to do it, Meatman. All the immune will." She shook a clump of mud from the wiring of her siltshoe. "No one thinks of Mother Nature as a butcher when she kills off the weakest of the species—it's Darwinism, survival of the fittest. It's the natural order of things." As we walked on, she wrapped her arm around mine. "You've got Hy's boy helping you, and I know you're close to him. I'm not pretending this is going to be easy—it shouldn't be—

but Eden hasn't given us any choice. This planet is raping itself into us, making us hard people. It's time to use that hardness to our advantage."

Lady Malic waited for me to speak, but there was nothing I could say, nothing I could force between my lips. I could only stare beyond her.

"Something holds you back," she said. "In time you'll see this is the way." She slipped her arm out from under mine then slowed her pace to fall back in with the rest of the group. "Lead on, Meatman," she told me with triumph in her voice.

What Lady Malic was selling made so much sense it scared me. Even if I didn't agree with her completely, here was someone who finally had a plan. What if, in the future, we could rid our colony of the disease completely? Eventually create generations who are immune to it? What if we could beat this place—have something approaching normal lives? Hope is a dye; just a few drops in some water and you can color a whole well any shade you want. Still, the thought of being without Nessa in this new world crippled my hope. I couldn't imagine a life without her, much less a life where I'd allow someone to take her from me, even for the greater good. And yet with each step I took with this old woman and her family of followers, I felt a little less alone.

But after I cast my selfishness and fear aside and ignored all the philosophical claptrap, there was only the truth. When the good intentions were stripped from the bone, what we had at the Reapers would be a family slaughtered at our hands. And I couldn't change that. As I looked back at those men—their faces so full of fight, if only for the satisfaction of having put one up—I wondered if it occurred that way to any of them as well. I hope it did.

9

We were another hour in the mud before I spoke again. My skin was a wet sheet slung over muscle and my feet fell onto ground that was as soft as batter. Stopping briefly, I surveyed the land. "This gives way to black rock soon. It'll be easier to walk then. Reaper's place is just beyond that."

"Not to sound droll but, *well done*, Meatman." Lady Malic laughed to herself and lifted her siltshoes with a renewed spring.

Soft soil morphed into the ebon shine of volcanic stone and we sped to a trot before entering the scrublands behind the farm. The home was similar to many settlers' farmhouses—a small conglomeration of various Edenwood and brickstones, ramshackle with hasty repairs pocking the exterior like sores, tumoral additions bulging from its sides. The bush had invaded; vines slithered over the walls and crept into every aperture, growing and expanding, pressuring the brick, slowly ripping the home asunder from its core. Prismatic florets and a muscular sheath of cirri only served to disguise the fact that Eden's assault was ongoing here.

The sheets of warm rain mixed with a sea of steam and fog to mask any hint of our arrival. Lady Malic pointed out the side door of the farmhouse where a seepage of light crawled out from underneath into the pitch of night. She gave the signal and we gathered in front of it, steeling ourselves in preparation. Owen's lips stretched into a wicked smile, which spread to Lyin Cubb, his teenaged boy. Baxter, Guy Idler, The Frey, Smith, and Ackerman all gripped their cudgels tightly.

I had an uneasy feeling in my gut, like it was trying to tell me something. Something I wasn't allowing myself to hear. Lady Malic nodded to Chamberlain. The archer lifted a bent leg, cocked his knee back, and kicked open the door. We rushed through the house like water.

Reaper was the first. His appearance had altered even from that morning; he was larger and less human-looking, his frame filling the room. His midsection had widened, and his hands branched out into immense brown mitts. There were several jagged new arms now reaching from his trunk. When he saw us, his mangled vocal chords emitted a screech so shrill it startled us long enough for him to escape to the front room of the house.

Awestruck as we were, we gave chase.

He barricaded the narrow hallway with his body, flaring his extremities to the walls and ceiling. More screams—staccato, full of fear.

The group stopped dead twenty feet from him until, empty-handed, I approached the thing with my arms raised. His facial features had sunk into his skull and the lengthy protrusions that budded from his torso curled and flexed like dark, skinny fingers.

I said gently, "Let me talk to you."

"What are you doing? Owen said. "We didn't come here to talk to it."

I ignored his words and kept my focus on Reaper. "Maybe we can avoid all this," I said to the hulking mass.

The easement had barely passed my lips when his bony hands grabbed me. A number of his jagged arms reached down the hall and held me while the remainder wrapped themselves around my neck. I clutched at the wooden fingers puncturing my skin but couldn't pry them loose. As I struggled for air, the room began to go dark. I had to act. Breathing would have to wait a few more seconds.

With one hand, I freed my scimitar then wheeled it around my head, audibly slicing the thick air. I brought it through and severed the arm. Feeling the fingers immediately go limp, I tore them from my throat. I charged down the hall, leaped forward, and planted the sword into Reaper's left shoulder, a blow so well-struck it would have felled even the stoutest of men.

But this was no man, not anymore.

The blade lodged into his pulpy flesh and remained there. An amber syrup of lifeblood flowed from the wound. Frantically, I tried to remove the sword, but it was tightly embedded.

Although I feared his vengeance, Reaper took none. His face was strangely placid, his eyes empty. The men swarmed the hallway like ants, but Reaper was far heavier than he appeared and continued to block our passage. Smith tried to kick out his legs, but they seemed bonded to the floorboards, and we piled up in front of him.

"You're bottlenecked," Lady Malic shouted from outside the hall. "Somebody go round and cover the front door."

As more of Reaper oozed onto me, I loosed the scimitar from his body, yanking it upward, but he brought his hand down onto the blade and held it with a supernatural strength. His diseased face was straining and he growled at us. He was fighting for his family. And even if it wasn't completely human, it was admirable.

Our assault must have taken its toll on the giant though. A gap opened under one of Reaper's arms and Cubb squeezed past. Then Baxter slid through…then the rest of them.

Handy appeared in the hallway in front of us, a poker wrapped in her fist. She hadn't changed to the degree her husband had; she looked much the same as she did that morning, more than enough human to give a few of the men pause. As she shuffled forward, Ackerman wasted no time bludgeoning the woman before tipping her stiffened frame against the wall. She crashed against the wood with a dull *thud* then slid down.

Reaper turned his head toward me. The sight of his wife's corpse seemed to take any remaining fight out of him, and as I finally extracted my blade, he fell to the floor as well, the air escaping from his body in a hideous burble. Lying beside his wife, he looked directly at me and whispered a single word.

"*Never.*"

The wet wind howled through the front door, announcing the children's escape. When we got there, Chamberlain was pointing across the sward to the deep brush. "They were already out of the house when I came around," he said. "I didn't have time to bring any of them down, but they ducked in there."

One by one, we charged into the bushwoods hedging the front of the house. We hacked away at thick cables of vine and branches that crisscrossed our path like cage bars, often catching a glimpse of *something*. It was always just ahead of us though, darting through the soft moonbelt light that trickled through the bush. These glimpses carried us forward desperately through the nettles and brambles that tore away at each of us by inches.

"It hurts!" Cubb screamed, his disembodied voice floating among the trees.

My vision grew blurry and a hot pain ran through me as I staggered over the path of trampled vegetation and out of the bushwoods. Owen pulled his boy into the dark light of the clearing, and we huddled around him. Boils pushed out of his exposed skin. Someone else called from deep inside the briar. Lady Malic stood in the yard, waiting for the rest to emerge while Cubb lay on his back with his chest heaving.

"Help him, Cardinal. Somebody, please, help my boy," Owen said.

"Cutter, we need you out here now," she yelled. Then she paced around the men. "I can't believe we let those damned kids lead us right into a poison patch."

My arms swelled and searing lesions formed on my skin.

A voice cried out from the bush again, "I can't breathe."

Lady Malic paced between us. "Where the hell's Cutter?"

"I think that *is* Cutter, ma'am," Chamberlain told her, nodding to the bush. "Shall I fetch him?"

She waved the archer into the patch.

Ass down in the mud and waiting out the plant toxins, I took out my journal to write while Lady Malic corralled her troops, their faces filled to bursting with rosy pustules.

"Are we done?" she screamed. "Is this all it takes to stop you *men*—a few pricks and rashes?"

"No, Cardinal Justice," they said in near unison, their faces wet with rain.

Chamberlain emerged, covered in burrs, Cutter slung across his back, huffing desperately. Malic took a seat on the soil and instructed Chamberlain to lay the doctor on the ground in front of her, where she watched as his face twisted into a death rictus.

Lady Malic took a long moment before letting out a small groan as she lifted herself from her knees and then asked, "Is anyone else here going to die?"

No one answered.

"Is anyone else going to die on me?" she said again.

"No," a few voices answered her, and none of us did die. At least not in that field.

"What about the Reaper kids?" Guy Idler spit the words out through inflated lips.

"They're lost to us," Lady Malic said. "But tomorrow we'll go through the whole damned colony. We'll recruit the healthy and put down the rest!" She put her finger down onto my open journal. "Alpha colony's salvation started this night—write that down in your book."

I imagined Nessa in bed the next morning with a fanatical throng cresting the hill beside our house. I closed the journal and forced myself up. "I'm leaving."

"What?" Lady Malic said, "I still need you."

"No, you don't. If this crusade of yours fails just because I'm not there, then it was meant to die."

"The strong will survive this, Meatman, and strength will beget strength. Once the weak perish, they'll rid us of their rot. Have faith in that."

I cleared my throat. "Look maybe you're right, and maybe you're just stabbing at the truth. I really don't know. But you're talking about killing people I came here with—people you came with. We're all trying to stay more human, right? Then explain to me why I feel like less of a man now?"

Malic had no answer for me.

"Now, I'm not saying you're wrong, Cardinal—I'm not saying that at all. I'm just saying it's late, I miss my wife, and I'm just plain tired of listening to you talk. It's time I got back home. Follow me or stay here, it makes no difference to me."

Lady Malic pursed her lips and waited a moment. "Gentlemen, what we have here is a case of receding spine. He might not be so closed off to our cause if he wasn't protecting his own."

My whole body started to shudder, but I hid it from them. It felt as if Malic's own icy fingers had grabbed hold of that receding spine she accused me of having.

"A blind woman could see that your Nessa's taken ill," she said.

Inside, my body was raging. My heart fluttered in my chest and dropped.

She knows.

There was silence. Then Malic waved her finger nonchalantly in my direction.

"Well, go get him before he decides to run off."

The men flanked me.

"Don't any of you touch my Nessa!" I gritted my teeth and pulled a blade with each hand, spitting and flailing.

A flying club caught the side of my head and brought me down. They were on me in an instant.

"Take his steel and keep him close," she told them. "Tonight's little hunting party has left me unfulfilled. I say why put off until tomorrow what can be started tonight. Let's pay a visit to your beloved Nessa."

The toxin-pain wore off and was replaced by a soreness my body had never known. With pikes at my ribcage, they led me back over the same route we'd just taken to Reaper's farm.

"What are you doing?" I said.

Lady Malic told her men, "If he speaks again, cut out his tongue." Then she faced me. "I'm not saying you're wrong to ask, Meatman... I'm just tired of listening to you talk."

I knew what they were doing. I also knew this land in every direction for miles, so when we passed the last middy tree Chamberlain had marked and there wasn't a trace of phosphorescence to be found, I started to wonder.

Where were the markers?

It didn't really matter. If the trail was truly lost to them, they'd never find my house. It was just a matter of how long it would take *for them* to figure it out.

A little less than an hour of incompetent tracking later and Chamberlain had managed the task of throwing even me off my bearings. For the first time in years, I didn't recognize the land.

"How much longer to the first marker?" Lady Malic asked.

"We should've reached it by now, ma'am."

"Then why haven't we? Do you know where we are?"

Chamberlain didn't answer.

"Mr. Chamberlain, are we lost?"

"I believe we are," he finally said.

Lady Malic marched back to me and waved the men to lower their pikes. I was rubbing the soreness from my legs, anticipating that she was about to ask me where we were. Now it sounds like an easy thing to think up a lie on the spot, but when you're not practiced at such things, it turns out to be a lot harder than you'd expect. My mind was searching for a plausible mistruth when Malic began to speak, but before she could utter a word, a vibrato reached up through the mud and rattled our feet until our knees buckled.

"We need to get on solid ground," Chamberlain said with a flutter in his voice. He scanned in every direction. "Over there!"

The archer had spotted a ridgeline in the distance that was shrouded in shadow from those of us without the artificially-enhanced night eyes of his strigiforme vision. We raced for it, kicking up sludge just as the ground began to hum over the sound of the rain. Chamberlain scooped up the Lady Malic and dropped her over his shoulder. I didn't see any of the others. While I kept focused on the growing silhouette ahead, I'd passed the group, and I figured to be hitting a platform of ground rock soon. The ridgeline was just ahead.

Angry soil roared behind me and I craned my neck to watch a fissure open violently across the land and a spray of black liquid erupt like an oil strike, blotting out the light from the moonbelt. The glistening scales of several lissur broke the surface. They gulped the air then disappeared again. My heart pounding, the breath ripping from my lungs, I kept making for the bluffs just ahead, waiting for the rock to materialize beneath my feet. The lissur were close. Too close.

Fear and adrenaline fueled me. My mind was bewildered. My body—tempered muscle and sinew, the only things I could trust—controlled my movements. The bluffs were less than a hundred feet away now. Even without ground rock to save me, I could climb to the top of the ridge and hold out until morning, or until the monsters left.

The world shook with a deafening fierceness. My nerve endings had all been numbed by the sound. I peeked behind me again. The men lurched forward, wild-eyed, punching through raindrops, reaching for the stony oasis somewhere ahead of them. The marshy land finally began to harden. I tried to gain my footing, but my ankles folded over and my knees waggled.

I fell hard.

This ground wasn't smooth like blackrock. It was corrugated with roots. And they were moving.

I looked up with unbelieving eyes as the rock formation directly in front of me transmogrified and stood. Dozens of slender figures slowly unfolded themselves and splintered off from the whole. The low creak of great weight accompanied each of their movements. They stretched out their immense limbs and unfurled hidden foliage. Somewhere in that stirring, dark collection of leaves I could almost make out the faces that we'd lost. As those pitiless visages looked at the group, they pulled their rooted legs from the sod and gave slow, lumbering chase.

We fled from these new behemoths of Eden, the enemy Lady Malic had warned us about. But the trees marched toward us with the deliberateness of time and, like that very passage of time, we could not escape them. Every step they took covered a field. It was clear there was no sanctuary left, so we circled the leg of one and tried to climb its trunk; but it reached down and, with the swipe of one leaf-encrusted arm, removed us utterly.

The beings attacked. Their legs clopped slowly in the mush and their roots dragged behind them like loose shoelaces. We tried to scatter, but serpentine vines wrapped themselves around us and pinned our feet to the ground. And the air echoed with the sound of dragonsong.

Lady Malic, that tough old crow, wriggled an arm loose and picked up a machete. But instead of hacking herself out of her bonds, she tossed the weapon at *my* feet. "Get the Meatman his steel," she cried.

The men did exactly as they were told, and a pile quickly grew before me, hopping in time with the lissurs's subterranean movements directly below us. I grabbed a blade and slashed at the viny shackles until I was free.

"Cut us out. We'll help you," Ackerman said.

Although it pained me to acknowledge it, this bloodthirsty group was my people, and I needed them now. So I chopped away the ivy and gathered the group into a tight circle.

"Listen to me. Stay in formation. We fight back-to-back. Follow my lead, and when you feel someone move, move with them. The lissur are predictable. I know their minds better than they do. But don't try to kill one yourself. They're too big. If we can discourage them, they may just look for an easier meal somewhere else." The men started to look more at ease. "You hit any piece that gets close enough. Don't attack the body, you'll only tire yourself out."

In a garden of vortexes all around us, the wet turf crumbled away and the scent of fresh decay filled our nostrils. The first lissurs appeared. They bent their heads slightly and their tips blossomed open, allowing tendrils to spill out like mounds of spaghetti. They slithered forward on the air, reaching for us, but our frantic swings kept them at bay. Two dove back under the surface, and I stepped sideways. The men responded nicely to my pull until we were engaged in a type of dance, drifting as one synchronous entity rather than several.

The ground we'd just stepped from disappeared into a gaping maw and a full-grown Quintha rose from the hole, tipped itself over, and retched the soil from its gullet. It shook its head like a dog and strands of muddied saliva whipped to either side of the huge beast. The tip caught me in the leg and its spur gashed my knee. My blood spilled everywhere. The other lissurs retreated underground and the Quintha followed. The thumping ceased and the ground settled, but somewhere far below, a rumble still echoed.

"No moves," I said meekly, clutching at the fresh wound on my leg.

Time passed. First Ackerman whimpered and broke down into a crying fit, then Cubb began to shriek uncontrollably.

"Quiet!" Lady Malic snapped. She looked at them, her lips in that familiar pursed position. "And you dare call yourselves men."

We tried to corral the boy, but he could bear no more. He fled the circle and sploshed across the clearing. Owen gave chase. I watched in horror as the two figures sprinted through the mist, growing smaller and smaller until they vanished into a milky darkness. I kept listening. Listening. Listening for their demise.

A hungry silence ensued and the men's gazes fell on me for answers. I was about to speak when another leapt from our ranks and ran off to fade into the nothingness of fog.

"Don't be fools," I told them. "You won't survive!"

Then another.

Another.

And three more.

Were they the fools, or was I?

When the rumbling returned, only the Lady Malic and Chamberlain remained. Chamberlain turned to me. "Why don't we run for it like the rest?"

"I don't know if they'll chase us," I told him.

"They didn't chase any of the others," Chamberlain said. "If they're coming back up, let's be gone when they get here."

"If they surface and we aren't here, there's no reason for them to stay," I said. "They'll be on the move, and they're a lot faster than we are. It won't take long for them to catch us." A bolt of pain shot through my knee and I clutched my blood-soaked pant leg again. "I wouldn't make it far anyway."

"Why don't you stay behind, then?" Lady Malic asked. She pulled up her dress and drew a rusty streaker out of the holster strapped to her calf. She pointed it at me.

"You won't need that to keep me here. Look at my leg." I showed her the mangled appendage. "I couldn't outrun *you*, much less one of those things. Does that streaker even work?"

"Sure, probably the last one around here that does. I managed to save a few rounds and keep the juice in them active."

"If you think that'll stop a lissur, you're wrong."

"Oh, I know it won't. It's not meant for them," she said. "It's meant for you—to keep you behaved long enough to listen to me."

Chamberlain furrowed his brow. "Excuse me, ma'am, but why are you doing this? He's helping us."

"And he can help us more just by staying put," she said. "We're not cut out for this fight, Chamberlain. You're just an archer, and I'm not even that. We don't stand a snowflake's chance against one of those dirt dragons." She shook the streaker's barrel at me. "But he does."

Chamberlain looked hesitant. I could almost hear his loyalty chip kicking in.

"Come now, it's not as if we're stranding him here. He's armed and he knows these creatures—he said so himself. The Meatman will keep them tied up long enough for us to get out."

"And why the hell would I do that?" I asked.

"Because I can keep Nessa safe. I'll even let her cross over, if that's what you want. But if I die, the boys will eventually get to her. And without my guidance their behavior can sometimes be so... how should I put it... *distasteful*."

Then she took her finger off the trigger and handed me the streaker. I stood agog clutching the weapon.

"On my word, no harm will come to her," she said. "Just stay here and keep those things occupied."

Thump. Thump. Thump. Time was short, and people were harder to read than monsters. I made my decision.

"All right. Both of you, go now." I handed the gun back to her. "Take this—you might need it to keep your word. I wouldn't know what to do with it anyway."

"Feel free to make it out of here alive, Meatman," Lady Malic said. "Then at least you'll know I kept my promise."

"I intend to," I told her.

Chamberlain knelt to lift the woman again, but she waved him off. "My legs are strong enough," she told him.

He turned to me. "Don't think too harshly of our Cardinal. She only does what's necessary."

Lady Malic tightened her siltshoes and wagged a finger at me. "Be good bait and Nessa lives, I swear it." She tinkered with the streaker in her hands for a moment. "The thing about bait," she said, "it works much better if you chum the water first." Then, with a slow and deliberate ease, the Lady Malic turned around and fired a shot straight through Chamberlain's gut. His insides spilled out like hot soup and the bowman dropped facedown into the mud, his gaping wound feeding the soil.

I reached for him and screamed.

"I promised I'd never let Eden take him over, and now it never will." She backed away and crossed herself, then inspected the streaker. "I told you it still works. Now, don't take any of this to mean I lack confidence in you, Meatman. Remember, whether she lives or dies is entirely in your able hands. Fight a good fight and I'll see to it she's left free to enter the bush when her time comes. Don't know why you'd want such a thing but I'll swear to it if those are your true wishes."

"They are," I said, getting up from where Chamberlain's body lay.

"Then so be it." She turned and scampered off, her voice still ringing in my ears.

I took several steps forward and readied myself for the impossible trial. Deep, controlled breaths calmed my mind. The rains came again, flooding the field. Lightning sprites flashed in the distance.

The monsters came.

The first group of lissur emerged, their skin a blotchy patchwork. Calicos. They came at me in singles instead of packs. They weren't smart. Chamberlain's corpse attracted some nibblers. It kept them off me, though, so I had to admit the Lady's methods had merit. But one lissur in particular struck me. Its eyes, to be exact. Its ocular ring wasn't white like all the other lissur I'd encountered on Eden. Instead, they were a deep brown. A familiar brown. This couldn't be…

No matter.

The rest soon found me. I counted seven, maybe eight.

Slice, slice, slice.

I'd fought multiples before, but never this many. I could see Nessa's face in my mind's eye. Her old face, soft and bright, the way she'd been. I had to stop thinking about her. I had to forget everything but the lissur. Thought is slow. Action is fast.

Thrust, twist, recoil.

It was getting harder to swing these damn blades. My attacks grew weaker, and my whole body felt like a fresh bruise. Muscles screaming. Every nerve turned on to full. I couldn't stop the pain.

Chop, swipe, chop again, and again, again…again…again.

Blood everywhere. Thick and dark, a gravy of it. It hung from my clothes. It dripped from ringlets of hair and eyelashes.

And then I realized it:

I couldn't stop them.

I couldn't kill them all.

I was only The Meatman.

I dropped my steel into the mud and unfastened my belt. I took off my vest and let it fall, too. My body melted to the ground. It was time to rest. Finally time to give up. Time to sleep.

I looked up at overstuffed clouds and the lavender streaks of lightning escaping them. Thunderclaps filled the sky. I spoke to Eden, "You've won at last," I told it. "You beat me. Now come claim your prize."

I waited for Eden to wrap me in its shimmering skin, to pull me down, far from the rain. The drops splashed hard against my face. Pinned to the dirt by fatigue, by poison, by doubt, I trained my senses on the earmarks of the lissurs' presence: felt for the reverberations, waited for the low, sepulchral hum, sucked in that cool stench of death that heralds them.

There was none of it.

The dragons had forsaken me. Eden doesn't stoop to respond to the whims and wishes of mankind. Breaking me was enough, I suppose.

11

I lifted myself up onto my hands and crawled to my feet. My good leg began to churn once more, dragging the dead one and beating a slow path home over the abandoned redfield. At the edge of the sink, just before the safety of the bushwoods, I found the land scarred and dimpled with cavernous holes. In each were pools of manblood. At the edge of the woods, I spotted a body—or most of one—in a red frock lying against the bole of a tree.

Lady Malic was still alive when I approached, but blood darkened her clothes and streamed from her mouth. "I thought you'd gone and gotten yourself killed. I cursed you for a charlatan," she said to me with a gurgling laugh before her face grew somber again. I told her not to talk, that the time had passed, but she felt the need to. "I was a just woman, wasn't I? Wasn't I right for trying to save us?"

"It doesn't matter what I think of you," I said, bending over her. "Eden was all that matters, and to her you were just the easier meal."

She opened her mouth and took a final quiet breath. The life quickly left her eyes, replaced by something else. Something of Eden crept in and stared back at me. Not quite alive, but not dead either. I stood while the grasses around her body wiggled and reached upward, covering her. Wrapped in a blanket of green and gold, her body was pulled down into the soil. Then she was gone.

Eden *had* chosen to claim a prize on this day, but for reasons unknown, it was not me. It was time to go. The night was getting old, and Nessa was waiting.

As a flush morning sun dried the world out, I dragged myself back across the safe route. With my game leg, the journey seemed endless. Finally, I came over the little ridge and caught sight of the almond blossom tree and my house. Though it felt like I was running, I was barely upright. I reached for the twistwood door, pushed it open, and called her name.

Nothing.

I stumbled to the bedroom.

Empty.

Outside, clumps of soil, still moist to the touch, dotted the floor leading to the chop house. The door was gone, shattered into a thousand slivered fragments on the chop house floor. The huge tub was overturned, my jars smashed, and their rainbow contents spattered across the room. More mud, like breadcrumbs, led me outside. I tracked a pair of footsteps over the furrowed terrain of the yard and into the bushwoods, but lost the trail in the boscage. I searched for any sign of her. There was only the stillness of the trees. I was alone now.

"Don't leave me. I'll do anything!" I screamed. "Take me with you. Claim *me!*"

On a curl of wind, through the filter of the coppice, a sibilating response crept into my ears. *Never*, it said.

My body collapsed onto the grass, and I wept there until there was nothing left inside me to purge. Only then did Eden make its cruel request. I climbed to my feet and sucked in the air. The damp journal was still in my pocket, so I pulled it out along with a nub of lead and began writing. Someone had to leave a record of what happened here, what came before, and what was yet to be.

Now I was ready to fulfill my promise to Eden. "I renounce them." I released the words into the sky loudly. The wind immediately whispered my new purpose.

I took an unsteady breath and put pencil to page again. Tremors overtook my writing hand, and it shook violently as I pressed the dreaded words out onto the paper.

The colony needs me.

I shoved the book back into my pocket and spoke to the skies again, "You have me. I've sworn to do what you ask," I said. "Now for God's sake, bring her back," I pleaded.

This time there was no answer. Eden is patient, so very patient, and as I was reminded, she does not bend to the whims and wishes of man. I would learn to be patient, too.

AFTER THE FALL

12

Chronicle Entry Z9.14.38:

There are no such things as monsters. There are only those pitiable creatures who are compelled into being. And they are only monsters to those who've never been enslaved by their compulsions.

I am happy.

God help me but I am happy again.

The transport yo-yoed to the surface like a pregnant spider. The hulking, fat-bellied thing alighted onto the wet of Eden's ground and buried its skinny legs in the soil, an ocean of timespace in its wake. It dwarfed the bug of a starhopper we came down on a lifetime ago.

The door of the great machine whooshed open and a young couple— man and woman—emerged, immediately swelling their lungs with Eden's ambrosial air.

I kept to the bushwoods, listening to my people.

The woman turned to the man. "Think there's any Alphas left?"

"If they're here, we didn't pick anything up," the man replied. "I doubt they could've made it by themselves for this long."

But I did make it. I made it all these years and now they were finally here to save me. I prayed I wouldn't have to be alone much longer.

The hydraulic legs of the ship exhaled, and the entire bulbous hull squatted into the mud. The couple stepped onto Eden just as thousands of other faces began to fill thousands of other doorways. In the ship's bloated shadow, the man stopped and picked up some soil, pinching it between his thumb and fingers then putting it to his nose. This brought a smile. He dropped the dirt and wiped his hands together as the woman chuckled at him.

"What?"

"Is that how you clean yourself off?" she asked, wiping her hands to mimic him. "Distributing the dirt evenly? That's ridiculous. You're just getting the other hand dirty, too."

The man paused in mock thought. He took her hands into his, twirled the matching wedding band that clung to her finger, pulled her body close, and kissed her. Then he whispered, "You're absolutely right. It makes so much more sense, mathematically speaking, to rub as much of the dirt as I can onto *your* hands."

She playfully yanked her now-soiled hands away and looked out to the thick curtain of dark teal bush. "There's so much out there," she said quietly. "We might never be clean again."

It was my time.

I shambled out from my perch in the bushwoods. My head and face were covered in gray hair, and the shabbiest clothing hung off my bones. I could see their disbelief at the sight of me. But as more of the new arrivals joined us, they accepted the vision of an elderly man—a human being—with eyes still as blue as spring, surviving on Eden. They encircled me.

"Can you understand us?" someone asked.

I nodded.

"You're an Alpha colonist then?" the first woman asked.

I nodded once more.

"We're the Beta group. Gamma arrives in two months." She gave a wide smile and hugged me tightly before her partner admonished her. The touch of another felt surreal after all this time.

"Is there anyone else left from Alpha colony?" she asked, then quickly shook her head. "I'm sorry, this must be a shock. I'm sure you have questions of your own." She flitted back and forth between myself and her crewmembers. "There are supplies and medicines on board and a whole bunch of new neighbors for you."

It had been so long since I'd used my vocal cords that it took some time to awaken the muscles. There was an uncomfortable pause as I opened my mouth to test my voice. A few plaintive moans were all I was capable of.

The woman stopped me. "Give it time, it'll come," she said. "We're not going anywhere, I promise you."

I smiled what I hoped was a genuine-looking smile and rubbed the heartstone necklace that hung down in front of my chest. Someone handed me a pouch of cloudy liquid and as I raised the straw to my lips they squeezed the elixir into my mouth. The taste was foreign and made me cough, but it felt good. I cleared my throat and croaked out the words from the script. "Alpha colony welcomes you to Second Eden, your new home."

I struck me as odd that the Betas eyed me with a superior mien, as one would a crippled child. I didn't hold it against them though. They were the real children. The newest children of Eden.

A path unzipped before me and a tall gentleman strode toward us. Even from a distance, I could see he had shinier bits pinned to his clothes than the rest of the Betas. He seemed to me not a very patient man. That would change.

"I am Fifth Division Major Marius Cory of the Beta colony," he immediately said. He stuck out his hand and I reflexively shook it. "Are there more of you?"

I nodded.

"We can't locate them. Where are they?"

"Close," I said, my voice loosening up now. "Would you like to meet them, Major?"

A collective wave of excitement passed through the Betas. "We would very much," Cory said. "There's so much to show us. We want to know everything about this place."

"You will," I told him as Eden whispered to me its final instructions. I pointed into the darkness of the bush. "Wade into the thicket there and you'll see them on the other side. It won't take long."

"Thank you for sharing this beginning with us," he said with complete earnestness.

I felt the prick of something, a remnant perhaps, of a vestigial emotion, something I didn't think I was capable of feeling anymore. Was it sympathy? I couldn't remember. It quickly passed though.

"No, thank *you*, Major Cory," I said. "Thank you all for coming to our aid. We can always use some new soldiers."

Deep beneath me, Bean swam slowly in the soil, no doubt trying hard to hide his big, new self. But I could feel his faint hum. Eden's whispers were now a chant banging inside my head, and Nessa's sweet voice was an unmistakable note in the cacophony.

Forgive them their excitement, Mother, your children have been so patient.

Major Marius Cory reached up, barked out a command then dropped his arm like the Grand Marshal of a race. Down the line, a hundred other tall gentlemen and gentlewomen wearing shiny bits dropped *their* arms as well and the Betas rushed gleefully into the bush on all sides of the mammoth transport.

I reached inside the folds of my sleeve and handed the Major a ratty, weathered journal.

"What's this?" he asked.

I looked hard into his face. "Read it," I said and patted the mildewed cover. "It might help you better understand."

"Understand what?"

"That we all have a place here on Second Eden."

I turned my back on him and began to walk toward the bush, hoping I'd done enough to be with my Nessa again. I was wading headlong into the dark brush when he called out to me.

"And what exactly is *your* place here, friend?"

I paused only long enough to answer him, "I am the Meatman," I said. "I bring them the meat."

But I can't be certain he heard me, above the screams.

This was a piece of mine that was one of a few different "creation" stories that I produced in my earlier years. I think it was the most interesting of the lot though so I decided to re-edit it just a bit and give it a fresh coat of paint, so to speak, and a new life as part of this collection. I was clearly interested in the idea of beginnings, especially after I read Isaac Asimov's The Last Question. *Now, to be clear,* Man Farm *doesn't bear much resemblance to* The Last Question *but that's alright—Asimov's story acted as inspiration nonetheless and that's good enough for me to throw the man some credit here. For* Man Farm *I wanted to infuse this fantasy story with a Wonder Years-like narrative; the fond reminiscences of a grown man looking back to his childhood, and his first "man farm". It originally appeared in the magazine* OG's Speculative Fiction.

Man Farm

I can still remember the day I got a man farm. My father brought it home one day after work. He knew I was always a curious kid and, despite being a little young, I was pretty responsible. Dad helped me set it up. We fitted together its rectangular frame, screwed it to the base, and slid the pellucid magnifying walls into place. It was good-sized for a man farm, almost as big as the ones my friends had. It took up the whole back corner of my desk and I had to relocate my pencil can inside one of the drawers, but I didn't mind too much. We filled the farm with soft soil and stones from the yard, twigs, plenty of water, and fresh greenery.

"Where will they live?" I asked Dad.

"Anyplace they can," he said. "Men adapt well. They have pitifully short lifespans, but they can thrive, given the right environment. In the farm, they'll start out living in the shadows and crevices, eventually they'll build their own little homes. They can even live underground—men are good burrowers."

The kit came with a pouch of dried organisms that could be added to the farm to create an ecosystem. Now I'd never heard of an ecosystem, but all these critters looked to be good for decoration if nothing else. Dad had brought thousands of men home with him in a small white paper box, their pale bodies wriggling and rippling like living sand. I unfolded the flaps of the box and scooped some out hesitantly. I placed them on my hand.

"It's okay, they won't bite you," he told me. "They're far too small to even realize where they are."

I put some under the microscope I'd gotten for my birthday the year before. I could see them scurrying to stand on their tiny leg stalks.

"Look how funny they are, Dad. I can't believe they can get around like they do?"

89

"Pretty amazing, aren't they?" My dad looked about as charmed by these creatures as I did.

"They sure are," I said.

They were far smaller than the men teeming in the yard during the spring and summertime. My father told me these men were smarter than those and would make for a much more interesting farm.

"They're quite delicate, son. That farm will need a lot of attention or it'll die out. Do you think you can do it?"

"Absolutely," I told him. "I love it." Then I gave him a huge, tight hug.

It was a good man farm.

Dad and I spent that whole week setting it up. We added all kinds of little flourishes. Then we rested. Years later, it's still one of the fondest memories I carry with me of my father. I decided to keep the man farm on my desk because it was nearer to the window. I watched in amazement as the farm grew from small groups huddled around miniscule orange flickers of light to villages of men with homes and roads and vehicles. Dad made sure to get some female men too. Unless you knew exactly what to look for, they appeared to all be the same. Even though Dad showed me how to spot the differences, I still got them mixed up. They would nest inside their dens until barely visible pink baby men would squirt out from inside them, one at a time (sometimes two).

It was a *very* good man farm.

The men worked tirelessly and they used every speck I'd placed in their world to their advantage. They could be tender animals, but as their numbers increased and the space inside the farm grew scarce, the men would choose sides, take up arms, and stage fierce battles. I found them to be fairly entertaining tactical affairs when viewed with the naked eye, but under extreme magnification, they were horrifically grisly. On a few rare occasions, when I simply could not stand the sight of the carnage, I would stop them and punish the ones I found fault with.

At night I watched over them from my top bunk. If they ever needed anything, I would get it for them. I felt like they understood that, even though I knew better.

I loved my man farm. My brother Denny, however, said it was queer to care so much about stupid men and he reminded me repeatedly. He said it was his duty as an older brother. Denny had a pet Golden Tiago spider that was the envy of every neighborhood boy and the nightmare of every neighborhood girl.

One wet afternoon, Denny and I got into a fight over nothing really while playing a board game on the living room floor. I love my brother dearly but, to this day, we still can't play a game with each other without a fracas ensuing and our mother being called in eventually (even as adults). Being the smaller and weaker sibling, I used the only effective weapon I had in my arsenal—unsparing fraternal razzing: I reminded him that Mom and Dad were secretly hoping for a girl when he was born, I teased him about his shit grades in school, I made fun of his complexion and how he could never get his hair right and it was no wonder that Julie Kempler didn't like him.

Too far. I'd crossed a forbidden line, even for little brothers. Denny proceeded to bloody up my nose and I proceeded to hit the waterworks once I got within earshot of my parents. Mom and Dad heard me crying and saw my nose gushing. They grounded Denny for a month.

"But you don't even know what that punk said!" he told them. "Why do you always take the baby's side!"

He offered up his objection with all the earnestness of the too harshly convicted. *Let the punishment fit the crime* was a plea known throughout the kid world: When you can't beat the rap outright, try to inject a hint of doubt into the mind of the jurors, it may bear fruit. He stomped away to the bedroom to begin serving his time. *Dead man walking,* I wanted to call out, but I thought it belied the true mindset of a victim. Better to keep playing the role of the wounded.

When I went up to bed that night, the room was black. I fingered the wall for the nightlight and switched it on. Denny was in bed, pretending to be asleep. In the muted darkness, I caught sight of the man farm. It had been knocked over on its side. I rushed to stand it back upright. The soil had been shaken around and the landscape inside the farm had reshaped; what had once been level ground was now scattered everywhere, creating towering mounds and low gorges. Through the cross-section of the case I could see the dead men of the farm, frozen within the dirt. Not just below the surface, the way they buried their own, but lost deep beneath. I tried not to cry but found my eyes glazing. The charade now over, Denny watched me suffer with a wide, tight-lipped grin.

My brother would pay.

I ran downstairs and promptly told my parents what Denny had done. My father shook his head. "What are we going to do with that one?" he asked my mother. I nodded my head in agreement.

She stopped her knitting and placed it in her lap. "I told you a month is a bit much, John. We've never grounded him that long before. Don't you think three weeks would've been plenty?"

My father splayed his fingers over his cheeks and knit his eyebrows the way he always did when he was thinking hard. "Maybe," he said, "But Denny's old enough. We should expect more out of him."

"He makes a good point, Mom," I said.

"John," my mother replied with doe-eyed compassion. "He's still just a boy."

My father had grown up quickly. Grampa died when he was fifteen and he had to take care of Grandma and Auntie Cass by himself. My mother had four older brothers and sometimes I think she remembered what it was like to be an adolescent boy more than my father did.

"All right, I'll talk to Denny tomorrow," my father finally said.

Wait, what was happening here? If I thought that telling on my brother would result in a lesser sentence, I would've just kept my mouth shut. For crying out loud, what do I bother coming to you people for?

My brother now only had three weeks punishment, which you would've thought might improve his mood, but it didn't. He was as ornery as ever. I mean, I'd snitched on him twice—in one day. Let the tortures of the damned begin! He would shoot me glares all through dinner until my stomach started to ache as if under some voodoo curse. Then, shut up alone in our bedroom and expecting his brutal worst, he would ignore me completely. He was a master of psychological warfare.

A few days later I came home from school and Denny was sitting in the kitchen, stuffing himself with sweets no more than an hour before dinner. He looked right at me and grinned a crumbly-cookie grin. What an emboldened prick! He knew I couldn't rat him out again to our parents; I'd passed my quota for the week. My tattling had reached that invisible ceiling, that nebulous grey area that all astute kids recognized could push you in your parents' eyes from *loyal informant* to *whiny nuisance* with one too many squeals.

He covered his mouth with a napkin but I knew he wanted me to see it. His school let out earlier than mine, Mom had to run to the store, and Dad wouldn't be home from work until later. Denny had been left alone in the house with the farm.

I bounded up the staircase and threw open the door to my bedroom. Inspecting the man farm I found, to my great relief, nothing seemed out of sorts. Within its walls, there was evidence that the men had begun to rebuild and were adjusting well to the new topography.

Then I saw the thing.

In the corner, nestled beside a clump of forest, was Denny's Golden Tiago spider, with its thick, striped legs curled underneath its body. It was feeding itself contentedly on a living pile of men it had netted within its web strings, dipping its incarnadine fangs down into the writhing mass, its plump abdomen engorged. The majority of the men were fighting to detach their bodies from the death thread with little success. For others, there was simply no fight left in them. They hung helpless, screaming their soundless screams while the Tiago drank their insides.

I became incensed. I took out the sharpest pencil I could find from my drawer, unlatched the door on top of the farm, and stuck the pencil through the fat midsection of the spider. Then I lifted it and planted the impaled monster upside down in the soil, its legs still churning the air.

The rest of the men came out of their hiding spaces inside caves and underground tunnels. They hastily freed the survivors and surrounded the creature. At the base of the pencil, the men set off small fires that merged and climbed the wooden pike, engulfing the arachnid. Its lifeless carcass spit and wilted under the sway of the flames. I left it there for Denny to see knowing he wouldn't dare tell on me for fear he would have to explain how his Tiago got in the man farm to begin with.

My sweet revenge was short-lived though, as I knew without a doubt Denny would retaliate. He was still confined to our room for another two weeks and I couldn't be there every second. I could transplant the farm to another room of the house, but Denny would get to it eventually. The men needed protection; they hadn't done anything wrong. They were innocents in a larger celestial game playing out on a plane of existence they couldn't even comprehend, the poor bastards. They deserved a peaceful life where they could look up to a bright blue sky, free from my brother's retribution. If I wanted to save the men, I had to do something drastic.

I wasn't positive it would work, but if it did, it was one sure way to keep the men out of Denny's reach. There would be no school the next day, so I decided to execute my plan that night.

I spirited a man away from off the top of the highest mound of the farm. I held him in my palm and spoke as quietly as I could so as not to damage his ears with the thunderous booming that my voice must have been to him, whispering the same instructions to the man over and over and over even though I had no reason to believe he would understand me. Finally, I placed the man back atop the mountain and waited all afternoon for him to rejoin the colony. All that was left now was the arrival of nightfall.

That evening I stayed up late, pinching myself to keep awake and praying that my brother would fall to sleep quickly. When I heard his familiar snuffling beneath me, I knew that he had. It was well past midnight before I finally alighted from my perch, tip-toed to my desk, and secured the farm in my hands. I brought it to the edge of my brother's bed and opened the top, carefully lying it down on the mattress. Then I slid Denny's covers down to his waist. I gently tipped the farm on its side and waited.

Nothing happened for a long while and I began to worry. Then, warily at first, the men came out from their homes and forged toward the bed. Their exodus, stalled briefly by the folds of the bedsheet, continued once

I'd carved a pathway for them with my finger. The men acted exactly as my voice had instructed them. They faithfully left the safety of the farm and crossed the badlands of bedding, climbing to the edges of the covers, where Denny's body and the sheets met. Some spilled over and disappeared beneath the linens, the rest fanned out over Denny's bare body. The mass of men hung there over him like a cumulonimbus cloud then slowly dissipated into a thinly-spread mist. Finally, the dark patch faded into nothingness, leaving only a faint roiling under my brother's skin. A moment later that ceased as well.

My father's words echoed in my head. *Men are good burrowers.*

The next morning, I slept in. The instant I awoke I plunged my head down over the side of the bunk. Denny was gone. I rushed downstairs to find my brother sitting at the kitchen table with my parents, his head buried in his breakfast.

"Good morning." I sat down next to Denny and gave his elbow a nudge. "How do you feel?"

He lifted his face a few inches from the plate. "Leave me alone."

"Dennis, be nice to your brother now," Mom demanded.

"But Ma, he's bugging-"

"Denny," Dad cautioned in a low growl.

My brother slumped in his chair, frowning.

"How do you feel today?" I asked again.

Though it seemed to cause my brother actual physical anguish to address me against his will, he finally acquiesced. "Fine." He motioned to his back, rubbing it against the chair as he spoke. "Just a little itchy."

"Let me see it," Mom said. She examined his back. "It looks irritated—dirty, too. What have you been doing, Denny, rolling around in the yard?" "No," he replied quizzically (The concept of sarcasm was something my brother clearly struggled with).

Mom completed her diagnosis. "It's just a little raw. You might have scraped it or it could just be sunburned. Don't scratch it, sweetie, it might get infected."

"Yeah, don't scratch it," I blurted. My parent's heads swiveled my way, funny looks plastered across their faces. "It's better if you just leave it alone, that's all I'm saying."

Again with the looks.

I put my arm around Denny. "What? Can't a guy show a little concern for his big bro?"

Denny shrugged my arm off. He was speechless. I'm not sure if it was out of surprise, if he was still mad at me, or because he finally figured out that some questions are rhetorical.

Whatever the reason, he turned his attention back to my mother, who was swabbing his back with a washcloth. "I won't touch it," he promised. "My tail doesn't even reach that far."

"Well then, it's a good thing," my mother said.

And with that, to my great delight, the family went back to eating breakfast with no further discussion on the subject. Denny slid his fork across the plate and gobbled up the last uneaten portions of his meal, sublimely ignorant to his role as my newest man farm.

"Dad, I think I'm going to get rid of that farm," I said.

"What's wrong? I thought you loved it."

I dropped my head in faux shame. "I'm getting tired of taking care of it, that's all. It's a big responsibility."

Dad looked at me with something akin to bewilderment. He lifted his palms skyward. "All right then, I'll get rid of it later this afternoon."

"That's okay," I told him. "I took care of it already. I found a spot nearby that's perfect for them."

I knew I had to let the men go, but knowing didn't make it any easier for me. I finished my breakfast that day with a smile painted to my face and a hidden dolor locked away in my gut, wondering if the men of the farm would ever remember my face, or my voice, or that I existed at all.

One of the newest pieces in this collection. This was a story interrupted. It was started (and stopped) only to be restarted and finished years later. I don't think I ever had a clear path for what I wanted to do with this story, what I wanted it to become, and that halted me dead (as happens so many times with writers). I didn't follow the advice that I give to all my writing students to push through and force a story into being, which is sometimes the only way that stories get written. So, when I needed stories to round out this collection this premise came back to me and simply would not let me abandon it again. And I'm thankful that it refused to be forgotten.

Grizzled hunter Colonel Everett T. Allory wants a challenge. He seeks to bring down the galaxy's deadliest prey—if he can find it—a mythical beast known as the Shi'roc-Su. He wants its head on his mantelpiece... but the animal's not just going to hand it over. Influenced by so many fantastic "hunt" stories that I love from the likes of Richard Connell, Harlan Ellison, George R.R. Martin, and several others, Shi'roc-Su is, I suppose, my version of The Great White Hunter tale.

Shi'roc-Su

"It is said that the Shi'roc-Su cannot die. That the beast is the everlasting spirit of the planet Mylau itself and draws its power from the molten innards at the core of its home," the withered, tawny man said. "It is immortal, a god."

Everett Allory yawned and exchanged a benign smile with the pilot, then continued wiping down his tracer rifle. "I'm well aware of the stories, Rinku, even the hippy-dippy, mystical bullshit ones." The helipod rattled down through the upper tiers of the planet's atmosphere towards the surface of Mylau.

"Then you must also be aware, Colonel Allory, that it is entirely likely I'll come back next week and there will be nothing left of you for me to retrieve and return to your mothership for its long voyage home—it would not be the first time the Shi'roc-Su has claimed an expert huntsman such as yourself," the old guide said, his wispy voice barely escaping from pale and wormy lips. "I'd think you would know this better than most—you were friends with the renown Ahlmo Veidt, if I'm not mistaken?"

"*Friends* might be a bit too strong a definition of our relationship—we were friendly, but not exactly friends. I knew the man, respected him, but he was a rival. After he vanished on Mylau chasing the legend all those years ago, I knew I had to come here and track the thing for myself. Anything that could take Ahlmo out was something I needed to try my hand at hunting down," Allory said. "How many would you say you've lost to the beast, hunters and locals?"

"The Shi'roc-Su does not ravage our meager numbers, we Mylauans have learned how to protect ourselves from the creature for some time now. We do not venture into its territories, do not invade its sacred grounds." He offered Allory a stern mien. "We simply do not seek it out," he said. "There is no need. We stay safe within our high walls and never venture out into spaces where we would not be welcomed. For this reason, it does not seek us either. Perhaps, also, because we offer it up so many like yourself to sate it's considerable... appetite. There's a kind of symbiosis there, I think. Who's to say though?" Rinku placed his hands upon his lap. "We know the Shi'roc-Su better than you outworlders. We honor and worship it, from a safe distance."

"Sounds to me like you people don't want to screw with your cash cow," he said. "Smart."

Rinku offered a nod and a half-grin. "There is that aspect too, I suppose. Men like yourself, with so much coin in their coffers and so much to prove to themselves, keep Mylau flush and thriving. Our, what shall I call it? *Tourism industry*, pays for many of the conveniences we would otherwise go without. So, you see, the Shi'roc-Su provides for us as well. We bring it sport, it brings us riches. As I said, symbiosis."

"And you never worry about what might happen? It doesn't consume your every thought that one day someone could end all this with a single shot?"

"If that is the way of fate, then so be it," the old man said. "But that time may never come. That skilled a hunter may never touch down on Mylau's soil. They certainly haven't yet."

"About that?" Allory said. "How many men has it killed?"

Rinku sighed deeply. "I do not see the prudence in sharing such knowledge—the sheer starkness of the number might serve to discourage you, and I'm afraid I don't know your heart well enough to be an adequate judge."

Allory squinched his face, deepening his already myriad wrinkles. "You can quit it with the psyche-job, I'm not an easy scare. I've devoted an entire lifetime to this, ever since I could hold a tracer. It's in my veins. That's all my family ever wanted for me, and all I ever wanted, too," he said. "And when you have as much as I have, you get to do exactly what you want. I may not be quite as famous as a rockstar gunner like Ahlmo Veidt was, but you *do* know who you're talking to, right?"

Rinku bowed his head. "Forgive me, sir, I let my tongue get away from me. I meant no harm. Everyone in wild questing circles knows the name Everett T. Allory. The great man, from the venerated Allory lineage, descended from sportsmen and stalkers. This is known. You are an honored guest here and among the finest trackers I've ever escorted to Mylau's surface. You've paid the agreed-upon price and I've brought you here to hunt the mythical Shi'roc-Su. I assure you it will be an adventure you will not forget in all the time you shall live. Please accept my sincerest apologies."

Allory stared at Rinku while he stroked the stubbly growth of his chin—dark shoots of hair frosted bone white—before clapping the bantam man on his shoulder. "Forget about it, I can be kind of an overbearing prick at times, a defect of my upbringing, I'm afraid. I know you're just doing your job, regaling the clients with macabre folk tales about the Shi'roc-Su. Heightening the experience for them, I get it."

"Thank you for recognizing that. Nevertheless, I am most sorry, Colonel. The failures of others surely in no way speak to *your* unique capabilities as a hunter of deadly game. Besides, I would never wish to frighten you off. Considering your stature, that would be foolhardy of me, not to mention very bad business."

"If this thing is everything you claim it is, it'll be my greatest challenge, but I never came across an animal I couldn't get inside my sights." Allory cupped his hands to the porthole and leaned in for a better view. "I guess the same could be said for Ahlmo Veidt, at least before this one."

"From what I can recall of Mr. Veidt's expedition, he was an exemplary hunter in every way. He acquitted himself well," Rinku said. "He battled the Shi'roc-Su with honor."

"I'd expect nothing less from Ahlmo. Our rivalry aside, the man always had honor. He treated the prey with respect, always reverent."

"Reverence is good. To hunt the Shi'roc-Su you must have reverence for it, as well as a good dose of fear—it's not a beast to be trifled with. As you say, you've heard the stories. A head ringed with dozens of baleful, glowing crimson eyes; a body swollen with muscle; with row upon row of snarled, wavy teeth like kris daggers and claws like swords; poisonous, tentacle-like growths covering its body, able to paralyze a man with just the slightest touch. And lest I forget to mention, it's savage as a demon, sir," he said. "A walking, breathing nightmare."

Allory gave the guide a chuckle and slow, mock applause. "My god, that is great stuff! How long did you have to rehearse that little speech? I hope you're not building this thing up too much though."

"You don't believe the legends?"

"Oh, I'm sure there's some truth in there, to a degree. From my experience the natives are always given to more than a little exaggeration about their myths."

"Myth, you say?" Rinku twisted in his seat. "Colonel, believe me, it is no exaggeration when I tell you that the Shi'roc-Su is also *the cleverest* game you will ever encounter. You'll find it's cunning quite surprising. That is, if it allows you to find it at all. It is as illusive as smoke, dear Colonel. Whatever you've seen in the past, it is no matter, you cannot fully prepare for a creature such as this."

Allory's eyebrows lifted. "Are you telling me you've seen it?"

"Indeed, I have, sir. Once, as a young man. A very reckless young man. I will not bore you with the rudimentary particulars of the pursuit, but suffice it to say I was, how shall I put it, *outsmarted*, by the Shi'roc-Su. And fortunate to escape with the memory of it. That is why I can make the claims that I do—because I know them to be true beyond all question." Rinku bowed his head again. "I trust I have not unnerved you, sir."

Allory burst out in a supercilious laugh. "Let me tell you a secret," he said, pulling a Bowie knife from his pack and fogging the silver of the blade with a warm gust of his breath. "Fear is nothing more than doubt disguised. A man is utterly free of fear when he is free of all doubt—doubt in his abilities, doubt in his equipment, doubt in his intellect. Doubt is the mother of cowardice, Rinku, and that cowardice is the enemy of success." He polished the weapon to a gleaming, mirror shine and returned it to the sheath on his belt. "Remove all doubt in your mind that you'll fail and there is no seed for fear to grow out of," he said. "Doubt is a disease of which I am not a sufferer."

Rinku nodded. "A very philosophical perspective, my friend. As an argument, it's quite convincing."

"Thank you."

"Though, if you'll forgive an old skeptic, I can't help but wonder how well your philosophies will serve you when this ship lands and that hatch door opens and we let you loose in the Shi'roc-Su's domain," he said. "Tell me, Colonel Allory, being an espouser of wisdoms, you must be familiar with the writings of the earthling, Aristotle?"

"Can't say that I am."

Rinku smiled politely. "No matter, sir. Aristotle would say that the behaviors you exhibit are not truly courageous because you are keenly aware of the dominance you hold over your prey. He would argue that the only true test of courage would be in the face of an equally-matched opponent."

"Is that so?"

"Quite so, Colonel."

Allory craned his neck to peer out of the helipod's back window, made obsidian by the darkness of space. But all that was visible to him was the reflection of his own face in the glass, bronze and creased with crows-feet forged by the light from a thousand different suns on a hundred different worlds.

"This Aristotle," he said. "He ever do any big game hunting?"

Rinku gave a snicker. "No, I don't believe so."

"Well, you tell your man Aristotle to come out with me sometime. I'll put a plasma rifle in his hands and carefully explain to him that there isn't a living thing in the cosmos that can take a blast from that gun and keep coming. I'll make certain he fully understands the immense advantage he has over... let's say a starbelly buckhog, like they have over in the Krell Nebula. I'll flush that monster out of the bush straight at him, all teeth and warm snot flying, bearing down on him like pure malice, and you try to convince him that it's not *real* courage that lets him stand there and squeeze off a round."

"I don't think-"

"Because your philosopher friend would piss himself like all the other uber-elite assholes that pay me to take them on safari. Then let's hear him lecture me about the true nature of courage on the way home while he's sitting in a suit of his own urine."

"Again, I meant no offense."

"I'm not so sure," Allory said before giving the guide a strong, albeit friendly, pat on the arm. "But that's what I like about you, Rinku. You keep me guessing."

"Thank you, sir. I am genuinely enjoying our discussion, as well as your frankness on the subject. I hope it's not too banal for your taste."

"Not at all," Allory told him. "I'm sure we've got a few more minutes, any other questions for me before we land?"

Rinku brought his hands together as if in prayer and rested them against his mouth. "You spoke of honor before, Colonel. Tell me more about where the honor is in felling beasts."

Allory grinned and wagged a finger at the old man. "There you go again. I can feel your condescension all the way over here. Listen, people like Ahlmo Veidt and me can't help that we have all the advanced tech, the training, and decades of experience on our side. I offer my prey their share of concessions too—I hunt them only in their natural surroundings, and only for a week. If I can't find them in that time, they win. They beat me." Allory leaned back in his jump seat. "They can always kill me, too," he said. "It's a fair fight."

"Excuse me for saying, sir, but that is only *your* definition of fair."

Allory shrugged. "Someone has to set the rules. The animals can't very well do it, so that leaves me. At this point, it's the only way to test myself," he said. "I'm so bored with traditional hunting parties—I want a real challenge again. I want to feel that blood surging and that adrenaline filling up my system. I haven't had that in a good long while and I'm beginning to think it's never going to happen again. How dismal would that be?"

"And you say no prey has never eluded you?"

"Not once. Mythical or otherwise." Allory again gazed out the porthole. "How much longer?"

Rinku leaned back, tapped the man in the front chair, and directed his eyes toward the Colonel. Allory pointed to his wrist.

"We're nearing the drop zone now," the pilot announced.

Allory checked his gear and locked his gun into place on his pack. "I know a whole lot of guys who wouldn't even bother coming after the Shi'roc-Su because they're afraid they'd never find it."

"Or more likely," Rinku said. "They're afraid they would."

A tantrum of rain erupted from a neighboring cloudbank and dropped to the surface. The cabin rumbled and violently shook. Allory tipped his head back into the cradle of his shoulders as the helipod yo-yoed downward through the storm. The pod set down amidst the low plinking of raindrops against the hull. It alighted in a brightly-marked clearing surrounded by a lush, verdant forest. Rinku deactivated his magnetic harness and crawled out of his chair. He extended a solemn hand to Colonel Allory and escorted him to the hatch.

"What's the matter, Rinku—no more spook stories?"

"I'm afraid not. But as you've pointed out, they're all just part of the grand production—a bit of showmanship on my part. I try to give the clients their money's worth."

"Well, you've certainly been most entertaining company."

"Thank you, sir." Rinku began to close the hatch before pausing. "I do hope you find success in tracking the Shi'roc-Su."

"Thank you," Allory said. "But you don't really mean that, do you?"

"To the contrary, Colonel. I've grown quite a fondness for you in our short time together."

"Then I suppose I should be apologizing."

"Whatever for?" Rinku asked.

"Why, for putting you out of a job, of course."

The guide smirked. "I'll leave you to it then. See you in a week's time, my intrepid sportsman... if it takes you that long. Happy hunting!"

*

The helipod dropped onto the surface and released Everett Allory. He watched the vessel rise and float through the Mylau air until it finally vanished into a blue-black bruise of a sky. Overhead, thunderclaps crunched, goldenrods of electricity splintered the darkness, and fat drops of rainwater beat against his helmet, deafening him.

Who wants an easy hunt anyway?

The ground was a quagmire and held onto his feet. Cables of thick vine and deep green, veiny leaves ensnarled his legs, furthering his difficulty. Yet Allory stood with resolute purpose. He inhaled deeply, filling his lungs with the oxygen-rich air. This type of atmosphere perfectly fed the species that roamed Mylau. Sizable, impressively dangerous game. No true hunter wanted feathers or scales or shells on their wall. They preferred flesh and fur and bone. They wanted meat, beautiful dead meat. And if you came to Mylau hoping to bag the Shi'roc-Su and failed, like all the rest, at least you could leave with some other exotic prize, if you left at all.

Allory trudged into the forest, his sensors all the while taking readings, clicking away, gathering data. Mylau was a most foreign world, but he'd hunted in hundreds of galaxies across the stars and there were always commonalities—always things he could count on. He began to catch sight and sound of familiar elemental combinations: the scent of ammonia coming off a nearby alkaline lake, the shrill cries of a terrygault flock (or some relative of them), the acrid taste of silliq dust—a pheromone—in the back of his mouth. These sensations were all as clear and obvious to him as his own face, as was an acute awareness that eyes unknown were watching and studying him from behind that vast curtain of flora. The Shi'roc-Su was waiting. The game had begun.

This is the realization that the huntsman must always face. He is the intruder, the interloper, the alien. *Mylau does not want you here, great hunter.* The great hunter must know this... and he must not care.

Soon the rain slowed to a spitting trickle. After several hours hiking and just before bedding down, Allory discovered the first track, unmistakable in its uniqueness. He knew it must be that of the Shi'roc-Su because he'd never seen anything remotely like it in all his years, in all those worlds.

He took a spade from his pack and buried the head into the ground. The drowned soil came up easily, surrendering itself in hairy, grass-filled clumps. He dug a shallow hole and laid down in it. The rain washed over him and his naked face shimmered with the thin coat of lacquered water. Within minutes he was lightly asleep, weapons in hand.

*

Allory awoke to a clear, lavender sky. His clothes were dank and dirty after a night pressed in the soil. He gnawed at a vitabar and downed a jugful of liquid before heading out for the day. He spotted a group of thin-trunked trees with sallow bark at the far edge of the clearing and made his way over to them, a shock of blond hair crossing the dark meadow. Large, velvety-skinned leaves drooped from their branches like hanging drapery. The hunter pulled a machete from his pack, took hold of one of the low-lying branches, and hacked it off. The tree spewed a clear viscous substance. Allory quickly held the branch above his head and showered himself in the fluid. It mixed in with the dried mud and sediment and humicolous organisms that covered him. It would all sunbake throughout the day and Allory would be *of* this place, this planet; he would now be practically indistinguishable from the rest of the indigenous species that roamed this forested plain. It was one of the tricks he'd picked up in his countless expeditions.

The hunter was one with Mylau.

Allory haunted the countryside for the next two days before he eventually discovered another set of tracks. A strong set. He'd studied the characteristics of the beast, as much as one could any chimerical creature, before arriving. He cobbled together as many of the scant details as were available, cataloged and compared them to his existing knowledge of all things wild. There were a few mutual attributes and Allory worked these up to create a profile. Based upon the size of the tracks, the animal was not as large as legend would have it, but he chalked that discrepancy up to what he called, 'Tall tales told by small males.' Every hunter wanted a better story than the last, after all. The tracks did have a signature five-padded paw print with the occasional drag of a talon on the backmost pad though. That part was accurate.

At points over the next few hours the trail would disappear from the master tracker altogether, but Allory took notice of nearly undetectable claw marks left on the soft bark of a neighboring rot willow and he would pick up the scent again. He would lose the trail off and on, the prints mixing with those of other game: a striped howlem, a marshcat, a larger tangierslade monkey—all very similar to less expert eyes. But the depth of the print may have been too shallow, betraying the weight of the animal, or the gait too choppy, or the pad pattern was slightly askew. Allory knew the differences well; the mark of the Shi'roc-Su was unique.

But there was something else, too. Something wholly unexpected. Something intricate.

There were instances when the trail would lure Allory into a thick coppice that hid a morass of swamphole akin to quicksand. Or toward unstable rock footing that would end in a precipitous drop and certain death. Or still another that would've ensnarled the man in a grove of strangle-vine, had he taken the bait. He escaped each and continued on, carefully untangling and unraveling the subterfuge that the beast was using to hide itself.

Rinku wasn't kidding. There's a craftiness at work here, you devilish animal, some real guile to you. Covering your tracks? Setting traps? I bet Ahlmo figured you out as well, and I bet he was as eager as I am to bag you. Maybe too eager. Maybe he lost his head and forgot the bounty of deadly defenses Mother Nature blessed you with. Forgot that you're a savage killing machine at heart and nothing more. Perhaps it bewitched your mind and dulled your senses... before it inevitably decided to strike.

Days passed.

More traces of the Shi'roc-Su. More following. More signs, more clues, and still more and more following. Forever following. Allory never seemed to be able to catch up to it. The thing was like a ghost. Many other huntsmen, most others Allory knew of, maybe even Veidt, would have given up the search, or lost the trail by now. The Shi'roc-Su scarcely left any evidence that it existed at all. But it *did* leave evidence. To Allory's eyes it was clear.

The man pressed on.

On the fifth day Allory believed himself close enough to activate his scanner and pinpoint the exact location of the creature. Once he did, he caught sight of, for the first time, the Shi'roc-Su's outline on the infrared.

Only for an instant. Then it was gone.

He pursued in full sprint on the sixth day, certain it was only now yards ahead of him, only to lose it again in an especially unruly chaparral. At every turn foiled, every trick undone. The beast was besting the man, but Allory would not—*he could not*—accept it, could not allow it. This was the adversary he'd craved for so long. He would not fail this test.

On the seventh and final day of the expedition, breathless, Allory stumbled along a faint trail the Shi'roc-Su had left in dampened soil. The trail led to a wide mossy cavity that descended into the ground as if it were the immense maw of Mylau itself.

Have I finally cornered it, or myself? Does it need me in close quarters, to unleash its fury?

The hole dropped at a thirty-degree angle and Allory carefully ducked into the void. This was his chance. His final chance. And he knew it. The Colonel hoisted his tracer rifle and, switching on his infrareds again, he entered the darkness. He was on edge, twitchy, waiting for the ambuscade. All of his senses were alive and raw, ready for his attack, or to fend one off. He steeled his mind and kept moving. Step after step.

But there was nothing. Nothing but empty blackness. He pushed further in.

The underground grotto was expansive and he wound through a network of tunnels until he'd lost any sense of how long he'd been there. And still the darkness. No light, no breeze, no escape for the thing that had eluded him this long.

Is this the den?

His heart thumped like a hammer in his chest. His pulse ran out of control. The hunt was nearing its end, he could feel it within him. He'd used all his tactics, tried every strategy against this foe, and now, finally, it would bear fruit.

Up ahead he could hear... breathing.

It wasn't even trying to hide itself anymore. The Shi'roc-Su was trapped. Allory himself was exhausted, body and mind, and even though they were barely more than thoughts in his head, he formed the words.

"I got you," he said.

He turned a final corner and was stopped dead by the sight of so many glowing red eyes, not more than twenty-five feet in front of him. That, and the radiating warmth of live flesh that was not his own. He flicked the scope-light of his rifle on and caught his first real look at the Shi'roc-Su. It was everything he imagined it would be, everything he was told it would be, and still more somehow. He tilted the gun aside to get a better look.

The beast was crouched against a back wall, its ghastly head upturned with frightful teeth showing, all aglisten. Its entire face, in fact, was refulgent with sweat and spit. It was panting ferally and Allory watched the poison ribbons of its body heave in and out.

Simply magnificent! Such a glorious prize!

But the man was aware that he did not know this prey the way he knew the others. He didn't know *all* that it was capable of. *Was this merely a ruse, or had the thing finally been beaten?* It was folly to allow it to live any longer, the tempting of fate. Allory wasted not another second. He adjusted the plasmatic weapon into his shoulder and retrained his sights on the Shi'roc-Su.

He pulled the trigger and fired a glowing pellet straight through the animal. It slumped over and stretched its majestic body out onto the soil with, what Allory perceived as, a strange sense of relief.

The great hunter hadn't even the time to approach the kill before the gun was swatted from his hands and a ferocious blow came down on the back of his skull. Before he lost consciousness he saw, all around him in the murk, sets of eyes converging on him. Bright, hungry eyes. There was movement everywhere and an instant later, they were upon him.

*

Allory awoke on his side in the clearing just outside the opening of the subterranean cave. He heard a cacophony of voices jabbering loudly in a tongue he'd never confronted before, not in all his days. His hands were tied behind his back with a familiar figure's diminutive feet directly in front of him, just touching the end of his nose.

"Congratulations, Colonel Allory," Rinku said as the group quieted itself. "You have defeated the Shi'roc-Su!" He circled round the man and, with the help of several locals, propped his body up against a log. The carcass of the animal was lying just in front of them.

Allory tried to shake clear his senses. "Wh-what is this, Rinku? Let me go this instant."

"I'm afraid I cannot, great hunter," the old man told him as he turned his back to face the others. "You see, you have slain the Shi'Roc-Su." He reached down and stroked the back of the animal's neck.

Allory gritted his teeth. "That's why I came here, or don't you remember?" His voice grew louder. "If you people didn't want me to shoot your precious beast-god you shouldn't have taken my money."

Rinku's fingers searched through the thick fur. "To the contrary, we depended on you to do just that. Ah, there it is," he said. He raised his arms and backed away as the illusion of the fearsome Shi'roc-Su flickered and disappeared, leaving only the image of a limp, scraggly human body in a sim-suit.

"Is this some kind of joke?" Allory said. "Where's the Shi'roc-Su?"

"Why," Rinku said, "This *is* the Shir'roc-Su. This is the animal you've been seeking the entire time. A person, simply costumed in superstition."

Allory's face soured.

"Come now Colonel, chin up, you've done yeoman's work here. You should be quite proud of yourself. This was no mean feat. The people of Mylau will celebrate you tonight, they will celebrate your sacrifice."

Allory twisted in his bonds. "What sacrifice?"

Rinku sat down in front of the hunter and crossed his legs. The words rolled sweetly from his lips. "As I mentioned earlier, we Mylauans have needs. Before the Shi'roc-Su we were a poor and dying rim planet on the outskirts of the stars, with nothing to offer, nothing to bring travelers to it. Before the Shi'roc-Su there was no reason for important men like you to visit us." He unfolded his legs and rested on his knees. "But important men will pay obscene amounts merely for the chance to hunt the galaxy's apex predator." He got to his feet. "So, we simply created it."

Allory's face flushed. "This isn't right," he said. "I beat your monster. I won! And you stole it from me!" He closed his eyes and let out a weak, sad laugh. "There is no Shi'roc-Su." He shook his head. "There never was."

"Don't be silly, Colonel Allory, of course there is. I promised you a grand hunt for the deadliest, most elusive animal in a thousand worlds," Rinku said. "I kept my promise—the Shi'roc-Su is all these things." He kneeled down and palmed the skull of the corpse in the sim-suit. He swiveled the head so its face met with Allory's. The lips had been sewn shut and the face, wan and weary, was a familiar one. The hunter's eyes widened.

"Ahlmo?"

"Yes, your friend was a most excellent hunter, indeed. His reputation as a slayer of dangerous game was well deserved and it's a good thing because it takes the best to triumph over the Shi'roc-Su," he said. "Mr. Veidt tracked down the previous Shi'roc-Su, a young upstart named Kordavius who came to us some years ago from a planet out in one of the dark constellations if I'm remembering it correctly." He paused in thought for a few moments before giving up the recollection. "It's of little matter anyway, allow me to continue," he said. "Mr. Veidt successfully stalked and killed him and now you have successfully stalked and killed Mr. Veidt. As I said, no mean feat. We were beginning to think we would never get a new Shi'roc-Su... and then you came along." Rinku sat down and leaned back on his hands. "In all your research and fact-finding, in your studious analyses of Mylau, amidst all your fanciful dreams of this day, did the great Everett T. Allory ever bother to wonder what the word Shi'roc-Su means in our language?" Rinku crawled along the grass until he was eye-to-eye with the bound man. "It means *honorable fool*."

Rinku clapped his hands sharply and called out, "Get Colonel Allory into his suit, give him his claws. Our next guests will be arriving soon enough and the Colonel needs time to recuperate and grow accustomed to his new surroundings. He needs time in the wild to become a beast. He needs to learn how to be the Shi'Roc-Su," Rinku said. "We want this to be a fair fight after all, isn't that right, Colonel?" He turned back to Allory and whispered in the man's ear, "You'll learn what it's like to be the hunted now, to have only your wits and your legend to aid you in the face of overpowering force. You'll learn how to run and hide and stay alive. *That* is the only objective now. Not to kill, but simply to survive, as long as you can," he said. "But kill if you must." He put his hand on the man's shoulder. "Don't worry, my formidable friend, I will bring you other monsters to battle with—some *real* monsters for you to test yourself against."

Several Mylauans held Allory down and sewed his mouth shut with catgut while the others prepped him for battle. As they stretched the Shi'roc-Su suit over his body and affixed his terrible claws, there was a blood beat in his ears and a solemn Everett Allory, to his great surprise, stifled a smile.

For this story I wanted to combine elements of Southern Gothic, H. P. Lovecraft, and voodoo into a tasty stew of a tale with a twist. It's a familiar setup that owes a little to a lot of different stories like Richard Matheson's Button, Button with some Neil Gaiman and a dash of The Twilight Zone mixed in for good measure. But I also wanted it to have something else, some original take on this oft-adapted storyline. So... would you give up just a couple inches of something to turn your fortunes around? It was originally presented (and beautifully I might add) as part of the inaugural horror podcast of Parade of Phantoms. And I am happy to present it again to you here.

Béba Daio's Inches

The dark woman wore a kerchief the color of tangerines. It was knotted into a hive atop her head.

"Béba Daio ain't taking no prayers," she said without looking up at the man.

"Tell her it's Clem Watkins, from the neighborhood over." He approached the counter but the woman paid him no mind. "Please ma'am," Clem said. "I grew up here—you know we all like family on the bayou. Tell Béba Daio I got to speak with her."

Her head lifted. The woman's cheeks were saggy, she looked like a mudslide; the whites of her eyes two moons reflecting in the rolling ebon sea that was her face.

"You can ask all you wants to, mista," the woman said. "She ain't listening. I told you, Béba Daio ain't taking no prayers tonight."

"I've never come to her before now," Clem said. "Please... just ask."

Her eyebrows gathered and she gave the man a damp look. "Hold on right here," she said, then disappeared through a beaded curtain behind the counter.

Clem's foot drummed the floor awhile and he felt the gathering sweat from behind his neck race down the groove of his spine, gathering at his belt. He edged slowly toward the door, backing almost completely out of the loggia when the woman suddenly returned.

"Come on, she's expecting you now."

The woman escorted Clem through a labyrinth of backroom doors. In each room there was wooden plank shelving stocked with mason jars of various sizes, the contents of which were hidden in thick, opaque substances while others housed strangely unnatural forms suspended in the glow of amber liquid. The woman stopped at a curtain of hanging seashells, rapped her bony fingers on the door frame and motioned Clem to enter. The room was candlelit with a thick aroma of mold and brine.

"Sit down, child." The low voice garbled from behind a translucent dividing wall at the far end of the room. Next to the partial wall sat a small round table and single chair. Clem slid himself down into it.

The shadowy figure slipped a hand out through a slit in the screen. It was small and looked frail to Clem. The flesh on the hand was almost limpid and, if not for the murkiness of the room, he felt he would be able to see right through to the meat and blue-green veins of it. He took it in his own hand and the gossamer skin bunched up beneath his fingers. Covering the pinky was a ring with a cloudy, oblong opal set in dull silver. Clem bent over and kissed the stone.

"What you want from Béba Daio?" the voice asked.

"I came to ask a favor of you, I need you to hear my prayer. I wouldn't have bothered-"

She raised her hand.

"You here now, Clement Watkins. Speak yo' prayer to Béba Daio, this ain't no place for the timid man."

"It's my grocer's shop—a couple blocks over on Saint Ann—been there the last two years or so," he explained. "Maybe you recognize the place?" Clem paused but the woman didn't answer. "Anyway, I put all the money I ever had into that shop, but I never get no business. I don't really have no regular customers and the ones I do got steal from me." He paused again for a response, but heard nothing. "I got nice fruits and vegetables though—I'll bring you some if you want. And my prices are real reasonable. If people just knew about my place..." His voice began to strain. "Béba Daio, I got a family—a wife, a girl and a baby boy, and another one comin'. I'm a good man, a Cajun man, born and raised here, and this is where I wants to stay. I need you to help me. Take my prayer, Béba Daio, please."

The old woman cleared her throat. It sounded like a backed-up drain. "Been waitin' a long time for you, Lil Clement Watkins, to come in here and ask Béba Daio for somethin'. What you got to pay me with?"

Clem cackled. "Well, you know I never wanted to be owing nothing to no one 'cept the bank," he said. "I can't afford no more debt."

"We all end up with debts need paying, that's just life."

"I was hoping we could work out some kind of arrangement. They say you always helping out folks in need."

"Is that what they say?"

"Sure, ever since I can remember." In the prolonged silence that followed, Clem noticed that his hands were trembling and he made a concerted effort to still them.

"They say anything else about Béba Daio?"

Clem's mouth had gone dry. "Nah, Béba Daio, that's 'bout it.

Another long silence followed... then, "I'll pray on it for ya, Clement Watkins."

Clem drew in a deep breath. "I sure am obliged to you, ma'am," he said.

"That's good," she murmured. "Now I'm gonna need somethin' from you—call it a token of your gratitude."

"What you need from me, Béba Daio?"

"Spirits say just a couple uh inches."

"Inches? Inches of what?"

"Oh, an inch a strength, an inch a will, an inch a nerve. Nothin' you can't make do without, I promise ya," she told him. "You think you could part with a couple uh nothin' inches, Clement Watkins?"

Clem didn't answer.

"You in need, ain't that so? That's what you come all the way out to Béba Daio's house for."

"Yes, ma'am."

"Well, help is what I'm offering," the old woman said. "Provided you agree to my price. Say the words, boy, say you'll give Béba Daio her inches."

Clem squirmed in the chair. "Will it hurt, giving you these inches?"

"I cannot imagine how," Béba Daio said. "But even if it did, what other choice you got? If you had any, you wouldn't be here, now would ya?"

Clem thought hard. "I'll give you da inches," he finally said.

Béba Daio again reached through the slit and laid a large, dirt-brown sack on the table in front of Clem. Whatever objects were inside that sack made a crunching, cracking sound as they rubbed against each other, their shapes jaggedly denting out the skin of the bag. She loosened her grip on the neck of it.

"First, you got to reach in this here bag for me, Clement Watkins," she instructed him. There was a moment's hesitation. "Go on now, I can't do it myself."

He dipped his hand into the bag and buried it to his wrist.

"Pick one out," Béba Daio said.

Clem waded through the bag, allowing the more minuscule objects within to pass through his fingers like too-tiny fish in a net until he clamped down on a hard, sharp piece and plucked it out. It was a single stone, scarlet red.

"That's plenty good," Béba Daio said, closing the bag and dragging it back through the slit to her world of darkness and shadow. When her open hand emerged yet again through the screen, Clem handed her the gemstone and she carried it behind the wall.

"You all done, Clement Watkins. It's gonna be alright now. You come back and see me tomorrow night and I'll collect my inches."

"I'll come tomorrow like you said," Clem told her. "But how will I know if your prayer worked?"

"You'll know... and then you'll come back to Béba Daio."

Clem nodded and quickly left.

*

"What happened?" Clem's wife asked.

"I tell ya, Cherie, it wasn't as bad as all that," he said while he closed the bedroom door. "She ain't tried to string me along or charge me nothing crazy like priestesses from the other parts do."

"How much she ask you for?"

Clem hesitated, then began fidgeting with the stubborn buttons of his shirt. The last one finally slid through its hole and he removed the sweat-spotted garment. "I don't know exactly... no money though."

"Good thing," Cherie said. "'Cuz we ain't got none just laying around."

Clem chuckled. "Yeah, I know that's right." He stepped out of his pant legs and climbed into bed. "Don't know why folks put up such a fuss about Béba Daio. She's been selling prayers to people down here for as long as anyone can remember. Even back to Willie Tyne, and Willie's been in this neighborhood forever."

"Who's Willie Tyne?"

"You know Willie," Clem said. "Old man hangs out down by the Tarot place, goes by Redd."

Cherie nodded her head. "Oh yeah, I know ole Redd." She turned over to switch the light off then rolled back to her husband and kissed his face. "Y'know, Clem Watkins, you a good man."

"Cherie Watkins," Clem said. "You a good woman. Makes being a good man an easy thing to be."

*

The next morning, Clem kissed each member of his family goodbye. He descended the wrought iron stairwell behind his store with cautious optimism for some sign of the prosperity that Béba Daio's prayer may have begotten, some sign—any sign—of her influence. He hopped off the last step and turned the corner of the alley to a loud, indistinct hum coming from the street in front of his store.

A group of people, customers was his only guess, were waiting in a line that curled from the small stoop of his storefront all the way down the sidewalk three storefronts over. As he approached the people, he could hear them going on about produce that was the freshest in the Quarter but not too pricey. They needed French bread for po' boys, milk, rice, eggs, red beans, and while they were there they'd pick up some cayenne, chicory, and boudin. Clem unlocked the front door to the shop and one woman asked him, "You got crawfish?"

Clem's lips split into a wide smile. "Why, we surely do, ma'am. Come on in." Then Clem reached out his arm and waved them forward. "All y'all, come on in!"

And they did. The hours passed and more and more people came by the store. More people than Clem had ever seen. That afternoon a young woman approached the counter slowly.

"How's business?"

"Hey Zoe," Clem said. "Ain't it something?" He gestured dramatically, his arms sweeping the air. "Things are really picking up around here."

"Sure are." Zoe grabbed a Nectar soda and a pack of chewing gum and brought it to the cash register. "I'm happy for you, Clem. You deserve it, you do. You got some of the best stuff in town." Her eyes wandered away from his. "I know you been busy today but you hear about what happened to Willie Tyne?"

Clem cheerfully packaged the soda and gum in a small paper bag and shook his head. "Nope," he said. "What's going on with ole Redd?"

She took the soda from the bag and opened it, took a swig. "Some young villains broke into his place last night, stomped him dead. Didn't take nothing." She took another and gulped it down hard. "Shoot, everybody around here knows he didn't have nothing to take."

"That's terrible. What's wrong with the kids these days?"

Zoe grabbed her bag. "Everybody's talking about it, calling it a tragedy. How Willie Tyne was an institution. I know I'm gonna miss his freckles and his nappy hair walking around up in here. Neighborhood won't be the same without him, I know that." She turned to leave. "What with ole Redd last night and you being so busy today, well like I said, everybody been talking."

"Talking about what?"

She looked Clem stone square in his face.

"You been down to see Béba Daio recently?"

She waited a moment. When Clem didn't answer she walked out on him without so much as a goodbye. He went back to work that afternoon and, even though the store had never had a more profitable day, his mind was muddy with thoughts of Redd Tyne and his visit to Béba Daio's house.

Clem returned to the old woman's home that night just before midnight to settle his debt. He walked the canal and cut through the old cemeteries just a few blocks outside the gas lamps and the stink of the Quarter. These were the Cities of the Dead, with their crypt-lined streets.

Votive candles threw a ghostly light upon stone cherubs that sat atop sun-bleached, shadowy tombs. Hoodoo money was strewn across a few of the graves. It was through territories such as this that Clem had to travel before he reached the old Creole townhouse with the sunrise painted across its door. He was once again escorted back to the little back room where the high priestess sat behind a veiled wall.

"How's things, Clement Watkins?" Béba Daio's voice curled around the divider like a water moccasin.

"Things is fine, Béba Daio, better than fine even." He took his seat at the table next to her silhouette. "We was real busy today and I know it was something to do with that prayer I asked you for."

The old woman gave a burbling laugh. "I told ya, boy, the spirits always listen to Béba Daio's prayers. Ain't you pleased?"

"Yessum, surely I am." Clem rocked in the chair and gritted his teeth a bit. "Ole Redd died last night, got kicked around like a dog. Y'heard?"

"Mmm-hmm, I heard," she replied.

"Béba Daio, there's something I got to know. Does your helping me and what happened to Redd got anything to do with each other?"

Clem could see the shadow of the woman move closer to the veil.

"Sometimes a good thing happens to folks, sometimes bad things happens too—ain't no telling either way. Willie Tyne had his share of good fortunes, I seen ta dat," she said. "Can't go expecting all fortunes to be good though."

Clem's face soured.

"Aw, don't have no sad eyes, Clement Watkins. You gots real nice eyes, bright, like your daddy. I likes da color, too—the way dem blues shine." Béba Daio reached around the wall and placed a polished cobalt stone near her edge of the table, the most brilliant blue Clem had ever seen. She produced the enormous sack once more, holding it open just beneath the table's edge, beside the cobalt stone.

"What's this?" he asked.

"Dat's *your* stone, boy," she said. "You ready to pay Béba Daio what you owe? You ready to give me dem inches?"

Below the bag on the floor Clem spied the shattered remnants of another stone. It was a stone he'd seen before—the scarlet one he'd pulled from Béba Daio's bag the previous night, all blood red and busted now.

Willie Tyne's stone.

While the grim realization crept upon him, Clem's muscles petrified, unable to move but for his jaw, which allowed his teeth to chitter.

"C'mon, boy, it's time to cast your lot. I can't do it for ya—even Béba Daio gots rules to follow. Just put your hand to that there blue rock and slide it off the table into this here bag. Come join your new friends," she said. "It's an easy thing to do, Clement Watkins, it ain't nothin' but a pebble you gotta slide just a little ways." Her final, haunting words rang in the man's ears. "It can't be more than a couple of inches."

Clem forced his arm over the table and touched the stone with his fingertip. He eased it the inches-length across the wood, swallowed down hard, and guided it over the edge and into the bag. The cobalt stone disappeared with the faintest tink.

Béba Daio leaned forward and choked the top of the bag closed with both hands, sealing its contents. As she did, Clem peeked through the slit in the veil and stole a single glimpse of the witch's face.

But what he caught sight of beneath her thick black hood was not so much a face as it was a slimy tangle of undulating tentacles and gelatin flesh; her skeletal visage an explosion of spiny white bone and suckers and matted sea fronds. Holes in her mottled skin opened and closed, gulping and venting the air, and somewhere, hidden in all that, Clem knew there was a smile. He leapt from the chair and covered his mouth.

Béba Daio shook the bag. The stones jangled against one another and settled. "Welcome home," she said.

Clem bolted through the curtained door, cutting himself on one of its shells. He navigated desperately through the byzantine passageways until he emerged back in the sitting room. He threw open the front door of Béba Daio's house and bounded down the steps onto the dirt road.

Clem Watkins paced the Big Easy streets like a zombie for hours before somehow ending up in front of his own grocery store as night became day. Raymon, from the nightshift, was standing by the window and saw Clem. He ran to his boss, frantic.

"Mr. Watkins, thank goodness you here, we ran out of fresh food yesterday on account of it was so busy and the next shipment ain't due 'til Tuesday! What do you want to do? You want me to go over to the all-night market and bring some back?"

Clem thought for the briefest moment and then shook his head. "Nah, just put out anything we got left in the back."

"But, Mr. Watkins," Raymon said, more than a little perplexed, "we just got all these new customers. That food in the back is old. You put that out, they might not come back here no more."

"They'll keep coming," Clem told him.

Raymon gave his employer a sideways glance. "You sure 'bout dat, boss?"

"Yessir," Clem said. "I'd bet my life on it."

This was another earlier story of mine that I never felt reached its full potential in its original form. I got the chance to do a wholesale rewrite of it for this book and I'm so glad that I did. The Starway Pass (a shortened version of its original title) was the longest story I'd ever published at the time it was written. It appeared as a three-part serial in the webzine Space Westerns. Truth be told, I wrote the piece specifically for inclusion in Space Westerns when I saw the beautifully-rendered pictures they created for each story they chose. The pictures were evocative, anachronistic, and just plain cool—sometimes that's all it takes to get you writing. And how much fun would it be to write a sci-fi western?

The story takes westward expansion to cosmic extremes in depicting one young man's fight to either fit into an isolated society that doesn't accept him or find a way out of it. A gateway between worlds known as a starway pass offers hope of an escape for our hero, Bil-Li Kay. But he's not the only one with eyes on it.

The Starway Pass

With his body stretched fully over the white dirt of Exoterra and his hands clasped behind his neck, Harland Cherry's gaze swiveled leisurely from left to right. The moonless night sky, alive with pinholes of starlight, scrolled for the old man beyond the prairie horizon like the tuneless paper roll of a Pianola. The three other men busied themselves several feet away.

"I reckon you fellas don't think much of people like us, living out here on the edge of the universe, cut off like we is. Folks must see this place as forsaken—halfway to hades—and it shows sometimes in our ways." Harland sat up. "But I think we're real lucky."

"How's that?" one of the men asked in a brusque voice.

Harland's grey eyes were still lost in the sky, wide as a child's. "We got the stars and all the rest of creation on one side of us see." He pointed to the brightness of the constellations before turning one-hundred eighty degrees. "And a sun burning all alone on the other side, with nothing behind it 'cept empty space. Just think, if that ole white fireball was on the same side as everything else, we'd never see the stars. And every night'd be as black as a bag of assholes." The three younger men stopped their activities and eyed Harland. "But instead we got this skyful of lights, so I says we're lucky."

"You got a peculiar way of looking at things, olden," one of the other men said. "The glass is always half-full with you Outridgers, isn't it? I guess it'd have to be, stuck way the hell out here." He unpacked his saddlebags. One of the others poked at the fire seriously while the sound of static from frying meetsprouts on a flame-licked skillet hung in the air. Harland got to his feet and snuffed the aroma. The last of the burly trio of men stood at an outpost, guarding the camp.

"This is hard living—natural living," Harland continued. "It ain't for everyone, I know, but I been living this way from the beginning. I got to live this way." He pulled a few clumps of breadmeal from his pocket and held them at the mouth of his sectis. The beast's antennae curled down to inspect the food. It snatched a piece of the breadmeal with its mandibles and carried it into its mouth. Then it opened its gaping maw, allowing the old man to handfeed it. "There you go, boy," he said, stroking the fur of its antenna. "I hear you can't find real food inside the hub galaxies anymore. It's all pills, powders and pastes now." He shook his head. "Ain't nothing else in this world like real food. You boys will realize that once you get back home to the hub."

The men grunted.

Harland rubbed at his back and eased his body down onto the blanket. He pulled off his boots and stretched out again under the wide velvet sky.

"I'm through talking," he said, then added, "Folks can live however they want, I s'pose. You can live stacked up like bricks if you want to—that ain't no life for me though. How 'bout you boys?"

Only the sound of dust crickets remained. The two men were in their bags, eyes closed, before Harland even finished talking. The other remained on watch on the outskirts of camp.

"Go on and get you some shuteye now. We still got a ways to go before we reach town. It ain't right making you boys ride the whole way, but the fuel's been dried up for some time. I guess we always figured-"

"Quiet," the watchman growled.

He grunted out a warning to his fellow lawmen and cryptically motioned the team into action. The threesome moved with militaristic precision: The fire was stomped out and covered, removing that light source; Harland, the secti, and all supplies were gathered together in a small circle; and the three men formed a perimeter around everything, waiting in silence. Suddenly, there was the sound of footfalls from somewhere out in the darkness. The great simultaneous *whooshing* of the men's dusters was followed immediately by the *swish* of rayzer guns being unsheathed from their holsters. Movement in the deep distance from the southeast. The men stepped majestically in that direction—ivory Stetsons low, winds billowing their coattails like comic strip capes, rayzers at the ready. Harland hid behind a decayed log.

By full starlight a silhouetted figure materialized into view, striding toward the men. The tailless, twin-armed outline and erect gait identified the figure as not Skelt, but man. The distinctive hip bulge of a gun belt and the thin, unmistakable line of a hat brim completed their assessment.

The men took aim, maneuvering into stiff poses, their bodies all straight lines set at jagged angles, meant to invisibly camouflage themselves into the mountain range behind.

"Hold, you!" the watchman called out. The figure did not answer. Instead, he continued to amble closer. "I said, HOLD!" The weapons screeched with a flutter of high-pitched beeps, alerting the men of their readiness.

Harland, still hiding, called out to the stranger, "You best listen to them, mister. Y'see them longcoats, don't ya? These boys are sanctified... rangers—

Order of the Black Guard—from back east. They ain't the playful sort, neither. Don't give them an excuse to redline ya."

"The old man's right," one of the rangers bellowed. "Live or die, stranger, it's your choice."

The arms of the shadowy figure immediately shot up. His answer coalesced in their ears as softly as if it were planted there by some direct means earlier and only now flowered into existence.

"My choice?" the voice said. "I think, die."

The silhouette twisted and vanished. The men attempted to adjust their aim, but they no longer had a target. Their trained eyes scanned for some hint of movement. Their ears strained for any possible sound. Other than a hushed Harland and the oblivious secti, there was none.

"Show yourself," the ranger hollered out. "What do you want?"

Again, from everywhere and nowhere, the answer crept into their skulls.

"To feed the soil with your blood."

Three angry bolts of crimson materialized in the darkness and streaked towards the men like comets. The luminescent streams collided with the rangers in a lava spray, their chests bursting forth molten bone and blood that poured over their chaps. The smoke from their charred flesh rose above the fallen men before evanescing into the night.

Silence.

Harland emerged from behind the log, stammering. "I got nothing to do with these boys. Like I said before, they come from somespace back east, I was just escorting them to town. Whatever beef there is 'twixt you fellas got nothing to do with me."

"Where is the starway pass?" he heard from behind him. Harland flung himself around to face the stranger, still shrouded in shadow. He showed his empty palms and lifted his arms until they nearly stretched out of their sockets.

"I never heard of it, mister," he said.

"Is the starway pass here?"

"I been around these parts a long time and I ain't never heard that name. I swear it."

The stranger stepped out of the night and into the dying glare of the fire's embers. He was tall, bean-thin with a biscuit-colored suit and checkered vest that clung tight to the lines of his body. His slouch hat, a tawny flat-top, sat just above his eyes, the wide brim obscuring his face. But the old man could see that the outlaw's skin shimmered vermillion and gold. He stepped closer. Harland saw deep lines mapping a glistening face and dark, jeweled eyes that lent him a distinct reptilian appearance.

"What are you?"

"The name's Lomac Zhinn," Harland heard the reply, but he would swear Zhinn's lips remained still. From inside Zhinn's jacket, two stunted, puny arms reached out and pinned the old man's hands to his sides before he could pull his gun.

"Show me the starway pass."

Harland whimpered. "I told you, I never heard of it. Lemme go now, there ain't no starway pass around here."

"You're telling the truth?"

Harland nodded.

Zhinn took a long while then released his hold on the man, taking his rayzer from him and skipping it across the ground.

"I believe you," he finally said. "And because I do, it's a rightly pitiable fact that your death will forever be a mystery to you."

With a free hand, Lomac drew his sidearm and fired a globule round straight through the old man's gut. Harland folded into the white soil and died burbling.

Lomac ransacked the camp, finding nothing of interest. He rolled one of the ranger's bodies over and took a seat on top of it by the remnants of the fire, stoking it back to life. A glint of metal leapt out at him from inside the fire. He kicked the woodpile and stomped it out. Then, using the dead man's hand, he sifted through the ashes. There he discovered a small, silver-chrome saucer.

"Catch a falling starway, put it in your pocket," he said, grinning, as he slipped it into his vest. He untied each sectis and sent them click-clacking away, leaving the hollowed remains of the men to rot. "I've got to live this way," he murmured to the still faintly smoldering corpses. "Other folks can live however they want, but I've got to live this way."

*

Bil-Li Kay wore a tightly-fitted bib shirt with a tangle of hair growing off his chin. The young man sank lower in the chair, one hand over his cards, the other shielding his eyes. The blond sunlight that crept across the saloon floor was a couple hours old, but Bil-Li and the other two men at the table, Rory and Ginger, had yet to wrap the previous night's game. Each one had a pile of clear rocks in differing sizes in front of them. Bil-Li's eyelids shuttered slightly as he reexamined his cards.

The heavyset man in overalls across the table leaned forward in his chair and pushed his entire pile of stones to the center of the table. "Fifteen crystals. In or out?" Bil-Li squinted at his hand. The tiny markings blurred and multiplied the harder he focused. "Well... are you in, or are you out?" Ginger stayed silent, choosing only to gnash the nub of a cigar and look on with great interest.

Bil-Li straightened himself up. "Don't act so damn anxious, Rory, it's a tell. Now I know you got something."

"I'm not anxious. I just want to get through this hand and win some of my money back before you fall dead away right here at the table." Rory sat the front legs of his chair back down on the floorboard. "Of course I got something," he said under his breath. "I'd have to be plum foolish to try and bluff you."

"And why's that?" asked Ginger through his clenched jaw, still holding tight the cigar stub.

"'Because you can't bluff a man who doesn't give a shit about losing."

Bil-Li half-laughed. "That's a real persuasive theory you got there." He took a swig from the bottle at his feet and shook his head vigorously. "And if I gave a shit, I might've listened to it. But like you said-" Bil-Li pushed a pile of crystals to the center of the table. "I'm in." He smiled. "And I raise."

Rory told his younger brother Gem, who was seated next to him at the table, to loan him some crystal. Gem leaned into the older sibling's ear. "Bil-Li's got an angle, but damned if I know what it is. What's he thinking?"

Rory sneered. "Bil-Li's *always* got an angle, little brother. But sometimes you're dealt a hand you just can't win with, no matter how clever you get."

Gem glanced down at the few crystals remaining in front of each player. "I don't know, seems like there ain't no hand he can't figure a way to win with."

Rory glared at him. "Listen, I'll pay you back double after I take this hand—you know I got a winner here."

Gem's fingers disappeared into his pocket and reemerged with a handful of gleaming jewels. He gave them over to his brother, slowly.

Rory dealt himself two cards while Bil-Li took none. "Bil-Li boy, don't you think it's time you sold your place and moved into town, started a family or something?"

He fanned out his cards face down on the table. "I had a family."

"Folks round here might treat you differently." Rory peeked at the upturned corners of his new cards.

"Folks around here treat everybody just how they see fit. Proximity ain't gonna change that. Things get hairy and I suspect you'll be right there with 'em, friend."

Rory gave the young man a scowl. "That's a hell of thing to say."

Bil-Li shook his head. "I'm sorry," he said. "I'd like to be wrong but-"

Rory's face suddenly cheered and he gave a nod to the door. Bil-Li craned his head round for a looksee. A comely younger woman—laced knee-high boots, patterned dress, parasol, and Saturn hat dipping down in a wave across her face, ice white from tip to toe—entered the saloon with her parents. A droplet of sweat slid down her jaw, her body's only betrayal to an otherwise grand entrance. Her father spoke to the two women briefly before heading to the bar. Mother and daughter waited just inside the swinging doors.

Her eyes found Bil-Li's.

"I fold," he said. He dropped his cards and headed swiftly toward the door. He tipped his hat to the women. "Mrs. Doil, Clementine—I swear you ladies get prettier every time I see you. You're both lookin' right fine today."

Clementine stifled a smile and wound up blushing instead. Her mother looked to the bar.

"Well thank you kindly, Bil-Li Kay," the elder woman offered stiffly.

"Fine as cream gravy," Bil-Li said, adjusting his hat.

A voice boomed from behind Bil-Li. "If you're supposing that my bringing family in here while I conduct some business gives you license to make advances—it don't," the man warned. Mr. Franck Doil was a stout man with a thick mustache under his Skimmer hat. He stepped between Bil-Li and the women. "We're not ten minutes out of Sunday service and you're in here sullying my girls with your eyeballs. I should've known better than to bring proper ladies around the likes of you, Bil-Li Kay. Go have your fun with Annabeth Traynor or some other trollop, not my daughter."

"Father, that's really not necessary," Clementine said. "Bil-Li didn't mean nothin' by it."

Bil-Li's gave an obliging glance to Clementine and turned back to her father. His face hinted of a smirk. "Apologies for my insulting behavior to you and yours—especially on the Lord Mother's Day. You seen the Lord Mother at church today, Franck? You talked to her recently?" The smirk finally emerged on Bil-Li's face. "Yeah, I didn't think so." Franck Doil's whiskers bristled. "I'm thinking she's just made-up by people like you so you can dress up on Sunday mornings and sing out loud while the rest of us heathens are trying to sleep. Hell, Franck, if I'd a known Sundays mattered so much to you, I would've waited 'til tomorrow to sully your girls."

The saloon went hush and Franck Doil's eyes darted.

"Ah hell," Bil-Li said. He approached Mr. Doil with an outstretched hand. "Dammit all, Franck, don't get your back up. All I said was your girls look fetchin' in their new dresses, that's all. I didn't mean no harm by it. Go home and enjoy the day with your family. Don't mind me, I'm just tired."

"And drunk," Mrs. Doil blurted.

"Yeah, maybe a little drunk, too."

Franck spoke low. He pushed the words out past gritted teeth. "I would ask that you keep your eyes off my wife and little girl."

"She ain't so little," Bil-Li said before chastising himself under his breath. "Damn it all, Franck, I didn't mean that—I just couldn't help myself." He stifled a giggle.

"You're nothing but a mudsill, Bil-Li Kay, still full as a tick at eight in the morning. Sure as you're standing here, your folks are in their graves rollin'."

Bil-Li froze up. Rory came up and pulled at the back of Bil-Li's shirt, but Bil-Li shrugged him away. "I would ask *you* to keep my parents' names out of *your* mouth. This whole town owes them that much, and a damn sight more. As for your gals, it ain't my eyes you should be worrying about."

"Whoah now, ease up, Bil-Li," Rory whispered.

Franck pushed a finger into Bil-Li's face. "Hobble your lip, boy, or I'll have some satisfaction." His skin flushed bright red. He moved his hand to his belt. "It might've done you some good to come to church instead of living wild out on that farm. Your daddy should've taken a lash to your backside, but he was too busy dealing with them Skelties—and look where it got him. Yep, I reckon your folks done you a powerful disservice raising you around those Skelties like they did."

"I asked you to keep my folks out of it, Franck."

The big man quickly drew his rayzer and buried it under Bil-Li's jaw.

Clementine stepped forward. "Daddy, stop this now!"

Franck Doil ignored his daughter. "That's *Mister Doil* to you, boy. Don't ever forget what kind of man is standing in front of you." Franck twisted the barrel into the soft of Bil-Li's neck. "Why do you think I opened a gun shop? You don't sell rayzers without knowing your way around one." He pushed harder into Bil-Li's flesh. "I've killed men."

Bil-Li hard swallowed. "Oh, I know you have."

Franck grimaced and raised the pistol up to Bil-Li's cheek. The skin bunched up around the young man's eye, partially closing it. He released the safety.

Bil-Li could hear the excited hum of Franck's piece warming. He moved his hand slowly down to his waist.

"Go ahead," Franck said. "Skin it and watch me melt your head clean off. I heard what they say about you, but nobody's that fast, not even a Skeltie." He grinned with the smugness only a man with a drawn gun possesses. "I got a real lively hand myself, and you're testing me."

Bil-Li's hand edged away from his gun.

"Drilling choo birds off of a fence post is easy, redballing a man is different. It takes some doing. Tell me Bil-Li, you ever killed someone?"

"Nah, I ain't like you."

Franck lowered his rayzer. "You sure as hell aren't. Now mind your manners, boy." He carefully stepped back, holstered his piece, then turned and motioned his wife and daughter to leave.

Bil-Li's voice was slow and clear. "I ain't like you at all," he hollered. "Because I'm not a coward, *Franck*."

Franck Doil turned back and fumbled for his gun. He pulled it finally and held it on the young man. "Get your ass outside."

Franck led Bil-Li out into the morning sun followed by most of the patrons of Delpit's saloon. The two men stepped onto the plank porch walkway and Franck gave the young man a hard push off the steps into the dusty street. A crowd quickly amassed from all corners of the town. The air grew thick with malice. Franck bounded down the saloon steps and onto the blanched soil with his second in tow, a big-bearded townie by the name of Trick Jim Kettenden.

"You're real brave to come at me like this, but you're wasting your time, Franck," Bil-Li said. "I ain't duelin'."

"Suits me fine, I'll shoot you anyway," Franck said. "Time to settle up. You can stand there and piss yourself or just stand there and bleed—makes no difference to me. I'd rather you take an active part though. Either way, you're gonna wear the red river, boy." Franck turned to the townspeople. "What say you good people of Purlieu, the usual thirty paces sound fair?" The crowd cheered their approval. "Thirty apiece, Bil-Li, sixty paces, that's a long way—my eyes ain't what they used to be. You may win yet!"

Bil-Li leaned in. "Talk as loud as you want, you lily cur, I'm not negotiating rules. You shoot me and it's murder, you know that."

Franck stared into Bil-Li's glazed, veinous eyes, turned to the throng and announced, "I guess terms have been agreed upon, thirty paces a man."

Trick Jim lined the men up back-to-back. "You heeled, Bil-Li?"

"He's ready, Jim, just count 'em off," Franck said. He inspected his rayzer, eyeing the clear liquid in the cylinder and testing the power cells. Bil-Li fingered the gun in his belt, but checked nothing else. Franck could feel the young man fidgeting behind him, struggling to stand in place. He looked over his shoulder. "I'll end it real quick, Bil-Li. They say you only feel it for a second."

"I won't let this happen," Bil-Li said.

"It's happening, boy," Franck looked off into the sky. "I admit your family was wronged, but I'm going to take all that pain away forever, you just let me do it for ya."

Bil-Li broke into the crowd for cover, but the townsfolk spread out as if there was an opposing magnetic field all around him. Trick Jim aimed his gun at the young man and motioned him back. Bil-Li sulked along the dirty white street to where Franck waited.

Jim instructed the men to turn their backs to one another again and started the thirty-pace count. Bil-Li's dark eyes, closed by the sun, fought to sharpen themselves.

"One…"

"Two…"

"Three…"

"Four…"

Bil-Li drew his rayzer and spun around just before the fifth step. A twine-thin round of beaded plasma blasted from his tiny rayzer gun and snaked through the air, connecting with Franck Doil's body above the arm. Opened up, bleeding and with his gun hand totally immobilized, the man fell as carelessly as a decayed oak. The chalk dirt kicked up and mixed with the thin pillar of smoke that rose out of the hole in Franck Doil's shoulder.

He only felt it for a second.

Gasps echoed everywhere. Bil-Li locked his aim onto Trick Jim before the man could grab the pistol from his belt.

"Set them heaters free, Jim," Bil-Li demanded. The brawny man unbuckled his gun belt and tossed it up onto the awning of Delpit's. An uncertain moment passed before Bil-Li let out a holler and swung his gun onto the crowd. The townspeople cowered as he waved the barrel nonchalantly past them. Clementine Doil and her mother watched from in front of the church with the other good women and children of Purlieu. Bil-Li trained his sights on the cluster and shouted at them.

"You would have me shot down in the street! Why?" His voice cracked slightly. "Because I remind you of what you are? Is it too much to bear? Tell me that's what it is because at least then I'd understand it." He scanned the shocked faces. "I swear I will haunt this town until the day I die. But first things first, I'm going to show you all what I'm capable of at sixty paces."

Bil-Li took careful aim and fired a blast line directly into the crowd outside the church. The townsfolk screamed. The laser streak zipped through the air toward a wailing mass of children. Amidst the cries, the ray disintegrated into a flaccid shower of sparks only a few feet in front of a tow-headed boy, his blue eyes wide.

The street fell silent.

"Had this made up special—concentrated low-level stream, minimal spray," Bil-Li announced, holding out the gun that was not much larger than his own hand. "I'd use it to get rid of jackhops. Mama liked it 'cuz it'd do the job on anything up close without setting her whole garden on fire." There was a sadness in his voice that was quickly replaced with anger. "But it can't so much as give you a blister from sixty paces!" he told them. "Franck Doil knew that." He motioned over to the man being tended and helped to his feet. "That man would 'ave put me down like a dog, and all you people can think to do is watch." Bil-Li shoved the gun back into his holster.

"You should've said something," Jim said. "Tell me how Franck was supposed to know your piece was just for garden jacks?"

Bil-Li wiped his eyes. "Because he's the one who made it for me. Ain't that the truth, Franck?" Franck Doil wouldn't answer. He only wore a shameful look as he hobbled to the Doc's office. "You're right about one thing, Franck," he continued. "It ain't nothing like drilling choo birds."

Bil-Li unhitched his sectis from in front of Delpit's and mounted the beast. While the crowd watched, he rode across the street to Clementine and reached his hand down to her without a word. Mrs. Doil held her daughter's wrist but Clementine yanked it away, grabbed hold of Bil-Li's arm, and allowed him to pull her up into the saddle behind him. She wrapped her arms around his waist and nestled her head into his shoulder blade, filling her nostrils with the stale smell of rotgut whiskey and day-old sweat that Bil-Li shed like a snakeskin. She held tight as the sectis picked up speed and a cool zephyr ran through her clothes.

*

Sheriff Bennett Tepper maneuvered through the jagged crystal field behind the Kay farm. In front of him, overgrown shoots of deep blue vegetation rose up out of jaundiced soil and peppered the remainder of the property. Tepper's sectis walked through the plants hoping to cloak his approach. With each step the animal would shake its legs. The sectis labored forward; blue weed tangling around the intruder. The beast's thorny legs ripped at the infernal vines, but for each stalk that was severed, three more spiraled up to take its place. Tepper gave a reassuring pat and urged the animal on. The sectis fought through the heavy brush.

The sheriff noticed that behind him a powdery residue was lifting off the torn vines. Along the path he'd trodden, an indigo smoke unfurled itself against the sky. Tepper hurriedly grabbed hold of one antenna and squeezed. The sectis shot up with a screech, pulling itself free, and galloped to the edge of the field toward the house. The sheriff was still a few hundred feet away when a laser bolt streaked over his head like a scarlet javelin. It spooked the sectis even further and the animal nearly threw him, but Tepper held on and, sinking low in the saddle, drew his weapon. In one motion he dismounted the animal, curled around to the front of the house, and approached the porch steps.

"Bil-Li, what in the hell do you think you're doing? You nearly took off my head!"

Bil-Li stepped off the porch, a dual rayzer rifle in his hand. "Don't blame me, Ben. You nearly got yourself killed sneaking around like that."

"I just come to talk, son," the sheriff told him.

"Stay where you are, Tep." Bil-Li brought the rifle to his shoulder. "I can assure you, this one ain't for jackhops."

The sheriff's voice was stern. "Bil-Li, how long you known me? I came around back because I figured this is how you'd react when you seen me riding up. I thought if I snuck up on you and showed up at your front door you couldn't turn me away. I guess I forgot how much Skeltie you got in you, boy. I'm alone, Bil-Li, I promise ya, now let me up. I don't have the time to stand around and argue with you... and neither do you."

Bil-Li wasted a few moments, just to prove that he could. "Put the ray in your satchel and come inside."

Tepper stuffed the gun inside the pouch of his saddle and climbed the steps to the door. The house was a big family octagonal. Too big. When he got close to the door, Bil-Li appeared again. Sheriff Tepper could hear the hum of a cyclone rifle they called The Sandman, but he didn't see it. Then, peeking out from between the curtains of an upper window, he spotted the double barrel of The Sandman. A sideways eight. The *infinite sleep*.

Bil-Li opened the door. "What brings you around, Ben?"

The two men shook hands. "Trouble, I'm afraid. You got Clementine Doil in there with you?"

"Yessir I do."

"You mind telling her to put that rifle away?"

"That depends, Sheriff. You come to take me in for what happened in town yesterday?"

"That's what I told them."

"I wouldn't do that if I were you, Ben."

The sheriff gazed up again at The Sandman pointed at him from the window. "I don't plan on it, son."

Bil-Li smiled. "Good. Come on in then, breakfast is on." He called out, "Clementine, sweetheart, put that thing away and come join the sheriff and me."

The thick aroma of spiced aduana and tarburd eggs filled the kitchen. The men sat down and Bil-Li filled the sheriff's cup with oil-black coffee. Clementine came down in her knickers, dragging the rifle, her tousled hair falling down around her shoulders. She propped the rifle up against the stove and flipped the eggs. Ben grinned sheepishly.

"You're mighty comfortable around guests, ain't ya, Clementine."

"We wasn't expecting any," she said. "Besides, I don't mind none, sheriff. How 'bout you?"

"I s'pose I don't, ma'am."

"Breakfast will be ready directly, boys," she said.

Ben tipped his hat and leaned over the table to Bil-Li. "The whole damn town's in an uproar—you took things too far."

"He was going to shoot me, Ben. For nothing, for words. Hell, just for being."

Clementine bent over and emptied the pan out onto dull-colored plates. Shards of sunlight cut into the kitchen, making sheer her blouse and outlining the grandeur of her frame.

"Much obliged," the sheriff said. Clementine smiled and sat down.

"They sent me out here to fetch you, bring you back for trial."

"Bring me to trial? On what charge?"

"On the charge of pissing folks off. And when people get pissed off they come to me. It's my job to make things right, Bil-Li. You shot a respected member of the town board. That just don't fly, boy, no matter what."

Clementine broke in. "What was he gonna do, Sheriff, just let my daddy kill him? I feel bad for what happened and all but Daddy had no right to try something like-" She shook her head. "I don't even know that man anymore."

Tepper waved the girl off and turned back to Bil-Li. "You could've said something about the pistol earlier. You could've sent Rory or one of them other boys to get me or you could've just kept your goddamn mouth shut in Delpit's. You could've done a hundred things other than what you did. Now it's too late."

Bil-Li dropped his head and heaved a tremendous sigh.

"We both knew this was coming, Ben. I was either going to end up with a hole in my belly or swinging by a noose. It's too hard having me around, being a reminder to them all the time."

The sheriff put a hand on the young man's head. "Maybe that's all there is to it, son—when those Skelties came through here and killed your folks, and didn't no one from Purlieu come and help—maybe that's a shame they just can't live with. Maybe you're right. Maybe it's just easier to kill off a bad memory than it is to go on living with it."

"I'm not going back to town with you, Ben."

"I'm not asking you to. I told them I'd bring you back, but when I ride in with just Clementine, they're going to come for you and I can't stop them," he said. "But you're not gonna be here."

Bil-Li's eyebrows furrowed.

"You'll already be headed south, to the Skeltlands," Ben told him.

"What's he mean, Bil-Li?" Clementine said. Bil-Li shrugged.

"You ever heard of a starway pass?" the sheriff asked.

"I don't believe so."

"It's a hyperdrive—like a bridge between galaxies, at least that's what I'm told. It's going to clear the way again for lots of people to come out here and settle, like it was before the debris fields and the sinkholes and the damn pirates. People back east won't have to worry about getting through the quads in one piece anymore, they'll be able to take this here starway pass from practically anywhere. I'm talking universal expansion, Bil-Li, and this is one of the places that's going to explode once they get that starpass up," he said. "And people like you will be able to get out of here and start living again, as far away from here as you need to be. Go get yourself a life, Bil-Li, because whatever it is you got going on here doesn't qualify."

"You wouldn't lie to me about this, would you, Ben? Because that would be about the cruelest thing a man could do."

"It's all true, but you didn't hear none of it from me, got it?"

"You hear that Bil-Li, we're finally getting out of here!" Clementine giggled and threw her arms across the table to hug him. They embraced for a long while before Bil-Li pulled her off and his face suddenly soured. He glared at Ben, whose features were still hard as a stone.

"Why ain't you smiling? There's more to this story, isn't there?"

Ben took a gulp of coffee. "Seems they lost track of this starway pass."

"Lost track of it?"

"It was stolen."

Bil-Li scoffed.

"How do you steal a bridge?" Clementine said.

"The bridge wasn't stolen, just the gate disc. It ain't more than a trifle of a thing—looks like a pancake—but it opens up and allows the starpass to anchor itself. Without planting and activating it, this bridge has nowhere to go to." Ben said.

"Why don't they just get another disc?"

"There ain't no other discs, not for us at least. We don't get this one down and they won't risk planting another here again. Not for a long, long time. We're too far out, and there's lotsa other systems could use it."

Bil-Li nodded. "Who took it, Skelties?"

"No, they were gunned down so it doesn't look like we're after the Skelt for this one. We think it was some rustler, name of Lomac Zhinn. I think he might have had some help but we didn't see no other tracks at the site. Lifted it off three couriers—Black Guard, no less—a couple nights back. We found them less than a day from here. Their guide wrote the name out beside him in the dirt before he died.

"Do you know anything else?"

"Yeah, we know this Lomacs must be one nasty sumbitch. He takes out a whole Black Triad and a guide by himself, steals this damn flapjack of the gods starpass thingy, and then just walks away."

Clementine grabbed hold of Bil-Li's arm.

"His trail points south, to the Skeltlands," Ben said. "You grew up around those things, maybe it'll help. They might know something we don't."

"*Those things* murdered my family."

Ben leaned back in his chair, his face pensive and grim. "Bil-Li, I never claimed my way was going to be easy, but if you want to save your skin and get off this rock, this is the best way I can think of. I also know your folks were as friendly with some of those Skelties as with their own kind. Your best friend was a Skeltie, wasn't he? You know about them—their ways, how they move, everything—more than anyone else."

"I just spent some time around them, that's all. I ain't no expert."

"At least you speak their language. You're the one person that might be able to go in there, find the starway pass, and bring it back. I'll deputize you, put you on the payroll, and send you off with a few toys I dug up if you agree to do this."

Bil-Li gave the sheriff a sideways glance. "I don't know, Ben."

"Listen, if you manage to bring that starpass back with you, well, more than a few folks will be showing their gratitude monetarily, and otherwise—I'll see to that. Once the pass is up, it won't be a thing for you and Clementine here to just up and leave Exoterra whenever you please."

"Why should I do any favors for this town? They never gave a damn about us. They sat in their houses while my parents were being slaughtered. They knew there was a Skelt raid going on and they chose to do nothing. Aside from you coming out here to save my hide, no one did a damn thing."

Ben stared into his cup for the right words.

"They were scared, Bil-Li. Shit, I was scared, but it was my job to ride out here and protect you, not theirs. That's why you've got to get out of this place. You're always there, reminding them. You're a living, breathing manifestation of their shame, boy. As long as you're around, there is shame in their souls."

Clementine shook Bil-Li's arm.

"Don't you go and help them. Don't you leave me, Bil-Li Kay. Do nothing of the sort for those people."

Bil-Li slouched down in his chair and crossed his arms. Then he stroked the whiskers of his chin. "I reckon I don't have much choice in the matter."

"It sure don't look that way," Ben said.

Clementine shook her head. "Well goddamn you both then." She stormed out of the kitchen.

"Ben, I appreciate you coming all the way out here for me."

"Old habits, you know."

Bil-Li rolled a cup in between his hands. "Why would Lomac take it? What does he want with a starpass?"

"Ransom, maybe," Ben said. "I doubt it though. Lomac or the people he's working for will probably go to the highest bidder with it."

"Then you can buy it back? What are you worried about?"

"No one around here's got that type of scratch, Bil-Li. There's a few million edge settlements cut off from the civilized worlds that would kill for a chance to anchor that pass—big settlements with a lot more to offer Lomac than we can afford to. When word gets out there's a starpass on the dark market, we're done. No one was even supposed to know it was here. I don't know how this villain got hold of the intel, but if that disc leaves here, it's gone forever. The suits back east don't believe in second chances for planets like ours."

Bil-Li pursed his lips and nodded. "I hear ya—I'll leave as soon as I can. I need to grab some things."

"Take whatever you think you need," Ben told him. "I've got a few things in my bags for you. It ain't as much as I'd like to give you, but it ain't a little, either. Consider it a going-away present."

Clementine came back to the kitchen fully-dressed. She sat down with the men and wiped her moss green eyes with the back of her hand before they could swell with tears again. Ben touched her arm.

"Your boy's a survivor."

Clementine reached across the table and slapped the sheriff hard across the side of his face, scraping the inside of her hand raw against his thorny beard. Bil-Li grabbed her at the wrists.

"I'm sorry, Ben, she-"

Ben raised his hand. "She cares about you," he said, rubbing his cheek. "She doesn't want to see nothing bad happen to you, that's all. I ain't mad. If I was a smart enough man to figure out another way I would, Bil-Li. But I ain't that smart."

Bil-Li pulled Clementine against him and stroked her long, flaxen hair. "It's a fine way you come up with, Ben. Just fine."

The lawman got up from the table and drained the last of his coffee down his throat. "I'll be outside when you're ready."

Sheriff Tepper tramped out the front door leaving Clementine and Bil-Li alone in the kitchen, facing each other.

"It's okay, Lemon, I'll be real careful, I promise," Bil-Li told the girl.

"You can't guarantee me you're coming back," she said.

"Nope, I can't."

"Things could happen to you out there. Terrible, awful things."

"That's right."

Clementine sighed. "Why don't we just go. Let's leave here. We can head off someplace where no one will ever find us—to the mountains maybe, or I'll even go to the pits. This is a great big place—we can ride northwest and be out of the territories inside of a week. We'll carve out a life for ourselves up there. I know I'm not accustomed to living natural and it'll be real hard for me at first, but I won't complain, no matter what."

Bil-Li took Clementine in his arms and held her sweetly.

"I could hide out the rest of my life in the highlands or the lowlands if I had to, but I couldn't take you with me, not my Lemon." He took her face in his hands. "I could belong there, but you never could. And you shouldn't have to. All we ever needed was a direction to follow. When I bring back this starway pass, we'll finally have one."

"What if you don't come back?"

"Then I guess you'll still have a direction," Bil-Li told her. "It just won't be the way I've gone."

Clementine pushed away from him and steeled herself. "All right then," she said. "If that's how it's got to be. You've got to promise me something, Bil-Li Kay."

"Anything," he said.

"You know there ain't no place for good men out here. Things like honor and mercy are just things that get you killed out in the wasteland."

"I know that."

"Promise me you'll leave the Bil-Li I know—the real Bil-Li—here in this house with me. And when you walk out that door, make your blood cold, put a stone where that big heart of yours is. Don't try to be the stand-up Bil-Li, the righteous Bil-Li," she told him. "Just be the Bil-Li that comes back."

He took a deep breath and nodded his head. "Clementine Doil, on my word here and now I will make that promise to you." Clementine kissed the young man deeply and ran up the stairs without looking back.

Bil-Li turned and walked out onto the porch. Ben was there. He had one of his saddle bags unbuckled. "You got something for me there, Sheriff?" Tepper removed a burnished, copper-hued rayzer and handed it to Bil-Li.

"Nothing terribly special, but it's the cleanest sidearm I got," he said.

Bil-Li twirled the pistol frontward and backward, stopping the barrel for a split-second at different shooting angles. The brown metal was a blur in his hand. Ben watched in amazement as Bil-Li turned his hand over and spun the weapon horizontally, his index finger pointed squarely at the ground, the weapon defying gravity. With the other hand, Bil-Li took his own rayzer off his hip and wheeled it around selfsame. He brought the two whirling pistols to a stop, one following the other, like the halting reels of a slot machine. He jammed his rayzer back down into its holster.

"Sweet Jesus, you can sling," Ben said. "Can you shoot those things too, or do you just lead the band?"

"Bil-Li started to reply when, without warning, Ben hurled a stone high into the air and Bil-Li, almost instinctively, drew his new piece, released the catch, and fired a red stream that disintegrated the rock before it reached its apex.

"Ooo-wee, you sure froglicked that sunnuvabitch!" Ben said. That brought a smile to Bil-Li's face. "Boy, if you ain't the fastest draw, I don't know who is."

"Aw, that ain't nothin'," Bil-Li told him. "You see them cans over yonder, lying on their sides?" Bil-Li pointed to three large perritree stumps in the field. "I see 'em," Ben said. "You fixing to knock 'em off?"

"Nah."

Bil-Li wiggled the fingers of his right hand, touching each one to his thumb with increasing rapidity. He pulled his rayzer and fired three bursts in quick succession. Ben squinted. "You missed 'em, Bil-Li, they're still there." The two men walked through the clearing toward the stumps. "Well I'll be damned," Ben said to himself as he got closer.

Each can remained on their stumps, but they were, all three, now standing upright. Ben shook his head in disbelief. "What you been doing out here, boy?"

"Practicing," Bil-Li said. "Not much else to do. You get hungry enough and you can learn to hit just about anything. Give me enough time and I can knock the shoes off a fly. Plus, I guess it was just something to keep my mind whole."

Ben lifted his saddle blanket to reveal another rayzer. He pulled it out and handed it to Bil-Li. It was far bigger than any handheld Bil-Li had laid eyes on before. On its side was a clear panel where thick plasma threads churned and twisted like pulled taffy.

"Is this a-"

"Yup."

"Ben, where did you get it?"

"Never mind, just take it,"

Bil-Li took the gun and caressed it reverently. "It's a lot heavier than it looks."

"Go ahead, try her out. She'll kick though."

The young man hefted the gun to his eyeballs, aimed at a stretch of pasture, and fired. He felt the rayzer's energy surge through his hands to the back of his spine. The constant burst of wide redline from the barrel disappeared into the distance and splashed down beyond the field. He held back on the trigger as he moved the gun slowly to the right, creating a laser blanket in midair. To the left, the plasma residue fell, hissing against the scorched sand. Bil-Li released the trigger.

"You're gonna have to give her a short spell to power up again. A second or two at most and she'll be ready to go again," Ben told him.

Bil-Li's mouth was agape. "I never handled a sluice rayzer before. What do you do with it, cut down trees?"

Ben laughed. "I figure a sluicer's good to have. I ain't gonna lie to you, Bil-Li, I got no idea what you'll run into down south. I'm not pretending to give you the sluice for any special reason I can think of. I'm giving it to you for all the reasons I can't."

Bil-Li raised his eyebrows and nodded. "Got anything else?"

"Just one more thing," Ben said. He reached into his shirt pocket and removed a pair of spectrum-tinted eyeglasses. "The Skelt see better at night. When you put on these nocturn glasses, you'll see as good as they do." Ben rapped on the lenses with his knuckle. "They're strong, too. Those lizards try to spit in your eyes and these glasses will help. But they can't do you no good unless they're on your face, so make sure to wear them. They blind you with that poison and you're good as dead. They'll tear you apart, Bil-Li. You know that better than most."

The two men shook hands.

"I'm in debt to you, Ben."

"Not once you leave here, you ain't. Not to me, not to anyone."

Bil-Li gazed out on the horizon. The electric white sun of Exoterra was still hanging midday high, casting sharp, small shadows on the planet's surface. "There's a little border town called Rya Delsa. My father used to bring me along when he'd go there to trade with the Skelts and do some handiwork they couldn't manage. It's quiet, as far as Skeltie towns go."

"Your Daddy trusted those savages?"

"They weren't savages, Ben. Not all of them anyway. Not to us."

"You see things a little differently now, I bet."

The sun closed Bil-Li's eyes to slits. "A lot has changed, that's for sure."

Ben called to Clementine, who was now leaning up against the doorframe of the house. "C'mon miss, it's time to get back to town. Your mother needs you."

She kicked the frame with her boot heel.

"Don't go fussing now," Bil-Li told her. "Head back with Ben. I'll come for you when I'm done."

"You better, Bil-Li Kay," she said.

*

Bil-Li rode into Rya Delsa late that night. He hitched his sectis up to one of the pillars that held up the town's only solid structure: a squat, ramshackle building constructed of thin, corrugated metal sheets bent around ground stakes and covered with more metal boarding. The place looked like a house of cards.

Bil-Li cocked his head to the side and ducked in. It was a den of moist, writhing Skelt bodies, sleek and scaled. They gathered around a network of holes in the ground that were filled with a clear, gelatinous soup, dipping their tongues into the thick liquid as they communed with one another. Bil-Li had to watch his walk to keep from accidentally stepping onto any twisted Skelt bodies or into any of the drinking holes.

The noisome scent of Skelt-thought permeated the air, a stale miasma of chemicals that attached themselves to Bil-Li as he walked past. His brain was swimming trying to recollect the pheromonal language.

It comes easy if you let it, he remembered. Some folks pick it up right away even if they never heard it before, real natural-like. For others like him, with bad memories, they sometimes block it out.

He had to remember.

Bil-Li stopped and shut his eyes behind the varicolored lenses of his nocturns. He breathed their thoughts deep inside his lungs, filling his alveoli and passing them into his bloodstream. He opened his mouth and stuck out his tongue like a boy in the rain, tasting the air and letting it soak into his capillaries. Time passed. Slowly, gradually, the language came back to him.

"You a 'lil lost there, Hugh? You not belong here," the Skeltie below him said. The viridian creature stood about four and a half feet high—tall for a Skeltie— at least the ones who stood upright. Bil-Li was no longer consciously aware of the chemical odor in the air, but he understood perfectly now the confabulations that were taking place all around him. The tall Skeltie beside him opened several small slits on either side of his neck and vented another message into the air.

"You must gotta be lost," he said, then cackled. *"You no even understanding me, eh, Hugh?"*

Bil-Li looked down at him. He thought the words as he mouthed them. "Of course I can." The creature slunk back in astonishment. "Why do you keep calling me, *Hugh?"* Bil-Li asked.

The Skeltie sniffed around Bil Li's torso and nudged its snout into the pit of his arm before it fully understood the man's question. *"That's what you be, a Hugh-man. We not take kindly to no Hugh-mans round here. Why not you go?"*

Bil-Li was too relieved that the Skeltie understood his chemical-speak to care much about his tone. He remembered now to lift his arms slightly whenever he communicated his thoughts.

"I won't be long, as soon as I get what I'm looking for. You feel like helping or do you want me to stick around here with you and your friends all night?"

"Fucker off, Hugh!" the reptilian creature said. His acrid message quickly reached the neighboring groups of Skelties.

Bil-Li surreptitiously slid back his jacket to reveal the rayzer on his hip. "What's your name?" The Skeltie gave no answer. "You look like an Abe," Bil-Li said. "We'll go with that. Abe, my guess is judging from your attitude you're not going to be much help to me in here, which is okay. I never make anybody do something they don't want to." He glanced around the room. "But I know you could use some dew because... what Skeltie couldn't? Tell you what, I got my sectis hitched up outside. I want you to go out there and watch him for me. When I leave, if anything's happened to it, I'm going to hold you personally responsible. But if not, I'll throw you some coin. You understand me, don't you Abe?"

The Skeltie hissed. *"Take a lookee where you be, Hugh. You wanting to die?"*

Bil-Li moved in close.

"Maybe, but not tonight, friend," His aroma was taut. "I already told you, I got work to do. If I walk out of this shack for some reason in a foul mood— and Abe, I *will* walk out—you're gonna be the first one I come see. So go outside and don't be riling anything up on your way. If I don't run into any trouble while you're gone, I'll make knowing me worth your while."

Abe stood with the two talons of each hand clicking away in thought. "*We see,*" he finally said. He lowered himself down to four legs and skittered out the door. Another Skeltie rose up beside Bil-Li.

"*What you needing, Hugh?*"

"Who are you?"

"*Me name's Trubbull. I get you whatever it is you came for.*" He browsed the room. "*Don't be pay no mind to none of these here louts, they not got no sense of hospitality,*" he said. "*I, on the other hand, is a real accommodating fella, for the right fee.*"

"You don't say."

"*Trust in me, big Hugh, I is the Skeltie you looking for.*"

Bil-Li laughed. "How do I trust anybody named Trubbull?"

"*Aw, it ain't nothin', Trubbull just middle name. Call me SeptichaTan if it ease mind.*"

"It really don't," Bil-Li told the Skeltie.

"*Righty right then, Trubbull, it is. What Trubbull do for you, Big Hugh?*"

"I'm looking for a man, goes by the name of Lomac Zhinn. He may have come through this way."

"*Lomac, you say?*" Trubbull replied. "*Real mean-spirited, this man is?*"

"Rumor has it."

"*I suspecting he ain't want to be found, neither.*"

"No, I don't expect he is," Bil-Li said. "You know anything?"

Trubbull unfurled a wide grin. "*Plenty,*" he said. "*What you got for Trubbull if I be tell you?*"

Bil-Li held out his smallest pistol. Trubbull spit on the ground at Bil-Li's feet.

"*What a Skeltie s'pposed to do with that, huh? You make joke of Trubbull?*"

"You could trade it to someone like me, someone passing through."

"*If you not figuring out by now, Hugh, we no get many tourists in Skeltlands. Ones we do already carrying cuzzin' they ain't no idiots, so I'm 'fraid ain't no market for that there rayzer.*" Trubbull placed a finger on his tiny skelt head in mock thought. "*Lucky be for you I flexible—I take either dew, or dew. So I ask you again, what you got for Trubbull?*"

"I got some, not a lot. Shit's no good for you."

"*Easy now, Hugh, I's already got one mama, don't need no others. Now how much is ya got?*"

"I'll give you the rayzer and ten jacks of dew if you tell me which way he's headed," Bil-Li said.

"*I's tell you what, you keeps the gun. For twenty jacks I do you one better and takes*

135

you right to him."

Before Bil-Li could respond, another Skeltie hopped up behind Trubbull. "That you, Pith?" Bil-Li said with a guarded smile.

"Is me," the Skeltie answered. *"Is very good see your face again, Bil-Li. Been like ages, old friend."*

Trubbull's head swiveled between the two. *"You know 'dis Skeltie?"*

"Pith and I used to play cross sticks with each other when I'd come down here with my father."

Pith nudged Bil-Li with his elbow. *"Then we pick meloi bush bare and fill bellies, eh Bil-Li?"*

"Only one of us picked the berries," Bil-Li said. "Pith here would dive in snout-first and scratch himself up something hellacious. Funniest damn thing you ever seen."

"Cosmic Mother not bless us Skeltie with beauty hands like you," Pith said. The odor of his response had the unmistakable lemon piquancy of sarcasm.

"You did all right," Bil-Li said. "Y'know, I used to get such a charge coming down here to see you, pal."

"Yeah, was whole different time," Pith said. There was a pregnant silence. *"Why you back in Skeltlands, Bil-Li? This not good place for Hughs."*

Trubbull interrupted. *"Your Hugh-friend Bil-Li and me do a little business, that's all."*

"Really? I want in."

Trubbull's smile drooped. *"Run away, shave tail, this is Trubbull's show. Don't be need no partners."*

"You be bringing him to Lomac?"

Trubbull covered Pith's ruffled skin slits before another word could escape. He shook his head and looked at Bil-Li. *"Young folk, talky talky talky, what can you do?"* he said. *"Pith, can work out for everyone if you keep neck shut."*

He pulled Pith away into an empty corner of the room. Bil-Li could see the two Skelties talking just out of his scent—calmly at first—then with some tumult. When they returned Trubbull said, *"Bad news, Hugh, price go up—thirty jacks 'o cris."* Bil-Li's eyes narrowed. *"But now got two guides, what a bargain,"* he added persuasively. *"Something happen to one, other take you to Lomac. Make Hugh feel better?"*

"Thirty's a lot of dew," Bil-Li said.

Trubbull unzipped a toothy grin. *"Bil-Li, I's know you no come all this way for nada. Whyever you need Lomac probably worth thousand jacks. Just 'cuz I's being reasonable no mean I's stupid."*

Bil Li looked into the Skeltie's dead, pupil-less eyes.

"All right, but we go now."

He flashed some dew and Trubbull's eyes somehow came alive. The three of them stepped outside. "You get paid when we get there, not a drop before, savvy?"

"However you say, Hugh. You the big boss," Trubbull told him.

They emerged from the shack and Abe was there cleaning the sectis's chitinous plates with his tongue, to the animal's considerable delight. He saw Bil-Li approach with Trubbull and Pith and handed over the reins. Bil-Li poured a half-jack of dew out onto the Skeltie's tongue and mounted up. Through his glasses, the night lit up in front of him. He set off with his two guides leading the way and the trio soon faded into an inkblot horizon.

"How far are we headed?" Bil-Li asked.

"*Less than day's ride,*" Trubbull said. "*We make camp few hours, start again first thing. Be there just after nightfall tomorrows. Suiting you fine?*"

Bil-Li wanted to argue. He wanted to insist they ride straight through. He knew that each stop increased the probability that dark events would befall him. But he was far too wayworn and he'd never make it another night without sleep.

The Skelties were sidewinding up ahead of him about thirty feet on their stumpy legs, leading him like bloodhounds. They were muttering covertly to one another. Bil-Li could glean remnants of their conversation in the air, but they smelled harmless.

After a few hours they stopped. Bil-Li welcomed the simple comfort of Exoterran dirt and a warm blanket while Trubbull and Pith rested as all Skelt do, standing motionless with their eyelids pinned open. Bil-Li left his glasses on and dropped his hat down low, shadowing his face. If he had to sleep beside Skelties, even friendly ones, he'd keep them guessing. He left his fingertips tucked inside his belt, thumbs perched atop the cloudy, mother-of-pearl gun handles. The sluicer was packed in his saddle nearby. Hours passed and the fire had worn down to neon orange embers. Bil-Li's face was shrouded behind his nocturns and hat. A barely audible snore was escaping his lips.

He awoke at once to a sharp spike of pain in his right wrist and the sound of scampering in the darkness. Trubbull and Pith were gone, leaving Bil-Li by himself with two puncture marks in the soft flesh inside each wrist. The pain ran hot through his arms and his right hand—his gun hand—burned intensely. He brought the wounds to his mouth and extracted as much of the venom as he could by sucking the pink toxin out and spitting it onto the ground beside him. He tore a swath of sleeve, tied it off at his bicep, and tightened the makeshift tourniquet with his teeth. It wasn't working well enough. He then slipped a stick underneath the strip of cloth and twisted it, making the tourniquet still tighter.

His right hand had swollen up like a hothouse tomato. The skin of his engorged fingers had split and gone to stone. His two Skelt guides were no doubt waiting for their vile juices to incapacitate him completely. Bil-Li stumbled in the dark before collapsing in the dirt. A short time later Trubbull sauntered out from behind the curtain of night and made a beeline to the man, his fangs still leaking mixed strings of poison and saliva. Bil-Li managed to pull the sluicer from his saddlebag and fumbled for the trigger, but his fingers had grown too large to slip inside it.

Trubbull slinked closer. "*Look at Bil-Li Badass now,*" he said. "*You was thoughting that you was gonna ride down here and tells all us poor Skelties what's what— you thinks those perfect gun hands gives you the right, just like all Hughs. Well, those hands no looking so perfect no more. We Skelties can be figuring things out too, Bil-Li boy, like you no be able to pull no trigger 'less you got fingers small enough.*"

Bil-Li tried to jam his pinky inside the trigger guard without success. He dropped the gun in the dirt beside him.

Trubbull smirked and made his approach. "*I's gonna crack your pretty skull with me's jaws,*" he said.

Pith appeared on Bil-Li's left, his teeth still glistening.

"Pith, why? We were friends."

"*I's sorry, brother,*" the Skeltie said.

Bil-Li clenched his teeth.

Pith turned to Trubbull. "*I's truly am... so so sorry.*" He tapped Bil-Li's left hand with his snout and nudged it towards the rayzer in the man's other hand. Bil-Li switched the gun over to his left hand and jammed his index finger just inside the loop in front of the trigger.

Trubbull's smug grin melted away.

Bil-Li squeezed off a bolt, point blank, that threw the Skeltie's entrails across the plain. He then fixed his aim on Pith.

"*I's no sting you hard, Bil-Li,*" Pith said, his arms raised. "*I's coulda filled Bil-Li Kay with poison and you be dead now, but I no did.*"

The Skeltie's words settled into Bil-Li's head and slowly, steadily, the man lowered his rayzer.

"You two were never taking me to Lomac and his gang, were you?"

"*Sure we was, Bil-Li, but we be serving you up to him. He a maniac, Bil-Li, crazy bad. Trubbull want kill Bil-Li and split dew instead of get cut from Lomac.*" Pith put a hand on Bil-Li's shoulder. "*But Pith not agree. We brothers, Bil-Li and Pith. I not say that back at bar, but that the way Pith feel.*"

Bil-Li placed his hand on Pith's shoulder too. "So you'll take to me Lomac?"

"*Helllll no, why would I's do a fool thing like that? It be like I kills you myself. Why you want with Lomac Zhinn anyway?*"

"He took something, and the people he took it from are in a bad way if they don't get it back. I just want to retrieve their property, I don't want to kill the man."

"*Bil-Li, you not be know what Lomac is.*"

"He's an outlaw, plainly. Got some folks in his employ too, I reckon."

"*He want you believe that,*" Pith said. "*He got no boys with him, don't need none. He ain't even no Hugh—he Skelt to the core, but no like any you ever seen. He shaped like you Hughs—he got 'dem long legs and long arms, killin' hands—but he one of us. He walk on two as well as he do four, he shoot a rayzer just like hugh-mans, but he got eyes of a Skeltie, speed of a Skeltie. He what you call an abomination, that one.*"

Bil-Li waved his hands. "That's impossible."

"*That ain't even scary scary part. He hate your people, as much as you Hughs hate the Skelt. He got Skelties all over believin' he gonna deliver us from the hugh-mans and free Exoterra of your kind. He on a crusade and he got whole damned Skeltlands behind him.*"

"And you believe him?"

"*No matter much what Pith believe, but it prime fucking important that you believe Pith because if I's take you to him, he kill you.*"

"He won't talk terms?"

"*You no talk terms with Lomac. Even though he Skelt he scare the shitting out of most of us. You best find other way if you want keep breath same air as him.*"

"Okay, so I've been forewarned. If anything happens to me it won't be on your head." Bil-Li looked deep into his friend's dark eyes. "I need this for myself too. This is another chance for me. Maybe my last."

The Skeltie turned and paced around in the dirt. "*I's hear 'bout what happen to Bil-Li's folks.*" He wagged a finger in Bil-Li's direction. "*I's want you know me and mine had no hand in it. We would never-*"

"I figured as much."

"*Some Skelt see a thing and call it evil for all the evil that's been done to them. Same way you Hughs seem to look at us, I's reckon. I's ain't sayin' it's right, what happened and all, it just is.*"

"I suppose so," Bil-Li said. "So you'll take me to Lomac?"

Pith lifted his head to the night sky and let out a quavering laugh. "*You's one crazy-ass Hugh, Bil-Li Kay.*" He fell down to four feet. "*Poison be in your blood still, give it some time. You be real stiff tonight but feel lotta better in morning. I's can take you then if you want.*"

"Thank you," Bil-Li said.

Pith scoffed and burst out again. "*And he thanking me for it!*" He shook his pointed head. "*Crazy-ass Hugh.*"

*

The pale face of the rock bluff was freckled with iron deposits embedded beneath its surface. It bulged out of the soil and pushed upward, to the sky. Pith led Bil-Li along a clandestine trail zigzagging up the side of the giant stone mountain, in between crevasses and sidestepping pitfalls. Near the top, they came to a triangular entrance that had been formed by two great slabs resting upon one another. Darkness obscured all but the first several feet of the cave's interior. Pith stopped at the threshold.

"*No too late go back,*" he said.

"I think it is for me."

"*I's no go in with you. I's afraid he kill me, too.*"

Both of them laughed a sad kind of laugh. Bil-Li faced the mouth of the cave.

"What will they do to you in Rya Delsa if they find out you brought me to him?"

Pith shook his head. "*No one find out, Bil-Li. You walk in cave, you not come out. I's sure you gots a good plan, but it no work. You never beat him. Lomac hate all hughmans."*

"What if I surprise him?"

"You no surprise him neither, Bil-Li."

"He's that good?"

Pith nodded slowly.

"Y'know, I'm not too shabby myself."

"No matter. If you be fastest Hugh who ever live, you never outdraw him. He Skeltie, you understand? A Hugh like you never be as fast as us. Lord Mother not make you that way—ain't your fault," Pith said. *"Please, Bil-Li, no go in there. You never win."*

Bil-Li looked around the sky in a desperate kind of way and kicked at the dirt. "Never?"

"No," Pith told him. *"Never."*

"Well shit, then why am I even doing a fool thing like this? I don't know what the hell I'm thinking. If this motherfucker don't kill me then Clementine will for doing something so stupid." He held back a sob and chuckled. "But I gotta try. I've gotta find a way." Bil-Li started into the opening. "What if I told you that if I somehow walk out of that cave alive it'll change Exoterra forever—it'll mean the end of the Skelt."

"Well," Pith thought for a moment. *"If that be true then—it make Pith sad sad to say—you not meant to walk out of cave."* Pith grinned. *"But that be up to fate, I's got no say in that. No Skeltie do. If we Skelt no meant for this place, we goes someplace else. I's still wish you luck, Bil-Li... my friend."*

The Skeltie dropped to the ground and shuffled away.

Bil-Li affixed his glasses, curling the thin wire behind his ears, and stepped through the sheet of darkness just inside the mouth of the cave. He could see clear to the back wall a hundred feet or so away. It looked empty. He eased forward slowly, checking for booby traps and trip wires as he moved.

He found none.

Lomac Zhinn isn't afraid of anyone, much less a Hugh. He thinks I'm beneath him in every way. Pith told me to find another angle. So what's my angle? He's better than me, and worse yet, he knows it. Think, Bil-Li, think—where the hell's the angle here? There's got to be one.

At the back wall of the cave, a ghostly amber luminescence hung in one of the corners. Bil-Li moved nearer and discovered that the back corner of the cave had been hollowed out; a squared opening led to a tunnel that cut straight through the interior of the bluff. The entire tunnel was lit up by the yellow, striped phosphorus rock. Bil-Li removed his nocturns and strode forward. He walked the path, marveling at the bright striations until the tunnel opened up into an enormous stalactite-encrusted cavern, the far end of which contained ever smaller semi-circular layers of bedrock, stacked atop one another, jutting out from the cavern wall itself and rising up to a craggy throne. Upon it sat a lonely figure, its hands resting imperially over the arms of a stone chair. He had thin, bulbous-jointed fingers and spiny Skelt nails that wriggled with portent. An ill breeze circled the cavern.

Bi-Li quickdrew his rayzer.

In an instant red light splashed against the walls of the cavern and Bil-Li raised the melted stump of a gun to his eyes. The barrel of the rayzer had been shot off at the front sight and plugged with the molten remains. It was useless.

"Six inches up and I would have hit the plasma chamber," the figure told him. "That would've been a hell of a thing for you. Pieces of you would be sliding off these walls now?"

A voice. An actual voice. It took Bil-Li a moment to tune his ears back to the frequency of the spoken word. "You can talk?"

"I can do a great many things." The figure seemed to glide from its perch, its powerful legs carrying it down the huge slab steps with a danseur's grace. It alighted upon the cavern floor with nary a speck of soil disturbed.

Bil-Li's stomach tightened. "My name is Bil-Li Kay. I didn't come here for a fight. I don't want that."

"Bil-Li Kay," the figure said. "You come into my home uninvited and the first thing you do is pull a rayzer." He shook his head. "Manners, manners, little Hugh. How can I possibly trust what you say after that?"

"You're right. I don't blame you if you don't trust me, or any other human for that matter," Bil-Lil said. "I'm not gonna lie to you because you're not stupid and I'm not gonna tussle with you because I'd lose that gunfight. I'll put it to you simply... I came for the starway pass, that's the god's honest truth. I'd like to bargain with you, if you're agreeable to it. You're Lomac, right?"

"I am Lomac Zhinn and the starway pass will never leave this mountain while I live."

"Name your price," Bil-Li said. "Everyone's got one."

"I don't."

Bil-Li inhaled deeply and rubbed his hands together. "Okay, what do you want most in this world?"

"I want all the Hughs off Exoterra so I won't allow wave after wave of your kind to travel that starpass and settle here, to claim it as your own—you have no right to it. The Skelt were born here, it's where our spirit lies. Where were all the hugh-mans born? Your people can't even remember. You're nothing more than soulless nomads."

"But aren't you part hugh-man?"

Lomac instantly had his rayzer under Bil-Li's chin. Bil-Li felt the heat emanating from the gun barrel on the underside of his jaw.

"I AM SKELT! I am a harbinger of freedom, heralding a new Exoterran age! The sound of my voice is the death knell for the Hughs! I was born as I am now, touched by Braam, the Sky God!" Lomac raised his free hand, four fingers and a thumb. "I have been blessed and burdened with the one physical gift that has allowed the Hughs to reign over us. If I could I would burn this impurity from me, but I have much work left to do."

"And all this time that gun hand was the only thing holding the Skelts back?"

"That should be obvious to you, especially now," Lomac said as he tapped the rayzer against Bil-Li's whiskers.

You are fast, there's no denying that," Bil-Li said. "But can you shoot that thing as well as a man?" Lomac didn't speak. The hum of the rayzer was the only sound. "I'm no threat to you, we both can see that. But I'm pretty good with a rayzer myself, maybe even the best shot on Exoterra." Bil-Li said. "How about we have a little contest? See if you Skelties *really* are just as good as hugh-mans."

Lomac remained silent.

Bil-Li shrugged his shoulders and tried to put on a smile. "You can shoot me later if you want. In the meantime, what's the harm in having a friendly competition first? You think you can prove yourself or don't you truly believe what it is you're selling everybody?"

Lomac slowly lowered his gun.

"Open your hand," he said. Bil-Li held out his palm and Lomac gave his gun to him at the same time he pulled another from his holster and trained it on the man. Bil-Li lifted both arms in mock surrender.

"No funny business," Bil-Li said. "Just a straight shooting contest to see who's the best, Hugh or Skelt." Lomac sidled around behind the man, his rayzer-sights never veering from Bil-Li's head. He lifted Bil-Li's sluicer ray from off the man's hip and inspected it.

"Nice piece. Much obliged to you, Hugh." He holstered the gun. "Now find us a target so we can get on with this?" he said. "Guest's choice."

Bil-Li's eyes searched the cave before he spotted an oddly-shaped, elongated stalactite that was bulbous at its bottom hanging near the far wall. "See that funny looking cave icicle over there, the long one?" He carefully took aim and pulled the trigger. A plasma burst nicked the bottom of the rock and a chunk fell harmlessly to the dirt floor.

"There's the target, except you got to hit the tip otherwise the whole thing falls, and you lose. You can miss it, as long as you don't *knock* it down." The Skeltie nodded and held out his hand.

"The gun, please."

"Of course," Bil-Li said politely and handed over the weapon. "Now you got to use the same rayzer as me or it won't be fair, agreed?"

"Agreed." Without looking at the man Lomac trained his sight and, with one outstretched arm, squeezed off a round that shaved a thin layer of rock off the stalactite leaving a cloud of dust hanging in the air.

"Excellent shot!" Bil-Li said. "You're good."

"Thank you." He handed the firearm back to the man. "Your turn."

Bil-Li took aim again. "Gonna get harder and harder to hit this thing without bringing it down. Hope I can get lucky here one more time." His bolt shot across the cave and knocked another section off, a larger piece this time. But the stalactite held in place. He handed the gun over. Lomac immediately got into a firing position. "Don't all this phosphorus in here bother your eyes? Hell, it's bright enough in here that I don't even need my glasses. But I know you Skelties don't see so good in the light."

Lomac held his shot for a moment. "It's dark enough," he said. He shot a burst and handed the rayzer back to Bil-Li without watching it land. It cleaved off the bottom corner of the stalactite knob as cleanly as his first shot had. "Give up yet?"

Bil-Li stepped up and fired off a round that ripped off the other corner. He blew away the smoke that emanated from the barrel of the rayzer. "I was just about to ask you the same thing."

The two gunslingers kept lopping off pieces until the ball at the bottom of the stalactite was no more than a nub. Bil-Li fired the first shot at the shaft and grazed the side. Lomac then wasted no time in taking his turn.

He missed.

"Oops," Bil-Li said. "You sure the light in here ain't bothering your eyes?" The Skeltie fired again. Another miss. "Keep going, just be careful not to knock the whole thing down." He kept firing, missing each time, until finally he sliced the entire bottom nodule of the stalactite off. Cracks began to form at the top of the stalactite. "I'm afraid it ain't gonna get any easier for you now." Bil-Li took his next shot and it hit the bottommost portion of the thin stalactite shaft. "I make this look easy," he said.

Lomac fired and the bolt sailed wide once more, splatting against the cave wall in a shower of sparks. "Maybe the light *is* bothering my eyes," he said. He shot again and again, missing each time until the rayzer only sputtered in his hand.

"You're out of ammo," Bil-Li said.

"Piece of hugh-man junk!" Lomac cursed and dropped to all fours. He slammed the gun into the dirt repeatedly and it shattered to pieces.

"We can use the sluicer if you like, it's got a wider stream. The way I see it it's only fair considering you got problems with your eyes. That ain't really your fault and I'd feel bad beating you that way."

"You will not beat me!" Lomac said before composing himself. "But you are right, it's only fair that I use the larger gun." He pulled the sluice gun with some effort and fired an even, controlled thread at the stalactite. The shot perfectly eviscerated the bottom third of what was left of the target. The stalactite wavered slightly and the cracks at the top of the cave lengthened, but it hung on. Lomac drew the second, smaller rayzer from his belt and held the sluice gun out to Bil-Li.

Bil-Li motioned to Lomac's other hand. "Do you mind? I'm no good with a sluice, damn thing's too heavy for me even though it can slice a piece off that rock thin enough to see through."

"Fine by me." Lomac handed the smaller rayzer over to Bil-Li.

Bil-Li took his time. He raised the gun to his eyes, lowered it. Raised it again. Lowered it. Raised it one more time, took a breath, and fired. The globule made the faintest contact with the stalactite. The crack widened and the rock swayed more than it ever had. Both of them took notice. Bil-Li grinned and handed the gun back to Lomac. The Skeltie jammed it back into his holster.

"This could be it for our little game," Bil-Li said. "Maybe you were wrong about some things."

Lomac growled and turned to the target. He held the sluicer low and fired a beam below the hanging rock formation. It splashed against the far cave wall and an inferno of sparks ricocheted off. Slowly he raised the red beam until it was just below the stalactite. He held it there a moment, grim determination and effort etched across his ophidian features, hoping just to touch the precarious stalactite and singe the end. He brought the plasma beam ever closer, ever closer. Nearly there now. Just enough to tap it. The cave was alive with fire. Bil-Li watched. Breathless, anticipating. He edged closer.

"You ever heard the story of the tortoise and the hare?" Bil-Li said.

All at once the back wall of the cave gave way to the onslaught of the sluice gun. A giant hole burst forth and rocks tumbled down from above it allowing the white-hot rays from the Exoterran sun to stream in.

Bil-Li made a grab for Lomac's holstered rayzer.

Whether it was the blink of an eye that Lomac was blinded by that sunlight, or the extra time it took him to wheel that heavy gun around, or the second it took the sluice to reload itself, or it could've been the jump Bil-Li got on him anticipating the wall to give way, or maybe it was a combination of everything. Whatever was the cause, the result was Bil-Li holding a blaster on the unconquerable Lomac Zhinn.

He leveled the rayzer and shot Lomac's gun hand. The Skeltie's perfectly-formed fingers were now nothing more than a mangled garden of seared flesh and cracked bones. The sluice gun fell to the floor of the cave.

"Now as I was saying when I first walked in here, I need that starway pass, and I'm willing to bargain for it," Bil-Li said. "Problem is you got a whole lot less to bargain with now, friend. Here's my proposal—if you give the disc over to me now, I'll let you live. That's my first, last, and best offer."

If it were possible for a Skeltie's face to flush, Lomac's would've. If it were possible for his dead eyes to show emotion, they would've screamed out. If rage had a name, it would be Lomac Zhinn. The Skeltie bore his dripping fangs. The talons of his good hand trembled with latent energy. The entirety of his body tensed like a spring.

"I see," Bil-Li said.

He eased back his index finger on the trigger and the rayzer fired. The shot hit Lomac square in his gut. Bil-Li kept his finger on the trigger and the red line burrowed through the target and exploded out the other side. The plasma spread outward from the hole in his center, steadily dissolving the outlaw and stewing the surrounding innards. Eventually his body folded, collapsed in on itself, and fell. The starway pass clanked in front of Bil-Li's feet while the puddle that was Lomac Zhinn slowly arced in all directions around the steaming mass. He picked up the disc, wiped it clean, and slipped it inside his coat, near his heart. He tapped his pocket and climbed out into the sunlight. He sat there in the dirt for a long while.

"So long, Mama. So long, Daddy," he said to the wind. "Me and Clementine are leaving this rock in a big hurry, and going..." He looked at the sky in every direction. "Ain't that something? After all this time you'd think I would've figured it out. I guess if you don't rightly know where you're headed," he told them, "any ole road will take you there."

I enjoy fantasy football. I enjoy it for many reasons that I can't fully explain in detail here but suffice it to say that my real-life gridiron fandom; i.e., the team that I root for, usually (read: always) results in my disappointment long before the actual season ends. So, I like having a dog in the fight even after my real-world dog of a team's season is long over. Now, I've been playing fantasy football for well over a decade, drafting a new team each year and acting as its virtual general manager. And while I greatly enjoy the prospect of creating and running a team of my own design each season, I've discovered that the whole exciting endeavor is not without its drawbacks. I think probably any passion project elicits the same sort of feelings. And it was those feelings that became the basis for this story.

Originally it was conceived as simply a "break up" scene between a superhero and his arch-nemesis. That was the jumping-off point—the thing that got me writing. It eventually turned into a deconstruction of sorts of the whole superhero genre, its tropes and rules, and is therefore probably best appreciated by those readers who are familiar with them. It's a fun little deep dive into the conventions of the genre with a few little easter eggs sprinkled in for the well-initiated. As I mentioned in the introduction to this book, I grew up reading comic books (and just about anything else I could get my hands on). Because of this I was steeped in the mythology of these characters and felt like, as a fan, I was at liberty to poke a little fun at their relationships with one another. Like I said before, it helps if you're somewhat familiar with these tropes, but honestly, it's not totally necessary. It may be enough that you've only played fantasy football.

Marvels of the Burger King Parking Lot

"Why are we here, Scourge? This isn't our regular night." An ivory and azure clad elbow was perched just outside the Dodge Durango's open window. His other arm rested on the steering wheel.

The Scarlet Scourge was cloaked in his signature cardinal robes. He lowered his hood to reveal his face. "It's important, Bill."

"I have told you numerous times," The brawny man's head swiveled back and forth, scanning the lot. "Call me Captain Keen when we're in public."

The crimson-clad villain reached into his to-go bag, pulled out an onion ring, and popped it in his mouth. "Are we really considering *this* to be," He made air quotes with his fingers. "In public?" He chuckled. "Method superheroes, so devoted to craft."

"I don't break character when I'm in costume, you know that," Captain Keen said. "And as a matter of fact, we're not exactly in public. We're actually in a Burger King parking lot at midnight, at least midnight." He lifted his gauntlet and glanced at his watch. "I stand corrected, quarter to one. The point being, it's late." He suddenly ducked his head and gave a side-eye out the passenger window where a lone figure was entering the restaurant. "Y'see?" Keen said. There's night owls like that everywhere, creeping around fast-food joints in the dark. What if he'd spotted us?"

"A rando with the munchies is nothing to worry about. He didn't even look over here. He's got other stuff on his mind, I'm sure."

"It's a big risk being seen together like this is all I'm saying. All it takes is for one person to snap a picture of us with their phone. We should just stick to our regular night when we know it's safer."

"You're right, but this couldn't wait. Besides, look around. There's no one else here, Bill."

"*Captain Keen.*"

Scarlet Scourge threw up his hands. "Have it your way, Captain!"

The superhero shushed his nemesis. "I'd feel a whole lot better if you were out of sight, so get in the truck already, will you?"

Scourge ambled around the Durango's back bumper and climbed into the passenger seat. "The only person who could possibly catch us is the girl working the drive-through and look." He pointed to the small window embedded in the brick wall on the side of the restaurant. "She's nowhere to be found. She didn't make either of us out when we ordered in our civvies and she sure as hell can't see us now in the dark." He lifted a Whopper with cheese out of his bag and unwrapped it. "No one's going to find out about us."

"Alright," Keen said. "You've convinced me. So why are we here?"

Scourge carefully lowered his flame-grilled burger down onto his lap. "I need to tell you something," he said. "I think it's time we…" He paused and squirmed around a little in the Corinthian-leather-upholstered seat. "I think this is it for me," he finally said. "I think this is goodbye."

Captain Keen stopped chewing and his body straightened up. "What do you mean?" The merest bit of white French Fry guts dropped from his mouth.

Scourge continued. His voice was even and clear. "I think it's time I moved on. You've got your life, your career to think of—and I've got mine. We can't do this forever."

"We can't?"

"Well, I guess what I'm saying is… I can't."

"So, you're quitting the whole superhero-supervillain game?"

Scourge looked away, out the window into the deserted lot. "I didn't say that."

Keen's face grew flush. He brought his hands to his chest. "Then you're just quitting *me*? Is that it?"

"Don't say it like that, Cap."

"How else should I say it? You're supposed to be my arch-nemesis for godsakes, and I'm yours. We have history together—you can't just go and shit all over that. This is insane!"

The Scarlet Scourge recoiled. "Whoa! I've never heard you swear before," he said. "Besides, it's not like that." He waved his hands and a speck of ketchup from his burger flew toward Captain Keen's immaculate costume. The superhero flicked it away at an impossible speed, nearly cracking the windshield.

"Then what's it like?" Keen's voice grew louder. "Is there someone else? Please tell me you're not going over to Capital City—there's nothing Amazing Man can offer you that I can't."

"This has nothing to do with Amazing Man. I don't even really talk to that guy."

"Then who is it? That Canadian superhero? The one who uses the electric hockey stick as a weapon? Serge Protector?"

"No."

"Is it White Nite? It is, isn't it? I knew it! You always liked him. You thought that dumb outfit of his was *so cool*, so young and hip. How friggin' ridiculous!"

"It's not White Nite."

Keen brought a clenched fist to his mouth while he thought. Who have you been talking to? Who's giving you this crazy advice?"

"No one."

"Is it one of your supervillain friends? Adam Bomber? Or that lawyer, Lex Loophole? You know he's jealous of you, right? That's the only reason he's telling you to do this."

"Stop!" Scarlet Scourge said before he let loose a heavy sigh. "Believe me, it's nothing like that."

Keen looked deep into his friend's eyes. "You swear?"

"I promise you," Scourge said. "This is all about me, no one else."

Captain Keen took several deep, calming breaths. "Okay, I'm sorry, but I had to ask," he said. "I should trust that you wouldn't go running around being someone else's villain."

There was a loud noise outside. Captain Keen and The Scarlet Scourge both ducked down in the truck cabin as a group of people emerged from the restaurant and hurried to their cars.

"Again, see that?" Keen said. "That's why we have to be careful out here."

Both men slowly eased back upright in their seats.

"Listen to me, Cap, I have too much respect for you to go behind your back. I'd never let anyone else handcuff me but you." This brought a smile to Captain Keen's face and his perfect teeth shone brilliantly. "But I'm always the bad guy in this relationship. We're always on different sides, you and me. Why is that?"

"Well, how can I put this nicely," Keen said. "It's because you're a bad person. You do bad things—break laws, steal stuff, occasionally kill someone, etcetera, etcetera."

"Pfft, thanks for sugar-coating it. *That's* putting it nicely?"

"But it's all true, Scourge." The lights of the Burger King sign suddenly went dark. "Hey, I guess they're closing up."

"Yeah, earlier than usual. Fine by me. Gives us a little more privacy," Scarlet Scourge said. "Now what's this about me being a bad person just because I'm a criminal. The two things don't have to be mutually exclusive, y'know. I *need* to be a criminal mastermind just so you'll have something to do. You totally love the challenge."

Keen nodded. "You may be right there."

"Of course I am. I may be a criminal but I'm not a bad dude underneath. We're all criminals, I'm just better at it."

"We're not all criminals," Captain Keen said.

"Sure we are... even you." The superhero's face soured. "Are you going to honestly tell me you don't break the law from time to time?" Scourge asked.

"Never!"

"All those times you tear-ass around town in the Keenmobile, you're never speeding? You never ran a red light? A stop sign? I seriously doubt it."

Keen stammered. "That's different."

"Ever cheat on your taxes?"

"No."

"Not even a little?"

The Captain balked. "Certainly not."

"How about Lois? Does she cheat on her taxes?"

"Well…" He shrugged and looked away. "I wouldn't know. I'm her boyfriend, not her Dad."

"Yes, you would know. You know damn well she does, and you'd never turn her in. Not in a million years. I told you, you're not perfect either."

Captain Keen wagged his finger in Scourge's direction. "Now, I never said I was perfect."

"I know you didn't—which is so like you, by the way—you'd never say anything so boastful." Scourge shook his head. "Jesus, even your confession of imperfection somehow makes you more perfect. It's fucking unreal!" The Scarlet Scourge slammed a chicken piece down onto his lap and a smattering of dipping sauce nearly landed on the superhero's codpiece.

"Good god, man, can't you see I'm wearing white? Be careful around the costume."

Scourge exhaled a heavy breath. "Shit, I'm sorry, bro. I can't seem to do anything right tonight—this is a lot harder than I thought it would be," he told his counterpart. He extended an arm across the center console. "You want an onion ring?" he asked, waving the carton of deep-fried food in front of the superhero's eyes. "It's got Zesty Sauce."

Keen put up a hand. "No, thank you."

"Now why the hell not?" Scarlet Scourge huffed. "I got the large because of you! We always share."

"Whoa, pal, I don't know where all this hostility is coming from. You eat the onion rings. My body needs to be in tiptop shape to run around in this outfit," he said. "I'm wearing a unitard, or haven't you noticed? You get to wear the flowing robes. You can put on a few pounds and not worry about it. I can't even fight crime around the holidays, for Pete's sake. Ever heard of social media? Forget about it, that's all I need is for someone to post a picture of me at an unflattering angle. There are no fat superheroes, bub, look it up. There's plenty of fat villains though. Total double-standard," he said. "And don't think I haven't noticed that your biggest heists always happen right after Thanksgiving or Christmas."

The Scarlet Scourge flashed a coy smile. "Guilty as charged. But it's all part of the chess match, isn't it? You've got to learn to lay off the eggnog and snickerdoodles, my friend. A moment on the lips, you know the rest."

There was a silent moment before the two men chuckled it off.

"Well, you get the point at least," Keen told him. "It's not all rainbows and unicorns for me either."

"Okay, point taken. That one's on me."

"So, what is the real problem here, Scourge—why are you doing this? Still thinking about changing your villain-name? Do you think that'll get you out of this funk you're in?"

"Nah, Crimson Chaos is cool and all, but it's a major hassle to switch names. Everyone knows me as The Scarlet Scourge. I've built a brand, I can't just trash it because I'm in some sort of mid-career, emotional crisis. I'd have to redo all the merch, make up new business cards, it would turn into a whole thing, hard-pass. Besides, I don't think that's the problem."

"Then what is it?"

"I don't know," Scourge said. "I guess I'm in a rut. Same old thing, something's missing. This whole setup just doesn't work for me anymore."

"Did you see that shrink I told you about? Dr. Q is very good. She really gets guys like us, understands what we go through. Easy on the eyes, too." Captain Keen's attention turned to the building. "Hold on a sec."

A young couple approached the restaurant doors and rattled the handles. Keen rolled down his window. "Hey, it's locked, I think they just closed up." he called out. He turned back to the supervillain. "Sorry, buddy. You were saying?"

"Yeah, it's just that I work all these long hours, plot these massive crime sprees, real elaborate stuff, y'know?"

"Oh, I know. Believe me, it shows. I can see the effort you put into it. You go all out."

"I know, right? Spare no expense, none whatsoever," Scourge said. "I put in all this planning, coordinate my henchmen's schedules, work in a little *me* time, and then it all goes to hell when you bust it up."

Keen sucked a breath between grit teeth. "Yeah," he said. "That's kind of what I do though. Like you said, it's a chess match. You knew that going in."

"I did know that, and I enjoy the game. The mano-a-mano stuff with you is the whole reason I do it. I'm alone down in my lab, cooking up schemes. You're in your man cave trying to figure out what I'm up to next. Then we play it all out and see who wins—I like the cat-and-mouse part of it, that's very cool. I'm not as crazy about the whole going to jail thing though, that part blows."

"Need I remind you, I always speak on your behalf in court," Keen said.

"Yes, you do."

"Always recommend a minimum-security facility where they might rehabilitate you instead of punishing you."

"It's true. You do that."

"And you always end up escaping."

Scourge smiled widely. "I do, don't I?" he said. "But you go easy on me because, admit it, you enjoy this part of the job as much as I do. Our late-night parking lot talks over some junk food, reliving the capers, comparing notes, *sharing*. I can't do this with anyone else in my life." He lifted the straw to his mouth and took a swig of Mello Yello. "I think I'm just lonely."

Keen placed a hand on Scourge's shoulder. "Guys like you and me, we weren't meant to have normal lives, buddy. Our families, friends. So many sacrifices would have to be made, by us and them."

"Exactly. I'm not ready for those kinds of sacrifices." Scourge said. "I can't be expected to come home for dinner, or to drive the kids to tee-ball. I mean, these banks aren't going to rob themselves! If I don't try to take over the world, who will?"

"I hear ya, pal. You're lucky though. I gotta do the normal guy thing every single day. Hold down a nine-to-five, mow the damn lawn, keep the girlfriend happy, all the while trying to deal with you and every other small-timer in this town. It's exhausting. I have zero hobbies."

Scarlet Scourge gasped. "You're chasing other people while I'm home working?"

"Oh," Keen said. "They mean nothing to me. You're never around, and I have my needs to think about, too—wait, we're getting off track here. What I'm trying to say, if you'll shut up and let me get to it, is... I get lonely too."

"You do?"

Keen nodded.

"What a relief to hear you say that, Cap. I thought I was the only one."

"No sirree."

"Wow, that's crazy. Did I ever tell you I got so desperate once, I even decided to train a sidekick? He showed a lot of promise actually."

Keen started to laugh. "Who? The one with the hook for a hand? Always shivering? Had to wear those thick, cable-knit sweaters?"

"Yeah, Cold Cut, that's him. He was good."

"Meh. I wasn't crazy about the costume. He looked like an Irish fisherman."

"Whattaya want? The guy had bad circulation."

"What ever happened with that?"

"He couldn't take the winters so he bought a place down south, turned into a snowbird," Scourge said. "I don't need no part-timers, I'm pretty big on commitment." He scooped a dollop of soft serve ice cream into his mouth. "What about you?"

"I tried the sidekick thing too. You remember Kid Liberty?"

"Nope."

"Before your time maybe. What about Rad Lad?"

"Vaguely."

"That's not surprising, he never stuck either," Keen said with an eye roll. "Much too young to be fighting crime, child-endangerment charges just waiting to happen—not a good look for me. Plus, I just can't deal with teenagers, they're too quirky. I never had the connection with them that I have with you." Captain Keen downed his soda, slurping the last bit loudly. "Hey, I know some up-and-coming supervillains looking for junior partners if that's the kind of thing you'd be interested in doing—Phantom Master, The Big Chill, Ms. Trigger Finger, Doc Danger—you want me to ask around for you?"

Scarlet Scourge's eyebrows gathered. "I'm not a fucking sidekick, Bill," he said before burying a spoon into the low-fat frozen treat of his sundae cup. An awkward silence lingered until the ruby racketeer pointed inside the Burger King. "Do you see that?" he asked.

"See what?" Keen said. "I can't see a thing, that window is totally black."

"Exactly! Why is it so dark in there? We've been here a million times after this place closes and we always see them cleaning up. Wiping down tables, taking out trash."

"It is a little strange that they closed early tonight," Keen said.

"At 12:45, no less. Isn't that a weird time? Name me one business that closes at 12:45?"

Keen stroked his chin. He pointed to Scourge. "If you were going to knock over a Burger King-"

"This is exactly when I'd do it."

Captain Keen immediately swiped the crumbs from his costume and checked his teeth in the rearview mirror. "Alright, wait here. I'm going in."

"Like hell I will! Why do you get to have all the fun? If some fucknugget is cutting into my action then I'm going in with you. No one jacks a BK in my town without at least running it by me first. There is such a thing as proper etiquette, y'know."

Keen drummed his fingers against the dashboard. "Suit yourself," he finally said. "But please let me handle it."

Scourge gave a mock salute. "Roger that, Captain." He reached inside the hood of his costume and lowered his night vision goggles.

"Are those new?"

"Yeah, picked them up a couple weeks back."

Keen's eyebrows raised. "Nice. The red goes with your outfit."

"Thanks, I thought so too," Scourge said before turning his attention again to the inside of the restaurant. A masculine figure in a ski mask holding a pistol in one hand and a long flashlight in the other peeked out of the enormous front window. The powerful beam from the flashlight illuminated the upper portion of the thief's body. "Oh man, will you get a load of this guy. Not too obvious, is he?" Scourge lifted the goggles that covered his eyes. "It's like amateur night for Christsakes. I swear you should have to pass a test to get into this line of work."

"He definitely picked the wrong night," Keen said, eyeing the crook. "What kind of gun is that he's holding?"

Scourge lowered the night goggles once more. "Nine-millimeter, looks like. Everyone loves the nines these days—the Glock 19, Sig Sauer, Springfield XD, good old Smith & Wesson, whatever floats your boat."

Keen's eyebrows raised. "You really know your stuff."

"Well, we all bring something to the party," Scourge said, still watching the window. "You know, this guy's probably just a lookout. My guess is there's at least one or two more perps inside."

"*Perps?* Well listen to you, you sound like one of the good guys."

"Do I?" Scourge shrugged. "Honestly, I feel for these poor bastards," he said. "Hey, how about you go inside and give them the whole spiel about not having to do this. How they still have time to turn their lives around. How crime doesn't pay, blah, blah, blah. All that bullshit."

Captain Keen leaned in. "Sounds like me," he said. "Go on, I'm listening."

"And while you're distracting them, I'll sneak up from behind and blast them with the Scourge-shooter until their insides liquefy?" he said. "What do ya think?"

"Uh... no."

Scourge groaned. "How about I shrink them down and let him fend for themselves against the microorganisms of the world?"

Cap shook his head.

"It would teach them a good lesson though," he said. "You superheroes love that kinda stuff."

"Absolutely not."

"Alright, I could hypnotize them to think they're walking around in a field of flowers, and then guide them into oncoming traffic?"

"You're a very morbid individual, do you know that?"

The Scarlet Scourge grinned. "I prefer to think of myself as simply more creative than most."

"Hmmm," Keen said. "Interesting interpretation. Tell me, have you ever come up with an option that doesn't end in someone's murder?"

Scourge thought a moment. "To date, no."

Keen arched an eyebrow.

"Well, that's all I can come up with on the fly. What can I say? I'm ill-equipped, man."

"How about this time you just hang back and watch me, until you get the gist of it?"

"This time?"

"Sure," Keen said. "I mean, there's no reason to think we couldn't try this again when you're better at being... better."

"A team up?" The Scarlet Scourge tried in vain to hide his smile. "You mean it? What am I saying, of course you mean it. You never lie! That's kinda your thing, too."

Captain Keen suddenly got a faraway look in his eyes. "Together we could thwart the nefarious plans of all this city's wrongdoers."

Scourge's head bobbed. "Yeah, that's right, and we can have little tactical sessions to learn how to best engage villainous scum in tandem."

"We could have weekly meetings and go over our strategies for taking down the criminal underworld," Captain Keen said, his voice rising.

"With snacks?"

"Of course with snacks."

"Definitely snacks."

The two men playfully exchanged body slaps.

"And…"

"And?"

"Aaaaaand…"

Their eyes got wide.

"Stakeouts!" they screamed in unison.

"Hey, maybe we can even alternate," Scourge said. "Next month you can help me pull a job or something?"

"Ehhhh, I don't think so, partner."

"Hey, no problem," Scourge said, his hands raised. "We can talk about it more later, maybe?"

The duo hopped from the Durango and sauntered toward the restaurant door, their exquisite costumes billowing out behind them in the fierce Autumn wind.

"Scourge, this is gonna be so great."

"Really great."

"The best."

"The *absolute* best," Scourge said. "It's gonna be, can I say it?"

"I'd rather you didn't."

"I think I should."

"Please don't."

Scarlet Scourge breathed in deeply the cool, crisp night air, then emptied his lungs completely with audible satisfaction. "This is gonna be… SUPER!"

This was one of my first published shorts (all the way back in 2007) in the now defunct magazine turned e-zine known as Blood, Blade & Thruster. I was very proud at the time to be the featured author in the same issue of BBT that had interviews with the likes of a fledgling young writer (and member of literary royalty, even if very few at the time knew it) named Joe Hill as well as the legendary George R.R. Martin who discussed his hopefulness at the possibility of HBO adapting a little book series he'd started several years prior called A Game of Thrones (I wonder how that worked out for him.) Needless to say, I was flabbergasted by being in such esteemed company.

Flash forward to now and I have to choose which of my past stories to include for this current collection. I initially passed over this one because, though I loved writing the satirical piece about a modern-day messiah being confronted with American culture, I didn't feel like the writing was strong enough to warrant its inclusion. But since I had already re edited a few older stories for the book, I thought The Book Of Judy (original title: Jesus Christ Supersize) might work as quasi-flash fiction if I could condense it substantially. In the end, it's still a bit too long to be considered flash but it's just the length it needs to be to work, and ultimately that's all that really matters. I hope you enjoy the read.

The Book of Judy

I met the messiah at a gas station in northern Arizona. I was making a pit stop on my way to work outside of a town called Eagar. He appeared to me among the cactuses in the distant sands, silhouette dancing like a flame over the oil-streaked interstate. He strode out of the rust-red desert, a purpose in his step.

He was shirtless, mid-to-late-forties and a little paunchy, not exactly the abs of savior. His cheeks were rosy with sun so I asked him if he needed some water. I gave him a bottle from my car and he took a sip.

"Bless you child," he said. The words escaped from lips that had been sewn shut by the mid-morning heat. "Your kindness will not go unnoticed in His eyes."

"It's no big thing," I told him while I plunged the nozzle of the gas pump into my car.

He took a seat on the asphalt in the shade of my Chevy Malibu. "For I was thirsty and you gave me water to drink. You do not know of me; I am but a stranger to you. Whatever you do for one of the least of these brothers of mine, you do-"

"Jesus Christ," I muttered. "They're out of regular unleaded—now I've got to get the good stuff. I don't think this beater even knows what to do with super premium."

The messiah got to his feet, removed the pump from the side of the car, and placed his hands over the hole. "You are no longer in need of gasoline, Judy."

I chuckled, but only for a second. "How do you know my name?"

He smiled coyly. "Judith Ritasico, your tank is filled with high octane fuel." Then he sat back down on the pavement with his drink, his back resting against the wheel.

I lifted the nozzle again and started to pump. The car regurgitated gasoline down its side and onto my feet before I noticed to stop. I crammed the nozzle deeper into the tank and tried again with the same result, the pump spitting all over my knockoff Manolos.

"This can't be," I said under my breath. I'd made a mistake, nothing more. It was that simple. It had to be. I returned the nozzle to its holster on the pump.

"I could sure use a ride," the messiah said.

Now you might think I'm crazy for giving this rando a lift, but I'm not. I swear to you I'm not.

"The A/C's broken," I told him.

"Not for long."

*

On that long drive into work, he told me all about his dreams and visions of the past few months, about The Voice. I suppose I should have been at least a little frightened but, for some strange reason, I wasn't. He told me he'd been given a mission.

"Real faith is waning, Judy, and those who claimed to know The Word only twist and pervert it to their own ends. The Day of Judgment is coming, but God doesn't feel like it's fair to judge anyone until a true messenger has delivered His Word first. So, I was sent to clear things up for everyone."

And you know what, he was right. He was absolutely right. Too long had good people turned their backs on God because one more pompadoured preacher was found coked-up in a sleazy motel with a fifteen-year-old on the ministry's dime; because the holiest rollers roll around in Rolls-Royces instead of piece-of-shit Chevy Malibus; because the Pope wears a hat shaped like a shovel and no one asks why; because Catholic priests have a taste for young boys; because Allah recruits women and children to be detonated, their entrails painting shop windows along the Gaza Strip; because a wife in New Delhi is burned alive by her husband, her murder sanctioned by her religion; because the children of Africa are lost and the rest of the world doesn't give a fuck; because boys are trained to kill and die in His name; because no one knows who's right and who's wrong, the time is upon us... The time of The Great Clarification.

"I'm in," I told him.

Even still, I would have had a real rough time believing it all but for a conviction in his being that would not allow me to dismiss him completely. There was a power undeniably present within him and his words galvanized the dead muscle my own faith had become. That, and I'd been driving in cool comfort for over a half-hour now in air conditioning that had somehow been resurrected after three days on the fritz.

That was the day I became his friend and follower.

I'm a thirty-eight-year-old, unmarried receptionist from Tucson. My psychiatrist thinks I'm depressed, my sister thinks I'm high-maintenance, my parents think I'm a lesbian, and my boss thinks I'm interested. I'm a middle-aged Latina woman with a few extra pounds and graying hair so the rest of the world doesn't seem to think much about me at all.

The next few months, spreading The Word westward were a blur: Winslow, Flagstaff, Scottsdale, Phoenix, Tempe, Yuma. People were flocking from as far away as Utah and New Mexico to hear the messiah speak. We packed everyone we could into a convoy of donated school buses. The Second Coming Tour was headed for the California coast.

With very little money the messiah nonetheless made certain we were all fed. He had a McDonald's gift card he said God had provided him (in the guise of a radio station prize giveaway). It got us a never-ending supply of Filet-O-Fish sandwiches

"The Lord really does move in mysterious ways," I said.

The tour was going just as we'd hoped. We were preaching The Word and converting the faithless in every burg we passed through. I watched him take the beaches of San Diego, crisscross up the coast to San Francisco and Oakland, into the streets of Los Angeles. I walked with him through Anaheim and Compton and up the steps of the Capitol Building in Sacramento.

I witnessed the miracles, too.

I saw him instill the spirit of hope into the people's hearts. I was right there when he walked over the La Brea Tar Pits. I was in attendance at the wedding in Beverly Hills where he turned water into *bottled* water.

Things weren't moving fast enough for me though. We'd been on the road for nearly a year and gained a loyal following wherever we played, but we had yet to pop nationwide, where we were still seen as little more than a West Coast, granola-fueled cult of weirdos. I was growing restless with the Second Coming Tour, but not its message. I was a disciple to the glorious end and I would follow the messiah, no matter where it led. I loved him. Not in a romantic way but in the way that a little girl loves her father or brother or just some nice gay bestie. He was my teacher and my protector. He was one of the few men in my life who would love me unconditionally no matter what I'd done in the past. But he was my friend too; he trusted and relied on me. We'd stay up nights on the bus, giving each other the giggles. A group of us on the tour formed a really close circle with the messiah. There were about a dozen of us all told, but I was the first. And I was getting worried.

The messiah was looking beat. I could tell he was exhausted and wouldn't be able to keep up this pace for long. So, I instructed everyone on tour to return to their homes and concentrate on spreading The Word over the internet in the hopes it would go viral. And lo and behold, it did.

We were approached one evening in Oregon by a representative from the Mars candy company. They offered us an ungodly sum of money and all the candy bars we wanted for the tour in exchange for signing a licensing agreement. It sounded like a great idea to me. The messiah charged me with the marketing of his name.

By the time the ads hit the airwaves touting Snickers as "the official candy bar of the Second Coming", I had brokered a slew of other sponsorship deals. I had the messiah's face plastered all over the TV, internet, and satellite, peddling everything under the sun. The public ate him up.

The messiah himself was far too taxed and uninterested to participate in the promotions, but I made his name, image, and likeness available. His face could be found on lunchboxes and talcum powder, from Holy-O's breakfast cereal to bottles of Viagra. A messianic body double swooshed down the slopes on a Rossignol snowboard and Nike boots sipping a Sprite. The video game, Saturday morning cartoon, and action figure were soon to follow. He was the Gerber baby, Colonel Sanders, and Mickey Mouse all rolled up into one divine pitchman. His face became as ubiquitous as the products themselves. He was bigger than the Beatles, a marketing phenomenon. A superstar. All thanks to me.

That's when the whole thing started to fall apart.

It didn't take long for journalist snoops to figure out that the messiah had a name, Gerry Kublick, plumber from Nogales, divorced father of four who failed the third grade and pulled down 22K a year after taxes. Not exactly the resumé everyone expected.

Little by little, we started to hear the blasphemer's prattle. The messiah? That sell out? Puh-lease! He is, like, so last year. My parents listen to him. No thanks.

Messiah fatigue set in. His Q rating was down and his fifteen minutes were up. He fought it as best he could, but how do you fight something you don't even understand?

"But it's good that people know who I am, isn't it, Judy? That I'm no different than them." I didn't have the heart to tell him that people don't like their saviors to be too real, or too much like themselves. Month after month, the crowds on tour got smaller and smaller and even the miracles ceased to impress any longer.

Oh Lord, I'm scared. I'm scared that I failed you. I'm scared that the wolves came out and I brought them right to you. It wasn't supposed to end like this. I'm scared, Lord. I'm scared for all of us.

Once the tour suffered its final death throes, I moved to the West Coast permanently. I got a little house out on the water in Chula Vista, nothing fancy. The ocean is violent and beautiful. Sometimes I feel closer to you, Lord, just listening to the waves. I heard somewhere that the messiah went back home to Arizona. He just sits around his apartment now... waiting for his agent to call. As for me, I'm just waiting too. Watching and waiting for those *really* big waves to roll in.

I began the rough draft of Every Good Stud Comes to His Senses *almost a decade prior to its completion. When the story meandered for about 35,000 words without an end in sight, I put it away and assumed it was destined to be just a failed attempt at a coming-of-age, dystopian novel. Flash-forward several years when it was time to start a new piece and something was pulling me back to the halls of the Fairchild Institute for Young Learners.*

Every Good Stud's Anthony Burgess-esque dialogue is unmistakable and I don't shy from the comparison. The kids in my story, though, have their own post-modern vernacular, they have invented words, and they have some more modern slang that's evolved. However, I wanted them to speak with a uniquely American vibe so I tried to veer away from anything that sounded too Alex DeLarge. Burgess's dialogue is, understandably, very British and could be a little on the precious side for me. While I loved that in his book, I wanted to strike out in a different direction with Tig, Cheza, and the rest of the crew in my story; I wanted to make them kids that are (hopefully) a bit more relatable than Burgess's droogs, even if you still can't **fully** *relate to them. So basically, they're kids. I always hoped this novella would share the aesthetic of A Clockwork Orange with a little bit of the heart, humor, and poignancy of a John Hughes film. At least that's what I was shooting for.*

Here's a fun fact: the dentist story in the book is actually based in some truth from my own life. When I was growing up there wasn't a lot of extra money floating around the DelGuercio household, so when I got a cavity it was no Novocain for me. My first few fillings were pretty excruciating and the thing I remember most about those trips to the dentist was the scent of burning enamel or dentin or whatever it was as the drill burrowed into my teeth. I remember that, and the pain of course. But mostly the smell. To this day it makes me sick to my stomach just thinking about that unique odor. Every Good Stud Comes to His Senses *appeared (in its original form) in the webzine* TQR Stories.

Every Good Stud Comes to His Senses

"What's the know on brannyspank here? He looks dim as a bulb." Alfa says, motioning to the figure at the table. That's me, Tig Fynch, he's pointing at, by the way.

The stud with him named Pooch, all muscly and menacey, leans over to me and goes, "My bestbro Alfa wants the know on you, brannyspank—what say you give it up."

I don't answer him. This is the way it has to be.

"Going clam on me, eh? Then let me give you the know on us," Pooch says. He drops his own tray of foodstuffs down onto the table and pulls mine away from me. "This is our spot, brannyspanks eat someplace else."

"Where's that?" I ask. "Where do all the brannyspanks eat?"

"I don't know, maybe in Brannyspank-land."

Oh, the boundless wit of the understud mind.

Pooch turns up the intensity on his electralime hair holograph for effect. "But they don't eat here, you get?" he says.

Everyone slaps Pooch on his back in encouragement and teehee loudly. Then one of the more observant studs speaks up.

"This kiddie's in sensory confines," he tells everyone. "He's down the hole, Pooch. Poor stud probably doesn't even peep you."

"I'm real hard to miss," Pooch says before he picks up a wiggly chunk of gelatin-D with his fingers and smears it all over my face. I scowl all blackhatter at him. "Yeah, you see me all right. Get up, brannyspank, time to find yourself a new table."

I wipe the slime from my cheeks. "You studs are right. I *am* down the hole." I stand up and turn to face Pooch. He's so big that I've got to strain my neck, but I stare straight into his dark little peepholes anyway. "But I see you," I tell him. "I'd have to be real dead-like not to notice a gigantic nudge-weasel like yourself standing right in front of me."

His face goes all radish and he balls up his fists.

Oh joy joy, another beating. Color me surprised.

He glances over at Alfa, clearly the stud to know in this group, who gives him the o-kee-dee sign. "Commence with it already, I'm hungered," the boy tells him and he waves Pooch on to give me the pummeling I'm so clearly asking for. So, this frankenstud comes at me with a pile of no-good in those black orbs of his. There's no fullgrowns in the nosh house yet so he figures he's got the time to beat me like he owns me. He cocks his fist and lets loose.

One direct hit to my jaw and I crumple like an accordion. The studs at the table all start whooping it up, real Lord-of-the-Flies-craze-like and all. I manage to get to a knee when he rears back and throws a fist at me again. A real Gentleman Jim, this one.

Just stay down, Tig. Take it. Do your job.

Pooch doesn't disappoint. He keeps pounding away at me like the sadist I thought he'd be—*kiddies these days, so much anger.* After a few minis I can hear him huffing away so I know he must be close to spent.

"I'm finito with you," he finally says. "Now go away before I change my mind." A few of his bestbros are congratulating him, giving him high slaps and chuckly-chucks. I pick my specs and earpieces up off the nosh house floor and put them back on my noggin.

"But I ain't finito with you yet," I tell him.

Twenty-four karat silence. I kuffing love this part.

His face goes full cherry again and he starts throwing his fists into my body. But what all these studs don't have the know on is that I'm farther down the hole than any of them realize... and I can't feel much at all. I'd share this little tidbit of info with Pooch, but he seems so busy, what with the kicking of my ass and everything. It doesn't take long before he's all used up.

Now, I don't necessarily like doing this, just whomping away on a meatbag like Pooch but, c'mon, he deserves it. I know he deserves it. You know he deserves it. The studs watching all know he deserves it. Hell, deep down I think even *he* knows he has it coming. At least I'll try to make it look like I'm not enjoying it as much as I am.

I start in on him quickly, all feral, hammering down on his arms while he tries to block me and my fists a-flying. I know it hurts biggy time; he's dull but he's no blanket like me. He throws a few back, real weak-meek-like. I'll bruise up after all this but I won't feel the pain, not like he will. He starts with the cowering every time I bring my fist back for another go at him.

That's a good good sign. It means we're almost done here.

Now, instead of ending it all-dramatical by landing one atomic wallop like something you'd see up on-screen at the cineblast, I prefer the subtler, somewhat feline, method of peppering the prey with continuous, gentle slap-slaps of my hand. It subjugates in a way no haymaker ever could.

Just then, keeping to schedule, a sensor strolls into the nosh house and the mob scatters, burying their noggins in their trays. I stop with all the comeuppance and let Pooch slink back to his chair, his face all swolly, stretched skin and rosy lumps. I pant and collapse into the seat next to him, then lean over and whisper,

"Now it's finito."

He just nods. The thing about making an example of someone is, if you do it right right, you only gotta do it once. I hold my hand out and he begrudgingly rakes his fingers across mine in the universal gesture of bestbrohood.

I kinda feel like a deehole now.

I mean, this isn't who I really am, but here at The Fairchild Institute for Young Learners it's survival-of-the-fittest-jungle-law-type stuff, real Darwinian shizz, know what I mean? You've got to have the know on all the angles to win at this game. So, I played lame, I possumed a bitty. Truthy is there probably ain't *that* much difference between Pooch's nums and mine. But after everything that's happened to me, I guess I'm just more willing to take the pain than he is.

The duty sensor on watch walks by our table, his silken robes swishing like a loose sail behind him. We must've fooled the olden because he keeps to his rounds in the other sectors of the nosh house. Pooch looks all sheep-like across the table to Alfa. The boy with the blue blue eyes and matching holo of hair shrugs at him.

"Wowza," Alfa says, as he does a slow clap of his hands. "That was très unexpected." He unzips a smile and points in my direction. "So, what's the know on you, spank?" His tall holo sways like a methane flame.

"Tig ain't no spank, he's been around," a tiny understud at the end of the table squeaks. Clearly my rep has preceded me, at least some. This understud's holo is a close-cropped golden spiky that blazes in all directions.

(He ain't too too important to my tale so I'll just leave his name out.)

Alfa pitches his voice to mimic the understud's, going an octave higher even. *"He ain't no spank?"* he squeals out before returning to his regular baritone. "Then how come I never laid sights on him?"

"Because he-"

Alfa lifts a finger to his lips and shushes the kiddie. "If he ain't no brannyspank, let him share it himself." He turns to me. "I repeat, what's the know on you?

"The name's Tig," I tell him. "Tig Fynch. I got shipped down here from the north wing." The table goes all quiet-like. Alfa nods his noggin repeatedly.

"The hard arm, huh? What'd you do to get shipped up there?"

The studs are glancing sideways at each other but no one dares interrupt me. I reach for a handful of curdmeal from Pooch's tray and shove it in my mouth. "The olden over there's got real heavy sights on us." I give a stealthy chin waggle toward the hooded figure in the center of the room. "Any sensor hears I'm giving up the know on all things and it'll be the age treatment for me, maybe you studs, too."

Alfa offers a bitter teehee. "The treatment's a kiddie scare, spank. If you're trying to spook us, try try again."

"It's no false scare, best-believe," I tell him.

"So you say." Alfa leans back in his chair and splays his fingers down on the table in front of him. "O-kee-dee, what's your tale, Tig Fynch? Give us the know."

I got him.

"Sugar it for me first," I say.

Alfa sighs loudly. He twists his neck to peep around the table and sees a collection of hungered stud faces giving him their wordless consent.

"O-kee-dee, Tig, you win," he finally says, *"Pretty please*, give us the know."

"That's better," I tell him. I clear my throat. "So, have any of you ever gotten high? I mean *really* high." The studs bristle with the taboo excitement that can only be brought on by the promise of adolescent senseporn. Alfa's eyes go real wide-like.

"You know we haven't," he says. "Now enough with the bites, Tigger, give us the whole roll."

I smile, though I swear I don't mean to, and proceed to give up the know.

*

Rewind the tale. Summer was ending in eastwing and I was exactly eight days from my sixteenth annibirthary and not yet the smooth and collected individual who could perp that masterful bit of subterfuge on poor old Pooch that you just read about. If we're being truthy, you'd probably consider me a real average stud. If we're being *real* truthy—below average. I had bestbros I talked to, hung with, sure. Who doesn't? But there was no connection, y'know? They always just felt like space holders until somebody I really clicked with came along. Even worse, I always felt like I was just a space holder for them, too. I mean if I wasn't into them, that's cool, at least I was the one who got to decide. But when no one's into me either, well, that's just some real melancholia-like shizzyness. All us studs, we were all floating around Fairchild Institute like bacteria in a biggy petri dish. Bumping into each other, sharing goodtimes for a ticktock, and then bouncing back into the cytoplasmic pool. Endlessly floating and bumping.

Which would've been fine, I suppose, until SHE spoke to me.

"It's Tig, right?" This femmy was a full level older than me and peeping in on one of my lessons. "Tig Fynch? That's your name, isn't it?" I stared up at her blankly from my chair. "Intro to Quantum Mechanics," she said, peeping around the room. "Yeah, I remember this class from a few cycles back, straight crackerjacked it. You'll do fine, Tig, no nerves."

Cheza Gregory was a beautiful animal. Nevermind that crooked, raven holo on her noggin and the Kabuki Joe makeup. She only had that freakwear on to frighten understuds like me. And speaking only for a stud like me, it totally worked. But even with it, she was beauteous. When the other understuds around me in class with ears high enough to hear caught a listen of Cheza's raspy voice they got up and moved to a safe distance. You can't peep straight at Cheza Gregory up close for long. She's like the sun. Real bright-like. It's no wonder I was feeling so warm. No wonder I started talking to myself either.

Cheza Gregory knows my name. Cheza Gregory knows my kuffing name! She's talking to me, I'm sure of it. What does she want? She's peeping at me like she wants something. Does she want me to talk back to her? I think she wants me to talk back to her. She's STILL peeping... I should totally talk back to her. G'head, talk back to her, Tig. Maybe I'm overthinking this. Oh no, her lips are moving again.

"Hey, understud!" She waved her hand in front of my eyes. "Am I a bother to you or are you gonna join in this convo at some point? Maybe you should get your ears juiced next cycle."

I barely managed to spit the words out. "I'm... Tig. T-Tig Fynch."

She nodded her noggin slightly and went smiley on me. "That's a start," she said. "But I already said that. Now that we *both* know your name, whattaya say you come watch me get my box twiddled?"

"I'm Tig Fynch," I said again, louder this time, just to be certain she knew exactly who she was talking to, in case there was, y'know, a mistake. Because I'm thinking somehow, somewhere, she must have made a mistake.

"Yeah, we've established that, all thanks," she said. "You coming with, or not?"

My inner self started talking to me again.

You can end it right here, Tig. Go ahead, pretend like none of this terrifying-yet-strangely-exciting-encounter ever happened, I dare you. All you have to do is say 'no' and you can crawl right back into the safety of your previous, unremarkable state of existence. Wait, are you actually considering that? Christ on a cracker, I was being sarcastic! Now stop being a yellowass, Tig! For all your complaining, when push comes to shove maybe you're just not willing to step into some real funtimes. Maybe you deserve this shizzy life after all. I've had it, let me out of here!

Let's just say my conscience is a bitty more craze than me. I'm afraid I disappoint him most of the time.

"So, what are you gonna do, Tig?" Cheza asked.

*Yeah, what **are** you gonna do?*

I took a slow breath. "I'll come with," I said, finally.

"Wondrous!" She grabbed my hand, spun on her heel, and towed me to the headwoman's office. With my class scores I'm only there a couple times a year, but Cheza greeted the man at the desk and plopped herself down on one of the big, cushy chairs I'm pretty sure aren't meant for studs. Then she actually introduced me to the guy. *What-the-shizz?*

"Tig, say hey to Linklyn. Linklyn, Tig." I gave him a hey and he heyed me back without raising his hood from the work he was doing, tap-tapping on a compupad. Seemed pleasant enough. "It's Doc Linklyn here's last day for a while—he's on the way up. Gonna be the new headman at Fairchild when olden lady Toi finally expires." The young man lifted his nog and a comely face slipped a little farther out of his hood.

"I'm not a headman yet," he said. "And the word is *retire*, Cheza, not *expire*. Headwoman Toi can't expire, she's not a carton of milk."

Cheza leaned over to me. "Sometimes she smells likes she's expired though."

It was a pretty good one, but I was too uncomfortable to teehee.

"The headwoman will be with you momentarily," Linklyn told us.

My backside slid around the oversized chair and I pretended to study the office walls. "I didn't know you could bring other studs in here with you," I said.

"*You* can't." Cheza flashed me a wicked smirk. "But I'm a different grade of meat, or at least that's what they tell me. I've been watching you. You keep to yourself a lot, don't cha?"

"No, not really," I said to her, straightening up in the chair real defiant-like. "I have bestbros, just not a lot of them. I'm picky."

"Oh, don't get so tangled up, Tig—I'm not saying you don't. I'm sure you're the mayor of Understudville. But still, there's something else about you—there's a longing in there." She pointed to my nog. "Something that cries out to be heard in this, this... theater of the ordinary." It really spoke to my ordinary-ness that I couldn't tell whether she was flirting with me or insulting me.

"I don't think I have a longing," I said. "I'm not a longer. I don't long."

"Course you do! All human beings have longings," she said. "You just haven't figured out what yours are yet, you're still too dull to feel them. We all are, in truthy, but I'm getting closer to full senses."

"I'm not," I said, all dourpuss.

"Give it time, Tig Fynch. You'd be surprised how quickly your nums can rise if you hang out with the right studs."

"You think you can help me pull some better marks?"

"Better marks? Sure, I can do that, at the least least. What's in it for me though?"

A buzzer sounded. Linklyn waved us into the juice rooms and Cheza turned back to the young man at the desk. "Happy graduation, Link. I still have that gift for you."

"Next time," he said, his noggin still buried in the pad.

Cheza never even asked if I could go in with her. It was just sort of assumed. When we arrived at her door, Headwoman Toi didn't say much to Cheza. It was a well-rehearsed dance between the femmy stud and the olden: Cheza hopped up on the table and lowered her nog, Toi disconnected her holofield and her fingers probed the recesses of Cheza's shaved scalp. Then she went to work at the skin behind her neck.

"Fill 'er up and check the oil, Doc."

"You haven't a clue what that means, do you, Ms. Gregory?" Toi had the remnants of a Pan-Asian upbringing in her accent.

Cheza gave a scoff. "Please, Heady Toi, just because I've never piloted an actual gasoline combustion engine doesn't mean it's not clever. Besides, the jokey was only meant for you, not the understud." Her chin in her chest, she raised a finger blindly in my direction.

Toi peeped down her tiny specs and smiled. "They were called automobiles, Ms. Gregory, and you didn't pilot them, you drove them. I guess there's only so much you can learn just from reading about it, even for you."

"Will ya stop spoiling everything, you relic."

Headwoman Toi paused. "Alter your tone please, Ms. Gregory."

"O-kee-dee," Cheza said with what sounded to me like real sorriness, "But I think you're asking for it by wearing those antique goggles on your face."

"I like to wear eyeglasses," the headwoman told her. "There's a certain comfort in old-fashioned things. Now stop moving around." Toi took hold of Cheza's skull to keep it steady and turned to me. "This is like trying to operate on a meerkat. I should get out the harness, for goodness sake."

Then they both teeheed.

What the kuff was going on here? Cheza was talking to a school official like she was a fullgrown. And Toi was letting her! Curiouser and curiouser this new world was.

Headwoman Toi took out a lightscalp and made her incisions on the back of Cheza's neck. She lifted the skin and meat and rollyed it all up like she was opening a sardine can from one of those mid-20th century vids. From my vantage it was a full tummy-tumbler. It made me happy happy I can't actually see it the few times my box get cracked. As for Cheza's nogbox, it was now wide open for me to peep. It was a surprisingly unremarkable-looking chip-and-circuitry board. I'd never actually seen an exposed one before, just diagrams in my anatomy class. She picked up a buzzy, lightning wand in each hand, edged her glasses down the bridge of her nose with her knuckle, and prodded the embedded electronics. Seriously weirdo stuff to peep with my own two. When the headwoman finally juiced her, Cheza's left leg and arm spazzed a bitty, but otherwise she acted all norms. Finally, Toi stretched the skin back over Cheza's scalp and gooed the femmy shut.

"Give it a mini to dry then you can fire up your holo and take your new tongue out for a spin," she told Cheza. "You know the way out." The headwoman scuttled away leaving the hydraulic door to ease shut. Cheza immediately bounded off the table and switched on her hair.

"What are you doing? She said to let it dry. You'll catch the rot."

"Don't be so naive—nog rot's just a spook story, Tig. It's a silly myth perpetuated by the establishment to keep you from playing with yourself." She shook her noggin. "You've got about as much chance of getting the rot as you do of seeing the Easter Bunny."

I wanted to argue, but what could I say? I didn't know anything about anything, it seemed, and Cheza was a real insider with the know on all things. How was I ever going to impress this femmy?

"Ah yes, the Easter Bunny," I said. "What do we really know about him?"

That made her smiley at least. "You're a funny kiddie," she said.

Kiddie?

Kiddie!

NOOOOOOOO! I'm not a KIDDIE! I shave, for godsakes! I'm dangerous and enigmatically cool. Kiddies CAN NOT be dangerous and enigmatically cool—they need help buttoning their clothes. Kiddies are one step above babies. Babies are sweet. Puppy dogs are sweet. Overalls are sweet. Babes in overalls holding puppy dogs are sweet. ANYONE can be sweet! I'm dark and complex, like Batman or string theory. But I absolutely CAN'T be a kiddie!

At least that's what I was saying on the inside. On the outside I was totally mum... like a scared little kiddie.

She leaned over and ran her hand over my nog, shorting out my holo for a micro-tick before it flickered back to life. My whole body stiffened. I brought a hand to my noggin to capture some of the residual heat her fingertips may have left behind, just to verify to myself that it really happened.

Cheza Gregory touched me.

"Come eat with me," she said. "My tongue's at sixes-and-five now."

"O-kee-dee," I said. "Let's eat."

It felt more like a dream at first when we walked together through the halls to the nosh house. She held her noggin up so so high, she refused to even acknowledge the hungered eyes of all those peasant studs peeping us hard. I couldn't look away though; I *wanted* to feel their stares. It made it all seem trés real to me.

"So, how'd you bump your tongue so high?" I asked.

"I've been pouring all this cycle's marks into my mouth," she said. "You think that's manic, don't you?"

I shook my noggin all vigorous-like. "If you've got the nums, they're yours to spend. You earned them square-and-fair. I say put them wherever you want." We were shuffling through the line with the other studs. I caught a few gawkers and I shot them a few noddy-nods, all chilly and shizz. They nodded back, mostly confused. "I've never met anyone in such a hurry to come to their senses," I told Cheza.

"Aren't you?" she said.

"Sure, I am. I just don't pull the marks you do. I'm not as smart smart as you."

"Maybe you are, maybe you're aren't." She leaned close to me and whispered. "And maybe you shouldn't have to be so smart to come to your senses. That's what they're saying on the outside."

"Who's saying?"

"Lots of people. They're saying it's wrong to hold back the full senses we were born with just so Fairchild and every other school can keep us in line and have a carrot to dangle in front of us so we pull good scores. The Resistance is alive and well out there, Tig, even if we're never allowed the know about it in here. That's just what they want."

I shook my noggin at her. "How in the wide world do you know these things?"

"Like you said, I'm a smart." She grabbed a fruity-knot-fruit from the line and popped it in her mouth with a resounding moan. "God, I love this new tongue! You won't believe how good sixes-and-five taste," she said.

"Right now, I can't even imagine it."

She shrugged at me. "Someday you won't have to imagine." She swallowed the knot-fruit and leaned into my ear. "Some people are saying that not everyone in The Resistance is on the outside. There may be some sensory-symps right here among us at Fairchild."

"Sympathizers here? You mean some of the sensors are in The Riz?"

She smiled that crooked smile. "Maybe," she said. "Some look trés suspy to me."

"You're blowin' my brain biggy right now, y'know that?"

"Hey, we got a right to our own bodies, Tig. It can't seem too craze to you we're not the only ones who think so."

"But you're already sky-high, why do you even care? You'll be fully-sensed way before any of us."

"Exactly right," she said. "An understud blanket like yourself should care about being held down even more than I do... so why don't you?"

Cheza Gregory is so cool. So smart. So different from anyone I've ever met. She's right— I should care! I should care more than she does. Me and all the blankets like me being held down from experiencing life simply because we're less-than-extraordinary seems hardly fair-like. And it takes someone like Cheza, who's barely held down at all, to make me peep it. So, to answer her question, 'Why don't I care?' It's pretty simple: No one ever told me why I should, not like her. I've never known a stud like Cheza that would ask these questions. The real question—the question I was most afraid to find out the answer to was this: What does someone like Cheza Gregory want with me? What the hell am I doing here? It's time to find out.

I pulled Cheza out of the line and backed her into a nearby corner. "I need to say something to you."

"O-kee-dee," she said. "Say something to me."

"I don't know how you peep me, but I am NOT a kiddie."

She gave me an open-mouthed smiley. "I already knew that, Tig." She pushed by me and got back in line. "I was just curio if *you* did."

It was our turn at the foodstuff dispensers. Cheza flashed her sixes-and-five to the automated server and grabbed every plate she could hoist: tasty pastes, leafsies, darkalots, whatever she could get her little piggies on. Me and my twos-and-two got a stinking bowl of veg-a-rice and a cleardrink. She brought the super-stacked tray to her norm table and began to eat. While I watched her noshing hard, I forced down my own lunchy, silently cursing my low tongue.

"My fulls would never let me get all that," I told Cheza, motioning to her tray. "Even if I *could* taste it."

In between extended grunts of delight, she mumbled through her stuffed mouth, "Don't have both my fulls... just Daddy... he does his part... I do mine." She crammed in a glob of sweetcream and swallowed. "I mean, if I didn't spend all his cred and I *still* managed to pull top marks, he'd have the know that I don't really need any of it to be my brilliant self. I am not gonna let that happen, no chance," she said. "This way we both feel better about my educational experience here at The Fairchild *Penitentiary*—er, I mean, *Institute*." She over-smirked and pushed a salmon-colored mush out from between her teeth. I teeheed so hard the cleardrink nearly shot out my nose.

Cheza Gregory is even cooler than I thought.

She corralled another bowl from the tray with her arm and pulled it into her mouth's orbit. "If I'm being truthy though, my dad's Grade-A max. It's not his fault I'm the way I am."

"What do you mean? He's gotta be the proudest full ever. You're Cheza Gregory! You've got the most sense in school, everybody loves you. All the femmys want to be like you. And the boys, well, they want to be like you too."

Cheza groaned. "Try being me some time, it's exhausting," she said. "The sensors and all their expectations—I'm the only stud in school not allowed to slack for a mini. And what do I get for all the work I do? Sky-higher expectations! It's a shizzy cycle, Tig. I just want to get off the wheel sometimes and breathe breathe." She took in another spoonful. "And these other studs in school, always thinking they're gonna be the one who figures me out. Pathetic, man."

I wiped my hand across my face.

Mental note: Stop trying to figure her out.

"If it's so hard hard being you," I said. "Why don't you just stop?"

She tilted her noggin and gave me that look. That Cheza look. The one I was already beginning to get used to. The one that said to me, 'We're not there yet, kiddo, you don't have the full know on me yet. You're not my fulls or my bestbro or nothing. We ain't The Two Musketeers and you should know not to ask questions like that, Alexandre Dumbass.'

"And who would you have me be?" she asked, real snark-like.

I froze solid as ice.

This is where she drops me, tells me to get bent, push off, blow away.

She dropped her spoon and moved the tray aside, then gave me a real soul stare. "Sometimes I wish I was different, but it's not my nature to wait for things. I gotta have everything now. Daddy says it's the Veruca Salt in me." She grabbed my forearm. "Do you know what it feels like to have the wide world out there and you just wanna touch it, no matter what the cost?"

I gave her a pensive nod and a long, *Mmmm-hmmm.*

I have no idea what she's talking about. Don't give her the know though. Quick, flip the discourse.

"So, say it already, what's sixes-and-five taste like?"

She let out a rapturous grunt. "I bet you'd like the know."

"I've been in the twos so long I don't know what I'd do if I tasted the real real stuff."

Cheza slid the half-finito package of fruity-knot-fruits across the tabletop. "Try it. Who knows, you might catch a burst of something, even at twos-and-two."

"You *are* manic," I said. "My tongue's so dead I could speak Latin. And what if I get caught?"

Cheza gave me the pouty pouty face. "Oh, I'm sorry, I thought you weren't a kiddie?" She swiveled her noggin around the room. "There's no sensors here yet to catch us. Go ahead and do it. Even if you get caught, you're with me," she said, biggy smile plastered on her face.

I realized at that moment it was true true what they said about femmys always wanting the bad boy. Cheza Gregory wanted the Romeo-Rebel-kind, and at Fairchild nothing says reb like sneaking a spoonful of forbidden knot-fruit. I quick-like grabbed up the bag, took out a knot, and eased it past my lips. I rolled it on my tongue and waited.

"I don't taste anything too... *tasty*," I said, tossing the bag back across the table. "Kuffing twos-and-two!"

That's when, behind Cheza, I peeped a sensor practically goose-stepping his way over to our table. He slipped off the hood of his cloak to reveal a face-full of pale, saggy skin and a freshly-shaved nog. "Tig Fynch, what are you doing? You're not cleared for knot-fruits, understud."

I put up my hands. "Yes, I know Sensor Cull, I—I don't-"

"It's my fault, Sensor," Cheza broke in. "I'm the reason he ate the knot-fruit."

Sensor Cull's face relaxed when he turned to the femmy. "I hear you're tasting at sixes-and-five already, congratulations are in order, Study Gregory." While he bowed slightly, Cheza threw me a wink. "However, even though I realize this is a time of celebration for you, Study Fynch here cannot join you on this particular voyage of discovery," he said. "He's not allowed to taste the fruits of *your* labor, even if he could, which he can't. But I think you already found that out, didn't you? Study Fynch, did you imagine your sense locks were a mirage? What did you think would happen when you consumed that knot-fruit like a hyena, stealing away another's catch—that you'd be able to taste it?"

"She gave it to me, actually. I didn't-"

"Rhetorical!" Cull lifted a finger into the air and frownied. "Fruit knots are a privilege you must earn through hard work and dedication to your studies. If it happens again, it'll be a numbers dock, Fynch."

I lowered my eyes. "Yes, sir."

Cull began to leave when Cheza spoke up. "I was well aware of his locks, Sensor," she said. "I knew he'd derive no pleasure from his new job."

"New job?" he asked. "What's that?"

"I thought I could use Tig as a personal foodstuff tester, to make sure I'm not poisoned. As top stud here at Fairchild I'm sure you'll agree every precaution should be taken to keep me safe from the foul machinations of those who might wish me harm."

Cull gave us a joyless teehee and pulled his hands out of his robe. "Very medieval of you, Study Gregory, although I think your concern might be slightly exaggerated. This is a school after all, not King Henry's royal court. I think your beefloaf is quite safe."

"Clearly you've never tried the beefloaf," she said.

Cull gave a hard sigh. "Nevertheless, employing a food tester seems a bit extreme. But I'll let him slide this time." His eyes shifted between Cheza and I. "How long have you two been keeping company?"

"We just met," she told him.

I don't know how, but Cull managed to frowny even deeper. "What about that other stud—what was his name?" The sensor stroked his chin. "Or the one before that? Or the-" Cheza's face began to sour and she prattled on about something or other just to drown the olden out. Cull stopped and the merest hint of a smile turned the corners of his mouth up. Then he was back on me, all smuggy. "I'm afraid that although we can shield our learners from many evils and excesses, we cannot always protect them from each other." Cull slipped his hands back into his robe and glided off while Cheza thrust her tongue out at him.

"Clarence can be a crotchety knob of the highest order sometimes. Don't believe a word he says about me, o-kee-dee?"

"Yeah, sure. He's always spooked me out anyway."

I didn't question Cheza about what Cull said. I suppose it was partly because I didn't want the know and partly because I was still in shock to learn one of the head sensors at Fairchild was named Clarence. Besides, I was feeling too too good to let something as small as Cull's crotchetiness kill the karma of the happenings.

That was forty-two days ago.

*

"Sweetstuff, Tig, it really is. Warms the cockles and all that." Alfa's carving tracks into his mashed spudatoes. "If I was eight-years-old—AND A FEMMY—I might actually give a rat's. But as I am, to date, neither of those things, get to the gooden parts already or go piss."

"Bear with me, bestbro, we're at the tip top of the roller ride," I tell him. Alfa over-sighs. "Alright then, carry on... and on and on and on." He waves his hand for me to continue.

"O-kee-dee, buckle it up, bros."

*

Cheza was waiting for me outside the door at the end of my sixth lesson. "Come outside and play with me tonight, birthboy." Cheza said, her eyes alive. "Let's go for a stroll in the grove. I've taken the necessary precautions."

She clasped my hand tight-like and pulled me out into the hallway, fighting against the traffic of a steady stream of bumbling, sense-poor understuds. I dropped my volume and reminded her, "What about the Truancy Force? Going out after nightlocks is a violation majora."

"Only if we're caught," she said.

"I don't know, Cheza." I said in a slow whine. "Just for a joywalk? Doesn't seem worth it. Those truant officers are legit gonzos. They use fall guns on you, sick sticks—they put you in magbonds and everything."

"Who said it was just a joywalk, stud?"

Gulp.

"It's all about where the night takes us," she said. "There's something I want to show you. Be at my room before locks-on and we'll snake out of here." She pressed her palms together. "Pleeease."

"I'm still not sure."

Her hands dropped to her sides. "What are you so so worried about?"

"Well, let me think, how about... oh yeah, getting caught!"

"So what if we do get caught? What'll happen? They dock your nums a bitty, bring you down across the board—what's the biggy? You can't taste life with nums as low as yours anyhow"

"All thanks for reminding me."

"I'm sorrys, was I being too truthy? I thought I was just stating the obvious. My point is, I'm the only one really taking a risk here, and I'm doing it all for you. Come on, it's gonna be a total mind-scram. The least you can do is alter your 'tude—gimme more grati and less atti. Go a-scheming with me, Tig. I thought we were partners?" She doubled down with that same pout pout saddy face from before and flicked her holo over to a somber blue tint.

I was going with her. I knew it. Cheza knew it. It was just a matter of me grumbling the words now. No sense in dragging it out any longer.

"O-kee-dee, I'm in."

Her face beamed. "My door, tonight. Wear some darkies and douse your holo, you get?"

"I get."

In forty-two days spent with Cheza Gregory I learned it was best not to ask too too many questions. Just go with it. She was trés clever, real mastermindy, and she got us out of a lot of sticky sitches. Of course, she was the one who got us into those sitches to begin with, but she'd usually gloss over that part. As top stud she pretty much had her run of Fairchild and any little mischiefs we perped were quickly forgiven by the sensors because it was Cheza Gregory, after all, and an indiscretion or two was to be expected of such an active mind.

They had no idea. Like absolutely zero.

*

"So you're just gonna jam with her?" my older quartersmate, Ralen, asked me as he played with the settings of his holo in the bathroom mirror to achieve the in-look. "Are you totally gonzo? Those tru-blue meanies are everywhere after dark. You'll get nibbed for sure."

"I have to go," I told him.

"Why?"

"Because if I don't, Cheza will think I'm just a dim understud and wonder why she ever wanted to jam with me in the first place."

He dropped his noggin slightly, gave a low snigger, and rubbed his hands around his face. "Tig, hate to be the bearer, but you *are* a dim understud," he said with some force. "Just admit to yourself she's way too high for you, bestbro, before you get yourself in a heap. I mean, even you have to wonder what she peeps in you."

He was right.

I've wondered.

From the day Cheza and I first met I wondered what she peeps in me. But it doesn't hurt so much when *I'm* the one wondering.

"She sees... something," I said. "Something no one else can, apparently."

"Sounds like she's using you, Tigger. There's another game afoot here, that femmy must have some ulteriors to want to get into some tomfuckery with you." Ralen tugged at the collar of my shirt. "What is it about you anyway? Where's the special?"

The sense he was making was perfect, but there was ugly there too. Pure pure ugly.

"Why is it so hard to accept that she might just like me for who I am? Cheza Gregory might just be into *me*. Not you, not Harris Timmons and his dimples and his dreamy new rainbow holo, not Stex Rawl and his six-string and all his full's cred, not any of the other sky-high studs. She likey me... Tig Fynch!"

"Listen to yourself, bestbro, even you can't believe that."

"Well, I'm gonna find out, and not you or anyone else is gonna stop me. I don't care if she's weird or sketch or even a little gonzo—I'm having goodtimes. She makes me happy. For the first time in my whole life, it's not about my nums. She doesn't care about any of that. I don't know why, but she doesn't. I don't know why she wants to be with me either, but she does." I shook my nog. "And for some reason that just eats the insides of studs like you. Now why is that? Are you even a true true bestbro, I wonder?"

He waved his hand at me and walked back to the mirror. "Don't flatter yourself, I'm just saying she sounds like troubles, biggy troubles."

"It's Cheza kuffing Gregory! Who cares if she's troubles?"

Ralen turned and leaned against the sink. "O-kee-dee, Tig, what happens when she's finito with you? Everyone in my level's got the know on her. They say she's a real animal lover."

"What do you mean?"

"It means she likes keeping pets, you cool with that? Do you like being her pet?" I didn't answer him straight off. I was too too busy getting steamy at him. "You're not different, Tig. You don't have the special in you. You're just easy to domesticate." He pulled on his shirt and zipped it. "If you're not just a pet, please share how you're so so different from the rest of us studs?"

I didn't have the know at first, didn't have any answer for him, until I did.

"The only difference I can peep is that I'm leaving this room tonight to go be with Cheza Gregory, and the rest of you ain't."

I tapped open the door to our quarters and sauntered out, all not-givin'-a-kuff-like.

*

I opened her door a few minis before locks-on. She was dressed in tightblack from peak to piggies, a cap stretched over her noggin. She grabbed my hand and led me with the stealth out of her quarters to a darkened portion of the school where heavy plastic sheets hung from scaffolding that was set up everywhere. There was some constructo work being done on the schoolgrounds and it made for decent cover. She pushed through a bunch of these sheets then suddenly dropped to her hands and knees and began

177

pawing all hound-like around on the floorboards. A moment later she lifted a loose piece of wood, giggled, and slid under it, immediately disappearing. When the board lifted again, Cheza was peeping out at me from a deep hole in the floor.

"You didn't think it would be easy, did ya?"

I lifted the floorboard and dropped myself in after her, making sure to cover the hole completely so as not to make the scene look too too suspy. She already had an electrotorch lit and was carrying it through this subterranean tunnel like she was in a scene out of an Edgar Allan.

"Follow me at all times," she said. "No exceptions."

"So so serious. Where are we going?"

She said again, "No exceptions."

"O-kee-dee."

She stopped to finger at her gutpad for directions and then we got a-walking once more. We were down in that labyrinth for what seemed like hours. I think Cheza got us lost a couple times but was too fraidy to cop to it. When we reached a small flight of concrete stairs Cheza checked her gutpad again, peeped up at me, and got all smiley.

"Come help me with these," she said. We ran up the stairs and pushed up on a set of metal doors that gave way in the center. The first thing I felt was the fridgy, night air rushing in on us. Normally I wouldn't be able to feel it too too strong-like, but we were stuck inside Fairchild's sweaty bowels for so long that the bitey air hit me hard, even with *my* low nums. I stepped from the stairwell out onto the grass and immediately recognized the white aspen trees of the west grove—we'd peeped pics of Fairchild's new arm plastered over the eastwing all last cycle.

Cheza had run a ditch job on all the east arm surveillance cams and truancy patrols and dumped us onto the westwing grounds that wouldn't have a stud population until next cycle. No studs equals no orbs equals no one even has the know that we're here. I told ya this femmy had brilliance! She vaulted off the highest step and bounded toward the grove like a fawn.

"We're here, Tig," she called out. "It's beauteous, isn't it?"

"Sure it is," I said. "Awful long way to go for some fresh air though."

"But this place has some special in it," she said as she reached the tree line.

"It's just woods." My voice trailed off as I gave chase. "There's no special here, just... wood." I fought through the prickers and the dense shrubbery that strangled the ground between the aspens, but I kept a-following. "Where you going?" Cheza stopped where the big grove broke and a field spread out in front of us. On the other side I could see the fuzzy brights of the city.

She pointed to my legs. "You're bleeding." I peeped down at my pants and saw that they were pocked with small crimson circles. "Don't worry, I am too," she said, lifting her calf to show me. The night air was so fridgy that we could peep it streaming out in front of our faces. Cheza sucked it in through clenched teeth. "Lucky you're so dull," she said to me with a devily smile.

I took a few steps in the direction of the field and *CRACK* my body halted and I ended up flat. Cheza held in a teehee. "I told you *follow me at all times*, didn't I? That means don't take the lead, ever." She helped me to my feets. I reached out and my fingers brushed against a firm, invisible barrier. "The thing they don't show you on all those maps of this place is the polyfencing that surrounds it." I shook my nog to clear the cobs. "Well, now you know." She spread her hands against the fence and did a vertical push-up while I brushed myself off.

"Is this what you wanted to show me then?" I asked.

"Not at all, stud," she said. "*That* is." She pointed beyond the field to the city.

"Don't tell me you wanna go there? Don't tell me that's what you want me to do with you?"

"O-kee-dee, I won't tell you." She teeheed to herself. "But that's where we're going," she said, then began to stalk the fence line.

"Why? I can't enjoy it, and neither can you—we're not high enough yet. You may have the most sense in school, but you're not a full, not even close." Cheza wouldn't answer me though. She just kept pacing the fence. "Besides, how would we even get there?"

Cheza stopped. "There you are tall, light, and handsome," she said. I half expected her real studboy—some sense-maxed, wild-one type—to appear from out of the shadows. But instead, she strolled over to one of the trees. Real peculiar-like, she was acting. The tree was white, like the aspens, but with a segmented trunk, like bamboo. She hugged it, wedged one of her feets against the bole, and shimmied up the thing. She used the deep crevices between its segments and its thick, outstretched branches as rungs before she stopped and settled herself so so far up, I could barely see her.

"I take it you've done this before?"

"I've done most everything, silly. She eased herself out onto one of the branches.

"What are you thinking, birdy?" I called up to her. "You're gonna fall out of your nest."

"No, I won't."

"You're gonna die," I told her.

"Don't be so so dramatic," she said. "It's called a lantillo tree, they're all over South America. Daddy had a baby one shipped up here from Venezuela for my annibirthary, before the Quiroga coup."

"Of course he did."

She gave a chuck-chuckle. "I told him it was an experiment for botany class." She sat down on the branch and, with her legs wrapped around it, crept out to the skinniest part.

"I can't watch this," I told her. "It's gonna snap." But she kept right on squawking like we were in a class and she was giving the know on all things.

"The lantillo is renowned for its strength and its accelerated speed of growth. During the war when Quiroga wanted information from the government soldiers he'd captured, his men would sharpen the end of a lantillo and plant it just below the soil while the prisoners watched." She crawled out onto the branch even farther. "Then, they would tie the prisoners to the ground with stakes and leave them there. The prisoners knew that eventually the tree would pop up out of the ground and burrow its way into them. That's all they'd think about for hours and hours as they lay there. It was a genius mindkuff," she said. "By the time they felt even the first prick of that tree on their skin they gave up the know on everything." She was at the very edge of the branch now.

"That's trés cool. How'd you hear about all this?"

"Tig, anything you want the know on is out there, you just have to look for it. Quiroga's a great man and they don't teach us a thing about him in school."

"I wonder why."

"Wakey wakey, little Tiggy. Because he's a revolutionary, that's why. He saw injustice and wasn't having it. Who woulda believed that a simple mush farmer like Quiroga could lead a rebellion and overthrow the powers that be when anyone who spoke up either got thrown in prison or executed? He knew he had to tear the whole system down to fix it—it was his solemn duty," she said. "That's how I feel too." She bounced on the end of the branch but it didn't so much as sway under her weight. "Y'see? This thing's plenty strong and I only planted it a couple months ago. What are you waiting on? Get up here!"

"I'm no Quiroga," I told her.

"Quiroga wasn't even Quiroga," she said. "Until he needed to be. Now start climbing."

I took a breath, real deep deep, and gripped on tight to a couple of the branches above my noggin.

I must be craze.

Then I carefully wedged my foot into a cleft at the base of the tree and lifted myself up, just like Cheza did. Up and up I went until I reached the branch Cheza was sitting on. When I inched my way out to meet her, she stood up, holding on to the branches above. She offered me her hand and even though my knees went wobbly-like when I stood, the lantillo was a steel beam under my feets. From that perch I peeped back across the canopy of aspens below me. It was a magniffy sight, even for my low eyes.

"The aspens are all engineered to grow exactly twenty metrics high, so they put the fence at twenty-five." She reached her hand over the border of the wall. "You get? No fence up here. By the time they notice this fella poking out, we'll already have had our goodtimes."

I took her hand in mine. "All thanks, Cheza," I told her. "All thanks for tonight. All thanks for the last few weeks. All thanks for everything. But we don't have to do this. I've had goodtimes with you already."

"Why stop now?" she said.

"Cheza, we don't have the sense to enjoy what's in the city brights. You might be close close, but I'm not. Their set-up's not like at school—it's dangerous for studs like us."

"Answer me one," she said. "Do you trust me?"

"Well... yeah, I guess."

"You guess?"

"O-kee-dee, I trust you," I said. "I do."

"Then stop leaning on your nog so much," she said. "And trust this instead." She poked a finger into my chest.

Was this actually going to be the first time in my life that I decided to blindly do something that took some true true courage? Or was I just a yellowuss who couldn't say no to his femmy? It's a pretty fine line. And speaking of fine lines...

Cheza pulled a wad of knotted, narrow-rope from her pack and tied it to our branch. She gave it a tug, dropped it over the far side of the fence, and repelled down. I followed and my feets landed firm-like in the tall grass on the other side a few ticktocks after hers. We crossed that field in minis and picked up the road that led straight to the brights of the city and the promise of bona fide actual-factual adventure.

*

Our feets were padding the concrete just outside the city brights when Cheza grabbed my hand and squeezed it real real tenacious.

"Listen to me this time, do exactly as I say, you get? I wanna make this a trés special night for you, but you were right before when you said the city's a dangerous place for blankets. Promise me, Tig."

"I promise." She spooked me, I admit, but I'd come too too far to let a bitty fear stop me now. "I'll do whatever you tell me to."

"Great-o," she said. "Follow me."

"Where to?" I asked.

She answered me all sing-songy-like. "We're off to peep the wizard."

The first thing I did peep when we got there, howev, was how there was no kiddies around at all and not a singly person had a holo—all the fullgrowns had their real fuzz. Some of them kept it covered, but it would still spill out the sides of their headtoppers. I guess there's no need to keep your skull shaved and sani if you never get cracked to have your box twiddled. Still, it was such an odd thing—everybody walking around with *real* hair—and all-nonchalant about it to boot. Sure, we'd peep our fulls when they'd visit on the rare freedays we got from school, but most of them wore nogtoppers or domeware so as not to make us poor poor studs feel bad about our bare braintanks. But this was a whole city of fulls giving zero kuffs about studs like us. They were everywhere! Just out there all shaggy and

181

whatnot. Up until then I always thought our holos looked essentially the same as the genuine article, but the lightfield of sim implants embedded in my scalp would never be able to touch the texture and richness of what I was peeping now. The sensors at Fairchild were all required to either be bald or hooded at all times so we never got to see their true true locks, which was probably a good thing because it was already starting to make me feel inadequate somehow. I patted my black stretchcap then peeped over at Cheza's thin-lipped grimace and realized she was feeling it, too.

Before that night, I never got how much the school was tailored to dulls like me. Everything at Fairchild was biggy and bangy and safe safe and came at you all slow and ease so even the dimmest studs could get a handle. But this place was a mishy-mashy hodgepodge of wonders: all the sounds, and the sniffs, and the sights! I couldn't focus in on any one thing. There was a true true newness in all the blurred minutiae, but it was always once removed—a shadow world I couldn't fully perceive, like going to a museum but only being allowed to peep through dirty windows. That was the tale of my life, really. All this beauteousness, and I couldn't really touch any of it. So I guess it never really touched me either. Cheza didn't waste a singly ticktock on the minutiae though. She tugged me along the sidewalk like a toddly-tike, a clear clear destination in her mind. A few minis later, she started bopping with excitement.

"We're here, we're here!" The femmy was posilutely giddy.

"This?" I asked her. "This is what we broke out for?"

It was a small, bricky building that reminded me of the gardener's shack back at Fairchild. No windows. A large metal door, all denty and in bad bad need of a new coat of paint. With a singly naked light bulb radiating above it and humming all loud-like. What paint there still was on the door, along the frame, was a sicky green color and peeling. Cheza dragged me into the alleyway and we wended around the back to another metal door with a peep slot.

"How do you know this place?" I asked her.

"Shhhhh... no talky. Need thinky."

I nodded and kept mousy quiet while my orbs settled on some real gutterpup types lying against the wall across from us. At least I think they were gutterpups. They looked the way every lazeabout bummy that had ever been described to me looked, only they stunk worse, which was saying something considering how low my nose was. They wore faces that were all sunk in, real hellathin skeleton, y'know? A couple of them reached out towards me all slo-mo and their fingers grasped at the nothingness like we were right in front of them, even though we were at least a dozen metrics away.

"Who are they?" I said.

"Cloudheads." Cheza rapped out a gonzo cadence on the door with her knuckles. "They're junkie freakshows. Don't let 'em touch you unless you've had your shots."

"Why do they do it?"

She sighed. "Why do you keep talking after I told you not to?"

I put my hand over my mouth.

I don't get. Here I was, all my senses underwater, working hard hard as can be to give myself some feels, and these people actually paid cold cred to turn theirs off. If something about being a fullgrown made you wanna do all that, maybe I'm better off staying fifteen. There was a sound coming from behind the door and Cheza gave me an elbow nudgy.

"Ready?" she said.

"For what?"

A smiley broke out on her face. "Your annibirthary present, if it wasn't already obvious."

The tiny slot opened and a peeper wiggled at us from behind the door. A few ticktocks later the whole thing swung open with a grindy creak. Cheza let out a short squeal and hugged the figure on the other side. He'd lost the robes and hood but I was sure sure it was Linklyn, the headman-in-training from Fairchild. He had some seriously wrinkled clotheware, the shadow of a beard darkening his cheeks, and an unruly tuft of genuine chestnut brown atop his noggin. Now actual hair of any kind was still a craze sight to me, but even more gonzo was to see a real h-do all mussied up. Holos are always so perfectly tame. Still, it was unmistakably Link. He peeped our tightblacks and caps, gave a loud groan, and let us inside.

"Very subtle," he said. "Where'd you buy those getups? Mickey Mouse's Black Ops Clubhouse?"

"Trés funny," Cheza said with sarc a-dripping. She dug inside her pack and handed him a small comp chip. "I brought your graduation present, as promised. Happy belated, kind sir."

Linklyn pocketed the chip and told her, "It all better be there, little stud. I'm sticking myself way out for you this time."

She glowered at him (Cheza gave real good glower.)

"When have I ever shorted you, Link?"

"Double juice jobs go way beyond the yoosh request," he said. "And there's a first time for everything."

Cheza winked at me. "It's a special occasion," she told him.

Linklyn stood there a moment, his orbs shifting between the two of us. "Alright rockers, let's get rockin'. Lose those stretch-scalps and climb on the tables." He made his way to the other end of the room.

"Is this safe, I mean, I thought you weren't a headman yet?" I said.

Linklyn stopped his prep. "Don't you see the medical degree hanging on the wall?"

I peeped around. "Nopers," I said. "I don't see anything."

"And do you know *why* you don't see anything, understud?"

I shook my noggin.

"Because you're dull as dirt, kiddo. So, if you want to stay that way, by all means, keep asking dumdum questions." He turned his back to us and began to scrub up at the sink. "I thought you said he was cool, Cheza."

Cheza climbed up onto one of the tables and threw me a harsh look. "He's o-kee-dee with everything. Tell him, Tig."

"Yeah, I'm down with The Riz. no dramas." I got onto the table next to Cheza's. "That's what all this is, right? A resistance-run facility or something?"

Linklyn choked out a teehee. "Nothing that romantical, I'm afraid... this is a business. Just a way to get me through med school without being in debt the rest of my miserable." He came around behind us and jabbed a syringe into Cheza's neck. When it was my turn, I flinched.

"*Tranquilo*, stud. This is just a local so you don't feel anything," he said. "Until you feel *everything*, that is." He plunged the needle into me and administered the anesthetic, then rolled a covered cart over to where we were sitting. He peeled back the white sheet to reveal a tray of glisteny silver tools. The shine jumping off the metal nearly made my orbs go all squinty. He picked up a lightscalp from the tray and the beam flared to life. "Who's up first?" he said. Cheza aimed both her thumbs squarely at herself. "O-kee-dee then, it's the bitty lady." He brought the laser to the back of Cheza's skull, but before Linklyn could slice—

"Just one more thingy," I said. "I know Cheza said there's no way we can catch the rot but..."

She threw me a murderous look, but Linklyn calmed the femmy down.

"No, no, let him take a mully on that one," he said, patting her shoulder. "I'm not that much older than you two." He started in on Cheza's neck. The lightscalp tracked across her skin, opening the flesh. "I remember the scare tactics they'd use on us, those gore films in class. Long before your generation, or even mine—back when it was a real problem—they called it *redhead*. Later it was *box rot*. Now all you studs call it *nog rot*. Every generation or so they come up with a new name, but it's not a problem anymore. They only tell that olden tale to keep you studs from playing with yourselves."

Linklyn's laser instrument wasn't as advanced as the ones they had at Fairchild so he had to remove the flesh in layers like he was shearing wool from a sheep (I saw a vid about it once.) I couldn't watch after long though, no tum-tum for it, I guess. When I was sure he was finito with the lightscalp, I peeped again as he pried open her box and used his surgical tools on her. He worked quickly and, it seemed to me at least, expert-like, considering what he had. It made me feel a little less anxious about the whole thingy. "Here we go," he said, and with a final touch of the lightscalp, the femmy's body jittered to life and the deal was done. He filled the empty space on her neck with pinkfat and closed her up. "Let the goo dry this time," he told her. She nodded all obligingly and turned in a sense-stupor toward the wall.

"You're next," he said to me. I swallowed real hard and sat up straight on the table.

"I'm glad I can't see you poking around in *my* nogbox," I told him while he did his toiling on me.

"You should be grati that you're too dim to hear the hum of the scalpel or smell the char from the incision. These are distinctive experiences, best believe," he said. He put down his lightscalp on the tray next to me and picked up his pinchers and prodder. "My great-gramps used to tell me this story about going to the dentist back during a time back when nogboxes were just for privileged families. He had so many brothers and sisters that his fulls couldn't afford a painkiller for them. So, when those unlucky kiddies had cavities that needed filling, they got to smell the burnt enamel and dentine mixed in with the raw raw pain of having their own living tissue ground into dust. He always said he'd never forget that smell until the day he died. That's something you'll never have to endure because of that nogbox you've got attached to you."

"You sure you're on the right side then?" I asked him. "You don't sound like you're Resistance."

"You didn't let me finish the tale," he said. "Great-gramps remembered those trips to the dentist and he made a promise to himself that if he ever had kiddos of his own, they'd never have to suffer the way he did." Linklyn craned his neck around my body to peep me in the eyes. "He became an orthodontist—the first doc in our family—and it all came out of that unpleasantness he had at the dentist's." Linklyn placed the dripping crimson instruments back onto the tray, took a peep at my box, and gave a snort. "Maybe I could've saved the needle on you, stud. You really are dead on the outside, aren't ya?"

"Twos-and-two," I told him. "Fairchild's a tough place to get high at."

"Not for this one." He waved his bloody prodder at Cheza, who was still too sense-drunk to take notice. "You're not like her though, huh?"

"No one is," I said.

"Don't feel too too bad. There's hellava more people like you in this world than like her. Maybe that's why The Resistance is so strong." He rattled his metal stick around my nogbox and I got the feel of new sensations a-kindling within me. "I was never the top stud, but I worked hard in school and got real goody nums. Why did I have to wait so long to come to my senses? Why should *anyone* have to wait for what they already have, what they're born with?"

"I guess they shouldn't," I told him.

"Jesus Christmas, Fynch, at least say it like you mean it!"

Linklyn seemed upset and I didn't want to further upset the man who was, literally and figuratively, getting inside my head. I thought it better just to clam. It was awkward for a mini, but I needed him to notch down. Didn't want him having any flubbys while my box was open.

"Sorry," he finally said. "I suppose you can't sound like you mean it unless you actually do." He kept tap-tapping at my circuitry. "You will soon enough though."

I was testing my peripherals and staring at Cheza on the table next to me. She stretched her arms as if she'd just woken up and then sprang onto the floor.

"Toilet?" she said. Linklyn pointed her toward a corner door. "Is he almost done? We've got biggy plans tonight."

"Real close," the young man said. Cheza gave me a grin and headed for the bathroom. The door slid shut and Linklyn leaned into my ear. "Don't ever think it's not hard for someone like her. It might seem like a real sweet-treat to be the first one up the mountain, but don't forget that the first one to the tiptop is always alone."

Then it happened. The whole room filled up.

The sound of air flowing into my ears was heavy as a bomb at first and everything seemed to swell up and get focussy for me. There was a sharp sharp pain at the base of my neck where Linklyn had me opened up. So sharp I swore I could smell it. And everywhere tingled. I was an exposed nerve, alive—*really alive*—for the first time.

"How do you feel?" he asked.

"Like I imagine a freshly-peeled orange does."

Cheza came out of the bathroom, ran over to me, and grabbed my arms. "Do you see now? Do you see what it's like?"

"Careful!" Linklyn said, quickly pulling his hands away from my neck. "I'm stitching him."

"Oh, sorry Link, g'head and zip him up." The young man wagged his noggin and went back to work sealing me up. Cheza took my hands in hers and rubbed our fingertips together. "I've been wanting to do something for a while but I had to make sure you'd feel it like I do."

She cocked her nog to the side and leaned in so our lips could meet. But her calculations were off and she pressed so hard that her front teeth clanked against mine. It was simultaneously the greatest and grossest ticktock of my life, and I didn't have clue one why... it just was. She must've felt it too because she pulled her nog back all swifty. "Not bad," she said. "But not quite right either." She took in a huge breath and leaned forward again, more careful-like this time. She closed her eyes (*I was watching*) and it was as if her lips were reaching out for mine, towing me in with a tractor beam of love (*Oh My Kuffing Gee! Did I really just say that?*) Actually, it was more like what I imagine docking a ship onto an orbiting space station would be like. It was this series of slow-moving maneuvers to get us in position and then BAM! we were locking.

Our lips met again... softly, this time.

We rubbed our warm, velvety pinkskin together, to what purpose I had no earthly idea other than it felt really, *really* good. Then we separated.

"Now that's a kiss," she told me.

It sure was.

Our fabtastic moment was poisoned only by the presence of Linklyn, who was mock-barfing over my shoulder "Ew, I forgot how awkward you studs are when you get your new juice. It sounds like a barnyard in here." Cheza smacked him in the arm. Linklyn just teeheed a snig and wheeled his tray over to the sink. As for me, I think I was still in shock. "Why would anyone want to take that feeling away?" I asked. Cheza looked so so proud of herself.

"It's real simple." Linklyn started the water and began to rinse his tools. "They figure no feely means no kissy, and no kissy means no sexy, and no sexy means..." He waved a finger toward my pelvis. "No sexy means no Venus diseases, no teeny bumps, and no melodramas—absolutely no distractions of any kind from your studies. Everything kiddies a century ago got away with are off-limits to you. Isn't it progressive that we get to pay for our ancestors' mistakes?" He patted the lightscalp dry with a rag. "Like I said, it's real simple. I didn't say it was real fair."

Cheza got all scoffy. "Kuffing fulls! They don't think we can handle it."

"Haha!" Linklyn said. "I hate to sound like one of those oldens at school, but you *can't* handle it. You're only teenys, you're not supposed to be able to."

Cheza's orbs went slivers and daggers. "What a punky Judas you are, Link," she said.

"Oh grip it, will ya, Cheza. Whether you realize it or not I'm being totally truthy. It doesn't mean I'm not for the cause. The fact that teenys can't control their urges isn't the problem. The problem is that most every full I know can't either—the quicker you're allowed to figure that out and deal, the better off this whole damn backass society will be." His face went all radish and his throaty chords went full cacophony. "Our senses weren't meant to be dimmed from the time we're prestuds to fullgrowns, it's kuffing barbaric!"

"Preach, teach!" Cheza yelled, pounding her fist against the table and hooting it up all craze-like.

Linklyn composed himself and gave a quick smirky-smirk. "I guess I shouldn't complain. If they didn't hold you studs down, I'd still be trying to figure out a way through med school." He toweled off his hands, unbolted the door, and held it open for us. "Now I'm sure you're both hot to hit the town and if I don't get nibbed for juicing, I could probably do time just for watching you two fumble around with each other. So go do whatever feels good, but do it somewhere else," he said. "You're welcome."

Me and Cheza stepped out into the alley, sky-high and ready to fly, in a new world of pungent, pulsing miracles. Cheza closed her hand over mine and we crept out into the streetway. I pressed my feets against the hard hard sidewalk and we set off. Her fingers were painfully tight around mine, but I didn't care—it was good to feel anything this much.

"Where are we going?" I asked.

"A funhouse," she said and she towed me along until we came upon a building made up of a long line of tiny rooms, all alike. She credded the guy at the office and he gave Cheza a code key bracelet. We entered the room number marked forty-two and Cheza collapsed onto the bed. "Have you ever felt anything so soft in your whole life?" she said, hugging the pillow. I walked over, sat down next to her, and hugged the other one.

"It *is* pretty amaze."

She wrapped herself inside the bedsilks and rolled around, still clutching the pillow. "This is how everything should feel, Tig. After tonight, you'll never peep the world the same way again."

"Wait," I said suddenly. "How long can we stay like this? They'll find out when they open us up again at school."

"We can stay high through the next grade cycle, right before new score grants come out," she said. "No one at the institute will have any reason to crack us open until then."

"And after that?"

"We just sneak back into the brights and have Linklyn dull us down again. They'll never get the know on us." She got up and glanced out the window, then turned back to me. My orbs were shut and my nog hung low. "What's the matter?" she said. "You're not having second thoughts, are you?"

"No, it's not that. It's just-"

"You don't want this? Just say it, Tig."

"I don't want-"

"What? What don't you want?"

"I don't want..." My chords got all strainy. "I don't want to ever go back to the way it used to be. I want tonight, forever."

Her face lit lit up and she went all octopus on me, wrapping me in her arms. "I had a feeling about you, Tig Fynch, right from the jumpy I did."

Then she kissed me, for the second time.

My whole body swelled with an energy I never knew existed inside me. I immediately took hold of her. I didn't have a choice, really. It was like I was on auto or something. We eased ourselves down onto the silkies and our hands went a-roamin'. Sometimes she'd take my hands and put them where she needed them to be and, wouldn't you know it, wherever she needed my hands to be was exactly where I needed them to be too. That can't be coincidence. I figured out that up until that night I was six-under, searching for a way out. Now I had the know.

Cheza was my way.

The moments that passed inside that room were a soul nourishment that stretch out to me still, to this very. We left the funhouse not a whole lot of minis later and even though we'd go on to trip the light fantastico that night, nothing would ever stick to my skull matter the way that bitty time I spent with Cheza Gregory in an empty room did.

And I think that's how it's supposed to be.

*

"What then, Tig? We needs the deets! Don't go skimpy now!" Pooch says. But the duty sensor's got a sneak-eye on me so I ease back down onto my chair, lips tight tight. The message gets through and one-by-one each stud loses their eager orbs and drops down into their seats. Alfa *shoo*s a few of the younger, lingering understuds away and we sit in deady silence, just chewing and swallowing. I can read it in every slow up-and-down chomp of their jaws; they're in agony. They want the know, and they want it now.

Patience, studs, it's coming.

The duty sensor's real diligent. He must be able to smell some of that forbidden fruit that I've been giving up the know on wafting over from our table, so he just satellites us. We keep our keels even though, biding and biding, when a foodstuff dispense luckily goes gonzo and demands his attention. He leaves and I start back in on my tale.

"After the funhouse Cheza and me hit the streets. We covered the sidewalks, the frontwalks, the backwalks, and all the walks in between. We saw all the sees, heard all the hears, and ate every eat we could." I lick my lips to great-o effect. "We ate and ate. We ate our way through that whole place." Every stud listens to my tell and they hoot it up and nudge each other so much you'd think they'd lived in my skins and done it all themselves. "We credded every vendo we came across and they'd play their blows and six-stringers so sweet-like that if it wasn't called music they'd have to call it candy. You've never heard notes like these, studs, best believe. We hopped the gate at the natural, simmed a few adventure times, and watched a tale at the cineblast. We were everywhere that night!"

"Did you meet anyone else from The Resistance?" Alfa asks me. "Is it for really real?"

"We didn't peep anyone else besides Link, but The Riz is real, alright. Real as cornmeal. The writing's on the wall," I tell him.

"What do you mean?"

"I mean there was actual writing... on an actual wall. I peeped it with my own two: **GOD GIVETH, MAN TAKETH AWAY; MY BODY, MY RIGHT; FREE THE FIVE.** Stuff like that. It was all over the place. Cheza was right, something's happening."

Alfa sits back all slow in his chair, a far-off look in his orbs. "Well, go on then, tell it some more."

I pause for a quicky thought. They should have the know on all things, I suppose.

*

Before we knew it the sun was threatening to rise up and glow all over our parade. It was time to get back to Fairchild quickfast.

"How was it tonight? I mean, with me?" I asked her. I had to have the

189

know. "Any regrets?"

Cheza touched my face. "It doesn't matter *how* you were, Tig. It only matters *that* you were, if that makes any sense to you." She took my hand and we began the trek back to Fairchild. "But you did real fine, stud." We reached the polyfence and the branches, like outstretched arms, of the lantillo tree. Cheza waved her hand out in front of her for the narrow-rope. She cursed to herself, put her hands on her hips, and peeped again. "It's gone," she said. "How could it-"

Light exploded everywhere.

"This is the Truancy Force," we heard them tell us on their megasounders. Those tru-blues on their glide-bikes shot up through the trees and hovered over us, fall guns drawn. More bikes. They fanned out and flanked us. I wanted to run, I did, but there was no kuffing place to go—they were everyplace. Cheza made a break, but the tru-blues corralled us both into a tight circle and threw out their shocknets. A ticktock later, they were on top of us like a bunch of Buzz Killjoys.

*

This new high sight of mine was really something. I was so so tired, but the early morn sun seemed to burrow through my lids right down to my orbs. I couldn't get a wink if I tried (and I *did* try). Cheza and I were in the back of a transport sandwiched between a pair of helmeted tru-blues. Cull was in front of us with another sensor I didn't recognize piloting the tranny. We zoomed around awhile until the cramped streets widened and the tall buildings shortened and there was nothing left outside the window but grassy grass and sky.

I opened my orbs a squint and whispered to Cheza, "What are they going to do with us?" Cull threw me a harsh stare and gave one of the tru-blues a bitty nod. The officer swatted me across my cheek with his dummy club and my jaw locked up. The pain was ferocious-like; I'd never felt anything to match it. *Oh, to be a blanket again!* I peeped Cheza. The Mighty Cheza. She was all sobbys and whimpers.

"It's the treatment," she mouthed. "The age treatment."

My insides went freefall. I wasn't savvy to the pertinents of the age treatment. Who was? But by the look on Cheza's face, it was all no good. When we finally stopped, a large orange-and-black building was stretched out over the land in front of us, emitting a purr, like a slumbery tiger. I could hear the echo of waves slapping against rock in the distance. The tru-blues pushed us forward and Cheza and I shuffled to the doorway in our magbonds. We were met inside by more tru-blues and an odor all rancy and rank. Hear me now, bestbros, I couldn't accurately describe it to you, but if I could, you wouldn't want me to. Even the description would make you go all gaggy.

Cull and the other sensor, an olden with empty orbs, escorted us down a long strip of floor to a collection of dark, frothy pools. Fear-frozen, I was.

They held me there while Cull told the tru-blues to deactivate Cheza's bonds and walk her out to the edge of the far far pool.

"I'm at least partially to blame for this, Ms. Gregory," the sensor said. "I warned you many times—too many times I'm afraid—because I can see now that they were nothing more than empty threats to you." He stood beside the olden sensor. "I've always been quite fond of you. We all were. You can't say we haven't been fair."

"Sure I can. *You haven't been fair.*" She stood with her arms real akimbo-like and gave that relic a saucy grin. "See, I said it," she said. This femmy had some iron in her.

Cull bowed his noggin. "That's our Cheza, defiant to the last. Your *resistance* is obvious, Study Gregory. What do you think your father would say if he were here?"

She shrugged. "He'd understand."

Cull pointed to me. "And will this boy's fulls understand as well? Will they be as forgiving? Perhaps you'd like to explain it to them—explain how you've corrupted their son, recruited him to join the ranks of your fellow delinquents."

"I wasn't recruiting anyone," she said. "I like him."

"Of course you do, you've liked them all I'm sure."

"No, he's not like the others."

"So, you admit there *have* been others?"

Cheza stammered. "It's different with Tig." She peeped back at me. "I mean it, it's different. *You're* different to me, Tig Fynch, and I'm different when I'm with you. You can feel it too, can't you?"

The tru-blue yanked her noggin forward.

"I'm sure you made them all believe they were special, Ms. Gregory. That's one of the keys to the indoctrination into The Resistance, isn't it?"

Her face started waterfalling, the wetdrops running down her cheeks. "You don't know what you're talking about! I wasn't hurting no one, I just wanted some goodfun."

Then Cull opened his arms. He approached the femmy and, would you believe it, she fell right into them. She started hugging that olden tight tight and weeping her little orbs out.

"There there now, that's not how relationships work, girl," he told her. He exchanged a somber glance with the other sensor. "I'm afraid that's not how Fairchild works either."

Cull lifted his arms high high and let those tru-blues snatch up Cheza and throw her into the pool. Her body sank beneath that mirror of dark liquid and I could feel my inners go to jelly. I tried to wriggle free from my mags, but it was useless. I was frantic. I scanned the cavernous room. Signs of a size that would've only been a blur to me before now jumped out to my new orbs: the shock reds, yellows, the iridescent oranges, and a large outline in the shape of a fish. *A fish?* Yeah, it was a fish—a fish curled around all circly with the words 'BioFresh Systems' printed on it. There were other words, other signs. So many. Cheza was still in the pool, all desperate and flailing and gurgly with black water. I kept searching for something in the messages on the wall. The Age Treatment. *What does it mean? Where are the words?*

Age Treatment

There they are! I peep them.

Age Treatment Facility

No, no, there's more...

SEWAGE TREATMENT FACILITY

And there you have it, folks.
Cull peeped while I dropped to my knees.

"There are drawbacks to being fully-sensed, Study Fynch," the olden devil said. "Not all the tastes life has to offer you are pleasurable ones."

Cheza's fingers groped the pavement for something—*anything*—to cling to. She reached her hand out of that wetfilth and hung on to the outside of the pool. All calm-like, Cull stepped to the edge and eased the femmy's fingers back into the murk with the toe of his boot, leaving only some dusty residue from her nails written on the concrete like a kiddie's chalk drawing. "Last night with your new senses you stole some fine experiences. Today, you suffer an ill one," he said.

*

Gaspy gasps. Slacky jaws and swapped expressions of terror. The table is silent.

"You studs wanted the know," I say. "That's all the know I got."

Alfa exhales a long breath and leans back in his chair. "Did you-"

"No, they never gave me the treatment, just Cheza."

"Jesus in January, Tig, what happened to her?"

"They scooped her out of the pool eventually, but only after they were sure her senses were on crud overload. Then they brought us back to Fairchild. She didn't say a singly word to me the whole way back. They dropped her off at the east arm. I can still peep her walking away, that blank look in her orbs. Nah, not blank, more like... broken." I tell them. "Toi met Cheza at the door with a buzz wand and took her down. The instant the wand touched the back of her neck she went jelly and folded to the blacktop. The sensors lifted her up and dragged her inside. I don't have the know on what else they did to her, don't think I want it either. I never saw Cheza again." I clear my throat. "Then Toi came over to the tranny and buzzed me, too. Don't remember much after that. I got dumped into sensory confines and shipped here."

One by one, the studs come over to give me some respects. Some offer a strong strong look, a chinny nod, or an awkward smiley. Others place their hand on my arm or my shoulder and give a real squeeze to be sure I can get the feels. It's what I imagine a funeral must be like.

Alfa wipes his babe-blue orbs. "That's a true-on wicked tale."

"I'm afraid to say it's still being spun. I'm seeing the Council of Sensors after this to beg beg for mercy. They're waiting outside now to take me."

"Femmys, man," he says, shaking his noggin. "They can talk you into the worst sitches. Will we see you again, bestbro?"

I force a smiley. "Give Pooch the know that I'm sorry for the pummeling," I say, then I walk out of the nosh house and into a set of waiting magbonds.

*

Sensor Cull calls me into his office and offers me a sit. I slink down into the chair. "All thanks, sir."

"No sense in mincing words, Fynch. Let's get right down to it." He reaches into his robe for a joystick, taps it out on his desk, and lights it. "You've made some regrettable choices, there's no denying it, but the school feels that Study Gregory is the real rot in the wood here. That she took advantage of a naive understud and manipulated him for her own subversive needs is, frankly, appalling. She was more brazen with you, but you weren't her first." He takes a drag off the joystick and sets it in a tray on his desk. "And you wouldn't have been her last."

My melon's all choly and it droops between my shoulder blades real sad sad.

"Your quartersmate, Ralen, was concerned for your well-being and, rightly, tipped us off to your nocturnal rendezvous with Ms. Gregory. If I can speak plainly, Fynch, she bewitched you, deceived you, and ultimately cost you dearly, understand?" He leans over the desk and pats me on my noggin. "I'd like to know where your mind's at right now. It may have an impact on how we treat your case."

"I'm embarrassed more than anything, sensor, a bitty angry too," I tell him. "I guess she used me, made me think she cared and now I just feel stump-dumb for buying into it. I mean, Cheza Gregory with me?" I make a loud snorting sound. "It's even more craze when I hear it out loud."

He nods his nog "Every revolution needs its foot soldiers and Cheza knows that. She would've told you whatever she thought you needed to hear to get you onboard. None of it was true, I'm afraid."

"Yeah, it's so obvs to me now."

Cull sits back in his chair with his palms together. He leans his chin against his outstretched fingers. "Tig, I'll be very blunt with you, this next part is important to us. It's important for you, too."

"What is it?"

"We need to know who on the outside juiced you. We're aware that there may have been an agent for The Resistance who managed to infiltrate the school. We need to know who this person is."

I go all squirmy in my seat for a ticktock. "I got real unease about it," I say. "They seem like a good person. I don't think they means anyone harm."

"I know you do, but this *good* person is a large piece to an even larger problem and if you can give us a name it'll reflect very positively on our opinion of you. Forgiveness is one thing we believe in here at Fairchild, but it has a price. Telling me right now who sensed you up would go a long way toward paying that price." He leans forward in his chair "What would you say if I told you we were willing to restore you to your previous sense levels, bypass any other punishments, and let you return to Fairchild? Wipe your whole slate clean."

I don't answer him immediately. I can only stare at the wall of his office, at the blurred letters on the diplomas hanging there, thinking how much better twos-and-two would be right about now.

"Is your aid turned up? Can you hear me? I'm throwing you a rope here, son. I suggest you grab onto it."

I go all clam on him, drape my hands over my face and ease them down my chin. "It was Linklyn," I say. "The guy who's training to take over as school's headman. He's the one who got us high."

Cull nods his nog repeatedly. "You want that second chance, don't you, Fynch?"

I exhale and a nervous teehee escapes my lips. "Yes," I tell him. "God, yes."

"Well, I'm giving it to you."

"O-kee-dee, all thanks, all thanks, Sensor Cull! I'll prove myself. I'll be a good stud, I swear. I just want everything to go back to the used-to-be-way."

He pulls another long drag from the joystick. "I'm thrilled to hear you say it. Of course we can't let you return to eastwing. Too much talk going on there as it is. You'll have to transfer permanently to the south arm of school. But I've been told you're already making friendly with the studs there."

"I am, they've been trés nice to me, sir."

"Perfect then," he says before his voice suddenly gets grave. "I don't think I have to tell you this, but if you stray from the path again, we'll have to come down on you…" He squints at me. "Extremely hard."

"No worries about that, no sir."

"It would please me greatly not to hear your name uttered for the remainder of your time here at Fairchild." He reaches over and gives me a pat all chummy-chum-like. "Some stud's names aren't really meant to be heard anyway, are they? Better to blend into the crowd than stick out for the wrong reasons," he said. "We understand each other then?"

"Clear and crystally, sir."

He grinds out his joystick and slides the remnant inside the sleeve of his robe. "Do you have any questions?"

I hesitate. "Don't read anything into this," I tell him. "But if you don't mind me asking, what happened to Cheza?"

He leans back in his chair real thoughtful and then breaks out with the, "I suppose there's no harm in telling you." line.

O-kee-dee, let's hear it.

"Ms. Gregory has been expelled from Fairchild. With her father's ample cred and her own natural aptitude some other school will no doubt take her on. She's not our problem anymore, or yours. I suggest you banish her from your thoughts, Study Fynch, it does you no good to dwell on her." He turns away and begins to tap tap at his keypad. "See yourself out, if you would. I'll have your records sent over to southwing. Headman Grigson will be awaiting you there to lift your senses."

"All thanks again for the chance, sir."

"Make it count this time and you won't be at twos-and-two for long. Every good stud comes to their senses eventually, Fynch."

"I know they do."

*

"How's it feel to be out of sensory confines?" Alfa catches me in the hallway between lessons.

"Twos-and-two isn't much," I tell him while we walk, "But it's better than being down the hole, that's for sure."

"You'll fit in just fine with me and my bestbros, none of us pull high marks either. You should feel right at home. And they've already taken a shiny-shine to you."

"Even Pooch?"

"Pooch won't have no beefy grudges if I tell him you're with us," he says. "We're getting together in my quarters around nineteen hundy tonight. You should come, it'll be funtimes."

"Yeah, sure, sounds golden," I tell him.

"Great-o." He smacks my arm. "You're clan now, Tigger," he says. "Remember, tonight, my quarters, number eleven-oh-four. We'll rowdy until nightlocks, o-kee-dee? See ya when I do."

"See ya," I tell him back. He pushes through the studs ahead of me and ducks into his class.

A smiley crawls across my face.

That night we rowdied at Alfa's and his bestbros all welcomed me with the openest arms. Even Pooch. I have to admit they're not a bad bunch of studs. They're dim like me, but they've got hungry ears so they love love my tales about that night I spent in the brights. In a few cycles, if they stay on the straight, they'll all graduate to full-sense and get the know for themselves. I keep telling them that, but it's almost like they don't believe me. I'll get there too, in time. It's autumn and things are a-changing all around me.

*

The semester rolls on like some kind of unstoppable machinery. Sensor Cull is a non-entity in my life, which is perfecto with me seeing as I'm studenta non grata to him, too. So it seems as if he's staying true-word about letting me go on with my studies without having sneak-eyes on me every mini of the day. That fall I half-thought that some word about Cheza would leak down to southwing, but I didn't hear a squeak. It's probably better for me that way anyhow. Ding-dong that witch is gone—who gives a figgy if I never get the chance to tell her off to her lying face. She's erased to me.

The calendar hits December and midwinter lacuna is upon us. Every stud is thankful for the freedays, but mostly we're looking forward to the upcoming sense boosts that accompany the handing out of last cycle's marks. I did o-kee-dee, I'll get my yoosh—a micro numbers jump.

Every stud's fulls get to visit Fairchild during lacuna. We aren't ever allowed to leave the institute's sense-protective care so my fulls, like most other studs', come to visit if they can. I haven't really spoken to them much since "the incident". Fairchild contacted them about it (shocker!) and set up a window for all of us to have a remote-style chit-chat, but I squashed the whole iddy. Not gonna be able to avoid it this go, though.

And peep on this: my new quartersmate's name is Ferdobern Taicin. Is that a proper moniker or what? He's a couple cycles newer than me and because of it we don't have a whole hellava of a lot in com but, all thingys considered, he's a good little pup. Trés respectful. He insists on me having the place all to myself that afternoon to entertain my fulls because his mom and dad leave that morn.

All thanks, Ferdy.

My fulls arrive, to my great not surprise, supes-early.

"Can you hear us, Tig? We're ringing the bell—are you in there?"

I swing the door and let them in. "Yes, I can hear you," I tell them. "My nums are back on norm. They have been for a long time now, you know that." I open my arms. "Happy greets to you, my fulls!" I can tell my mom, nogtop on her skull, wants to do the old squeeze-and-hold with me, but she's holding back today. She's trying desperately to keep that dourpuss stretched across her face. Dad's sporting his own domeware and the paternal version of the puss.

Unbelievable. Did they practice these faces in front of each other before they left the house?

"Could you at least step inside before you start with the frownies?"

"What's there to be smiley about?" Dad says.

"Well, it's a beauteous freeday and I got rid of the sleepys and you're both here for the first time in a multi and I'm staying out of trouble and it's a beauteous freeday and can we not talk about this right now guys? If I'm being real truthy, I'd just like to forget the whole thingy and I can't if you two only came here to beat a stud down. It's a new life for me and I just want to try try again. Can we do that? Can I just move on?"

My mother goes from zero-to-slobbery in about half a ticktock. "Of course we can, sweetie. We forgive you," she says, pulling me to her mombosom while my father grumbles something about babying. "Now that they've shipped that awful girl far away from here things can get back to normal for you."

"Well, I hope you learned your lesson," Dad says. "At least that way something good can come out of this whole mess."

I nod like the dutiful son. It seems to appease them and I true true am happy they feel better. I never meant to hurt them, really. We spend the rest of that beauteous freeday talking and lunching. They give me the know on the goings-on back home.

Life is good again.

But while I'm talking, I notice they both wear this real craze look. I can't explain it, but it feels like they see me different-like now. I remember thinking how I wish I could wipe that look off their faces and give them their old ones back. I wish I could be all innocent again, if only for their sakes.

But you can't unbreak an egg, and cracks can't be uncracked. There's some wisdom-words for ya. Outside, the snowflakes are dancing around in big swirly-swirls until they settle on the ground. When it's this so so cold, it's hard to imagine it'll ever be spring again, but it will be.

It will.

*

"Just let me see it and I'll never ask again," Alfa says while he trudges through some prickys.

"I don't like being out here," I tell him. I brush aside one of the aspen's pale branches. "If they find me back in the west grove I'm totally kuffed. You know that."

"Don't get all inside-out on me, Tig. It's a sunshiny day, the ice is melted—we're allowed to take a walk as long as we stay on the grounds. It's not suspy at all."

"O-kee-dee, I'll show it to you, but then we ghost this place, and don't even think about going up."

"You think I'm manic or something? After all the tales you tell, I just want to see it with my own two." I stare down at a twig with a few round aspen leaves attached to it. He begs me again, "Show me the lantillo."

I get, I really do. That whale tale I fed them is a pretty ripe fish to swallow whole. A little too hard without at least *some* proof. Alfa's been top-notch to me this whole cycle so I suppose if I owe anything to anyone, I owe it to him. After about ten minis in the grove, we're at the polyfence.

"Here it is," I say, pointing out a stained tree stump. "Or should I say, here it was."

"What's with the paint?"

"It's not paint," I tell him. "It's called dolorjuice—it kills the tree after it's been cut. Should've known they'd poison it." I clap my hands once. "That's it, you've seen it. Right where I told you it would be. Can we skidaddy now?" Alfa begins to pace. "What's wrong with you?" I ask him.

"Tig, I haven't been full-truthy with you." Far off in the distance I detect a sound, born just at the edge of my perception, and with each tick and tock it grows louder—an unmistakable *whirr*. "I always believed your tale, believed it all the way," he says.

My voice is low and troubled. "What did you do?"

"I just had to get you here, to this spot," he says. "They promised they'd let me in."

The sound of a motor rises. Alfa listens as the wind and the whirr washes over him. "D'ya hear that? They came, just like they said."

A pair of tru-blue gliders, a singly and a two-seater, shoot across the sky above our noggins, double back, and yo-yo down to the forest floor. It's an eerily familiar vid in my nog and it gives me the shivs. The pilots kill their engines and they both step ginger-like off the bikes and come up on me. One of them lifts off their dark helmet.

"Cheza?"

"Miss me?" she asks. She's ditched the long, raven holo in favor of a short coif of the *au naturel*-ist kind. Real, mousy-brown locks all over her nog. It's a nice fuzz on her. I want to answer the femmy, but the words won't come. Headwoman Toi takes off her helmet next.

"I believe we've already met," she says. "Good to see your face again, Study Fynch."

I stammer a partial response.

"How did you…"

"Ever play chess?" Cheza says, smoothing out her jumpsuit with her palms. "To be good at it—and I mean *really* good—you gotta be thinking three moves ahead."

"O-kee-dee," I say. "But I still don't get how-"

"Madelyn here," She motions to the olden beside her. "I mean *Headwoman Toi*, never dulled me into solitary confines—that was just a way to buy us time. You didn't think I'd let you get away from me that easily, did ya?"

"You did this?" I ask the Headwoman. Toi nods.

The two femmys leap up and straddle the gliders again. "Who do you think connected me up with Linklyn?" Cheza says. "Toi's been resistance for years. Now get on before we're made." She starts her engine and inches the bike closer to me.

"I gave Linklyn up," I tell her. "To get my life back, I had to."

The femmys peep at each other a ticktock, then turn back to me. "We know," Toi says. "Don't worry about that now."

"What about me?" Alfa hollers over the hum of the magdrives. "You told me I could be one of The Riz."

"That's right-o," Cheza says. "But your work at Fairchild ain't done yet, stud."

"It's not?"

"The Resistance needs more than just a few trees," Toi tells him. "We need a whole forest. And when you need to grow a forest, what do you do?"

Alfa shakes his nog.

"You plant seeds," she says. "Lots and lots of seeds." She points to the ground beneath his feets. Alfa bends over, wipes some dead leaves aside, and picks up one of the lantillo seedpods that encircle the stump.

"Get to planting, Johnny Alfa-seed," Cheza says before she turns her big, doe-eyes back to me. "Tig, get on, you're ruining the ending."

My feets shuffle back slowly. "I'm not going with you, Cheza. I just got my shizz straight. My life's a rose again after you kuffed it all up for me."

"Pffft, what life was that?"

"I'm up to threes-and-one!" I tell her. "I'll come to my senses in five cycles if I stick."

"Or you can jump on the bike and leave now, with me."

"But I hate you," I say.

Cheza flashes me a frowny puss. "Aw, you don't mean that, not really, Tig."

"Forget it, it's no use trying to darkside me, I'm not joining the dumdum Resistance with you."

"Then don't join," she says. "Just get on the bike."

"They'll follow us," I tell her.

"Yep."

"If they find us, it's the treatment. I watched you go into that sewage—that was really real. Why would you risk it?"

The glider's idling engine threatens to drown out our voices. She jumps off and grabs me by my collar. "I'd risk being thrown into a vat of shizz a hundred times over for the chance to feel the way I did with you that night!" she says to me.

I give her the squint-eye. "What about all those other studs—just recruits for the cause like me? Where are they now?"

"No iddy at all," she says. "I don't keep tabs on their wheres-and-whens. What's that tell you about them, and what they were to me?"

I shake my noggin all feverish and start pacing the grove. "Nah, nah, I've made my promises. Why are you doing this to me?"

Cheza takes my hands in hers. "Listen, that was my whole pitch, Tig. I got nothing else to sell ya with... except you and me," she says. She points to her wrist. "Tick tock, stud, tick tock."

I turn to Toi. "What happens if I go with you two?"

She shrugs. "Some things you don't always get the know on, kiddo."

I hear a hundred voices in my nog, all telling me what to do. But I know they all stop talking to me once she's gone. Once Cheza rides off, it's finito for good this time.

She climbs back onto her seat and revs the engine. The bike gives a squeal before it bucks just off the forest floor and hovers there.

"What are you gonna do, Tig?"

*

Welp, I've reached the tail of my tale and what's left to say? Oh, I get, you want the know on whether I climbed up onto the back of that glide-bike or not. Now, if I told you I joined The Resistance and did the happily ever after with Cheza you'd buy that romantical shizz, wouldn't you? That'd be a sensible resolution to my epic coming-of-ager.

But what if I told you that it doesn't matter?

Not really.

Hey, bestbro, I know that you like me. I can tell you care. Just have the know that I'm happy happy with the choice I made. So, you don't have to worry about Tig. If you have the know on that, then does it make a biggy diff what I did?

How about you decide instead? Whatever provides you with the most joy-like ending. I'm mirthy when you're mirthy, after all.

What? Not enough?

Well then let me pose this scenario to you: You just cellied your sixteenth annibirthary not too too long ago and you're at threes-and-one when the femmy in the raven holo shows back up to turn your whole kuffing world turvy-topsy. What would you do?

Yeah... me too.

This began as an exercise in flash-fiction and morphed into poetry. I use the term poetry very loosely as I am anything but a poet. That said, I did want to infuse my words with a consistent rhyme scheme and give it a flow. I set up some rules for myself and that gave the piece its form. Once finished, I liked Metal With Me *enough to send it out. To my great surprise the Irish magazine Ballista as well as the U.S.'s own Kaleidotrope liked it too. Being chronically impatient I submitted to them simultaneously and it was accepted by both publications. I then faced the unenviable task of emailing Ballista, declining the honor of appearing in their magazine, and fessing up to my indiscretion. They were far kinder to me than I deserved.*

The idea for the piece arose from the numerous doctor and hospital visits I was forced to make when my father's health was failing near the end of his life. It seemed like they were swapping out so many parts inside him that I wondered what the effect of all this might have on one's soul. I mean, what happens to you when you're more man-made than you are man? Metal With Me *first appeared in the magazine Kaleidotrope.*

Metal With Me

The day of my birth, amidst all the mirth,
I came down with a touch of bronchitis.
I would bawl and I'd choke,
A metal snake down my throat,
Felt alien, and I did not like this!

When I was eight, my life was great,
Then I went for my very first filling
Mama said, "You'll grow richer,
With a tooth sown in silver."
But, alas, it was not worth the drilling.

When I was eleven, my life was pure heaven,
'Til I fractured myself playing ball.
Took a stainless steel peg,
To make me a new leg.
Hardly noticed the difference at all.

When I was eighteen, my life was a dream,
Then to war, at my country's behest.
Caught an assload of shrapnel,
Tantalum plates my back skull,
Even more metal pinned to my chest.

At age twenty-nine, my life was just fine,

Metal With Me

When I crashed driving home on the sauce.
Nickel pins were affixed,
To my ankles and wrists,
To keep them from all falling off.

In my thirties and forties, I tired with more ease,
Iron pills kept my blood count from ruin.
Doc claimed me irrational, but
Eating metal's unnatural.
After dinner you don't swallow the spoon!

At age fifty-five, I was still alive,
A pacemaker plugged in to my heart.
If I clutched my chest wailing,
Nature's battery failing,
It would give me an instant jumpstart.

I was still a spry pip, when I got a new hip,
Took a tumble while visiting my brother.
But at just sixty-three,
Said it wouldn't slow me.
Fell at seventy and they replaced the other.

By eighty, I was weighty, trunk and limbs did betray me,
Pelvis, too, aluminum due to failure.
I looked like a gilt knight,
In King Arthur's high sight,
Sir Breaks-A-Lot with titanium genitalia.

When I turned ninety-four, swore there could be no more,
To be done for my life to prolong.
Then they swapped out my head,
For an alloy instead.
What can I say? I guess I was wrong.

Now I'm two-hundred one, my days finally done
Oil anoints the metal Almighty.
But nanobots are inclined,
To evict my strange mind.
Now I'm the alien, and my body doesn't like me.

This is a weird one (aren't they all). One day I'm listening to Neil deGrasse Tyson talk about the feasibility of interstellar travel via "solar sails" and I decide to do some research on the idea. That leads me down the internet rabbit hole for hours (pretty par for the course for me, actually). It gets me thinking about the likeliest destination of a manned interstellar voyage and, of course, I come up with our nearest star system, Alpha Centauri (or Rigel Kentaurus, the 'foot of the centaur', as it's also known). That's where I get my start.

As I'm writing, the story starts to take the shape of a very early piece I'd written some twenty years prior. Apparently, I subconsciously felt I needed to revisit it. Go figure. From there the plot morphs into something wholly unforeseen yet very familiar to myself and many millions of other fantasy readers worldwide I'm sure (I wonder if you'll recognize it.) It's a little bit Isaac Asimov mixed with Douglas Adams. That's how it goes sometimes: I start off writing one thing, then it turns into something else, and by the end it looks nothing like my original vision, but I'm still very oddly satisfied with it. That's writing for you.

The Arcadian Nights of Rigel Kent

Their photon sails having been stretched open for years, the fleet captured each speck of light in the dense tapestry of the cosmos and converted it into usable power. These supermassive miracles of science, reflective sheets of highly-durable aluminized material, were no thicker than a single red blood cell. Billowing, concave marvels dreamt up and developed by the eager astrophysicist minds back on Earth, they propelled some fifty-thousand souls on their interstellar crossing. A silent, gliding armada of colossal Japanese sedge hats, each attached to its own globular ship by wires that fanned out like a spider's web. They pushed the settlers a percentage of light-speed toward Proxima Centauri b. Their new home. Humanity's new home.

Or so they hoped.

"It's surreal," HeHarald told his wife in their cramped bathroom. "We've been waiting half our lives for this. I hardly remember what it's like not being in this tin can. I don't know what a real world even feels like anymore, at least not one that isn't a simulation. Grass, dirt, sky, it'll probably all feel weirdly artificial to me."

"At first, maybe, but I bet it'll all come back to us." SheZahda was looking at herself in the mirror and drumming her thigh with her hand. "I'm trying not to expect too much. I know this isn't gonna be a lot like home." She began to comb her fingers through a head of cropped hair, mostly the shade of rust, streaked with shoots of dull silver. "But why shouldn't I get my hopes up? I mean Proxima's right in the Goldilocks

zone and-" She stopped. "No, no, no, don't do that to yourself, Zahdy."
The woman inhaled deeply and pulled the top of her pajamas on. "I
promised myself I wouldn't build the place up, just in case it's not..."

"Shhhhh," HeHarald said as he placed a finger over her lips.

SheZahda seemed to instantly become calm. "I'm just excited to
finally step out of this floating prison... nervous, too."

"So am I," HeHarald said.

She continued to swipe at her hair in the mirror. "Proxima b is such
a terrible name for a planet, don't you think? What was wrong with Rigel
Kent? That sounds very homey, very... hospitable," she said. "God, I
hope it's as livable as we think. What if we get there, it's a disaster, and
we have to turn right around and go back to Earth?" She shook her head.
"Twenty more years in a can, I don't think I can do it, Harry. That's
twenty more years gone."

HeHarald carefully placed his toothbrush down onto the sink and
touched his wife's cheek. Her honey-colored eyes locked onto his. "I
know you're worried. I am too. But this is not helping, dear," he said.

"But what if-"

"We'll jump off that bridge when we get to it." He pulled her into
his chest and held her lean frame in his hands. "*If* we get to it."

"You're right, Harry, as usual. You're always right," she said. "It's
pretty annoying actually." She gave him a half-hearted smile and returned
to play with her hair that hadn't changed dramatically in the fifteen
minutes since she'd started playing with it. She smiled. "I hate you,
Harry."

"Hate you too, dear," he said to her reflection.

"It *is* exciting though."

"That it is." HeHarald inhaled deeply, lifted himself from off the
toilet, and squeezed behind her to exit the bathroom. "Now let's get
some sleep so we can be down at the observation decks bright and early.
I don't want to miss a thing tomorrow."

"I'll be ready," she said, following him out. She tapped the light off,
slid in next to him under the bed sheet, and draped her arm up and over
his broad shoulder. "Do you think the others back on Earth will come
here eventually? Will we be like a version of the pilgrims or something?
Space pilgrims?"

He rolled over to face her. "Well, they convinced us to sign up. I
think if Proxima b is even close to what we hope it'll be, it won't be too
hard to convince the rest."

She shifted onto her back and stared at the ceiling. "Half the people
on The Mayflower didn't even survive that first winter, y'know."

"But half of them did," HeHarald said. "Try not to get too cynical,
honey. They've prepared us for every eventuality, brought everyone we'll

need, all walks of life. It's not just the scientists and engineers and biologists. We've got all kinds of regular folks like us—worker bees. Have faith it'll be enough. Right now, in this moment, life is rich with possibility. Let's just hold onto that feeling for as long as we can, okay? Worrying about a thing never did much anyway."

Her answer was a terse *uh-huh*.

"Baby, I'm not saying we should close our eyes to reality but so far, they've been dead-on about everything. There's no reason to believe Proxima b's going to be any different than we've been told. They wouldn't have sent us all this way-"

"Gotcha, positive thoughts," she said. "Sorry if I'm being a downer."

He stroked her head. "You're not. You're just being cautious, careful, questioning Zahdy, and I love that. I always have. We'll be ready for anything this trip throws at us."

A smile crept across SheZahda's face. "Okay, I believe you."

"Good," HeHarald said before promptly turning his back and chuckling. "Now go to sleep already."

The sleep cycle ended and everyone awoke well before the solar sail arrived at the Proxima Centauri system. The star itself was a glowing ember ball hanging in front of the fleet and the commandants of each orb ship coordinated their crews to make an approach, skimming by the exoplanets that could sustain life. Not much was known about the star system other than the meager tidbits that could be gleaned from images captured by earthly telescopes. They were reading tea leaves mostly: decoding colors to determine the elements that made up this world and if they were conducive to life, calculating its stellar flux, monitoring solar flare activity, determining acceptable ranges for a great many factors. Once it was ascertained that Proxima b had a good chance of housing water and an atmosphere, and that tidal locking so often a problem on red dwarf systems was no longer a concern, they made their plans to depart. They had done all the diligence. Checked and rechecked the data. If there was a time to leave, they thought this was it.

That was so, so many years ago.

HeHarald and SheZahda heard their commandant's voice ring out over the intraspeakers of their orb and they joined with the rest of the crew, gathering at the enormous windows of the observation deck to get their first real glimpse at the star Proxima Centauri and their new home, God willing, Proxima b. All the sail ships in the great astral fleet had slowed for the approach to the system and the assembled travelers put on their eye shields to view the star.

"It's unreal," SheZahda said to her husband. "Not at all like I pictured it."

"Magnificent."

Soon Proxima b came into sharp focus. It had that familiar, cloudy-blue-marble look of Earth, even if the shapes and features of its surface were totally unrecognizable. There were audible gasps as the orbs crept ever closer and the exoplanet grew larger and larger in the viewing monitor. HeHarald's entire body was tremulant with joy. He grabbed his wife's hand and held on tightly.

"I cannot believe this, Zahdy. I'll be damned if that doesn't look like another Earth."

The sails folded in upon themselves in an orderly manner, slowly disappearing until there was nothing left and the orbs could begin their descent into Proxima b's atmosphere. The people watched the monitor as the dark of space gave way to a white-hot slide into the clouds, like the orb ships themselves were so many fiery pebbles being thrown into a cosmic ocean only to emerge safely on the other side. For the first time since they'd left Earth all that time ago there was no curtain of night in front of them with pinholes of stars and galaxies forever away. There was only a lush green spread out everywhere on the land beneath them, bordered by great foamy seas. Euphoric shrieks filled the orb and the closer they came to making planetfall, the more and more like an Eden this place seemed.

"Will you look at that, it's like we never left."

"It sure is something," HeHarald said, ogling the picture within the window.

The orbs touched down on a grassy plain hugging a shoreline. Commandant Foley came aboard the intras again and told everyone to sit tight while they surveyed the area. After a long while, and with military escorts leading the way, the orb's hatches unfurled and dropped their stairs, and the people started to spill out onto Proxima b. SheZahda and HeHarald waited at the window for their turn. They watched as their crewmates poured out onto the planet's surface and, one-by-one, removed their helmets and biosuits and began to jump and dance around.

"What am I seeing?" HeHarald asked. "It's like a paradise. We have to get out there!"

"We will, we will. Be patient."

"The first thing I'm gonna do is roll around in that grass."

"I just want to touch it," SheZahda said. "With my own two hands. Just feel it in my fingers."

An armed detail of soldiers stepped forward and addressed the couple. "Are you the Bergs, HeHarald and SheZahda?" a tall, female member of the detail asked.

"Yes," they answered in unison.

"Commandant Foley requests your presence on the bridge."

"Right now?" HeHarald said. "We're about to go outside."

"Now, please."

They were escorted to the front of the orb where Commandant Foley was awaiting them in his dress whites. The detail remained while the man spoke. His voice was sharp and resonant and it shattered the silence of the empty bridge deck.

"Bergs, I'm glad as hell to meet you both." He extended his hand and the pair each took turns shaking it. "Come look at this," he said. He directed them to the bridge's huge window where, outside the ship, they could see people hugging and yelling and playing. "Look at them out there, Mr. and Mrs. Berg, they're happy as damn clams. And why shouldn't they be? This place is a wonder, simply breathtaking, wouldn't you agree?" They nodded their assent. "We've been taking readings and the whole thing checks out. I don't think any of us could've imagined in our wildest dreams that it would be this good," he said. "There's still a lot to do, but this is a great start."

"That's fantastic to hear," HeHarald told him. "What do you need from us? We were just about to head out and join the rest when you sent for us," he said. "So why *did* you send for us, sir?"

Foley stood up straight and tried to sound as official as he could. "The most unusual thing happened as soon as we touched down."

"What's that?" SheZahda said.

"As I was saying, just as our feet hit the ground, we got a communique."

"From Earth?"

"No," the commandant said. "It definitely was *not* from Earth." HeHarald exchanged a curious look with his wife. "It was from... out there." Foley pressed his hand against the viewing window.

"Out there?" SheZahda said.

"A message came through the transcom, we don't even know exactly how, summoning us to come to The Horn.

"*The Horn?*"

"That's right. '*Come to The Horn*' it said. Didn't identify itself, didn't tell us what it wanted or where to find this Horn," Foley said. "We were hoping you might be able to help us shed some light on it. Does any part of this message mean anything to either of you?"

"No, sir," HeHarald told the commandant. "Why would you think we'd know anything about this?"

"Because they asked for you two, by name," he said. "*SheZahda Berg and HeHarald Berg, come to The Horn. That would be lovely.* That's exactly how the message read."

After a long, quiet moment, SheZahda finally spoke, being the only one of the two who could manage to get a word past her lips. "I think I speak for Harry when I say we're both utterly gobsmacked, sir." She looked to HeHarald, who nodded at his wife and then at Commandant Foley. "How could-"

"We don't know," Foley said, shaking his head. "We don't know anything right now. We were praying you might give us some insight on this... fuck, I don't even know what to call it," he said. "You're both quite certain you don't know what this message means?"

"No idea," SheZahda said.

"Or who they are?"

They shrugged. "Not a clue."

Foley rubbed at his hands. "They're highly-advanced, that's clear enough. They have access to our data banks as well—how else could they know your names? And I'm being told that their message is coming through on every flotilla, in every language we have onboard."

"Who did they ask for on the other orbs?" HeHarald said.

"No one else, on any vessel," Foley told them. "For some strange reason, you're it."

"Maybe they think we're in charge?" SheZahda asked. "Some kind of error reading our data?"

"Doubtful," Foley said. "We've tried to get a message of our own back to them in various ways, knowing they have access to our datamesh weave, but we haven't gotten a response. Hell, we still don't even know what this Horn they're talking about is. We've sent up the probe drones to map out the area. Once we get a lay of the land, if there's something out there, we'll see it. But right now, it seems as though they're just waiting."

"For what?"

"My guess?" he said. "They're waiting on you two."

HeHarald began to pace the bridge, walking in small circles. "Was there any indication before this that Proxima b had intelligent life?"

"Never," Foley said. "I'm told it's more than likely they're not from here. Proxima b could just be an outpost for them—a place to meet other advanced species like themselves."

"So, they consider us advanced?" SheZahda said.

"Let's hope you can convince them of that," the commandant said. "In case you weren't scared shitless enough." He gave a weak smile and motioned to the biosuits hanging by the airlock. "Obviously we didn't prep for a first contact situation. We anticipated coming across lifeforms on Proxima b, but nothing close to this."

"Commandant Foley," a male officer's voice broke in on the intraspeaker. "We're getting the preliminaries from the probes," he said. "Look onscreen, about a mile to the west."

The viewing window blackened and flashed to a grid map with the fleet's location and an unnaturally perfect form at the precise location the officer had indicated. A triangular structure, long and lean, in the shape of a horn.

"I think that answers one of our questions," Foley said. "Mr. and Mrs. Berg, we want you to meet with these beings and report back to us immediately." His voice was somehow collegial and harsh at the same time. "I'm not sending you out there alone though." He gestured toward a squad of soldiers who were already suiting up. "These are some of our best, they'll accompany you." The couple signaled their understanding with slight nods. "Proxima b's atmosphere, as you can tell by now, is startlingly normal. The air is seventy-one point four degrees Fahrenheit, pressurized, and sufficiently oxygenated. It reads perfectly safe. We don't know exactly how but we don't understand a whole hell of a lot about much anything at the moment, so we'll have you wear the suits as a precaution. We have some recording devices we'd like you to wear as well." He attached a small pin to each of their uniform's collars. "This will record audio and video. We've also prepared a list of questions we'd like you to ask." He handed SheZahda a small electronic tablet. "Find out as much as you can before…"

"Before what?" she asked.

"Before anything... unexpected happens."

"With all due respect," she said. "If it's unexpected, how are we supposed to know when it's going to happen?"

Foley gave a defeated shrug. "Just get everything you can, don't waste a second. Understood?"

"Understood, sir," the pair said in unison, with HeHarald giving a half-second-late salute. SheZahda forgot the military protocol entirely.

Foley turned and took a few steps before HeHarald stopped him. "Sir, if they're as advanced as we think they are, will any of this—the soldiers, the technology—even matter?"

The commandant turned back. "Everything matters, Berg," he said, then resumed his departure. "Godspeed, both of you. We'll be watching."

The Bergs put on biosuits and joined their entourage at the airlock. They triggered it open and filed out of the outer bay hatch and down the slide stairs. The eight-member party headed due west, leaving their shipmates to gambol in the fields surrounding the orbs. HeHarald and SheZahda couldn't tell if anyone even noticed them leaving.

"Do you think they'll let everyone know what's going on?" SheZahda asked one of the squad members through the biosuit com.

"Above my paygrade, ma'am," the man replied. "But my guess is that everyone back there is on a need-to-know basis," he said. "And right now, they think no one else needs to know."

"Quit your tongue waggin', soldier," the sergeant barked. "That's not why we're here."

"Yessir," the young man said and quickly clammed up.

"Sorry," SheZahda whispered through the com.

"S'okay," he told her. "It's best we keep the talk down though."

SheZahda smiled slightly and made a zipping gesture across her helmet's visor where her mouth was. The group continued in silence, moving cautiously over the uneven, wild terrain. They covered the mile's distance in a little under an hour and, once they arrived at that point, there was no doubt they'd found The Horn. The starkly white, perfectly-conical edifice was plainly not Mother Nature's doing. Mother Nature created perfection through her imperfection. This was not that. It was a familiar perfection. A thinking being's perfection. A structure of intelligent design. Before the party was a gleaming spire that rose up out of the terra firma of Proxima b like a narwhal breaching the surface of the sea.

"This can't be real," HeHarald said.

"And yet, here it is." No sooner had SheZahda uttered those words than a voice rang through their headsets.

"The Bergs were requested," the voice said. "No one else. They will be taken care of and returned to you unharmed with all the details of this meeting. They do not require fellow ambassadors or envoys, nor any protections."

Commandant Foley's response came through the headsets. "Why do you ask for them? They're not our leaders. Wouldn't it be better to speak to me directly?"

There was only fuzzy dead air in response. SheZahda and HeHarald turned to face each other, then the soldiers.

"What are we supposed to do?"

"The instructions were explicit, Commandant Foley." The alien voice boomed in their ears. "It is perhaps best if your efforts at retaining even a modicum of power cease now. Send in the Bergs."

Several long moments of static ensued before Foley gave the order to the soldiers to return to the orb, and for the Bergs to enter The Horn. With some hesitation, the squad turned and started eastward, looking back over their shoulders every few meters until they disappeared into the brush.

"What do we do?" HeHarald asked through his headset.

"Approach The Horn," Foley commanded.

"Okay?" HeHarald told the man in a dying voice. They edged closer to the base of the spike.

"What do we do when we get there?" SheZahda said. There was no answer from the orb.

"I guess we wait," her husband said.

A moment later a tiny, dark speck appeared on the exterior of The Horn in front of the Bergs, like a single period being typed onto a pristine sheet of paper. The shape, its edges rolling and changing, this dancing droplet of ink, slowly grew and grew until those edges began to solidify and the shape was large enough for *something* to walk through it.

And that's exactly what happened.

The figure walking out from The Horn toward them was, by all appearances, humanoid. HeHarald and SheZahda could scarcely breathe as it advanced on them. Their eyes unable to look away from the sight of this creature. Mankind's first ever contact with an alien species.

"What is happening, Harry?"

"I wish I knew," HeHarald told his wife, without averting his gaze.

The thing moved in a type of glissade, with limbs rhythmically in step. The lanky figure continued until it was only a few feet from the two of them. Its features now were in full, vivid view: a pygmy-esque stature; greenish-gray, hairless skin; a distended belly with very little musculature on its body; a large, bulbous cranium; elongated fingers; nose slits; and prodigious eyes like black opals. The thing raised its head and unveiled a wide, toothless grin. Then, it waved its slender fingers, its mouth began to move and, miraculously, the words it spoke could be understood.

"Greetings. You must be confused and for that I extend my apologies. If you'll bear with me, I'm somewhat new at this, or at least it's been quite a while. Please remove your suits," it said. "The air is perfectly safe here. I'm sure you've been told this already."

SheZahda's thick-gloved fingers reached for her helmet, but HeHarald stopped his wife and signaled her to wait. He unlocked his own helmet with a de-pressurizing hiss. Despite the evidence he'd witnessed from the crewmates, who played so carefree on the proximan fields, there was the briefest instant of uncertainty as he removed the dome from his head. But with a few satisfying breaths, it disappeared. SheZahda followed. They unfastened their gloves, opened their suits, and stepped out of the puffy artificial skins.

"You're trusting. That's good," the figure said. "Come with me."

It turned and eased toward The Horn. They followed the petite lifeform who, as small as it was and as casual a stride as it seemed to possess, they nevertheless could not seem to catch up to. It moved toward the great pearly spur in the ground and, upon reaching it, it looked back briefly, waved the couple on, and strolled through the opening. SheZahda and HeHarald moved as if in a dream state and though The Horn was only a hundred feet or so away from them, the walk seemed interminable, as if they were on a treadmill. When they finally entered the dark doorway, they were hardly aware they had stepped inside it, the blackness seemed to simply consume them. Everything was now opaque, but they could still see each other through the murk, in an odd sort of shadow-light.

A conventional illumination quickly returned and they found themselves alone in what they could only perceive as a waiting room. At least it looked, or more aptly it *felt*, like an earthly waiting room. Fully-furnished, windowless, harsh lighting. The Bergs instinctively took a seat next to each other on the small couch and a voice sprung to life inside their ears. "Make yourselves comfy, I'll be with you shortly. Do either of you require a refreshment? A beverage perhaps?"

HeHarald's face was emotionless. "No, I think we're alright."

"What do you have?" SheZahda suddenly asked. Harry flashed his wife an incredulous look.

"Whatever you wish," the voice said.

HeHarald's eyes searched the room. "That's not possible."

The voice was resolute. "All is possible."

"Root beer," SheZahda blurted. "I haven't had a root beer in over twenty years. Do you have any really good root beer on this planet?" she said. "Ah, fuck it, I'll take *any* root beer."

"I believe we can oblige."

SheZahda leaned into her partner's ear. "There's something very familiar about that voice."

"It *is* familiar," HeHarald said. "It reminds me of a counselor I had in junior high, Mr. Plunkett. Great guy, real easy to talk to. He helped me through some awkward early teen stuff I had going on at a time in my life when I couldn't really talk to my parents."

SheZahda got up and inspected the perimeter of the room with a pensive look attached to her face. She ran her hands over the walls until she reached a picture hanging at eye level. "What is this?"

"What do you mean? It's a painting."

"I know it's a painting, but a painting of what?"

HeHarald straightened his body up on the couch and squinted slightly. "It's a vase, with some white flowers. What are those called again? Lilies? Tulips? I don't remember the names of flowers, you're the gardener. Snowdrops, maybe? No, they're definitely lilies, right?"

"I don't see any lilies."

"Okay, so they aren't lilies. What are they?"

"Harry." She snatched his arm and dragged him over to the wall. "I'm saying this isn't a picture of lilies or snowdrops or any other flower."

"What?"

"At least not to me," she told him.

"Are you blind or something." He pointed at the picture. "You don't see a bunch of flowers, in a vase, sitting on a wood tabletop?"

"I don't see one flower in that picture. And I don't hear some school counselor's voice either—I hear a woman, my Aunt Delia's voice," she said. "Harry, I don't think anything in this room appears to me exactly the same as it does to you."

"That's insane."

"What color is the carpet?"

"Brown, like a vomit-brown Berber."

"And the walls?"

"They're a type of green, an olive color. Army green or something."

"What about the furniture?"

He walked back to the couch and armchair and slapped at the material. "It's clearly black leather, Zahdy." He pressed the padded headrest. "Eh, probably faux-leather."

SheZahda looked at her husband with unease and slowly wagged her head. "We might be seeing and hearing similar things, but we're perceiving them in slightly different ways," she said. "That's what I think."

"How can they do that?"

"You heard what the alien said—anything is possible."

Suddenly a door that neither one of them remember being there opened and the lifeform stepped into the room holding a frosted mug of root beer wrapped in its spindly fingers. It handed the glass to SheZahda.

"One root beer," it said.

She took the mug and stared at the creature, then back at the mug. She lifted it to her eyeline and sniffed the bubbles gathered on its head. "Thank you." She cautiously lowered her lips into the froth and tilted the glass until the tide of brown liquid washed against her tongue. She let out a loud sigh. "Now that's good root beer," she said. She turned to HeHarald. "It actually is really good. I'm not just saying that."

"I hope you're both comfortable," the alien figure continued. "Are either of you distressed in any way?"

They shook their heads.

"I gather you must have a great many questions?"

Though still quite stunned, the pair managed to nod their affirmation. They shot furtive glances at each other, silently urging the other to speak.

"Yes, we do. I mean of course we do! How could we not?" HeHarald laughed. "Let me see, where to start."

"Let's start with this little trick," SheZahda said, lifting the mug. "How could you know what root beer is, and how did you just whip it up?"

The alien thing shrugged its slight shoulders. "It can't be a total shock to you that we would have capabilities far beyond your own. Anything you can think of—anything you've ever thought of—is known to us. We can extract any knowledge you have and produce-"

"But I don't know how to make root beer," SheZahda told the creature.

"Excuse me?"

"I said, *I don't know how to make root beer.* I get it, you're advanced. You can take anything we know and use it, but I don't *know* how to make root beer. I mean, I know what it is. I know what it looks like, what it tastes like," she said. "But I don't know how to make it, and I doubt anyone on those ships knows how to make it either. You can extract every last bit of knowledge from every cranium aboard those orbs and you still wouldn't know how to make root beer." She brought her hand to her hip. "So how did you do it?"

HeHarald nudged the woman with his elbow. "Honey, enough with the third-degree already," he said just under his breath. "Please excuse my wife, I have no idea why she's hung up on this root beer thing, we've just been cooped up an awful long time. I'm sure the inner workings of soft drink production is the least of what your race will be able to teach us. We welcome your help and we count ourselves very fortunate to have a neighbor like yourself just a star system over."

"It is fortunate," the alien said.

"Incredibly fortunate," SheZahda broke in. "Like, astronomically so. Like *winning-the-lottery-ten-times-in-a-row* kind of fortunate, wouldn't you say?"

"Uh, yes, as I already said, it's an exceedingly fortuitous outcome for your party."

HeHarald stepped in between SheZahda and the diminutive figure. "Fantastic! So, we've established that we're very lucky you're here. Let me apologize again."

"It's fine," the alien said. "I knew you'd have questions. I just hadn't anticipated so many of them to be about root beer."

"Excuse us a moment." HeHarald wrapped his arm around his wife's waist and gently turned her around. The couple took several steps away from their host. "What is going on with you, Zahdy?"

"None of this adds up. Not anything."

"The acoustics in here are very good," they heard the alien say. "Full disclosure, I can still hear you both quite clearly."

SheZahda spun around. "I'm sorry, none of this adds up, okay? There, I said it."

The skin of the creature's forehead corrugated. "What doesn't *add up*, exactly? Where's the problem?"

"That's just it. There are no problems," she said. "There are absolutely zero problems. That's the problem—this is all way too easy. We travel twenty years on the hope that this system will be able to support us. At best we're thinking this place is going to be a lot of work, y'know? A fixer-upper, *at best*. But no, we get here and Alpha Centauri's just right and Proxima b is just right and, oh yeah, just in case you thought there was no root beer in outer space, *voila*, here's a sarsaparilla for you in a nice, cold mug. I bet there's a whole lagoon of this stuff on Proxima somewhere, am I right?" She took a deep, measured breath and turned to her husband. "This isn't real, Harry, don't you see that? It can't be. This is Shangri-la, Disneyland, it's Willy Wonka's Chocolate Factory for Christ's sake! But it's not Proxima b, at least not the real one. And then there's you."

The alien figure leveled one long, bony finger at its own chest. "You take issue with me?"

HeHarald threw his arms up.

"Just think about it for one second, Harry. This being is exactly what we would imagine an alien would look like, exactly the way it's been presented to us since we were little kids. In every story, every science fiction movie, every drawing. The big head, the bulging eyes. It's a little green man—this is a Hollywood extra-terrestrial. Of all the possible forms of intelligent life an alien species might take, you're telling me that the first ones we run into look *exactly* the way we've always imagined they'd look?" She shook her head vigorously. "Color me skeptical but our unbelievable run of good luck seems, well, a little unbelievable to me. And when something seems too good to be true..."

"It probably is." HeHarald gave a sad smirk and his eyes fell. He collapsed onto the couch. "This is all a fantasy of some sort, isn't it?"

"That's my Harry," she said, taking a seat next to him. "Right again. You're always right... eventually. I sure wish you could talk some of that good ole Harry Berg sense to me and make this all work out, but I don't think you can."

"Nope, not this time, honey."

The lifeform grinned its toothless grin. "I knew I chose the right ones." It turned around and clopped toward the doorway. "I'm about to let you two in on something," it said. SheZahda and HeHarald cast a side eye toward each other. "Don't bother trying to run... you won't get far." It flung the door open and disappeared through the breach. Just as quickly, the door slammed shut. SheZahda rested her head against her husband's shoulder. HeHarald gave her hair a peck.

"I'm sorry," she said. "I ruined it, didn't I?"

"It's okay, babe, you didn't ruin anything. You were just being who you are, and I love who you are." SheZahda smiled secretly. "Still, would it have killed you to wait a little longer to figure it all out? I really could've gone for a cheeseburger, even a make-believe one."

"Me too, Harry," she said. "Me too."

A thunderous voice suddenly bellowed out all around them. "HeHarald and SheZahda Berg. Prepare yourselves."

SheZahda wrapped her arms around her husband's torso and closed her eyes tight. "Please, whoever you are, don't hurt us."

"That word, *hurt*, is a subjective one," the voice boomed. "I couldn't possibly assure that with any degree of certainty."

HeHarald clamped his eyelids shut as well. He gripped his wife. "Just do it already," he said. "Whatever it is."

There was a prolonged silence. SheZahda allowed the muscles of one eyelid to loosen and open a sliver.

"Let me just bring the volume down a bit," the voice said. It was still a deep baritone but not as fearsome as before. "That's better. I always have trouble modulating that thing. Now then, where was I? Ah yes, I'm afraid I haven't been totally up front with you both, that much you figured out on your own, but if you'll allow me, I'd like to make it up to you by being totally straight with you from here on out."

As the words reverberated in their ears, the image of the waiting room slowly began to dematerialize. It disintegrated before their sight, melting away as if a great vat of ivory paint were slowly being poured down each of the four walls simultaneously. It blotted out the previous scene, erased it, until the creeping alabaster blankness reached the floor and proceeded to fill that in also.

The Bergs stood suspended in a pallid nothingness. SheZahda spoke tentatively, in a voice that was barely more than a whisper.

"Hello?"

"You both are exquisite. You'll do quite nicely," the voice answered.

"Who? Us?" HeHarald asked. "Exquisite? No, no, we're just farmers."

"There you go again, downplaying your gifts. You are a great many things yet you choose to define yourselves based solely on what you offer your community. I find that extraordinary," the voice said.

Their response was a staggered, "Thank you."

"I suppose now I owe you that explanation." A pinpoint of light emanated high above them. Slowly it grew, gaining power, radiating brighter, reaching out in all directions until it engulfed the two humans in its pure, golden brilliance. "You're a clever one SheZahda Berg. You were correct in assuming my appearance was nothing but a ruse, but know that my intentions were wholly benevolent. I only wanted to make you both as relaxed as possible, to present you with a reality that you could understand and accept. In probing the minds of each of your fellow crew members, I came up with a composite of what an intelligent alien species might appear like to you. Thankfully, there was precious little variety in your imaginings."

"What are you saying? You're not an alien?" SheZahda said.

"Not exactly."

"Then, what are you?"

"That's a toughie. Let me see, how can I put this? If we're keeping close to what your idea of... wait a minute, no, let's back up... do you know how when you were little and you wondered... no, that's not right either... let's just say for all intents and purposes and really for lack of a better term... I'm God."

HeHarald and SheZahda said nothing. They tried, really and truly tried. They simply couldn't. They only stared into the soft flutter of The Light, entranced like two moths around a porch lantern. Finally, HeHarald was able to break the spell long enough to mutter the words,

"You're God? *The* God?"

"Technically, yes, I suppose so," The Light said. "God... or whatever you want to call me. You know what, it doesn't matter, none of the names your kind have given me are right anyway, but I guess none of them are wrong either, and in case you were asking yourselves about the light, and you probably were, I picked this form to put you both at ease because this is what your minds most accept as the shape of, quote-un-quote, God. Again, not my actual name—totally your word. But whatever, this light form you've chosen for me is a little garish for my taste. Just know that I don't actually look like this."

The couple were still mute.

"I get it, you have questions, and since I already know what they are because, well, I'm God, let me clear a few things up for you. First off, you can call this place heaven if you want to but that's not what I call it. I never actually gave it a name. I mean, seriously, who names their house? Very pretentious, considering it's the only one here. But if *you* want to call it heaven, whatever floats your boat, as they say. I realize it looks like an empty void to you, hardly paradise I know, but you have to realize that I've made it exactly as I wanted it. It is, in fact, quite beautiful to me but I'm afraid with your limited perception, just the five senses and all, you can't really enjoy the full view. I could help you see it the way I do but then I'd have to rearrange your entire biology, yadda yadda yadda, which I don't think you'd be too psyched about. Trust me though, these are *stunning* digs. Moving on…"

HeHarald slowly raised his hand.

"Yes, yes, you've got plenty more questions, Harry, I know. Loads and loads of questions for me! And I want to answer them all, in due time, so let's start with the biggies first, and then I'll get to some of the others. Number one, the cosmos is a fake—a trick, a gimmick, a hoax, a mirage, dare I say... a taradiddle. Just a little black lie I came up with. The whole blessed thing is just a gigantic planetarium really. Think of it as an intricate scroll of ever-changing lights on a canvas I've left rolling in your skies for billions of years. There to catch your attention, make you wonder, feed your dreams. It's a tantalizing view of a universe vast and mysterious and, unfortunately, not at all real. At least not yet. I mean it *could* exist, if I wanted it to. But I don't, so why bother making some new toy you're never going to play with, right? I just put it up there in the hopes that someone, somewhere would eventually reach out for it." The Light seemed to momentarily shine a little brighter. "And so you have."

"That's impossible," HeHarald said. "We've studied the cosmos for centuries, millennia even. We've seen so many... *things* happening up there, all over the place. Every corner of it. The universe is practically alive with activity. You faked all that, with some kind of eons-long program?"

"Hey, I said it was intricate."

"W-What else?" HeHarald asked, almost breathlessly.

"Uhhh, that's pretty much it, that's all of it."

"What do you mean?"

"I mean that's all there is, basically. Well, I suppose *technically* there's more to it but that's the big picture right there, all the broad strokes. I threw some stuff out into what you call space, had no idea what would happen. I set up some basic rules, some principles to act on the matter I put there, riled it up a bit, y'know, got things cooking a bit. Then I just put my feet up, so to speak, and checked it out while everything happened. What parent doesn't love watching their kids grow up? Never meddled, not once. I'm just a voyeur, that's what I do. I just sit back and observe. The deists had me pegged all along. All those things you blamed me for or credited me with doing, *Acts of God*, blah, blah, blah, I had nothing to do with. Wasn't me."

SheZahda's eyes widened. "Then we really are your children? We're special after all?"

The Light took a moment to answer, almost as if it were stalling. There was a low rumble and then, "I was speaking metaphorically before but, alright, you're my children, in a roundabout sort of way. My *creations* may be a better word for it. I mean, I never had you all in mind when I made everything. I work on a much smaller, subatomic level. You humans just kind of came together after a few billion years from all these elemental building blocks I threw into the ether. *My children?* Yeah, sure. *Special?* Eh, that one's up for debate—but don't take it the wrong way.

You're as special as everything else that came out of my tinkering. But hey, on the bright side, now that you know I exist, aren't you a little relieved I'm not about all that Jonathan Edwards, fire-and-brimstone crap? To get that worked up over anything would require me to give a shit. And after all this time, I'm not sure that's possible with me." The Light let out a sigh and a small flare bubbled up out of the corona at its top. "But now that you're here, you're definitely my favorites. That's good enough, isn't it?"

SheZahda shrugged. "I guess so."

"Well, it's certainly not a bad thing," HeHarald said, nodding.

"Not bad? It's a fantastic thing! I've been dying for someone to come visit me since I started this whole experiment, and now here you are."

"Experiment?" SheZahda said. "Forgive me but I can't help but be just a little disappointed that's all we've been to you, that's all everything's been to you. You're telling us that reality as a whole has been one big experiment?"

"You betcha! It's just one big science project and I, for one, am so pleased that it ended this way."

"Wait, what do you mean, *ended?*" SheZahda took her husband by the arm. "We just got here. What's going to happen?"

The Light flickered and dimmed. "This particular game is over. It's time to wipe the board clean and start a new one. It's been great fun though, believe me."

"No, no, I don't want to be wiped clean," SheZahda said.

"Don't worry, it won't hurt. It'll be as if you never existed. You'll be reused. Everyone. You, your friends, your ships, everything. Your atoms will be scattered again and they'll form the new pieces for another one of my games."

SheZahda clung to her husband's shoulders to keep from falling and HeHarald steadied her. "God, sir," he started. "My wife and I, and those people back there, spent years and years, came all this way to start new lives. We've still got a lot of those years left to live, or at least we thought we did. Does it really have to end right now?"

"I'm afraid so, Harry, but I'll offer you this." The Light paused for dramatic effect. "All the secrets of the universe. Everything you've ever wanted to know, every piece of knowledge your little heart desires will be yours before I end things. How's that sound?" It said. "Now go back to your friends and have a little powwow or whatever you people do, then come back here and tell me what it is you want to know." The two of them didn't move. "Scoot, you two. I'll see you tomorrow morning, bright and early. But not too early. I like to sleep in. Your Good Book got that one wrong too. I like to get a little rest in every day, not just on

Sundays, it's much healthier that way."

And with those words, the blank scenery slowly faded away, to be replaced by all the vibrant colors of Proxima's landscape. HeHarald and SheZahda were once again standing directly outside The Horn. In a type of daze, they began walking back in the direction of the orbs. They were met there by the military detail that had escorted them to the rendezvous point. The soldiers immediately ushered them to Foley's quarters. The commandant was breathless.

"What happened?"

"You saw everything, sir. We had the recorders on, like you asked," HeHarald said.

"You were in and out in a few seconds," Foley said. "They didn't pick up a thing. How could they?"

HeHarald began to speak, but his wife cut the man off.

"The aliens weren't there," she said.

The commandant's gaze alternated between the two of them. "What do you mean? We were talking to them right before you went in."

"I don't know, sir. We went in. Nobody was home. We came out."

Foley's lips parted, but it was a moment before the words came out. "This doesn't make any sense."

"I agree," SheZahda said.

"You're sure you didn't see anything?"

"Not a single alien, Scout's honor."

Foley made a tent of his fingers and he pressed them against his mouth. "Damned peculiar."

"We can go back tomorrow and look around a while longer this time," the woman said. "Maybe they're really impatient aliens. I bet we just missed them."

Foley made a fist out of one of his hands and rubbed it with the other. His eyebrows gathered. "Affirmative, let's try it again tomorrow," he said. "But take your time this go round. Then report right back with your findings."

"Yessir," they both said.

"Now go back to your room and get some rest, Bergs. You've had quite the day."

"With pleasure, Commandant," SheZahda said.

On the walk back to their room HeHarald moved close to his wife and spoke softly. "Why didn't you tell Foley what really happened?"

"Do you honestly think he'd believe us? Would you believe us if we came back with that story? Any rational person would think we're nuts, and all we got is rational people here. They won't go for this magical man-in-the-sky mumbo jumbo. They're not dummies."

"Still, at least a few of these folks must believe in a supreme being of some sort."

"Maybe," she said. "But not that sort."

"Zahdy, we were inside that thing today for a lot more than a few seconds, we both know it. How could Foley think we weren't?"

"Time must move differently in there."

HeHarald and SheZahda stopped at one of the viewing windows. Outside on the plains of Proxima b they could see thousands of their crewmates hard at work: testing the soil, excavating the land, laying foundations, planting seeds, preparing.

"Harry, no one's going to buy that whoever we spoke to today was God or Allah or Yahweh or Jehovah or anything else. They'll call us liars or kooks or worse."

"I can't imagine any of them are gonna be thrilled to hear about God's big plan for us either."

"We've got to keep this to ourselves until we can figure out what to do," she said.

"Agreed."

"So, what are we going to tell God tomorrow?"

"Well, if that was really God," HeHarald asked. "Shouldn't It already know what we're going to say?"

"That's a fair point, dear."

*

The next morning, not too early, Foley summoned SheZahda and HeHarald outside. On the way to meet the commandant they passed a group of other farmers surveying the land.

"Hey, Harry, Zahda!" one of the men called out. He approached the pair. "I saw you both heading out yesterday in your suits with a few soldiers."

"Yeah, scouting mission," HeHarald said.

"Why the heck did they want you two? You should be working the dirt with the rest of us."

HeHarald shrugged. "That's what I kept telling them."

"Noticed you came back empty-handed. Didn't find nothing?"

"You'd be surprised," SheZahda said.

"'sthat right?" he said. "Going back out today?"

"Yeah," HeHarald told him. "Probably a waste of time but, you know, I just do what they tell me to."

Their friend chuckled. "Well, be careful. Lord knows what's out there."

"Thanks, we will," SheZahda said. Once they were out of earshot, she turned to her husband. "I feel terrible lying to everyone, honey. They deserve to know what we found."

"What exactly have we found? Are you sure we even know?" SheZahda's shoulders slumped. "I guess not."

"Let's just see how it goes today." He pointed across the field. "There he is, let's go." They met Foley and the commandant accompanied them to the taller grasses south of the fleet, far from the others.

"Any new messages from the aliens?" SheZahda asked.

"Not a thing's come across since yesterday," he said.

"Stick around there all day if you have to, and keep the recording gear running. If they're a no-show again, poke around. See what you can find out about that place. Bring me back anything you can."

"Will do, sir."

HeHarald and SheZahda set off again through the southern woodlands toward The Horn.

"Look at it here, it's exactly the same as any forest we'd have back on earth," HeHarald said. "It's like this whole planet was created specifically with us in mind. Maybe God secretly wants us to stay."

"Then why is It tearing everything down and starting over again?"

"I don't know," he said. "So, what's the plan today?"

"I don't have one," SheZahda said. "Is that bad? It feels like it's bad."

"It's not good," he said. "But what can we do?"

They arrived again at the shimmering pale monument and, again, an ink spot of a door materialized and grew before them. They stepped into the black and were immediately greeted by The Light, as if It had been hanging there waiting for them the entire time.

"Let's get on with this, shall we? What would you like to know?" It said. Neither SheZahda nor HeHarald dared answer. "No plan, huh? Yeah, that's right, I heard you. I *am* God, remember? Don't worry, that's why I picked you. You're innocents, both of you. Of course you wouldn't think to make a plan to try and dupe me. Yours souls are too fine for that."

"We're sorry, sir, it's just that we don't know what to do," HeHarald said.

"You didn't tell your friends about me either, did you?"

"No," SheZahda answered. "But you probably already knew that too."

"You're right. I did," The Light said. "Also not a big deal. I get it, you didn't think they'd believe you and, even if they did, they'd take the news hard. You didn't want to cause them any anguish. You're good people, Bergs."

"I'm sure we're not the only ones," SheZahda said. "Why would you want to destroy us?"

The Light sighed (although it was hard to tell, but you could hear it if you listened closely enough).

"I'm just a curious sort," It told them. "I enjoy seeing what happens when I throw all the same ingredients into the pot, what new kind of stew it makes."

"But don't you want *this* stew? Why not stick with something you know you like?"

"I'm an aficionado of stews," The Light said. "I've made my share of them and, what can I say, I like to cook," It said. "So, what'll it be? Anything you wanna know, anything at all. Just ask."

"Okay," HeHarald said after some hesitation. "I want to know what it's like to have lived a *full* life."

"Oh, I see what you're trying to do, using semantics to trip me up, like I'm some sort of third-rate genie you can fool with some clever phrasing. Sorry, pal, that's not how this game works. Honestly, Harry, I expected more from you."

"No, that's not it at all, I swear," HeHarald said. "I really do just want to experience a full life, that's all."

"But you already have, my son. If your distant ancestors had lived to as ripe an age as you've reached, they would've counted themselves among the lucky. They certainly wouldn't have considered their lives to have been anything less than full. Do you have any idea what the average lifespan was during medieval times? Absolutely pitiful, believe me."

The man gave a bleating cry and doubled over. "But what does it all mean? I want to know the meaning of life?"

"No, you don't," The Light said.

"Yes... I do. You said you'd answer any question. Then I want to know what the meaning of life is?"

"Why does life have to mean anything?" The Light asked. "That is a very human trait, this need for meaning. No other species would ask me such a silly question. Meaning is something only you beings would attach to things, not me."

SheZahda rubbed her husband's back. HeHarald slowly straightened himself up and lifted his chin to God. "How can you not see what a huge letdown this is? Giving us the secrets to the universe is great and all but it doesn't mean much if, well, it doesn't mean much. Why bother—with any of this." He gestured wildly with his hands. "If there's no meaning to it all?"

The Light crackled and popped. "Let me ask you a question. I assume you always wanted to go to heaven someday, right?"

HeHarald's eyes narrowed. "Sure. Who doesn't?"

"I already told you, heaven doesn't exist. It's your invention and yours alone. I never promised any of you that, you all promised yourselves. It was a fairy tale made up by men and women, *for* men and women. How could you not have realized that? Eternal life hanging out with all your buddies? No work? No bills? No back pain? No hangovers? All the nookie and ice cream you want and nobody tells you when to go to bed? Harry, if something sounds too good to be true…"

"Yeah, yeah, I get it."

"So, tell me, where's the meaning in that?" The Light said. "There is none—it's an endless vacation, that's all. It's only what everyone *thinks* they want. Trust me, you'd get bored pretty damn quick. A few centuries in that hell and you'd be begging me to rip you to atoms. Your entire species' idea of a happy ending has absolutely zero meaning to it." The Light softened at its edges. "I thought you guys would be excited. All the answers to life's enduring questions are right here, just ask me. No more wondering. Aren't you happy to find out there really is a God?"

"One that doesn't give a shit about us?" SheZahda's voice was harsh and The Light seemed to withdraw, just a little, when It heard her. "A God we're just toys to? No, I'm sorry but that doesn't make me happy."

"Would you rather I hadn't revealed myself to you?"

"Yes," she said, pulling her shoulders back. "I'd rather be left in the dark. What am I supposed to do with all this great knowledge anyway? Tell everyone? Crush their hopes for a future they've waited years for? No thanks!"

The Light God went silent. Its gleaming rays still performed their effulgent dance, but it offered no words to the two mortal beings. HeHarald sobbed with fists tightened while SheZahda held his head in her hands and tried to calm him with whispers.

God's voice returned.

"Listen, I'm new at this. You both seem truly anguished and that was not my intent. I'm very pleased you're all here and I don't mean to cause any of you pain."

"You have," SheZahda said, still cradling her husband. "We're pained."

"I understand that, but what did you expect from me, if not the truth? What could I have offered you."

She shook her head. "I don't know, something more profound, I guess."

"I gave the universe existence when there was only emptiness, and that existence gave birth to you. I gave you free will to do whatever you wanted, to shape your worlds in any way you saw fit. I gave you creatures time to figure yourselves out, and you did that wonderfully. You're here, after all," The Light said. "I can't give it all meaning too. Only you can do that."

SheZahda nodded slightly. "That's it then?"

"That's it."

She buried her face in her hands and began to cry softly with her husband.

"Oh wonderful, now *I'm* pained," The Light said. "I'd hoped that maybe just talking to you would be enough."

"You would think it would be," SheZahda said through her tears.

"But it's not, is it?"

"Nope, it isn't."

"I suppose I didn't really think this through."

She sniffled. "Forget it, shit happens."

"Hmmmm," The Light said. "What to do, what to do... you really are an interesting bunch, aren't you? I did not see this coming, and I usually see everything coming. You human animals really are something."

HeHarald comforted his wife with a touch. "We appreciate everything you do, sir, and we don't mean to sound ungrateful. We're both just pretty shook up by all this," he told God. "That being said, we still would like to take you up on your offer. We have a million questions we'd love answered before you do what you're ultimately going to do."

"Yes, you've said as much."

"And you promised that you'd answer each and every one."

"I did, but a million?" The Light said. "I hope you're being hyperbolic because I didn't figure on that many. These have to be genuine questions you sincerely want the answers to, y'know? Don't try to pull a fast one on me, I'm being nice here."

"We give you our word," HeHarald said.

"Give me a moment to think on it, would you?"

"Not a problem."

"Still a Neil Diamond fan, Harry?" The man's eyebrow arched slightly. "Jewish Elvis? Are you still a fan?" God asked again.

"Uh, yeah, sure I am."

"Great, I'll be right back." The Light gently extinguished and a celestial harp rendition of *Solitary Man* played as the couple waited for Its return. When God's light reappeared HeHarald was humming along with the tune.

"Alright, I've mulled it over and I've come to a decision. I absolutely haven't changed my mind about starting everything over again, but until that time I think it only fair to answer all your questions first, no matter how long it takes," The Light told them. "So, what's on your minds?"

HeHarald looked to SheZahda, but she gestured for him to ask the first question.

"I guess I'll get the ball rolling," he said. "How did it all get started, the universe, I mean? Where did it come from? How does something start from nothing? Where did *you* come from?"

"Excellent question," The Light said. "Even though technically that was a few questions, but I'll answer them all. It's a bit complicated, I'll see if I can put this in a form that you can understand. Bear with me, this could get lengthy."

"We're not going anywhere," SheZahda said.

"Very well then, here it goes…"

The Light proceeded to regale the man and woman with the wondrous tale of The-Beginning-Of-It-All. It told them about The Great Big Nothing before The Big Birth and gave them the lowdown on The Cosmic Engine. God broke down all the Universal Law of Laws (and their various workarounds) and just as It was getting to the really juicy parts, SheZahda broke in.

"Begging your pardon," she said.

"Yes, what is it, child?"

She exchanged a few surreptitious words, a few knowing glances, with her husband. A married couple's shorthand. "Forgive us but, as fascinating as this is, Harry and I are only human after all and I'm afraid we do have our limits. We're really very tired, and we need to eat and drink something soon."

"And use the bathroom," HeHarald said.

"Yeah, that too," SheZahda told God. "Would it be possible for us to pick this story up later, say after a good night's rest?"

"Certainly," The Light said. "My apologies. I forget how fragile your little bodies are."

"Thank you."

SheZahda and HeHarald left The Horn and returned to the orbs to report back to Commandant Foley. Alpha Centauri still hung high in Proxima's heavens.

"Your coms gave out again the second you got inside," Foley said to them. "What happened in there?"

"The aliens were a no-show again, sir," HeHarald said. "We waited and waited."

"You were gone less than an hour."

"We were? That's funny, it felt longer," SheZahda said.

"Well, did you find anything?"

"Nothing to find, sir, it's empty in there. It's like they up and left when we didn't come running yesterday. Maybe we disappointed them?" she said.

Foley rubbed the bridge of his nose with his thumb and forefinger. "Really curious stuff," he mumbled.

"We can try again tomorrow."

HeHarald chimed in with his wife. "Yes, maybe another visit, before we give up on them completely?

"Alright," Foley said. "We'll do this one more time, just you two. If it doesn't work out, I'm sending a whole platoon over there to see what we can find."

"Sounds like a good plan, sir." SheZahda said.

The rest of that day HeHarald and SheZahda visited every ship in the fleet and spoke to every level of crewmember they encountered on those orbs. They recorded every question the people wanted an answer to. Every query, no matter what they were. Some were highly-scientific in their exactness while others were odd and ethereal in nature. There were the ones that begged contemplation and the ones that were purely unknowable. From the simplest and most straightforward to the daedal and byzantine. The metaphysical and the matter-of-fact. The profound and the pragmatic. Serious to downright silly.

The next morning, HeHarald and SheZahda set out yet again for The Horn, questions in hand. When they arrived, The Light welcomed the two of them heartily and finished Its story from the previous day. They thanked The Light and asked It one of the many other questions they'd compiled. The Light began to lay out the answer but, as before, it was long and detailed, albeit beautifully told. And once again, they asked if they might rest and replenish themselves before receiving the rest of the answer. The Light agreed to this because It hates starting something It can't finish. That's one of God's pet peeves.

"Why don't you both remain here with me instead of returning to your ship," The Light said. "Saves on travel time."

"I can't see the harm in it," HeHarald said. "Can you, honey?"

"Not really. No matter how many hours we spend in here, back at the orb it seems hardly any time's passed at all."

And so SheZahda and HeHarald agreed to The Light's proposal.

They were directed to the Holy Toilet before The Light enveloped the pair in Its warm embrace, filled their bodies with sustenance, and allowed them to sleep soundly and restoratively. The next morning (or what the couple conceived of as morning) they arose from their slumber, ate a most ambrosial breakfast, and listened to The Light finish Its story. They did this again the next day, and the day after that, and the day after that.

This continued every day (or what the couple considered to be a day) and every night (or what the couple consid—*oh, forget it, you understand*) for many, many days and nights. Evening upon evening, just after supper, the two people presented The Light with a different Great Big Question and The Light would explain to them the whole answer in exhaustive detail (this usually required quite a bit of background context and learning on Harry and Zahda's part; sometimes it felt like they were back in school again, which they didn't seem to mind) which ofttimes lasted well into the night.

One day HeHarald asked The Light, "Sir, how is the rest of our group doing, back at the orbs?"

"They're getting along just fine, Harry, don't worry about them. On this planet, I've provided them everything they'll ever need," The Light told him. "And even if I didn't, they look like a pretty resourceful bunch."

"Are they happy?" SheZahda asked.

"Seems like it to me."

"That's good then."

"It is good, isn't it." The Light said.

*

One day SheZahda announced that she was with child.

"I knew that," The Light said. "I was waiting for you to figure it out."

SheZahda snickered. "Of course you were."

Eventually SheZahda had the babe, a daughter she and HeHarald named SheMorgana, that they cared for with God's help. The family was treated to a splendid, emerald countryside inside the boundless expanse of The Horn, with a house there and a blazing sun very much like the one on Earth. They even had a dusty white pearl of a moon to hang in their night sky along with all those false stars that no one back home ever realized were just an elaborate mural. Each evening the new parents would pose another question and their divine host would unravel its mystery until the family invariably fell asleep. Between asking their questions and receiving the answers, The Light gave Its guests ample time to teach their daughter all the important lessons of life and allowed the family to frolic during the day. Then SheMorgana would fall asleep in her parents arms each night as the three basked in The Light's glow. HeHarald and SheZahda raised their daughter in love and happiness.

Eventually, God brought SheZahda, HeHarald, and SheMorgana neighbors. Those fortunate few from the orbs who stumbled upon The Horn were welcomed inside and invited to share this promised land with the Bergs. They didn't mind leaving the world of the sail ships behind, for this new place was a type of Elysian paradise. A virtual nirvana. They weren't certain how an Eden like this was at all plausible on Proxima b, or how exactly they'd gotten there, but they were thankful to be a part of it. They had many questions.

How did you find this place? they'd say to the couple. *And how did you manage to survive out here on your own?* But HeHarald and SheZahda were always possessed of a coyness that divulged only the merest of details of their situation. *How could you possibly have built all this?* their new neighbors would ask.

SheZahda and HeHarald would only tell them, *All is possible. We give praise to God the Almighty for these gifts and good fortunes.*

Oh! the people would reply. *God, you say? How very nice.* And then they would walk off, back to their own homes, eyeballing each other, thinking The Bergs were *those* type of people. God-fearing, churchgoing folk... holy rollers... nuts. And you know what?

That was okay.

HeHarald and SheZahda didn't mind one bit. Their new neighbors were still nice to them. They invited the Bergs over for dinners and birthday parties and cookouts and game nights. They helped them fix their roof and mend their fence. They joked with them and shared their innermost thoughts and hopes. They were their friends. And it didn't matter what they believed, or didn't believe. SheZahda and HeHarald couldn't blame them. They thought the very same things, once. But HeHarald and SheZahda had met God, and It didn't seem to be in a hurry to talk to anyone else but them.

"Should we let everyone know what's really going on?" SheZahda asked her husband.

"Why ruin a good thing? You know they wouldn't believe us anyway," he told her. "And even if they did, it would only spoil whatever time they have left. I think it's our burden alone to know God's plan, darling. It's probably best that way."

"I'm sure you're right," she said. "But I still feel terrible, being the only ones who see what's coming."

"Me, too," HeHarald told his wife.

*

Soon SheMorgana grew old enough to listen with her parents to The Light's stories and pose questions of her own.

"When are we going to tell Morg the truth?" HeHarald asked.

"I don't know," his wife told him. "But absolutely not right now, she's just a child. We don't want her growing up with that hanging over her head. Let her enjoy life, however much of it she has left."

"We're running out of questions, Zahdy."

"We're not out yet. Morgana has questions now we couldn't possibly think to ask. That's the beauty of a child's mind. Plus, we have all our friends—we could ask them as well." the woman said. "Have some faith."

HeHarald and SheZahda had more and more children, and with those children came more and more questions, a nearly endless string of questions that only The Light could answer. And each time, It obliged the family's curiosity.

One night, just before the Time Of Telling, as the Bergs gathered to await The Light's grace, God appeared and found a great commotion taking place. A now elderly SheZahda and HeHarald were hugging their gathered brood more than usual. Tear streaks dampened the two parents' faces.

"What's going on with my favorite humans?" The Light asked.

HeHarald and SheZahda were seated on a large cushion that resembled a cloud. They pulled their children, big and small, close to them. Harry spoke to God.

"I think we convinced ourselves years ago that this day might never come," he said. "But it's here now."

"What's here? What are you talking about, man?"

HeHarald looked to his wife. "We have no more questions that only You can answer," she said.

"That can't be, it simply can't," The Light said. "Think harder. Ask your kids. There must be something they still want to know. Why's the sky blue? How is a rainbow made? What are dreams?"

"We asked those a long time ago."

"How about, *Which came first, the chicken or the egg?*"

"Egg. Already asked that one. Unless you specifically mean a chicken egg, then it's the chicken. You broke it all down for us a few years back, remember?"

"Maybe I did," The Light said. "C'mon, there must be others. *Does anybody really know what time it is? Is cereal really just breakfast soup?* These are all valid questions! I can accept any of them! *If a tree falls in the woods-*"

"Those would just be tricks, and we promised we wouldn't try to trick you. Besides, we'd only be delaying the inevitable."

The Light paled until It looked to be nothing more than a hazy substitute of Its former luminousness. "You really can't come up with any more *genuine* questions for me? You've only asked me what... ten, twelve thousand?"

"We've been having some trouble for a while now," HeHarald said. "Just know that we're so grateful for everything you've done for us. You've helped give meaning to our lives, but we know the deal. We're ready for it to end now."

"Oh, this is an awful turn, positively terrible," The Light went silent for a long time. "I suppose I knew this day would eventually come, whether I wanted it to or not," It said. "Zahda, Harry, it was a pleasure answering your questions and watching your family take root."

SheZahda got up. "You've been more than fair, and we're at peace with whatever you decide to do."

"I am a supreme being of my word," The Light said. "And I told you both long ago that I'd answer all your questions before I scrubbed clean the cosmic plain. Are you saying that I've done that? That I've fulfilled my promise to you?"

"We are," the couple said together.

"You're sure?"

SheZahda and HeHarald looked lovingly at each other, then their children, and nodded.

"So be it," The Light said.

At that very moment, SheDuny, their youngest daughter, shook off her blanket, rose from the cushion on unsteady feet and said to The Light, "I have a question, sir." She clasped her hands behind her back and quavered in place causing her braids to swing slightly.

"Forgive her," HeHarald said. "She's just scared. She doesn't understand-"

"No, Daddy," the little girl said with little girl earnestness. "I have a question that we never ever asked our friend, really I do."

HeHarald smiled a sad kind of smile and tugged at SheDuny's pajamas to keep her from approaching The Light, but SheZahda implored her husband, "Harry, let her ask."

"Yes, let the child speak," The Light said. "SheDuny, I admire your courage. These years I've spent with you and your family have disarmed me, they've entertained me, and they've taught me much. In mind and in spirit you've nourished any soul that I might have. For your sweet sake, girl, ask your question and I will answer it. None of you need leave my side with an unanswered question upon your lips."

The girl took a step forward. She raised her eyes skyward and asked The Light,

"What's your name?"

Shards of light flitted above the family like sparks off a firework. The Light swelled in size and throbbed slowly before answering. Finally, The Light said, "I've had more than a few names over the ocean of time that mankind has walked the earth."

"Can you tell me one?" she asked.

"It would be my pleasure," The Light said. "I'll tell you about the first name I was ever given. It was uttered by the most ancient of your people, when Mesopotamia was still a lonely valley and only pockets of tribes haunted the caves of the world. Back then, one of you first called me *El*."

SheDuny giggled. "*El*? That's a funny name."

"I suppose it was," The Light said. "But it pleased me greatly."

"What else did they call you?"

"Well, I could answer you now," The Light said. "Or would you rather save that question for tomorrow night?"

SheDuny's eyes widened. "Can I do that? Can I ask you the same

231

question tomorrow?"

"Let me check our agreement, the fine print and whatnot." The Light could be heard mumbling words as if It were reading a contract. "Mmm-hmm... here we are, terms and conditions... no purchase necessary... uh-huh... void where prohibited, yes... not eligible to employees... well, well, I don't see anything here that says you can't ask me the same question—so long as the answer is different..."

The girl pursed her lips and her eyebrows closed in. She pinched at her chin. "How many names do you think you've had?" she asked.

"How many stars are there in the sky, little one?"

"A lot," she said.

"So," God told the Bergs. "I guess that means I'll be seeing you all back here tomorrow, and all the nights after."

The Light extinguished for a split-second and just as quickly returned. This coaxed a smile from HeHarald. "I think It just winked at us," he said to his wife.

God told them, "Looks like I'm gonna have more time on my hands now than I thought. Maybe I should start doing a little creating again."

"Not thinking about wiping the board clean anymore?" SheZahda asked.

"Nah, I think it'll be much more fun building an addition, make myself a proper universe, y'know? I've got the space."

"Sounds like a good plan," she told The Light.

"Yes, I think so." God's voice trailed off and Its light diminished until no one but the family remained.

SheZahda turned to her husband. "This sure isn't the kind of God I imagined, Harry."

"I'm sure it's not the kind of God *anyone's* imagined, outside of lunatics and storytellers."

She nodded.

"Good thing, huh?" HeHarald said.

"That God's nothing like we imagined? Nothing we even *could* imagine?" she said. "It most certainly is."

This story was one of a few ideas I had that revolved around the theme of imprisonment. I think this was the only one that I actually brought to fruition on the electronic page though. It's one where the imprisoners are just as, if not more, sympathetic than the imprisoned. I labored with the conclusion of this piece, endlessly vacillating back and forth hoping to strike the right balance between saying something but not being heavy-handed. I wanted, more so with this piece than any other I've written, to allow the reader to have an active part in the proceedings—to bring their own meaning to it. In the end, I hope I found that balance.

Farewell Luther

"We missed the cutoff for the water bill," Marjorie said. "And the cable's due Monday—we're going to miss that one, too. I'm sorry, honey, but we'll have to give up Luther."

"Absolutely not," Paul said after a prolonged breath. "We can't lose him. Everyone will know we're falling behind. We'll stall for a while. I know a couple tricks."

"It's no use, Paul. Our paydays fall late for us this month, and we had to get the minivan fixed, remember? We're going to miss at least two, maybe three, payments."

Paul paced the kitchen and rubbed at his face, wrinkling the skin into folds. "We'll ask for an extension, that's all, they have to understand. I mean it's not like we're the only people in history who've had trouble paying their bills. They won't just come in here and snatch our ward from us."

"Why not? When have you ever heard about the Overseers having any sympathy for deadbeat citizens?"

"We're not deadbeats, Margie."

Marjorie sighed heavily. "I know we're not, but that's how they'll see us. That's how everybody looks at people who lose a ward. So what, let them say what they want."

Paul's eyes widened. "So what? That's our civic duty you're talking about. We're better than that." He continued to pace the tile floor. "And what about Luther? We're his third family—three strikes is all you get."

"I know, it's unfortunate for him, but you can't tell me that what he has now is much of a life, sitting down there in that cell all day, doing nothing." She wrung her hands. "On second thought, yes, there is a name for it... a *dog's life.*"

"What if he was a dog? Would we give up on him, have him put down just because we couldn't afford the Alpo? We'd find a way."

Marjorie shook her head. "Oh, honey." She unfurled a great big grin and cupped her husband's cheeks. "You're a good man, Paul Nelsen, and I hear what you're saying. You're preaching to the choir, dear." Her smile shrunk away. "But there's no way we can swing it. That's nothing to be ashamed of."

Paul dropped his face into her palms. "Luther's been with us for so long now—he's practically part of the family."

"I know it feels that way, but he's *not* family, Paul. He's just a man who's locked up in our basement. Now if you'll go down and tell him I'll break it to the girls."

"They'll hate us."

"They'll understand, eventually," she told him. "Maybe not tonight, maybe not tomorrow, but someday."

Paul took a moment to collect his thoughts. "Alright, I'll speak to Luther."

He loitered in front of the refrigerator a minute more before finally deciding to go down the stairs. His footfalls were heavy on the wooden steps and the resultant creaking announced his arrival. When his slipper touched down on the basement floor, dust from the concrete kicked up and shone in the beams of light from the lone bulb attached to a rafter. On a cot inside the bars of a six-by-eight-foot cell a skinny, middle-aged man lay on his back tossing a red rubber ball into the air and catching it. Seeing Paul, he wriggled to his feet and fumbled through a group of papers atop a small table.

"Evening, Paul," he said. He slipped one of the papers through the bars and smiled. "I know Sarah likes them horses." Paul flipped the paper over to reveal several beautifully detailed pencil sketches of a horse—one with a little girl in the saddle. "I thought maybe Sarah could put it up in her room or something, y'know, if she wanted to."

"I'm sure she'd love that. Thank you, I'll give it to her."

"I know it's her birthday coming up."

"That's very thoughtful of you, Luther, but you don't have to get her anything. Sarah's our family, not yours."

Luther gave a scowl. "I know that. I'm not dumb."

"Oh, of course you're not." Paul raised his outstretched hands. He looked up into Luther's large, dark eyes. "I didn't mean anything-"

Before he could finish apologizing Luther broke into laughter. "I know what you meant, Paul, I'm just busting on you." He shuffled over to his cot, fell backward onto the mattress, and started tossing the ball again. "What can I do for you?"

"There's something that I..." Paul started before shaking his head and giving up on it. "The thing is, Margie and I, lately we've been..."

"Out with it, man!" Luther said, still tossing the ball.

Paul took in a breath and waited a moment. "Margie wants to know what you'd like for dinner tomorrow. Anything you want, your choice."

"My choice?" he asked. "What's the occasion?"

"No occasion," Paul told him. "You know Margie, she just likes to please."

"That she does, Paul."

"So what'll it be?"

"That's easy," Luther said. "Pot roast."

"Her Yankee pot roast?"

"Yep. Margie's Yankee pot roast all the way."

Paul clapped his hands once. "Okay, I'll tell her." He turned and made for the stairs. "A roast it is, tomorrow night."

"You know where to find me," the slim man called out. "Tell Margie if she doesn't mind leaving the door open up there, I'll be able to smell the pot roast cooking all night."

But Paul had already disappeared up the stairs.

*

"What do you mean you didn't tell him? Paul, he has to know. He needs time to process what's going to happen to him. We'll be the third family that's failed to keep him. Three strikes and he's out, remember?"

"He knows what it means," Paul said. "I tried to tell him but the words just wouldn't come. How'd it go with the girls?"

"I said I'd tell them, and I did."

"So, how'd they take it?"

"About as well as you'd expect a five and a nine-year-old to," Marjorie said. "They're upset. Sally even offered to sell one of her Sweet American dolls so we could get the money we owe. Isn't that something?"

Paul muttered under his breath, sounding like calculations. "It probably wouldn't be enough anyway... which one did she want to get rid of?"

Marjorie tipped her head forward and leered at her husband. "We are not selling our daughter's dolls." She reached into the cupboard and took out a pot and frying pan.

"Luther wants your pot roast. I told him you'd make it for him."

She sighed, shoved the pot and pan back into the cupboard, and pulled out the slow cooker. She gathered some spices from another cabinet and slammed them on the countertop.

"Don't get mad at me," Paul said.

"I'm not mad at you, I'm mad at this whole damn situation. It's hard on everyone." She lowered her head and her shoulders slumped. She shuffled toward her husband and Paul hugged her tightly. "We need to tell the Overseers we've missed a payment," she said, her voice muffled by Paul's chest. "If we don't tell them and they end up finding out on their own do you know what they could do to us? No, we come clean, we let them know what happened and they'll take care of the rest." She looked up into his eyes. "We're not bad people, they know that. And they won't issue us anyone else until we're back on our feet—that's how the system works. But you have to tell Luther. I don't want to see surprise in that poor man's eyes when they come to take him away. I couldn't deal with that."

Marjorie sniffled and wiped her eyes then opened the refrigerator to take out the beef for the roast. "I'd better get started on tomorrow's dinner," she said.

*

"This is delicious." Luther's voice traveled through the speaker. The closed-circuit television mounted on the wall transmitted video of the man eating Yankee pot roast inside his basement cell. Paul, Marjorie, and their two daughters were seated upstairs at the dining room table.

Marjorie pressed the button. "I'm glad you like it," she said into the intercom.

"Thanks for the picture," Sarah blurted before Marjorie removed her finger.

"Happy birthday," Luther said.

"You draw the best horses, way better than Dad."

"Well, Miss Sarah, your daddy is busy working hard every day so he doesn't have time to practice like I do," Luther said with a smile, staring into the camera's eye. "I'll make an even better one for you next year."

Sarah's lip began to tremble. Her fork dropped onto her plate with an echoing ting and the girl ran from the room as her chair tipped and crashed to the floor. Marjorie glared at her husband.

"Is everything alright up there?"

"We have something we need to tell you, Luther," Paul said. "It's not good news. If you're finished with dinner I'll come down and talk to you about it."

Luther pushed his plate away. "Sure, Paul. I'm about done. Why don't you come down."

Marjorie and the five-year-old, Sally, watched the monitor as Paul appeared in front of the bars of Luther's cell. "Why don't we give the boys a little privacy?" Marjorie turned down the volume as the two men talked.

"Hey, man," Paul said.

Luther spoke in his normal, heartfelt baritone. "What's the matter? You can tell me."

Paul's eyes wandered the room. "Margie and I are scuffling a bit with the family finances right now," he said. "This month it just snuck up on us."

"Go on," Luther said slowly.

"It's just that..." Paul stammered, "We missed a payment."

Luther's eyes glazed over and he sank to the concrete.

"I'm so sorry, Luther, I know we're your third family. I know what's going to happen to you. Believe me, I never expected things to get this tight for us. You have to know that if there was anything we could do to stop this-"

"I know," Luther said.

Both men were silent for a time before Luther spoke again. "It'll be a good thing in a way," he said. "I haven't told you or Marjorie but lately I've been real unhappy." Paul crouched down beside his ward, only the cage bars between them. "I been wondering what I could've been if I weren't down here, what I could've done out there in the world. Don't get me wrong, I appreciate all you do to try and make me comfortable but late at night, when it's real quiet, all those *could'ves* eat away at me."

Paul reached inside the bars and placed his hand on the man's forearm. "I've believed that about you all along, Luther. This life was never meant for you—you never belonged here. When they come for you Monday just keep telling yourself that you're going to a better place."

"I will."

Luther got up and stumbled to the bed, where he crumpled and lay motionless on his stomach. Paul remained for a long time until Luther, his head buried in a pillow, weakly motioned him away.

Sarah had already returned to the kitchen when Paul emerged from the dark of the basement stairwell. All three of the girls looked to Paul, who nodded slightly, and the entire family embraced each other. Behind them on the screen, Luther lay balled up on top of his sheets.

Marjorie wiped her own eyes then the eyes of her children. "Go upstairs now," she told them. "It's time to brush your teeth."

"We never brush our teeth this early," Sarah said. "Only television families brush right after dinner."

"Well, tonight we're one of those families. Now get going."

The girls galumphed up the steps with their heads hung and moaning, leaving Marjorie and Paul alone. She gave him a hug. "It's no big deal. The Ingersols lost one a couple years ago, remember? Tess and Frank lost one too—it happens, honey."

"If it's not a big deal then how come we still remember it was the Ingersoll's who lost their ward. People still look at Frank funny to this day. It *is* a big deal," he said.

"To the small-minded, maybe."

"Then there are a whole lot of small minds in this world."

She stroked her husband's hair. "When are they coming to get him?"

"First thing next week." Paul smacked his fist against the countertop. "I can't believe we're just going to let this happen. We owe it to Luther to-"

"We don't owe Luther anything," Marjorie said. "We've been good to him, taken care of him. We did what we were supposed to do. We're not going to do anything stupid when the Overseers show up next week. We're only talking about one or two unpaid bills right now, but if we get branded obstructionists we could lose our home." She grabbed Paul by the shoulders. "We could lose the kids, do you understand? I won't risk that much. Not for Luther, not for anyone. Say goodbye to him and get on with your life. It's the only way."

"So we're just supposed to sit here and watch them do it?" he asked.

"We have no choice."

*

The Overseers arrived at precisely nine o'clock Monday morning. The lead, an older man, and a woman in full scarlet-and-gold state regalia exited their cruiser accompanied by a five-person police extraction detail that pulled into the driveway beside them. The Lead Overseer twirled the key to Luther's cell on his finger as he approached the front door. Their paperwork was neat and in place, all legal. The screeching-eagle-with-nested-eaglets stamp was emblazoned upon the letterhead. All the required signatures had been gathered.

When Paul opened the door, the female Overseer handed him the paperwork, which he flipped through before escorting the team to the basement. Luther was sitting upright on his cot, head raised, eyes sharp.

"What's wrong with Luther?" Marjorie whispered to her husband. "You don't think he'll put up a fight, do you?"

"No," Paul said. "He's just preparing himself."

The Lead unlocked the cage door, stepped back, and three armed policemen entered the cell while the other two drew their weapons and stood outside either end of the door. Two police clamped down on Luther's arms and lifted him from the bed while the other came around the back of him with open cuffs. This seemed to awaken something primal inside the captive. He fought with the ferocity of several men, yanking his arms out of their hold again and again, grunting like a feral beast.

They managed to cuff one of his wrists, but not the other. When Luther tried to punch one of them with his free hand, the well-trained unit pummeled him with extreme prejudice and clamped the other cuff down. They shackled his feet, but even bound, Luther still wriggled and squirmed in their hands like an eel freshly pulled from the sea. It appeared to all in attendance that there was perhaps no man in history who wanted to be left in a cell more than Luther wanted to be left in his that day.

As they reached the door of the cage Luther tipped himself sideways and stretched his body out to such a length that they could not fit him through it. So they simply folded him up, knees into his chest, and harnessed him into a jacket. By this time he was little more than a living ball with nothing but a wobbling head occasionally extending his neck and snapping at the officers like an unruly turtle. They carried him to the steps. All five officers lifted him at once and ascended the stairwell on the way to the front door, stopping only in the living room to strap him to a carrying board. Once outside they brought him onto the lawn where the neighbors had gathered. The Lead Overseer pointed out a spot in front of the Nelsen family. "Right here is fine. Let's do it," he said. They laid Luther onto the grass, removed his restraints, and backed away.

The female Overseer faced the couple. "Paul and Marjorie Nelsen," she announced, "We, the government of the people, find you to be in violation of order five-one-six of the Forced Housing Act and have deemed you unfit for state service at this time." She then turned to Luther, who was still on the ground. "Luther Robinson, this being the third offense associated with your caretaking, you have been declared ineligible for any further welfare benefits and are hereby sentenced accordingly."

Luther hastily climbed to his feet.

When he moved toward the house the team lifted their rifles and pointed them at the man, prompting Luther to stop and raise his hands high.

"You are hereby sentenced accordingly," the Overseer repeated.

"This doesn't need to happen," Paul shouted. "It shouldn't end like this for him."

The Lead Overseer spoke calmly. "This is the only way it can end for him, Mr. Nelsen."

Paul took a step forward but Marjorie placed a hand on his chest to stop him and nodded at her husband.

"At least put the girls inside," Paul said softly to his wife. He turned to the Overseers. "Let my daughters go inside first, for God's sake. They don't need to see this." The Lead motioned to one of his officers who escorted the two little girls back into the house. A horde of neighbors were positioned just outside of the Nelsen's property line some twenty feet away. Luther looked plaintively at Paul and Marjorie.

"Don't you two worry none, I'll be alright," he said. "Take care of this family."

The team cocked their rifles.

"Give us the month to get on our feet, we're good for the money," Paul cried out.

"Please let us do our job, Mr. Nelsen," the Lead said.

"Two more weeks?"

The Overseer ignored Paul, instead turning to Luther. "You ready, Robinson?"

Luther swallowed hard and nodded. "Yessir."

"Good, I've got five more extractions to do this morning. Give him a three count, sergeant."

The police sergeant stepped forward and raised his arm as the four remaining gunmen trained their sights on the solitary man in the yard. It was only a mid-morning sun but Luther was sweating badly.

"One," the sergeant called out.

Luther began to back away.

"Two."

"We're so sorry, Luther," Paul said. Luther gave the couple a warm smile as he backpedaled to the edge of the yard. The crowd parted as if an invisible hand were carving a path for him.

"Thr-"

Luther turned and bolted. His government-issued sneakers hit the pavement with the merest of scrapes and he scampered down the road without looking back. When he reached the street's end he slowed to a trot. Then a walk. With his public assistance permanently revoked, Luther left the suburban neighborhood, and the Nelsens, forever. The officers lowered their weapons and the people spread out and returned to their homes.

"Good work, everyone," the Lead told the team. "Pack it up, let's get to the next one." He shook Paul and Marjorie's hands. "Thank you for your cooperation. I know this was difficult"

"What's he going to do now?" Paul asked.

The Overseer shrugged. "It's hard to say, Mr. Nelsen. I suppose that's up to Luther. It's not your concern anymore."

Paul gave a small grunt. The Overseer left the couple and rejoined his team. Paul turned to his wife. "Do you think he'll make it out there?"

Marjorie sighed. "He's perfectly capable. I'd like to think he will," she said. "Yes, yes, I definitely think he will."

Paul pulled his bathrobe tight to his neck. "The nights are still pretty cold, where will he sleep? How's he going to get a decent meal?"

"I don't know," she said. "He'll figure something out. Life's all about figuring things out, and you can only do so much of that from inside a cage."

"And what if he can't, you know, figure something out?"

Marjorie Nelsen could only shrug her shoulders. "I'm tired, honey. Let's go back inside now."

Paul nodded thoughtfully then took a final look at Luther in the distance as the man turned a corner and disappeared.

This one was always meant to be just a distraction for me. Something I worked on when I was blocked up or bereft of ideas. Something to keep my mind churning and my fingers from becoming too arthritic from disuse. Sometimes we need those things in our life: low pressure, lighthearted tasks to keep us going, keep us on track, something on the silly side to keep us sane. I played with this thing off and on for several years and in all that time it never materialized into more than it ultimately ended up being: a quirky little flash piece that I'm, nonetheless, quite fond of. And that's perfectly alright. I included it here, if nothing else, to show that writing doesn't always have to be deadly serious. It can be a whole lot of fun actually, if you let it.

Two Cups

"On the sixth day I created man, both male and female… and it was good."
-God

"Agree to disagree."
-The Devil

SCENE ONE - Tea for Two?

One afternoon a woman brewed a kettle of tea in the solitude of her home. She took a cup from the shelf and asked aloud, "God, if you're there, would you please join me for a spot of Earl Grey?"

Much to her surprise, God replied. "Personally, I don't go in for the stuff, but what the hey, pour me a cupful too."

The woman's eyes came alive and she beamed. "Thank you, O Lord, for answering me. I've waited all my life to hear Your voice."

God told her, "It was nothing, really, if only you'd asked sooner. I'm not a mind-reader, you know. That's a common misconception about me. Now make no mistake, I *could* be a mind-reader—I am all powerful, that part is true—I just choose not to be. I think you folks deserve some privacy and, full disclosure here, I'm not all that interested in every last thought you people have. Now what do you say you pour me some of that lovely dark stuff?"

"I can't believe I'm actually speaking with God!" the woman shrieked. "I have to tell my sister in Sheboygan."

God interjected. "If I may, madam, you're not actually talking *with* God just yet. You're talking *to* God. When I dropped in for this little visit, I gotta say, I imagined this convo of ours would be more of a two-way street, if you catch my meaning. *Capisce?*" There was a prolonged silence while God waited, and waited. "Helloooooo?"

But the woman was no longer listening. Instead, she was busy group-texting and composing an eye-grabbing post for her Facebook page.

"Please, I wouldn't do that," God warned. "How do you know I'm even

241

here, really? You could be schizophrenic or bipolar, did you even consider that? This could be early onset dementia for all you know. Or maybe it was something you ate? I might just be, as Scrooge says to Marley, 'some undigested bit of beef, a blot of mustard, a crumb of cheese, a fragment of underdone potato'. Don't tell me you haven't read Dickens! I could be The-Ghost-of-Christmas-Anything for God's sake, er, I mean, *my* sake. Just sit down and pour the tea, lady. We'll drink. We'll talk. We'll laugh. That's what you want, isn't it?"

The woman shushed God and turned away while her thumbs danced madly over the screen of her iPhone. "I'll show everyone," she said with a haughty laugh. "I always knew you were real. I knew you'd come down for tea if I invited you."

God gave an almighty sigh, as only God can. "If you were so cocksure," he murmured to himself. "Then why didn't you get out *two* cups?"

SCENE TWO - Wanna See Something *Really* Scary?

In his kitchen, over a steamy mug of cocoa, an elderly man wondered to himself if the Devil really existed when the demon lord himself suddenly appeared before him. The Devil seemed to the man a handsome fellow. He wore an immaculate suit of all-white and a straw Panama hat. He had large downy wings which he held tight to his body so as not to overturn the table, and a dachshund on a leash curled in and out between his legs.

"Who are you?" the man asked.

"I have many names: Satan, Lucifer, Beelzebub, Mephistopheles, Diabolus, Old Scratch, The Prince of Darkness, I could go on but I'll spare you any agonies, at least for now."

"Is there one you prefer more than the others?"

"Call me 'Devil'."

"If you don't mind me saying, Devil, you look very much like an angel to me."

"I *was* an angel... once upon a time. You must have read about it. It was in all the books."

"I'm awfully sorry. I'm old and I forget things, plus I'm not much of a reader," the man said.

"Well, it's true. I can assure you."

"I'm certain it is."

The Devil huffed the air above the pot on the stove. "Is that hot chocolate I smell?"

The man nodded. "With mini-marshmallows." He dropped two Hershey's Kisses into his cup and they mixed in with the murky beverage.

The Devil purred. "How decadent."

"Would you and your dog like some?"

"I'd love a cup," the Devil said, pulling one from the cupboard. "But none for the hound—you never give a dog chocolate. I'm sure you've heard that."

"Ah yes," the man said. "My apologies. I'm old and I forget-"

"Yeah, I got it the first time, pops. Just get to pouring already before you forget that too."

"Oh, of course." The man filled the Devil's cup.

"It's strange, you don't seem the slightest bit afraid," the Devil said.

The man supped his cocoa and marshmallows. "Why would I be?"

"Well, I *am* the Devil after all. That must still account for something up here. I truly don't have your best interests at heart, you know."

The man gave a snort and a rivulet of brown liquid streaked from the corner of his mouth down to his chin. "Most people don't have my best interests at heart," he told the Devil. "Besides, you're not terribly frightening."

The Devil blew on his cocoa. "No?"

"Not especially," the man said. "I saw *The Exorcist* when it opened the day after Christmas back in '73. People were running out of the theatre. Now that was frightening! You're not nearly as scary as that."

"But that was only a movie, it wasn't real. It was just makeup and pea soup and a chain-smoking actress with a raspy voice. That's not scary." The Devil grumbled. "*I'm* scary."

"Ha! '*I'm scary*' says the guy with the fluffy wings and the sausage dog."

The Devil's face flushed. "Enough!" He gnashed his perfect teeth, spread his now leathery wings, and transformed himself into an immense, horned beast; hairy and snarling with razor talons on its fingers.

"*Curse of the Demon* with Dana Andrews, saw it when I was a kid," the old man blurted, dismissing the Devil with the wave of his hand.

The monster instantly melted down into a pale corpse with sunken eyes and the stink of maggoty meat on it. "Saw that one too," the man said. "*Night of the Living Dead.*"

"Goddammit!" The Devil morphed back to his angelic human form and blew out his cheeks. He took a hurried sip of his hot chocolate and raised a finger. "Okay, how about this?" He inhaled deeply and all at once his body became a wriggling mass of tentacles exploding outward. Viscous fluid oozed over the organism's misshapen, roiling center and tumors of bone protruded from inside its saclike skin, threatening to burst forth and consume everything in its presence.

The old man simply smiled.

"*The Thing,*" he said. "John Carpenter's version, not the one with the guy from *Gunsmoke*."

The creature let out what could only be interpreted as an infernal sigh and deflated like a leaky balloon until only a puddle of pink flesh remained on the black-and-white-checkered tile floor. The Devil took human form once again, looked skyward and shook his fist.

"You see?" he said. "This is why we can't have nice things."

Just then a voice from the heavens, like thunder, rang out. "Fine, you win," God said. "I admit it, they're awful. But that doesn't change a thing. You're still not getting your old room back."

The Devil shrugged his shoulders and pouted. "Whatever."

Copycat Jack was to be the last original story I produced for this book (As it turns out, I ended up writing one more.) The idea came about after a true-crime kick I was on at the time. Truth be told, I'm fascinated by a good true-crime yarn and the mystery of Jack the Ripper has always been of particular interest to me (and many, many others). I'd always wanted to write a ripper story like Robert Bloch's famous Yours Truly, Jack the Ripper *or simply a serial killer story dripping with dread like Stephen King's* Strawberry Spring *or a host of other great murderer-on-the-prowl tales I've encountered over the years.*

I will say though that immersing oneself in the fictional and non-fictional lives and misdeeds of killers for weeks on end does begin to take a toll on your psyche. After I finally completed this piece, I felt like I needed to take a shower. But having just written a couple of lighter pieces, I needed to sate my darker side a bit. It ebbs and flows with me and I think that's part of the reason I like writing in the medium of short fiction so much; I get to indulge all the disparate tones I'd like to explore on a fairly regular basis. No matter how bored I get with a particular type of story, I'm never too far away from starting my next one. It's also what I happen to love about the genres of science fiction, horror, and fantasy; there's room for so many different shades of storytelling you can present your narrative in.

Copycat Jack

He murdered the waitress on a warm, summer night in a meadow outside of Haysville, Kansas, in a field of black-eyed Susans, her dark blood splashed over its xanthous petals. Edward would tell you it was a nice spot, secluded. Good for his kind of work. She was young and lithe but worn, he would say, like a lot of girls these days. She pleaded with him to spare her life as he sat atop the girl's body, alternately strangling and stabbing it. Her windpipe gave way with a soft pop and he thrust the knife in and out of her chest several times. He was astride the body for the better part of twenty minutes, waiting for it to die. When the life finally left the young woman's eyes and they glazed over like a doll's; when he saw the flowers he gave her, mottled violets and roses in a ring around her pretty throat, bruises she now wore like a scarf; when he saw the bloodstains blossoming on the front of her carhop's uniform; he spontaneously ejaculated. This work excited him.

Almost forgot.

He grabbed her hand and placed the ring finger into his mouth up to the knuckle. His tongue caressed the flesh which still tasted vaguely antiseptic from the cleaning solution she used on her shift that night. Moistened, he slid the finger out from between his lips and spit her class ring out into his waiting hand. A souvenir. Did you know that it takes the same amount of pressure to bite into a carrot as it does to sever a human finger? Edward does. He reinserted her finger into his mouth and bit down. From this one he'd take two souvenirs.

Instead of wrapping the body carefully and placing it in the trunk of his

245

LTD he decided to display his catch for the first time. He liked the way she looked. There was lots of space in the trunk of his Ford, that's why he bought it. In his old ride he sometimes had to hack them into pieces to fit them in the back. He'd gotten pretty adept at slicing them up. He'd pop out the exposed joints just like breaking the spine of a book. Then he would saw through the bone and separate the arms and legs from the torso. He'd gotten good at a lot of things that would make an ordinary person puke. But repetition builds perfection, as they say. And Edward would tell you it was just meat after all. Every surgeon in the world was at one time a tremulous tyro who'd never held a scalpel. Never opened someone up. It takes time, and practice.

Lots of practice.

Now was the time to introduce himself.

He spread the girl wide in that field near Haysville. Hollowed her out damn near completely. Vitals carefully arranged about the body, just like Jack would do. He was quite satisfied with himself except for the fact that he hadn't slashed her throat, The Ripper's signature move. Other than that, he was feeling sated. Like someone who'd just finished a meal. Sated, yes, but not full. Oftentimes he was, but not tonight. Not this time. He craved more. Just like Red Jack had on that fateful autumn night in London. The idea of feeding his urges again so soon brought a smile to a corner of Edward's mind that other people don't dare even acknowledge in themselves, much less feed.

He would tell you he was following in the footsteps of the cruel ones. The ones like him. How could he be expected not to when they shared so many of the same thoughts, the same appetites? He was discovering himself, body by body, by imitating his idols. These hunter-killers were his brethren, his kin. The whole world would see what he'd done and they would recognize the inherent virtuosity within him. He was merely a copycat now, but someday his deeds would be legendary. He wanted desperately to have a unique place in those annals, just like Jack. He was standing on the shoulders of giants but one day his accomplishments would be revered, his lofty place blood-secured. If only he had something avant-garde, something (if you'll permit me) *cutting-edge* to add to the histories, a calling card worthy of his inclusion into those great halls of infamy.

Wouldn't it be glorious to be immortalized like the rippers of old? From Whitechapel to The White City to that fellow from Dusseldorf... or the new one that's had them chasing their tales in San Francisco these last few years. He's a real original, with that costume and those cyphers of his. Now that's a neat gimmick. Oh, to be part of that pantheon!

He allowed himself to daydream a moment, but only just that long. She'd been an easy kill, this waitress. He had plenty of dark energy left. He checked the rearview mirror.

You're a handsome man, Edward. Handsome enough.

Unassuming, inviting, dangerous, but not in an unlikable way. All those women. They'd seen faces like his, and every one of those men's faces wanted something from them. They imagined they knew what Edward wanted too, but they didn't. They could never imagine a face like his wanting the things he wanted, needing the things he needed. His looks were the web, his cool blue eyes the silken threads, intricately beautiful false windows for behind those eyes he was soulless. And those women, all those tender, young lives, were merely flies to be ensnared. It was only at the end that he revealed his true spidery self to them, and by then it was too late. His fangs were out. His awful, dripping fangs.

Edward had already decided, this would be the night. A double-event, just like Jack had done way back in that late September of 1888.

You were so audacious, weren't you, Jack? Not satisfied after disposing of one of those Spitalfields whores who went by the name of Long Liz Stride, you had a bit of fun with Kate Eddowes over in Mitre Square later that night. Edward let go a chuckle. *And your black deeds live on to this day. How? What makes such an enduring monster?* he wondered.

It's a tough act for sure. Number one, you can't be caught, ever. It ruins the mystery, and people just love their mysteries. But you have to get yourself noticed, create an atmosphere of panic, of frenzied terror. You have to want to be heard and have your handiwork seen. You need to repulse *and* attract at the same time. You need both notoriety *and* anonymity. Not an easy task. We still don't have a name to put to those lurid events on the East End all those nights ago and that's part of the reason why Jack will forever be the ultimate bogeyman. It's risky business though; you have to really put yourself out there. And then one day you stop. You just stop, and no one can figure out why.

Always leave them wanting more, eh, Saucy Jack?

Edward spoke aloud to his reflection in the mirror. "But how will I ever be able to stop now that I have a taste for it? I guess that's a question for another time."

He needed gas. There was a station along a stretch of lonely road just outside of Haysville that stayed open late into the night. Thirty-six cents a gallon, not too bad. He'd fill up there. He pulled in and pumped the fuel into his tank before heading in to pay. The bugs in the air, uncontrollably drawn, were swarming the light above the door when he entered the gas stop. If not for the attached garage the place would've been scarcely bigger than the local Fotomat. A soda cooler softly humming with electricity, a candy display, and a large magazine rack against the far wall took up a good amount of the space inside.

What do we have here?

The girl looked new and fresh, but Edward knew better than to believe that—none of them were innocent. Couldn't have been more than a year or two out of high school, he guessed. She sat behind a large wooden counter, the top of her head obscured by the hanging cigarette dispenser. When she saw Edward walk in she slid her bottom off the stool and leaned forward on her elbows, eager to help. Bright eyes, she had. So very bright.

"Hey, sunshine."

Copycat Jack

"Hi there, Just the gas, mister, or can I get you something?" She flashed him a crooked smile. "Chewing gum? Pop? We got lots of sweets in here."

"Just the gas, uh..." He bent over to read her name tag. "Dorothy, and the key to your bathroom, if you have one."

"Anything for you." She reached under the counter and produced a key. "And everyone just calls me Dolly, in case you were curious."

"Thanks," he said, then, "I was a little curious."

His response coaxed another grin from the girl, this time more authentic. Edward could see one of her front teeth was slanted at the bottom. She handed him the key, touching the flesh of his palm as she pressed the metal into him. "Toilet's around back," she said.

"Thanks again," he told her before half-exiting the door. He paused and swiveled his head left, then right, before poking it back inside. "Sorry, which way?" he asked, with a perfectly rehearsed haplessness.

"You want me to show you, darling?"

"I'd appreciate it," he said. "And you can call me Jack."

*

In one elegant motion his blade drew a red line across her throat and unzipped the flesh, revealing the pink insides, and the rich, ruby juice spilled out in a flourish. Edward would tell you that the carotid can spout like the goddamn fountains at Caesar's Palaces, but he knew how to avoid the mess when he needed to. He'd done this enough. Instead, he painted the concrete wall inside the bathroom crimson.

Fine material, blood. Sticks to everything.

He eased the body down and splayed it out diagonally on the bathroom tile so he could work; it's so cramped in these backwater gas station shitters. He plunged the big-bladed knife deep into her belly above the pubic bone where the flesh is soft. *I slide it up up up past the ribcage to the chest, where things get a little tight,* he would tell you. *This sweet piece is all skin and bones.*

The blade sailed through parts of her and crunched through others, both equally satisfying to Edward. He had to lay her out like old Jack would: slick innards placed ceremonially about her body; intestines meticulously draped over shoulders; organs carved out, uterus removed; little nicks here and there, in all the sensitive places; weird shit like that. Something to get them talking and keep them talking. It all came so naturally to him.

He smiled while he cut; he'd tell you that he's not one of these joyless crazies, wracked with regret. He loved his work. He wasn't ashamed of what he was. It's how Mother Nature created him; it's what She intended him to be. They would have him believe that he had some wires crossed but he didn't think that's how it was at all. He thought his wires were dead-straight and everyone else's were tangled up. He would tell you that he was man at his most elemental, once-upon-a-time admired and respected for his ferocity, when it was necessary for survival. The majority have had those impulses conditioned out of their systems; they've been brainwashed to believe they're civilized. But

Edward's watched how man treats his fellow man the world over. He steals from him, enslaves him, and murders him by the tens and hundreds of thousands. How could *he* be abnormal in a world like that? He would say that he's not an outlier at all, he's just being honest with himself. Fuck that pussy John Locke and his social contract; that's just a way for people to avoid being feasted on, he'd say. Edward feasted when he wanted to. He knew what he was. He didn't question it anymore. A lion's got to lion.

He made a Y-incision between the breasts to the tips of the shoulders, peeled back the skin and voilà, it was all there, a showcase of his skill. It's all about the presentation sometimes, the showmanship. He left her to be found like this, minus her once-bright eyes. More souvenirs. They thought Jack might have been a medical man when they saw his victims gutted so utterly and expertly, but that's rarely the case. Edward would tell you once you open up your first it's not that hard to find your way around. He started out like a lot of them, our boy Eddie, as a kid, with small animals. Pretty soon he graduated. Now he was a master butcher, just like Jack. Before he opened the bathroom door to leave, he looked down at the body.

"Well, Dorothy, I have a feeling you're not in Kansas anymore," he said. "Bye, bye now."

After tonight the papers would surely have to talk about him, to pay him his respects. Give him a name. A new name, not Jack's but some dread moniker of his own. The press was good at that. It would be a very cool thing to Edward. He wanted to be known. He didn't want a mouse's life, always hiding, scurrying in shadow hoping not to be noticed, embarrassed of his fancies. Jack was never embarrassed, that's part of what made him Jack.

You've got to hand it to him, Edward would say. *Good ole Jack was a savvy man. None of this toiling in obscurity; he wanted to be famous. He wanted to be a star, the talk of the town every night. His name on all their lips, in all their thoughts every night they raised their petticoats for some stranger. He coveted it. And look at us, still talking about him. I wager he'd be pretty happy about that fact.*

The thought dawned on Edward: What if I pull off something even The Ripper didn't have the balls for? A triple-event! Yes, that would do it! He would need to take another girl, and it had to be tonight. But the night was still young, and so was she, wherever she was.

He drove along that country road, the beams from his headlights ever-searching and hungry. The hitchhiker he found was rail-thin, in tattered jean shorts. He pulled the car to the side of the road, leaned over to roll down the passenger window and told her to hop in if she needed a ride. She had a varicolored, crocheted bikini top strapped to her chest and a drab army jacket around her waist. Mousy brown hair she wore up, but not in any punctilious way. Just kind of thrown up there to keep it out of her face. Edward would've bet dollars to doughnuts that she was on something. The kind of hippie girl you see all over the roads these days. A kind of lost sheep. The kind Edward always seemed to find. The perfect kind. She unlatched the door and slid into the front seat beside him.

"Where you headed?" he asked.

"Wichita."

"What's in Wichita?"

"The Dead." Edward was silent, briefly taken aback by her response. She laughed. "The Grateful Dead, man, you dig?"

"Oh yeah, The Dead, I get it. So, are you one of those 'Deadheads' then, following Jerry and them all around? That's pretty wild."

"Nah, I wish," she said. "Just going to the show, fall semester starts up soon so I gotta stick around."

"You're a college girl?"

"Wichita State, man—go Shockers. I'll be a junior next year."

"Brains and looks, good for you," he said. He glanced over to see if his compliment had registered but she caught him looking. "Uh, what are you studying?" he abruptly asked.

"Journalism."

"A reporter? How fun," he said. "I'll be in tomorrow's papers, you know."

"Really? What for?"

"Just a hobby I have. Seems to arouse people's attention."

She gave him a smile. "Far-out, I didn't know I hitched a ride with someone famous. That's groovy, you get to do something you love and people are into it."

"It is, isn't it?" He smiled back at the girl and their eyes locked for a moment before she dropped her head demurely and giggled. "What do I call you?" he asked.

"Teresa."

"That's a nice name. Your mother's?"

"My aunt."

Edward nodded. There was a short silence while he navigated a curve in the road ahead. "So, tell me about yourself. What gets you going? What are you hoping for out of life?"

Edward liked to play with his food sometimes, but this time he was genuinely interested.

"That's a pretty heavy question, man. I don't know. I figure I'll finish school and then move away and start writing for one of the big papers. Probably win a Pulitzer."

"The Pulitzer Prize, just like that, huh?"

"Yeah, why not? Haven't you ever heard of women's lib? We're just as good as you men at anything we put our minds to."

"I have no doubt," he said, stifling a smirk.

"I should get the chance to be famous too, for the stuff I'm passionate about."

"Hey, I'm down with that," Edward said. "I'm always looking for something to get me recognized, help me stand out from the crowd. I want to be a one-of-a-kind but right now I'm not," he said. "If I can just figure my shit out. I'm kind of a work in progress."

"Aren't we all," she said. "When everything's said and done, man, all you can ask for is that people remember your name. That's all I want."

"I've got a sixth sense about these things," Edward told her. "Something tells me your name is going to be on everyone's lips sooner than you think." He gave her a reassuring nod and she smiled warmly at him.

"Thanks."

"Don't mention it," he said. "Hey, you ever get worried hitchhiking? I'm sure not everyone's as nice as I am. There's got to be some real wack-jobs out there."

"Don't I know it," she said. "But I can take care of myself, I'm scrappy. There was this one time though, this weirdo picks me up, a real creep. Keeps asking me these strange questions. What size am I? Do I like older men?"

"That *is* weird. What did you do?"

"What do you think? I got out of there, man. He was probably just horny but you never know, better not to chance it."

"I don't blame you. That sounds like every serial killer story I've ever heard."

She bolted up in the seat. "You get into that stuff too? All that Charlie Manson, helter skelter shit?"

"Sure, a little bit, who doesn't? There's just something about it—it's so macabre. I guess I've always been drawn to it, it speaks to me, y'know?" There was a prolonged silence. "Okay, now I'm the weirdo."

"Hey man, it's 1972, you can get into whatever you want to," she told him. "I ain't gonna judge, I'm right there with you. All those stories about murderers, it's a little exciting."

"Exciting?"

"Because it's a little dangerous, I think. It's kinda like hitchin'—there's an element of danger getting into a car with a complete stranger. Gives you a bit of an adrenaline rush, a little high. You never know what you're gonna get," she said. She reached her hand out the open window and spread her fingers wide to feel the wind rush through them while she pushed against it. "I suppose I'm a bit of a thrill-seeker."

"Well, I hate to disappoint. I'm sure this ride must be pretty boring for you."

"Who says you're a disappointment?" She gave him a coquettish grin. "Maybe you'll turn out to be a little dangerous after all."

"Who me?" He chortled. "No way, I'm as harmless as a dove."

"Somehow I doubt that," she said. She rolled up the window halfway. "You got any favorite, y'know, serial killers?"

"Jack the Ripper, of course. Who doesn't love his story? Can you imagine what the vibe must've been like in that slum with him prowling around like a phantom every night? All the killings in a one-square-mile radius. People packed in on top of each other like a sardine can and this madman, if you want to call him that, right there among them. The sheer terror on the streets at night must have been... delicious." Edward tried to catch himself, tried to stop his ranting, but he was too late.

Teresa's eyebrows raised. "Whoa! You really are into that dude, huh?"

He didn't want to appear too fevered, too anxious. Didn't want to blow his cover. He had this one in his hands and he knew it. "Not really, I just know the basic facts, like everybody else, that's all. It's a big mystery, who he was and why he was doing it."

"Maybe he was just trying to upset the established order, y'know? Shake things up a bit, shine a light on all that poverty and those terrible conditions everybody was living in."

"You're right about that. The crown did take some flack over it."

"And I bet those pigs trying to catch him caught hell too, didn't they?"

"I suppose they did, yeah."

"There you go then, the guy wasn't all bad! Anyone who can stick it to the man like that is doing something right in my book."

Edward fell silent for a moment. "That is quite an interesting take on it. I can't say I've ever heard it explained exactly in those terms. Spring-heeled Jack, hero of the people, that is a wild notion. You are going to make one hell of a writer someday, Teresa."

Just then Edward felt a tinge of something, something unexpected. Something almost painful to him. He didn't remember ever feeling anything like it before. But it made the thought of killing this girl somehow, distasteful. Like destroying a piece of fine art.

She turned her body to Edward. "You're pretty cool, for an old man."

"Hey, I'm only thirty," he told her.

She pulled her knees into her stomach. "How would you like to be *my* old man?" She placed her hand on his leg.

Edward looked down at the hand, then the girl, then the dark road ahead. "Did you ever want something so badly at first, and then you completely change your mind?"

"Sure, I mean that's pretty vague, but sure."

"Well, I was thinking I wanted one thing when I picked you up, but now I'm thinking I don't want to do that anymore." He looked over at her. "Not to you." Edward reached down and placed his hand upon hers. He could tell that a frisson passed through her. "I think it's probably best that you get out here, before I change my mind, or should I say my mind changes me. You see I have a... how should I say this? A weakness for young girls like you."

"Hey, I'm not *that* young. I've been around." She touched his cheek. "Don't be ashamed of what you're into, man."

"Oh, I'm not ashamed," Edward told her. "You're just not the one for me tonight, okay? Don't take it personally."

He leaned over her, lifted the handle, and pushed the heavy car door open. As he did this, she cradled his head in her arms and pulled it into her waiting breasts. "But sweetie, tonight, you're the one for me," she told him. With a single, swift motion she buried a knife edge into his neck below the ear and sliced him clean across. Blood erupted onto the dash and sprayed against the inside of the windshield. "Teresa is my name," she told him. "But you can call me Jill."

As Edward lay on the floorboards of his new car, losing consciousness, waiting for the lifeblood to drain from the gaping fissure in his neck, he would tell you that one final thought entered his fast-fading mind:

A female serial killer, now that's novel.

He would tell you this, but he can't anymore.

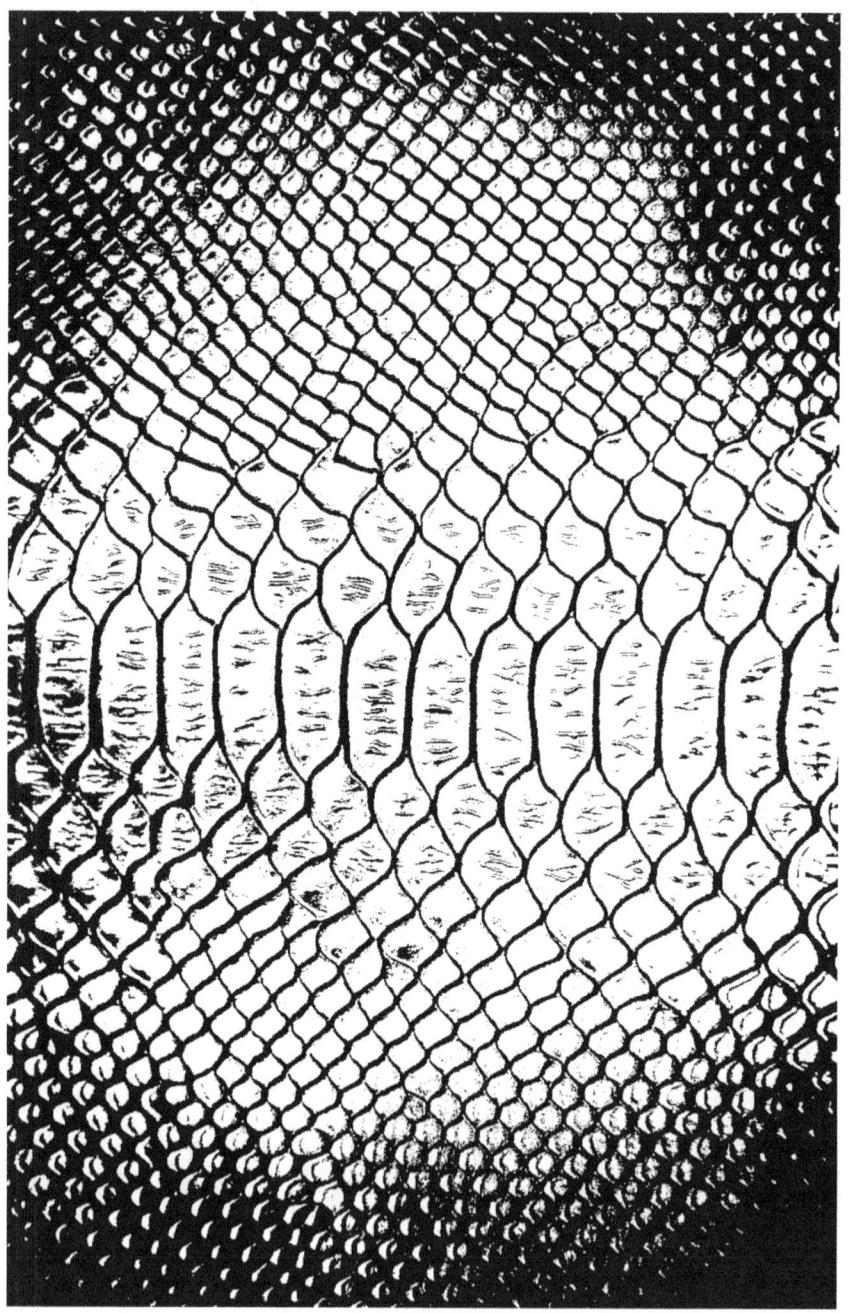

A very successful novelist friend of mine once compared this story to a Pokémon cartoon written by Quentin Tarantino. I actually rather like that description, it's pretty apt. The story represents a foray into the possible future of gene-splicing, animal fighting, and pimping. The original version of this tale found a resting place in serial form at the webzine Fried Fiction.

Unbreakable Yu was influenced more than a little by one of my favorite stories, Sandkings by George R. R. Martin, as well as Dogfight by Michael Swanwick & William Gibson. My aforementioned colleague coaxed me to turn one of my protagonists, the pimp character of Zeebo, into a full-on antagonist. So I did, and I think it worked out well. Of all the monsters that appear in this story, Zeebo could be the scariest of all because his want to succeed and make his mark in the world (or universe) is so damn relatable, even if his methods are grossly Machiavellian.

Unbreakable Yu

The Selvin-3 commercial transport bounced through a pounding methane rain for half an hour before finally alighting on a thin cover of regolith that had spread itself over the landing pad. The enclosure bubble slid shut over the plinking raindrops and the ship rumbled to a halt. In synchronization, the doors whooshed open and warm, fetid air replaced the sterile, temperature-controlled atmosphere of the cabin.

With a firm hand in the small of her back, Zeebo steered Lotus Blossom slowly through the aisle toward the door. Lotus wheeled their luggage in front of her with one hand while the other carried Dem-Si in his conical cage. The small creature grabbed the passengers' initial attention, but Lotus Blossom kept it.

The show had begun.

With her hands full, the bare skin of the girl's thighs just below her endorphin-emitting micro rubbed hard against the shoulders of the seated travelers. Eyes of deep jade collected the men's stares and her raven hair, stepped in the old Anduvian style, held them even longer. She slid by each with a geisha's grace, breasts exposed and her erect nipples painted a shock blue. The entire time she wore a barely-there smile: mysterious, coquettish, and perfectly rehearsed.

From behind her, Zeebo hunched his immense frame over the seats and tossed electrotape into the air. His contact code erupted like a firework in front of their faces, twinkled, flickered and dissolved as it fell. He straightened up, flipped his long dreadlocks over his shoulders and glanced back for an instant. One by one, the passenger dandies in their slouched fedoras and tailored spaceduds slipped their hands into their pockets as casually as their cramped seating would allow and recorded Zeebo's code for that time during their stay when the endless night of Newydd would become too endless to bear alone.

"I like this town already," he whispered in Lotus Blossom's ear.

*

NeoWynd's impotent sun kept its inhabitants in shadow, but the city's ever present artificial lights kept them awake. It kept them wanting. The streets were filled with the chirp of loaded mag-cabs, always on the move, and people packed tight. Pressing against each other. Commingling. The place was alive. It breathed. It sweated. A moist, sulphuric stench steamed out from the bowels of the planet through every concrete orifice. This was a city that dripped and oozed, and that was just the way people there liked it.

The unmanned mag-cab pulled up to the motel. It was a typical NeoWynd city block—a honeycomb of bulbous, egg carton housing piled up hundreds of feet and spread out for a hundred klicks in every direction. Zeebo ducked under the doorframe and triggered the slow, fuzzy birth of the ceiling lights. Lotus groaned.

"At least it's warm," he told her.

She took a last look at the methane plinking against NeoWynd's dome before stepping inside the tiny room. The ash-gray shelter was barren except for a bowl filled with colored stones sitting on a shelf. Zeebo pointed it out.

"Put Barbie in there," he told Lotus.

The woman emptied the stones into a sink and opened one of the luggage pouches, removing a bag of water with a thin, translucent red eel suspended inside. She poured it into the bowl.

"What about chitslugs?" she said. "I heard some got loose before a comp and now NeoWynd's crawling with them."

"That's just some nonsense story that's as old as you are, Lo. Probably started the same day these designer battles did, just adds to the mystique of this place. Chitslugs wouldn't survive here anyway, at least not for long."

"You're the expert," she said in a tone carefully ambiguous enough not to be construed as sarcasm. She opened the door to the adjoining room and unpacked some clothes into a wallspace.

"I *am* the expert, and in a few days everyone in the Greater Quadrant is gonna know it," Zeebo said. He pressed a shaded horizontal bar on the kitchen wall and the table top ejected from inside. He lifted Dem-Si's cage and placed it onto the table. A fine mesh of reinforced wiring held the animal inside. "Set up the tank," he told Lotus.

"Right now?" she whined. "We just got here."

Zeebo gave the girl a severe look and she quickly began to unpack the tank. Upright and clinging to the mesh, Dem-Si was just over a foot tall with seven distinct appendages: a pair of legs and arms and another amorphous set which sprouted from his midsection, each encrusted with tiny suction cups. He had a long, rapier tail with a brush of tendrils attached to its end and his body was shingled with hard, shimmering plates of gold and vermillion that conquered his green patches of skin. Though he was primarily reptilian in

256

appearance, he was possessed of an abnormally large skull with exterior ears, a short snout, and prominent dark eyes.

Lotus pieced together the wall panes of the holding tank while Zeebo began construction of a makeshift laboratory on the table top. His wrist strap began to flash and he glanced down at the screen.

"Your dates are lining up, Lo–you ready to make me some rod?"

"I didn't think you brought me along to be your handyman," she said, clamping in the final panel of the tank. There was no attempt to mask her sarcasm this time, but Zeebo ignored her and began to furnish the tank. Once completed, he placed Dem-Si down onto a stick hovel padded with straw, but the animal immediately left his hut, scampered to one of the clear walls, and raced around the perimeter of the tank. Lotus leaned over the perforated canopy to watch.

"He's familiarizing himself with the new surroundings," Zeebo said. "I taught him that."

She stared at the hybrid's face. "He looks a little like me, don't you think?" She ran her finger along the outside of the glass. Dem-Si chased it playfully.

"Why shouldn't he? A piece of you's inside him."

"It's a little strange, is all."

"You know with the big hybrid fights it's survival of the meanest and I ain't got the rod to afford some of these vicious, fringe exotics from no dealer. And I sure ain't got the rod to search all over the cosmos for them myself," he reminded her. "Ain't no one see the value of intelligence in a fighter. That's where you come in, Lo."

"I know that, Zee. I always help you out."

"That's my girl right there," he said. "Most of these street noobs got no common sense, I tell ya. Restraint is the key, you can't try to do too much. Any wannabe genejock can read the instructions on a splicer, but you gotta be real slick to make it all work."

"Why not use your own DNA though? He'd probably be a better fighter," she said.

"Nah, your genetics are perfect."

"Because I'm tough?"

"Because you're a *woman*," he said. "Dem-Si needs a certain type of cunning, and you have it inside you in spades, girl," he said. "Don't you?"

"I ain't saying I don't have none, but peddling flesh as long as I have taught me that women got, right in their nature, a certain..." he searched for the right word. "A certain *guile* that men don't. Remember how I taught you most men are just animals, real predictable?" She nodded, a knowing smirk crawling across her face. "But women... women are goddam marvels. They got a natural craftiness that serves them, you feel me? It's a gift, really. I love that about you women. Combine that with some nasty physical traits to

257

complement it, put it all in one body, train it, and throw it into the ring and you got yourself a winner." He shook his head in mock astonishment. "Everybody else can let their hybrids rely on instinct, but I'm gonna have Dem-Si actually *learn* as he fights, then use them female wiles to win me a shitload of rod *and* get me some respect."

"I don't know," she said as she walked to the bedroom. "I still think you could've tried your own DNA."

Zeebo scoffed. "Jesus, Lo, ain't you been listening? Well, that ain't never been a woman's strong suit anyway." He slipped his arms through the sleeves of a fresh shirt and followed her into the bedroom. "You still such a young thing." Then he stroked her cheek. "You gotta learn to take a compliment."

*

The arena was located in the basement of a dilapidated subscraper at the heart of the city, the first fifty-seven subfloors being used as a parking facility for mag-car owners who were either very brave or very desperate. But deeper still, on the fifty-eighth sub, there was a theater of battle.

Time had sunk the basement near its center, lending it the appearance of a shallow bowl. Many of the high-hanging lights no longer functioned or only flickered, save for the innermost ones, above the fighting pits. The entire shadowy expanse was littered with weight-bearing concrete pillars that sweat with dankness.

A group of blood-hungry young men huddled, hooting and shouting at the action within. The oval stage was constructed of basic starbrick and mortar with a clear polydome separating the combatants from the spectators. From his vantage point beside one of the outside pillars, Zeebo could see some plump, hirsute insect with too-small wings kicking up dust as it hopped around the arena floor, seemingly taunting a sluggish podshell.

"Is this the turnout I can expect tomorrow, Ohmav?"

"Don't be fooled, my friend," a voice responded from the darkness in a gravelly, Baltic accent. "They always hand the floor over to the indigenous the night before a build-battle." A diminutive figure in an indigo fez slid in between the onlookers like a stream of water. He had a jagged scar from the bottom of his ear to his artificial, metallic nose. This was the book, Ohmav Illic. "Let them have their day in the pit at such a callow age and they'll be back for life." He reached up to place a hand on Zeebo's wide shoulder. "Don't worry yourself, all the big rod that just flew in for your fight would rather partake in NeoWynd's other pleasures tonight."

Zeebo nodded and his skin flushed slightly with embarrassment over his concern. "You're right. The girl I brought has a full card already."

Ohmav made a waving gesture with his hand. "There, you see, you worry for nothing. But you didn't come here to talk about the crowds, now did you?" Zeebo moved in closer. "Dem-Si's opponent tomorrow night is a King Rat mix," Ohmav whispered.

"A long hair?"

Ohmav nodded. "It's a Fury alright. They've kept the splice within the family—sawdog for the teeth, a rotter for the claws. Nothing fancy, just mean stacked on top of mean."

"Typical," Zeebo said. "But at least they know exactly what they're getting with it. And now, so do I." He smirked at the little man. "I don't think I've seen that mix before though."

"I'm sure you haven't. You can't land in the five systems carrying that devil."

"God bless NeoWynd," Zeebo said.

"God bless," Ohmav echoed as he raised his hand in a phantom toast. "Anything else for me?"

"Is that not enough for you?" Ohmav said as he held out his hand. Zeebo pulled out a fistful of short, varicolored sticks and gave them over. Ohmav shook the rods around and thumbed through the different shades. Satisfied by the payment, he sorted them neatly into the pouches of his belt. "Now it's your turn, Zeebo, my friend," he said. "I want to know your lizard's honest-to-God chances?"

Zeebo thought about it long enough to watch the podshell skewer its moth-like foe with a blast of its tongue and pull the insect into its shell before the handlers could stop it. "It's looking really good," he finally said. "Dem-Si should figure this rat out. We've trained on Kings before, Furies even. Never this exact chimera, but he's seen the breeds before. And now that I know what it is, I'll whip something up to refresh his memory."

Ohmav was giddy. He slapped his hands together, light and brisk. "That is very good, yes, very good." Then he straightened out the lapels of his jacket with a quick tug and stroked his pencil mustache. "With the look of that Fury, odds on your hybrid might be awfully long tomorrow night. I feel almost guilty making this kind of rod off him without you seeing any. If you'd like me to place a wager for you-"

Zeebo dug into his belt again and handed over several more colored sticks. "Why not?" he said.

*

Zeebo returned to the motel, plugged in some U, and began to incubate new sparring partners for Dem-Si. Lotus Blossom trudged into Zeebo's room later just as he was removing the Fury's poison glands. She grabbed a bottle out of the kitchen and guzzled it down while her hand waded in the water of the bowl. The thin eel circled her finger and nibbled it innocently. She slapped at the trigger of Zeebo's slideout and dropped onto the mattress.

"Did the gentlemen remember their manners?" Zeebo asked without looking up.

"Mostly," she said.

"Did you take care of it?" he asked, now side-eyeing the young woman.

"He'll be fine, once he comes to. Don't expect any repeat business from him though."

"You never know. Some guys like the rough stuff."

"This guy didn't," she said.

Zeebo laughed under his breath. "Poor bastard."

"Just doing what you taught me."

He finished stitching the anesthetized rat. The Fury was now ready to provide Dem-Si with some practice. As a safety precaution Zeebo left it dazed and still wet with birthing plasma at one end of the ersatz battleground while he sheathed Dem-Si in a protective skinthin.

Lotus was on her back. She raised a leg and rolled off her fishnets, playing with the scented nylon for a few moments. "Do you ever feel like you were supposed to be someone else?" she asked.

"Like who?"

"I don't know, just somebody different from who you are now. It's like right now you're only pretending to be someone when the person you're supposed to be is still stuck inside you just waiting for you to figure it out. That's why you do these things, isn't it? You want to be someone else."

"I don't know, Lo. I'm busy."

She rolled over onto her side to face him. "Who do *you* want to be?"

Zeebo bowed his head and sighed, then pushed himself back from the table and swiveled his chair toward her. "I know when you get like this you won't shut up until I talk to you so..." he told her. "For one thing, I wanna be someone who's remembered for something more than just pleasure pushing," he said. "Next, I wanna have so much rod that I can build a house out of it, and I want all that real power that comes along with it." He paused. "And I wanna be someone people envy. Someone people look at and say, '*Goddamn, that muthafucker got it all!*'" Lotus stared blankly at him in the silent moment that followed. "That's all I want," Zeebo said before pulling himself back to the table top and returning to his work.

She grunted and rolled onto her back again, carefully slipping the other stocking off her leg. "You wanna know what I want?" she asked. Lotus gave Zeebo ample time, but he didn't answer. "I *don't* want things," she finally said. "I don't wanna be sore and swollen all the time, down there." She pointed to her crotch.

"I gave you pills for that."

She grimaced. "I know, but I don't wanna take those pills. And I don't wanna have to clean myself ten times a day. I don't want to be so, so *wanted*. I'm Lotus Blossom so much that sometimes I forget what it's like not to be her. You know what I mean, right?"

Zeebo threw his prongs down onto the table. "Let me tell you what I *don't* want, Lo, I don't wanna hear that kind of shit from you. You remember now it wasn't forever ago that you were an itchy little guttersnipe who needed a shower, and who gladly swallowed every pill I gave you because it made you feel good. I remember when you *wanted* to be wanted by just about anyone. You begged me to turn you into anything but yourself and now you miss that girl?" Lotus rolled over to face the wall and Zeebo gave a scoff. "I made Lotus Blossom. Lotus Blossom is beautiful, Lotus Blossom is unique. Lotus Blossom has value. You got the rest of your life to be plain old Yu, but for now you're Lotus and you're going to stay Lotus until I tell you not to. That's what you owe me." Lotus grumbled unintelligibly at the wall while Zeebo stood up from his chair and approached her. "There *is* one more thing that I want, Lo," he said.

He unbuckled his belt and summoned her with his finger. Lotus Blossom craned her neck to see Zeebo take his flaccid penis out of the top of his pants and dangle it over his waistband. She dropped mechanically down onto the floor in front of him and took hold of his cock while he combed through her hair with thick, dark fingers. Like a sculptor molding dead clay into something real, into something of use, she brought the man to life. Lotus tasted him, tasted his essence, and was finished. Affixed to the wall of the holding tank by his tentacled fingers, Dem-Si looked on with great interest.

*

Dem-Si's training went on through that night and into the next morning, causing Zeebo to oversleep and arrive late to the arena. Ohmav was right about the crowds: the place was teeming with spectators, but Zeebo sliced through them with Dem-Si's cage in his hand raised high above him. Ohmav was standing upfront and, when he saw the trainer, he made a signal to Zeebo urging him to make haste. As Zeebo neared the battle oval, the hordes of spectators slowly realized who he was, cheered, and pushed him along.

Ohmav pointed to the holding pen at the far end. "There's the rat, looks like they've been starving it for days."

"Then it'll die hungry," Zeebo said, unfastening the door of Dem-Si's cage.

Ohmav gave a smirk. "I suppose if you're not worried, I shouldn't be either," he said.

"An animal can only get so mean, and that rat was as pissed off as it was ever going to get the day they made it." He released Dem-Si into his own holding pen. "I'll take my chances with a pampered hybrid over a desperate one anytime. Loyalty trumps instinct."

"Nurture over nature, you say?" Ohmav nodded. "Unusual."

The fighting floor was covered with a thin layer of soil and furnished with several large rock piles and a smatter of browning vegetation. A man outfitted in a lustrous orange-striped animal pelt leapt onto the flattened portion of the dome. He did a jig to the pounding of a drum beat wearing the animal's head draped over his own like a hood. This brought the crowd to frenzy. Suddenly he stopped, spread his arms, and lifted his opened palms slowly as the gates of each holding pen simultaneously raised.

The animals cautiously emerged from their pens.

The Fury had an elongated snout for a King Rat species—no doubt due to some extra tinkering on its handler's part—with rows of long, crooked teeth serrated at the edges. The rat feverishly wiped its curled front claws against its mouth to spread the glistening venom it secreted. From its haunches, it dipped its head down and performed the same task to its back feet. Its black-and-silver coat was matted down and clumps of it protruded from its body in stiff cowlicks. The Fury looked to outweigh Dem-Si, but not so much that it would warrant a protest. Ohmav frowned slightly and he tapped his index finger against his temple.

Dem-Si began to meander from his pen through a maze of shrubbery and vines, stopping once he caught sight of the Fury. The rat then darted around its own coppice and surmounted the line of rocks at the center of the oval. Dem-Si remained frozen just below it, at the edge of the shabby grove, its skin plates already changed to an earthy, camouflaged brown. Undeterred, the rat charged headlong down the slope, slowing as it hit the dirt. It approached Dem-Si head-on, but the lizard would not move. The sound of the crowd grew deafening.

"What's he doing?" Ohmav whined. "The King's too close."

"Patience," was all Zeebo said, softly.

The rat moved in, baring its wiry garden of teeth. A froth of poison hung off its jaws and fell to the ground in bubbly strands, muddying its path. It crept by Dem-Si, pausing only slightly to sniff at the air. It stuck its head into the underbrush.

In that moment, Dem-Si's body sprang to life and he mounted the rat beast. The rat wheeled its head around, out of the foliage, as a black spray shot from inside Dem-Si's mouth, blinding the Fury. Dem-Si leapt from the writhing animal and circled it while the Fury thrashed about in a wild rage. He whipped his tail into the rat's side, gashing it. The thick coat of rodent hair parted and gave way to the bulging red velvet of entrails. Dem-Si scrambled back to the gate and scaled the slats to the top of his pen, his eyes searching for his master. Zeebo's face split into a wide smile.

"Bravo, sir," Ohmav said.

*

The faint glow of morning had been in the window for hours before Zeebo lifted his eyes to the new day. Lotus Blossom was sitting in front of the tank, arms draped over its roof, giggling to herself.

When he could no longer rest, Zeebo lifted himself up off the bed and, without his weight on it, the mattress slid invisibly back into the wall to be cleaned. He walked to the kitchen and took a swig off a bulb he'd left half-finished the night before.

"You're up early," he said.

"I couldn't sleep." Lotus wiggled her finger playfully at the lizard on the other side of the glass. Zeebo gave an apathetic chuckle and checked the time.

"This planet's too dark, I slept late again," he said with a shake of his head. "I stayed for the other fight last night–Dem-Si's up against a giant horn spyder from out on the rim somewhere, not sure which galaxy. I'll pick up some exotics today at the gene market and patch something together for him to train on." He reached down to power up his lab but, to his astonishment, the equipment was already on. He hastily checked the disposal; it was slick with plasma.

Lotus spoke into the tank. "My Dem-Si's finally awake," she said. "That's it, don't be a shy boy, come see what Mommy made for you."

Zeebo peered into the tank. There were now two glistening reptile bodies inside, intertwined with one another.

"*What did you do?*"

"I made her myself last night, while you were asleep. I thought our little boy could use some female companionship."

Zeebo fell silent. His face grew hard and ruddy.

Lotus's body stiffened. "You can say it's a concubine if you want. Didn't all great warriors used to have concubines?"

"You made Dem-Si a *girlfriend?*" Zeebo dug his palms into his eyes. "I bring you with me to NeoWynd and you fuck with my animal?"

Lotus tried to speak, but the words wouldn't come out. Zeebo shook his head for a long time before he spoke again. When he finally did, his voice was heavy, like thunder. "You better pray this don't mess him up, Lo," he told her. "Now separate them nicely and get rid of that bitch."

He made his hand into a tight fist and raised it. Lotus Blossom shrunk. Then all the muscles in Zeebo's body seemed to relax and he slowly unclenched the hand and brought it gently to the young woman's face. He cradled the side of her head, thumbing at her temple with the permanently silvered and calloused fingers of a mercury farmer's son.

"Marking that face up would be a real fool thing of me to do," he said.

Zeebo brought his free hand around and slapped Lotus hard on her ear. The force of the blow disrupted her equilibrium and she tumbled off the chair. With her head still abuzz and woozy, she slid herself into a corner.

"They're the exact same animal, the same mixture, I made sure of it," Lotus stammered. "She wouldn't hurt him, I know she wouldn't."

Zeebo opened his hand and raised it high into the air, then dropped it harmlessly to his side, seemingly confused as to what he should do with it. Rather than strike her, he grabbed a fistful of hair behind her head. "How you gonna know what another hybrid will do to him? She could fuck up his training." He wagged his head as he pulled her hair tight, causing her neck to bend unnaturally behind her. "All I need Dem-Si to know is what he learns in that tank, what I teach him, you understand? Everything else has an effect, Lo!"

Lotus's unblinking eyes moistened and the tears she tried so hard to hold onto left a trail down her perfect cheekbones. Zeebo stood over the sobbing girl in contemplation for a long moment, breathing heavily through flared nostrils. Finally, he stormed to the kitchen and brought back the bowl with Barbie, the red eel, inside.

"Do I like fish?" he said.

Lotus could only stare in response. Zeebo rolled his eyeballs and asked again, this time more forcefully. "*Do I like fish, goddamn it?* Have you known me to be especially fond of them? Do I breed them? Do I fight them? Have you ever seen me eat one?"

"N-No," she said.

"That's right, you have not. And do you know why?"

She shook her head.

"Because I don't like them, Lo. I do not like them in a box. I do not like them with a fox. I do not like green eggs and ham. I do not like them, Sam-I-Am. You get me?"

Lotus nodded.

"They wet, they slimy, they smelly, they nasty tasting, and they a hard-ass splice on top of that. So I don't fuck with no fish." He grabbed the mouth of the bowl with one unsteady hand and the eel flipped and twisted in the water like a streamer. "And despite all that, I own a motherfucking eel," he said. "Why do you suppose that is?"

Lotus carefully wiped the mixture of tears and snot from her face. She cleared her throat. "I don't know. For luck maybe?"

Zeebo gave a rattling, exaggerated laugh. "No, no, not luck," he said. "Insurance." His breathing slowed and he calmed himself with a couple of vigorous head shakes. He turned the bowl upside down. Water and eel hit the floor. Zeebo and Lotus both watched as the eel writhed, gulping at the air, its gills fanning for oxygen it could not reach. "In the Mondari quadrant the people call this eel a *sticky fish*." Lotus Blossom retreated to the corner of the room, dropped to the floor, and pulled her knees tight to her body. "So you've heard of it?" Zeebo said.

"Some of the other girls talk about it."

"What do they say?"

Lotus thought back to the times when the old prostitutes would cackle at her in their deep, throaty voices, mocking her innocence. "T-They didn't tell me nothing, but they said I'd find out all about it someday."

"And so you shall, my flower. So you shall."

While they spoke, the eel's labored breathing slowed. When it had taken its last, Zeebo dug into his travel case, took out an oversized pair of gloves, and slipped them on.

"This particular kind of eel has these bumps all over its body." He ran a gloved hand over its nodular skin. "The whole damn thing feels like a stuffed sock," he told her. "But they call it a sticky fish because the Mondari figured out, don't ask me how, that when one of these things die, millions and millions of microscopic spines swell out from the bumps on its body. And when you hit someone with it," He picked the eel up by its tail and snapped it like a whip, "those little spines stick right into their skin. Get it—*sticky* fish? Hurts like a sonuvabitch, or so I've been told. But the craziest thing about these little spines is that they don't penetrate the skin far enough to cause any real damage," he said, then he smiled. "And they don't leave any marks." Lotus's body began to tremble. "Not on the outside at least." Zeebo began to move.

"No, baby, no—"

He cracked the whip-fish again and paced the floor as he spoke. "You see sometimes I gotta train my girls too, get them to know their boundaries, but I can't have them all bruised up like old fruit either—that's bad business. Never damage the packaging, Lo. Now I suppose I could smack you in the ear every time you get out of line, but after what you did, I think I need to leave more of an impression." Zeebo approached the girl, the red eel undulating in his hand. "Stand up," he told Lotus. The girl shakily got to her feet, her weight still firmly pressed against the corner wall. "Turn around." The girl followed that direction as well. "Take off your clothes," he said finally. Lotus Blossom did exactly as she was told.

Face against the wall and blind to the man, Lotus heard only the whirr of the revolving eel as Zeebo readied himself. With the stroke of the lash imminent, Lotus clamped her eyelids down as tight as they would shut. The snap of the eel was followed immediately by a clap that reverberated in her ear. She opened her eyes to see the whip clinging to the wall a few inches from her head. Zeebo shook the eel loose and it dropped to the floor, leaving a gelatinous film behind. The girl exhaled.

"Don't worry about what Dem-Si needs. That's not why you're here." Zeebo went back to the kitchen to get a towel and Lotus panted out several weighty breaths. "Wipe that shit off the wall or they'll charge us," he said when he returned.

Lotus reached her hand up the wall to wipe away the clear streak when the eel snapped through the air and embedded itself into her forearm. She gave a wail as the hot pain shot through her flesh like her blood was on fire. Zeebo got in close behind her, his breath stale on her face. "I'm only doing this so you won't forget, Lo. Otherwise, I can't be certain." He peeled the diaphanous animal off her skin and handed her the rag soaked with warm water. "Clean yourself up," he said weakly.

Lotus covered her mouth to stifle the whimpers but could not halt the renewed welling of her eyes. She wiped her face dry with the rag and ran the cold tap over her arm for several minutes. While the pain lessened slightly it would never fully disappear, not for weeks. She managed to get the thin nightgown back on her body, wrapped her now throbbing arm in gauze, and moved to the tank. Dem-Si and his mate remained locked onto each other. Lotus pushed the roof of the tank aside and attempted to pry them apart using a shockbar. Initially, she mistook Dem-Si for the new lizard, nearly pacifying him before she realized her mistake.

She bagged up Dem-Si's unconscious mate, held it up to show Zeebo, tossed it into her room, and shut the door. "Come here, Lo." Zeebo was slumped in his chair, twitching badly, jacked on Uphoria. U was cheap, legal, and everywhere you looked on NeoWynd. Lotus Blossom crept toward the man. When she was within reach, he grabbed her by the arm and pulled her in. "I can forgive you," he said, his eyelids fluttering. "But if it happens again I won't be as gentle. You lucky we ain't home, I'd have to make an example of you then. You understand me, don't you?"

"I understand everything," she said.

*

Ohmav was seated at a floating table top outside a café called *The Neon* when Zeebo arrived later that afternoon. He sipped from a blazing lime cup while he watched the brilliant lights from a thousand miles of the city rail system crisscross in the distance like tangled necklace strands. *The Neon* was bathed in black light and the accompanying fluorescence augmented the dim glow of NeoWynd's nearest star.

"Zeebo, my good man, sit, try some of this local bean." He flagged the waiter with his handkerchief but Zeebo waved him off. Ohmav inspected the trainer closely. "I would be careful with the U on NeoWynd, my friend. The government here requires a minimum potency, it's harder than you'll find most anywhere, certainly harder than you must be accustomed to." Zeebo gave an obligatory nod to the bookie and Ohmav gazed into the horizon before waving his hand dismissively. "This place is all about the tourists now. I suppose people need a good reason to come out this far and NeoWynd is quite the devil's toy chest."

"Hook me up with a blast or two, man, that's all I need to finish this. I been working Dem-Si day and night, getting him ready for Teag's horn spyder."

"That is a wise plan. I don't have to tell you Boas Teag is a man of considerable skill. Anything he designs should not be taken lightly."

Zeebo nodded again, this time more spasmodically, as a U-induced tic twisted his facial features and caused him to repeat his words. "Teag's a master, I ain't blind to it. I'm not-not underestimating him, don't worry. I've come too far to let some Oedipus hubris shit bring me down. But-but I can't let sleep stop-stop me either."

"Uphoria certainly has its benefits," Ohmav said.

"*Whatever* I have to do-do this week is going to get done. It took me years to get here." Zeebo closed his eyes and slouched down in his chair while Ohmav dug out a vial of brown liquid from his jacket. He placed a few drops onto the corner of a napkin and handed it to Zeebo.

"Take this," he said. "It's called *whoa*, it's a suppressant. It should help jack you down. Zeebo tore off the corner and placed it under his tongue. The muscles of his face immediately began to relax. Zeebo breathed in deeply.

"Did you find out anything else about the hybrid spyder?"

"Teag is notorious for keeping his entire camp tight-lipped." Ohmav paused for effect. "But I was naturally able to obtain a tidbit which I hope will be of some use to you."

"What you got?"

"The giant horn spyder you know all about. A real tank: hard exoskeleton, powerful body, an antenna stinger, acidic venom, and fangs that could puncture spun steel. Its helix is a nightmare before you even get it into the splicer."

"Of course, but it's too docile, no one uses it," Zeebo said.

"You saw what it did to that split-tailed creeper last night in the pit. It's anything but docile now."

Zeebo conceded with a tilt of his head. "No doubt. So what's this new tidbit?"

Ohmav dropped his voice and leaned in over his cup. Steam rose up and framed the small man's oily face. "It doesn't outwardly appear to be anything but a giant horn spyder, am I right?" He swiveled his head left to right. "I've been told that it may not be much more," he whispered.

"What do you mean?"

"I mean the splicing was purposely limited to affect a new, aggressive nature and nothing else." He leaned back in his chair.

Zeebo's brow furrowed. "Why would a smart gene-swapper like Boas Teag only make a slight *instinctual* alteration when he could splice in any number of physical attributes to help his fighter out? I don't understand it, if you're going to give an animal a killer instinct, why not give it some weapons, too?"

Ohmav threw up his hands. "As I said, I didn't know if the information would mean anything to you, but it was so difficult to acquire, I thought it may hold some value. What do you think it means?"

Zeebo was quiet for a long time. Ohmav ordered another cup and sipped at it leisurely while he waited for Zeebo to mull over this new wrinkle.

"He's hiding it," Zeebo said suddenly.

"Who's hiding?"

"Teag's hiding it," Zeebo said. "You're even more clever than they give you credit for, Boas." Ohmav leaned in hungrily while Zeebo spoke. "Teag limited his splice to *behavioral* traits so he could hide the identity of the partner animal. That motherfucker knows that I can't possibly figure out what he spliced the spyder with if he doesn't give the spyder any of the physical characteristics of that animal, even if those characteristics would help it." Zeebo gulped in a chestful of air. "Which means he must know what I'm up to with Dem-Si."

Ohmav put his hands together in mock prayer. "Forgive an old gambler's ignorance of such things but–"

"Don't you see?" Zeebo said. "He did this so I can't prep Dem-Si for his spyder. He knows I can't teach Dem-Si to fight something if I don't know what it is, if I can't recreate it for him to practice on. He must've heard about me before we even came to NeoWynd."

Even in his panicked state, a sudden swell of pride rushed over Zeebo at the thought of Boas Teag, the great trainer, the virtuoso, preparing a hybrid specifically to counter the strategy of his own.

"As long as the recipe of that hybrid spyder is a mystery to me, ain't no way I can train Dem-Si to take it on, not with any certainty of success. He'll have to figure it out on the fly, and I don't know if he can pull that shit off," Zeebo said. "That's not how I built him. It takes him time to learn. Dem-Si can beat anything, I know he can, but only if I show it to him beforehand. He needs time to see it." Zeebo lowered his head. "Is there *any* way you can get to one of Teag's men and find out what's in that spyder?"

Ohmav shook his head. "I pulled every string just to get this, my friend."

Again, Zeebo disappeared into his own thoughts. "*You* may not be able to," Zeebo said as he slapped his hands on the table. "But I might. Go to that U-bar a couple blocks from the arena and wait for me there." Zeebo shot up from his chair, almost knocking it over, rushed out of *The Neon* and caught a railcar back to the motel.

*

Lotus was on the bed in her room when Zeebo burst through the door.

"Lo, get up, I need ya."

The young woman rolled over, her back to him. "I'm working tonight, remember?"

"There's something you have to do, Lotus, and this something, it has to be done now, understand?" Zeebo ripped the covers off her and she scurried to the far side of the bed.

"I'm up," she said. "What do you want?"

"Get pretty, and then you're coming downtown with me. I'll tell you once we get there."

"What about the johns?" she asked

"They can jerk off to the motel holo-porn tonight. This is more important."

*

Ohmav was waiting inside the door of the U-bar when Zeebo and Lotus arrived.

"My dear, you are a vision. It is utter cruelty that Zeebo has hidden you from me this long." He turned to Zeebo. "Perhaps we can arrange a liaison?" He fingered the motley sticks affixed to his belt before pulling one out.

"Keep the rod in your pants, Ohmav. She's not here for you," Zeebo said, scanning the bar. "Just tell me if you see any of Teag's men, I know you're familiar with them."

Ohmav's eyes covered the large room of patrons quickly. "There's Brother Luuce, he's one of them." He pointed to a sheer-curtained space where a man reclined on stacks of pillows with a sense hookah bridled to his head. "And that little fellow at the booth is Brother Drewell, he's one of Teag's as well."

"See anyone else?" Zeebo asked.

268

"No, I don't believe so."

"Then we'll take Drewell, it looks like Brother Luuce may already be too far gone to give us anything."

"What did you have in mind?" Ohmav asked.

Zeebo turned to the girl. "You got to be at your best tonight, my lotus flower. Do whatever you got to do, tell that man whatever he has to hear, but get him to leave this bar with you."

"And go where?"

"Back to the motel. I rented the room next to ours."

"The usual?" she asked.

"I'm afraid it won't be that easy tonight," Zeebo told her. He took hold of her arms and pulled her face close to his. "I want you to find out what they spliced their spyder with."

Lotus allowed a frown to form on her face, but immediately tried to brighten her countenance before Zeebo noticed. *I'm tricking for favors now*, she thought to herself, though she would never let those words escape her mind.

Zeebo grabbed the back of her neck. "I made you, bitch. I take care of you. You just as much mine as that animal is, so you gon' do what I need you to do, just like all the rest. Just cuz you my best earner don't change nothing, Lo."

She shrugged his hand away. "Alright, I get it. But what if this guy won't talk to me?"

"You my top girl," Zeebo said. "You'll get him to sing."

Lotus nodded and walked to the tiny windowed booth where Drewell was buying a U-drop from the tender.

"You must know how dangerous this is," Ohmav told Zeebo. "If Boas Teag discovers you strong-armed one of his men–"

"I'm not muscling anyone. That's why I'll have Lotus work him over. Brother Drewell ain't never gonna tell his boss that he gave away secrets to a whore. Have some faith, she can be very persuasive. An hour alone with her and she could make *you* want to leave your wife."

"She doesn't need an hour to do that," Ohmav said. Lotus Blossom sat down close to Brother Drewell, smiled, and began the process while Zeebo watched from the door.

Only a few minutes before she was the same rough-edged-and-wounded type Zeebo had found wandering the streets a hundred times before. Some of the girls he found just got rougher. Some got more wounded. But Lotus was perfect; she was just the right mix of both and she stayed that way through her training. Now she was in complete control. This was her field. Her every movement was an invitation, her every whisper an intoxicant, her very scent suggested to Drewell a silent yearning. And when she brought Brother Drewell home, her warm flesh would split open to him and be his confessional. He would kneel before her altar and share whatever secrets she wished to know. Of that, Zeebo was certain.

And then, as if on cue, Lotus led Brother Drewell by the hand out of the bar and into the NeoWynd night. The two men followed discreetly behind until they arrived at the motel. Lotus beckoned Drewell in with a curl of her finger. Entranced, Drewell shuffled forward into her lair. The door shut. Zeebo placed his finger into the key slot of his own room. His DNA verified, the door unlocked and he slowly twisted the knob to open the door. Once inside, he and Ohmav waited in the darkness beside the window. Brother Drewell left the motel just over an hour later. Zeebo opened the adjoining door and the men walked in on Lotus getting dressed.

"What did Drewell say?"

"*Phasmid?*" she blurted, grabbing a sheet to cover herself. "That's what he called it. They crossed it with a phasmid. Does that help?"

"A simple earth phasmid?"

Lotus could only shrug.

"That's genius, actually," he told Ohmav before turning back to Lotus. "Are you sure he wasn't lying to you?"

"I wondered that, too, but he insisted you could tell the splice was phasmid because of the way the spyder rocks back and forth and that there were some underdeveloped–*mandibles* I think they're called–if you looked closely at its mouth. He said they tried to cut them out but it never took."

Zeebo reached down and slapped Lotus's bare ass. "You did it, Lo, I ain't never gonna forget this. You should go lie down now and get some sleep. I'll be at it with Dem-Si until morning at least, with a little help." He took a puff of U and went to his room with Ohmav. Lotus collapsed onto her slideout.

Zeebo began the incubation of several phasmida hybrids, suited Dem-Si up, and prepared to train. The phasmids were a highly aggressive predatory species with an unorthodox fighting style. Zeebo knew that without the information Lotus pulled out of Brother Drewell, the spyder would've definitely surprised Dem-Si.

"Boas Teag was smart to partner these genes with the horn spyder's," he told Ohmav as the first batch of hybrids emerged from the incubator. "But I'm just as smart."

*

Zeebo's alarm warmed his wrist and shot an electronic pulse to his cerebral cortex, waking him. It was mid-afternoon. Lotus Blossom was coiled around him naked on the bed, still asleep. His waking stirred her and she stretched herself out like a cat, which allowed him to crawl out of the bed and sit up.

"What's wrong with the extra room?" Zeebo asked, tying his shoulder-length dreadlocks into a thick, black tail.

"It's lonelier in there," she said. "I'd rather be here."

Zeebo parted his lips slightly and exhaled. "It's good to hear you say that, Lo. I was afraid you wasn't ever gonna forgive me," he told her. "It's this comp, I just wanna win this thing so badly. You know what I'm talking about?"

"I know."

He stepped out of his shorts. "Why don't you come by the arena tonight," he told her. "You really should be there." Lotus's eyes widened. "But you'll have to wear a burka like the natives so you're not recognized."

"I don't mind," she said cheerfully. "I'll go out later today and pick one up."

"I'll leave your name at the door then."

"Thank you, baby," she said. "I would give anything to be able to see you tonight. When are you leaving?"

"As soon as I'm washed up. I want to make it there before the crowds this time and I want Dem-Si well-rested."

Lotus peeked into Dem-Si's hut. "Looks like that won't be a problem." The lizard was in a deep sleep. "How'd it go last night?"

"By the end of the training he was perfect. He was recognizing the phasmid's attacks and countering effectively. I was tempted to take off the skinthins and let him go at it for real, but I didn't want to take the chance." Zeebo checked on the sleeping animal then stripped off the rest of his underclothes. "I'm getting in the water. Pack up before you leave and be ready to check out in the morning."

"I can't wait," she told him and then whispered into the tank, "Good luck tonight, my killer."

*

Zeebo arrived earlier than the previous night, but the spectators had already begun to assemble. He had outfitted himself in his favorite suit, a scarlet five-button with his initials on the breast pocket in labstone. He was instructed to wait in a back room until just before the match was to take place. Ohmav met him in the crowded corridor and the duo stepped into the dressing room.

"How is our champion today?" Ohmav asked, rubbing his hands.

"Confident," Zeebo replied. He pulled the cover away from the cage. Dem-Si was lying on the floor. He was partially asleep.

"I must say, this sight does not exactly fill me with the same feeling," Ohmav said.

"He's fine, just tired is all. We were at it all night. Give him a minute." Slowly, as the men watched, the hybrid began to shake away his slumber, and with it, Ohmav's fears. "There isn't an ounce of worry in him. He knows exactly what to expect when he gets out there tonight."

"That's good. I've been taking bets for Teag's spyder at three-to-one odds and the suckers here have been eating it up. Most books have Dem-Si at five-to-one, or longer."

"Boas Teag's reputation always precedes him."

"All the better for me," Ohmav said. "When Dem-Si wins it's going to really stretch my belt."

The subsequent minutes passed with Zeebo quiet in thought. He prowled around the small room until he eventually spoke, it seemed almost reluctantly. "What are the longest odds out there on Dem-Si?"

"I've seen a few of the local thicknecks have him at about fifteen-to-one. Are you considering another small wager?"

Zeebo took in a heavy breath and flared his nostrils before he answered. "Tonight's my coming out, Ohmav. It's my gigantic 'fuck you' to everyone who thought I wouldn't make it. Everyone who thought I didn't have what it takes. Every piece of shit back home who thought I wouldn't ever amount to nothing but a small-time hustler." He waved his hands to the bookie. "Nah, nah, tonight's not a night to think small, oldboy. I got me plenty of rod stashed back at the motel. If I spread it all out on bets, I could make myself a real killing tonight," he said. "I think it's about time this playa stretched his belt too."

*

Three hours later, after an undercard of lesser bouts, there was the obligatory knock on the door summoning the fighters. Ohmav led Zeebo, hybrid in hand, through the labyrinth of dusty corridors where the trespassing, rust-colored pipes and heating shafts snaked across every section of wall and bulged from the ceilings. They moaned and sloshed. They sweated with condensation and filth, almost organic, almost alive, like the mucky innards of some great beast.

The men emerged at one high end of the basement. The frenzied crowd, even larger than the previous night's, greeted them with their noise and stink. Zeebo could see Boas Teag entering from the other end, his men cutting a swath through the crowd.

It was the first time Zeebo had ever seen Teag in the flesh. He was taller than Zeebo had expected, and more corpulent. His thick red beard had been teased out and swirled into hooks for the occasion. He wore his trademark bowler and plaids under a tailored straightline suit and he walked with the aid of two thick canes fastened to his forearms, hunched over as if he were an animal himself on all fours. His face had suffered the excesses of his life: a bulbous nose webbed in gin blossoms, ugly pits on any part of his cheeks that weren't covered in facial hair, and countless scars acquired in an adolescence of club fighting, before the ban.

Ohmav leaned into Zeebo's ear as they made their way to the pit. "He's a monstrous sight, eh? But he's also the most revered handler on four worlds. He procures huge fees any time one from his stable fights. Aquatics, aerials, sentient gasses, light forms, no matter. He's totally diversified and regarded as a true sportsman. A gentleman of leisure who lives life in the pursuit of his passions."

"That's just what I want," Zeebo told him. "A good life, but not too respectable, not too stale. I gotta still be underground, still be grimy. That's a just-right life."

Zeebo reached the edge of the combat pit and emptied his fighter into the holding pen, feeling the slightest shudder from the lizard as he did. The man in the striped pelt again performed his ritual dance and waited for permission from the trainers to proceed with the match. Zeebo and Teag both motioned their okays and the gates were slowly lifted.

The lizard was the first to move. He slipped out of his pen and meandered along the floor, beside the wallboards. A frisson of excitement shot through the assemblage. The horn spyder then crept out smoothly from the shadows of its pen. The reptile was sitting atop a small rock but quickly shimmied up the dome upon spying the giant spyder.

"Is this part of Dem-Si's training?" Ohmav asked.

"Yep, he's taking a high defensive position."

The spyder's eyes, posted on hundreds of short stalks around a single horn atop its head, branched out, searching for its prey. When it caught sight of Zeebo's hybrid, the spyder immediately marched toward it. The lizard shifted its position frantically as the spyder grew nearer but remained attached to the dome just above it. When the horn spyder reached the wallboard where the lizard was perched, the spyder fired its curled tail up but the hybrid reptile eluded it. The tail whapped against the side of the dome, leaving an oily poison streak.

Teag's spyder lifted its immense frame as high as its grounded quartet of legs would allow and hissed at its foe, the stridulation drawing oohs from the spectators. Fine hairs shot from its front legs and it bared a set of three-inch fangs. This display forced the lizard even higher along the curvature, where it remained.

"What's Dem-Si doing?"

"I don't know yet," Zeebo said. "He seems confused."

The people began to boo loudly and throw objects at the spot of the dome where Zeebo's fighter hung by its cupped fingers, in hopes of dislodging it.

"Zeebo, what's your boy doing?"

"Give Dem-Si time to figure it out, will ya! The spyder's not showing him anything new." He looked around at the irate faces in the crowd. "Let them cry all they want," he derided. "I don't care what it looks like, as long as Dem-Si wins."

"He looks scared," Ohmav said.

"So do you, just relax."

After several minutes the spyder retreated from the wall and laid itself down onto the floor in what appeared to be a mocking display, backing its body up more and more, almost seeming to dare the reptile to come down from the dome wall and engage it in battle. This coaxed laughter out of many of the spectators, after which Zeebo's face reddened. But the ploy seemed to work as the lizard suddenly and unexpectedly obliged, edging its way down the glass. At the top of the wallboard, it uncupped its fingers and dropped down onto the dirt. The arena quieted.

"He's ready," Zeebo whispered. "Now you'll see my training pay off. Get him, Dem-Si!"

The animal flitted across the soil to a craggy stone mesa at the center of the battlefield. It scaled the far side of the escarpment and waited, hanging there, suctioned just below the peak.

The horn spyder gave chase.

It reached the base of the rock on the opposite side, paused briefly as its eye stalks like tiny worms wriggled out in all directions, and began its ascent. It moved slowly over the steep, jutting rock face. Once at the summit, it crept along the perimeter, surveying the ground beneath.

The hybrid lizard's head swiveled nervously, looking for any sign of the spyder on the rock above him. Its photosensitive skin had blended with that of the stone. The spyder stepped onto the canted edge of the cliff, carefully reaching its legs out over the precipice. The reptile, seeing this, scrambled across the rock face below and wedged itself into a deep cleft.

"Dem-Si's pinned himself in a corner," Ohmav said, throwing his hands in the air.

Zeebo's brow furrowed. "No way, he's too smart for that. Give him some credit."

"Then what in god's name is he doing?"

"I can't be certain," he said. "But by the looks of it... he's baiting a trap."

The horn spyder began to crawl down the cliff face, its path carrying it directly over the narrow crevice where Zeebo's hybrid lay in wait, its orange-and-blue-pied underbelly exposed.

The lizard wasted no time. It ripped into the spyder's hairy midsection with its teeth, tearing off chunks of white spyderflesh and dropping them down the ridge. The horn spyder immediately jabbed at the enemy with its fangs but the lizard retreated into the fissure with each offensive. The spyder's legs quavered as it attempted to lift its hulking body farther and farther away from the rock slope, away from its adversary. But each time it tried, and failed, to remove itself from the fray, the lizard snapped at its bloodied midsection furiously until a tawny ichor stained its teeth. The swollen, distended abdomen was now an even larger target. The throng in attendance burst forth with a mixture of lusty cheers and groans.

"Do you hear that?" Ohmav asked. His fists were shaking with excitement. "That is the death knell for Teag's beast. The end is nigh," he said with an impish grin.

As the assault of the spyder wore on, Zeebo, too, began to beam, but with pride. "Teag's brute won't be able to take much more of this, I bet."

The spyder brought its body back over the mouth of the fissure and once again shot hair from its legs. The coarse shafts lodged into the reptile's hard-plated skin but had little effect, and it stayed hidden in the shadows of the cleft. Finally, it stiffened its pointed tail and brought it forward to lance the spyder, to finish it.

A hard thrust at the creature's maw instead punctured the skin beside one of its fangs and a clear liquid burst out, filling the small channel of the rock face. The lizard's scales began to steam and bubble as the dread spray consumed its body. Rivulets of acid burned the delicate cups of its hands and feet and carried it to the mouth of the fissure where the giant horn spyder impaled Zeebo's creation with its fangs, pumping venom into its body and liquefying it internally. The basement erupted. Lost in the celebratory din, Zeebo slumped over the holding pen and wailed.

The spyder carried its adversary's limp body to its own side of the oval where two of Boas Teag's wranglers prodded the beast until it released the lizard's carcass; it being considered discourteous to allow one contestant to consume another. One wrangler lassoed the spyder's eyestalks and led it back into the holding pen while the other entered the oval, lifted the defeated fighter's corpse with the top of his foot, and rolled it across the floor to the other open gate.

The masses hollered out their respects to Boas Teag and he acknowledged them with the slightest wave of his bloated hand. The dome was removed and Teag took in a wheezing breath and spit in the direction of his fallen opponent, as custom dictated. An event handler then bagged the body and disappeared into the bowels of the subscraper with it.

Zeebo's face was wan and bewildered. "I don't understand it. Dem-Si knew to stay clear of the venom sacks." He shook his head. "The fight was won. There was no reason for it."

Ohmav turned his back to the crowd and sighed. His voice was unnaturally even-keeled. "He simply missed then, there's no other explanation for it," he said. "Even the best laid schemes of mice and men go often askew, and leave us nothing but grief and pain, for promised joy." He patted Zeebo on the shoulder. "Forgive me now, my friend, for being so rude as to leave you, but as much as it pains me, I have debts to settle." Without hesitation, Ohmav turned and waded into the sea of hungry faces.

Zeebo waited above the holding pen for Lotus Blossom, whom he'd forgotten all about until now, but the basement soon emptied and still there was no sign of the woman. He found his way back to the trainer's room in the belief that she would be waiting for him there. Instead, he discovered two men, one much older and well-dressed than the other, standing above a body wrapped in plastic on the table.

"Is that my hybrid?" Zeebo asked.

"Yes, sir, it is," the elder man said.

"Well, if you're here to collect you'll have to wait along with everybody else. I ain't got the rod on me yet."

"Oh no, you're quite mistaken," he continued. "I'm not a bettor, I'm with the venue. The name's Cutter, most people just call me Doc though. I run this little sporting palace," he said. "Sorry about your animal, she put on one hell of a show out there. You're welcome to come back anytime." Zeebo could only muster a grunt in response. "I brought her back here in case you wanted to keep the body for some reason."

Zeebo looked down at the bag. "Just get rid of it."

"You sure? I salvaged what I could of her, but she was pretty burned up, inside and out, by the time they brought her back here."

Zeebo reached out, twisted the old man's shirt in his fist, and pulled him in close. The younger man immediately ran into the hallway and called for the security detail. "I don't know if you can tell or not but I'm not in the greatest mood right now, so are you trying to be funny or are you just senile, *Doc*?" Zeebo said. "Can't you tell Dem-Si's not a female?" He sighed loudly and released his grip. "You can't be no real doctor, or is Doc just an ironic nickname or some shit like that?"

The old man pulled his lapels straight and smoothed out his jacket. He looked up at Zeebo and his face soured. "I am a board certified cosmozooologist and have been for some time now, but you don't have to be a doctor to tell a boy lizard from a girl," he said.

At that moment, the doctor's young friend returned, followed into the room by three other gentlemen, each one brawnier than the last. They filed in and surrounded Zeebo. Doc Cutter opened the plastic and removed the body, laying it prone on the table. He splayed the legs and pulled aside a pocket of dead gray skin. "See for yourself," he said. Zeebo bent over the body.

"What the fu–"

Beneath his eyes, on what he believed were Dem-Si's remains, there was a stunning, complete absence of male genitalia.

"A *proper* trainer like Master Teag can at least tell what it is he's making, not like some of you upstarts," Doc said. "I'm afraid you're just not in the same class with a man like that, son. Not by a damn longshot." He scoffed and motioned to his underlings. The younger man threw the plastic back over the bantam corpse and disappeared into the hall with it. Doc Cutter followed with his crew in tow, stopping only momentarily inside the doorway to tell Zeebo, "Consider my previous invitation rescinded. I don't ever want to see you in my place again." Then he was gone.

Zeebo was alone. He shut his eyes and his mind raced in mad circles. *How could this be? What the hell happened?*

When all the puzzle fragments came together in his brain to reveal a full picture, his face morphed into a tight, crimson knot. He released a sepulchral bellow that would pinball off the walls of the tiny room, seep back into his head, and resonate in his skull endlessly. w

In that exact moment, galaxies away, a conservatively-dressed, comely young woman sat aboard an inbound Selvin. She was thoughtfully penning a message that read,

Dear Zee,

By now you've no doubt discovered why I didn't join you at the arena that night. You were always very sharp so I knew you'd figure it out eventually. I wasn't lying though, I really would've loved to be able to see your face!

I always considered myself your employee and, as such, I am tendering my resignation. Consider this my official notice, effective immediately. I took the liberty of keeping any rod you may have hidden in our hotel room as severance pay. I hope you weren't depending on it too much, as I know how difficult rod can be to get your hands on this far from home when you really need it. But like you always told me, you're such a smart boy, I'm sure you'll make do somehow.

By the way, feel free to keep the female hybrid I made as a souvenir of our time together (if she survived the fight). I'm afraid Dem-Si didn't like her after all. I guess they were too much alike.

Fondly,
Lotus Blossom

She dropped the letter into a plain-looking box and scribbled an address on the outside as the other interstellar commuters retrieved their bags and disembarked the transport. "Could you please deliver this package on your return trip to NeoWynd?" she asked a fresh-faced attendant.

"Sure thing," he said as he took the container. He pulled it close to his chest and sniffed the air. His nose immediately crinkled. "It smells... *strong.*"

"It's an eel," she told him. "And not a terribly fresh one, I'm afraid."

The young man only shrugged. He placed the box on a rolling belt that carried it away and eyed the overhead compartment. "Would you like me to get your bags, ma'am?" he asked.

"Yes, thank you, but please be careful with the cage."

"A pet?"

"Dem-Si's more like a friend," she said.

"Of course, that's perfectly fine," he replied, unzipping a sly grin while his gaze lingered on the emerald of her irises. Lotus wilted demurely, as a young lady should. "I'll get the rest of your bags down for you," he said. He spoke as he busied himself. "I noticed you when we left NeoWynd. You plan on going back anytime?" She responded with a knowing smile of her own and shook her head politely, no. The attendant pursed his lips in a mock pout. "That's too bad," he said. He helped her with the bags but remained in the aisle in front of her seat. "I don't mean to be nosy but, what brought you all the way out there, Miss..."

"Yu," she said. "And I came for a contest."

The young man looked a bit puzzled initially. Then, as the revelation struck him, he leaned in and whispered, "Big fight fan, eh? I get it. Not coming back though?"

"Never again," she replied as she slowly pushed him away with a single gloved finger. "Excuse me."

He straightened himself up immediately. "You really must've lost your shirt, lady?"

"To the contrary," she told him. "I made a killing."

She bid the young man farewell and tied the delicate cerulean strings of her new Saturn-ringed bonnet tight to her chin. She followed as the last of the passengers filed out of the Selvin and when she stepped out of the transport, a new sun shone on her face.

In its original form this may be the oldest of the stories presented in this collection. I must admit that the story changed drastically when I revised it years later. An obvious play on the title of the James Joyce novel, A Portrait of the Artist as a Young Man, *I was a relatively young man myself when I wrote it, but had aged considerably when I pulled it back out of the drawer after many years. Once I did, I discovered a very odd thing... the story didn't really represent me anymore. Words that I'd once written with a bellyful of emotion I now looked upon with a lifetime's wisdom. I vaguely remembered the person who wrote the piece and felt those stings, but that person wasn't me anymore. The emotions were real and valid but the story lacked any reasoning, any understanding. Now that I'm older the reasons behind such behaviors seem so much clearer. And with that understanding came a measure of acceptance, I think.*

I had to change the story some to reflect the newer, wiser me and because of this, what was once written in the intensely personal and raw first-person tense seemed now more appropriate in second-person. I realized that, even if it was originally just a story for me, it isn't mine anymore. It belongs to anyone who it speaks to.

A Portrait of the Artist as a Stung Man

Your car is busted. You need a ride. You follow your soulmate out the front door. Your thoughts dance in the air above your head, untied from your body, as they're apt to do. Your soulmate, noticing this, turns quickly and sucker-punches you square in the nose. They deliver the blow rightly, with no concern for their own brittle fingers. The blood runs down and seeps into your mouth, gets between your teeth, fills the crevices and frames them crimson. You slide your tongue over the enamel and taste yourself. It's a little salty... much like your soulmate. They drop you off at work. They tell you how very much they love you, and drive away.

Love you, too.

You are still bleeding out one nostril when you push through the glass double-doored entrance. You most certainly cannot arrive for your shift in such a state. You detour to the bathroom to clean yourself up until no trace of your state exists on the outside of you. You clock in, late.

Your boss immediately applies a full nelson and then moves that to a side headlock. He crooks his arm around your neck and coils it tighter with each exhaled breath you take, the way a boa constrictor would. The color of your face changes from your normal skin tone to a pinkish hue, it slowly reddens, then blues. You resemble one of those fiber-optic Christmas decorations.

The boss man is displeased. You have gathered this.

He releases his serpentine hold just as you were about to pass out from a lack of oxygen. Flickers and fireworks appear in your sight while you gulp in the air. You begin to work with your neck a pulsating welt.

You see Allison. Allison is pretty in a way that you like. You and Allison talk about the world outside the glass double-doors and you both laugh at the same times. Something tells you Allie is wonderful. She's sweet. She's honest. So when wonderful, sweet, honest Allison tells you that she's about to kick you in the balls, you have no doubt that she will. You prepare yourself as well as someone can, but you know the only real preparation for taking one in the nuts is scouting out a soft place to land until the pain subsides.

Allie looks hesitant (*she is sweet, remember*). Her right leg hangs like a loose pendulum, swaying. She cocks it back forty-five degrees and fires. You feel the raw sting first at the tip of your penis. A moment later a wall of pressure bears down on you—a five-G force that levels your body to the tile floor. You cup the epicenter of the pain, hoping to squeeze off the spread of the ache, but it doesn't work. It never works. The poison boils up from your groin all the way to your throat. Allison looks worried. She waits until you get to your feet before she tells you how sorry she is.

At least she apologized.

You go to lunch with your friend Rick. Rick used to work with you inside the glass double-doors until he quit to take on the world. To date, the world is winning. Rick immediately starts tagging you.

Jab.

Jab. Jab.

Jab. Jab. Jab.

He just flings them out effortlessly, like Ali—tattooing you in the face, almost as if he has no realization what it is he's doing.

He knows.

By dessert, a mouse swells under your eye. Within hours it will be all deep reds, magenta and fuchsia, the next day turning to dirty violets with jaundiced edges. The flesh is puffy and hard against your eye and a headache blossoms behind your temples.

Nice catching up, buddy.

You see your psychiatrist that afternoon. The doctor tells you that people act like this because they are unhappy, with themselves and others. They are unsatisfied. They are bitter. They feel unloved. They don't know how to cope with these feelings. You like your doctor. She never hits you. Of course, you're paying her.

You return home after work. Your parents are visiting (or it's your in-laws, you can hardly tell them apart anymore). You open the front door and step inside. You smell the casserole. Your father is there. He's a cinder block, small and hard and mostly hollow inside. He doesn't say a word, just balls up that calloused, sledgehammer fist of his and buries a haymaker into your gut. Somehow, you didn't see it coming.

The shockwave rumbles straight through your belly and rattles your spine. But you are able to tighten up some. Good thing. He may have killed you otherwise. A shot like that could rupture your appendix; that's how Houdini died. You take the blow. You fall. Hunched over, one hand on the carpet, your father steps over you and vanishes into the kitchen.

Dad's not a fan of casserole. You take some aspirin.

Later that night you go to bed. You make a promise to yourself that tomorrow will be different.

The next morning you wake up with that same thought still lodged in your brain like a splinter.

You will make today different.

Your friend agrees to give you a lift to work. They pick you up. The friend looks tired. Their eyelids droop down, covering bloodshot whites. As they speak your friend starts slapping you and spitting on your work clothes. You do not like this at all. At a red light your friend turns to you and hurls a forearm into your sternum. A dull thud echoes in your chest and a faint pop can be heard. You think something inside you has broken.

You are now resolute. You will try it yourself. You will hit your friend. But where?

The ear? No, too much hard skull behind it—you'll probably wind up breaking your hand.

The jaw? Nah, you don't want to knock the driver out.

How about the eye? Yes, you will pop them right in the eye—leave a nice big shiner to show everyone you mean business. And afterward your friend will still have one good eye to see the road with.

So you tuck your fingers into your palm and make a hard knot of your hand. You bring your fist covertly to your side and ratchet up the tension until you can barely hold it from flying loose. The friend isn't looking. It's perfect. You pull the trigger.

Nothing.

You try again.

Still nothing. You can't free the punch.

What's happening? It looks so easy, so natural, for the rest of them.

But you don't know how. You never learned.

A few minutes later your friend drops you off in front of the glass double-doors.

Thanks.

That night, very late, you are alone in your bedroom. You undress. You catch a naked glimpse of your reflection in the mirror. Your body is pocked with soft lumps and markings. Your skin is a highway of scars. There are bruises fading on you like wisps of smoke.

You notice that a tiny crack has formed down the center of your chest, where your friend hit you. You pick at the scabby skin around the crack, chipping off the pieces, even though everyone says you shouldn't do that. When there is nothing left to pick at you thump your chest hard with the flat of your fist and the crack branches outward in all directions as if your chest was a broken windshield. You flake away these new cracks and once you widen one just enough, you dig a finger into the groove and run it along the inside lining of your skin. You dig in with your other fingers and pull the rigid skin up. It lifts off the breastbone.

You continue to tug at the skin until a great fissure unzips itself, exposing the garnet of velvet flesh underneath. Your skin keeps its shape even after being removed. It separates from your body in thick, orange-peel plates. The uncasing proceeds until, finally, you lay the carapace atop the bedsheet you spread out beneath you on the floor. You wrap the shards of yourself inside the sheet, kick the whole pulpy mess under the bed, and towel yourself off.

You see yourself again in the mirror.

You are wonderfully grotesque, violently absurd. You'll tell them this was the real you all along. You were always this magical—always this fearsome. You will amaze them. You will twist their minds. You will haunt their thoughts. You will choke their hearts.

Tomorrow.

And tonight you will sleep, exquisitely.

Challenged by my place of work, The Downtown Writers Center, to craft a flash fiction piece in ten lines or less, I got to work on what would become Kings. *If I could manage to do it, the story would be transferred to an oversized placard and travel the streets of Syracuse, New York on a commuter bus for a month or so as an advertisement for the DWC. Many of my colleagues crafted work of their own, mostly poetry, for the event. During that unseasonably warm winter, the prose-form version of* Heavy is the Head *toured the city on a Centro bus, being viewed by hundreds (or thousands?) of riders, until it was removed and presented to me later that spring. It hangs in my office to this day.*

At the time, due to the size and shape of the placard, I was restricted to ten lines and needed to write it as straight prose to make it fit the board, but I always thought it worked better as a prose poem of sorts. Now, here in this collection, I finally get to present it in the format I always thought suited it best.

Heavy is the Head

When The Great Ones dropped
From leaden skies,
From clouds
Pregnant with dirt,
We quivered in corners

They leveled cities
As innocently as a boot
Wipes an anthill.
And like ants,
We scurried

They took away our toys.
There is no loss in crude baubles,
A Great Voice told us.
Though we were naked and ashamed,
Without them

You are not kings,
They boomed,
With what we came to understand
Was sadness.
We unburden you

And The Great Ones,
Restless
As they were,

Abandoned
The earth.

We wailed.
We stomped,
Our stubby,
Kid feet.
And we built

Our rocket ships searched,
Poking holes, zigzagging madly,
Over the celestial curtain,
Like a blind seamstress
Until there was no more…

Space

But we never met,
The Great Ones again.
Only others,
Like us,
Quivering in corners.

We wept,
For we knew,
Our kings were no more.
Long live the kings we muttered, now
Face to face.

To put it simply, this story wasn't supposed to happen. At least not for this collection. Allow me to explain: I was done writing new work for my book and was in the midst of doing edits for my publisher when the premise for this tale came to me (inconvenient and quite inconsiderate, these story ideas sometimes are). So, like any other idea I might have for a future story, I filed this one away, to be worked on at a later date after the publication of this book. Then a funny thing happened. I finished up with a round of my publisher's edits and while I was waiting for a new batch of feedback, I found myself with a little time to kill (key words: a **little** time). I probably should've just taken that time off and gave my mind a break while I waited for the next edits. But, for reasons I'll explain later, I can't seem to do that. Instead, I started allowing my brain to tinker with this idea of a new, more efficient form of state-sanctioned punishment. I figured I'd kick around some thoughts, create a few characters, maybe write a rough draft of a few scenes, nothing serious. I started writing, as I always do, in a very free-flowing, almost stream-of-consciousness manner (as I instruct all my writing students to try out with their rough drafts) and as the days and, eventually, weeks piled up, so did the pages. By the time I had to get started again editing the remainder of my stories for the book, I was overcome (read: obsessed) with the idea that **this** piece now absolutely **had** to be included.

Now, on to that explanation I promised. You see, I have a strong obsessive-compulsive streak within me. No idea where it came from. It's not a true 'disorder' per se (at least I think it's not), but more of a strong want/need to see a task—any task—through to its completion before moving on to anything else. Truth be told, it's a pain-in-the-ass habit to have. Impatience, tunnel-vision, single-mindedness, think of a dog with a bone. It's all-consuming, this "writer's curse". I can put it on hold, thankfully, for short periods of time, but it's definitely not my best attribute. Neither is this Felix Unger-like meticulousness I also happen to be afflicted with. They're not particularly helpful... unless you happen to want to get a novella conceived, written, and edited completely, in your spare time, in the span of a couple months. Then, these character "flaws" come in pretty damn handy.

A thousand thanks to my ever-understanding wife for putting up with, and making time sacrifices for, my mania on a too-regular basis (Sorry about all those missed dinners, honey!) Anyway, that's the skinny on this, the twentieth and very last story I produced for the collection you are now reading. Hopefully it was worth all the hassle I put myself (and my wife) through.

Tempus Servivit

"You've got fifteen minutes, counselor." The prison security guard's voice was gruff and emotionless. "Inmate, step away from the bars." The man in the cell quickly abided and the guard unlocked the door to allow the attorney inside. Both men took their seats. The lawyer leaned forward on his elbows and the small wooden table that had been set up in the holding cell gave off a creak that echoed through the jail's walkway.

"It's not looking good right now, Ellis," the lawyer said.

The orange jumpsuited prisoner across the table had a difficult time keeping his foot from tapping the concrete floor and his fingers from drumming the threadbare table, the surface of which had lost its exterior coat in spots so that the splinters of wood showed through like exposed tendons.

"How *not good* are we talking?"

"I'm supposed to tell you the jury could go either way but, if you ask me..." The lawyer inhaled deeply. "The witnesses' testimony fucked us over, your toxicology results didn't help, and we had that no show to court," he said. "On top of it all, the family's emotion was... compelling."

"That was all acting—they were playing it up for the jurors," Ellis said.

"Well then, that was some Oscar-worthy shit."

"Yeah, I saw it too, Doug," Ellis said, sounding perturbed. "I was there, remember?" Ellis looked up at the skylight and released a drawn-out sigh. "So, what do you think my chances are then, realistically?

"*Realistically?*"

"That's what I said."

"In my opinion," the lawyer told him. "Less than fifty-fifty."

Ellis shook his head slowly. "I've given you every cent I have and then some, how in the hell can this be happening?" The lawyer didn't answer. "What does this say about your *prowess* as a defense attorney?"

Doug sucked in a calming breath through his nose and exhaled. "You can't put lipstick on a pig," he told the man. "I worked my ass off for you. No one else could've done more."

"Jesus fucking Christ, this is unreal." Ellis Pritchard buried his face in his hands. "What are my honest-to-God chances of beating this thing?"

"Ellis, what do you want me to-"

"Tell me my chances!"

Doug grimaced. "I'd say, almost nil."

Ellis threw his hands up. "Well, fuck me I guess." He crumpled into the metal folding chair.

"Ellis..." the lawyer proceeded slowly, "I called a few people I know upstate when this trial looked like it might go sideways on us, and they brought something back to me. The DA's office isn't thrilled about it, but they'd sign off. They don't really have much choice, honestly."

Ellis replied without bothering to look up. "What are you talking about?"

"It's like a plea bargain, or a version of one. It's... unique," the attorney said.

"What's the deal?"

"So, they have this proposition. You plead guilty-"

"To a lesser charge?"

"No," the lawyer said. "You'd have to accept the charges brought against you."

"How the fuck does that help me, Doug? Please enlighten me as to how I'm going to avoid-"

The lawyer spoke over Ellis. "Shut up for a second and listen, will you," he said. "They'd convict you on all charges, but you wouldn't spend a day in prison. They guarantee it."

Ellis immediately stopped speaking as his mind processed what he heard.

"Interested?" the lawyer asked.

"How's that possible? How do I plead guilty to manslaughter and still get off scot-free?"

"Details are vague, but..." he said. "I mean, at this point, why not take a deal?"

"How did you-"

"I know a few people, who know other people, and let's just say I put it out there that to get out of this jam you might be amenable to something, uh, *unorthodox*. And not long after I baited that hook, I got a bite."

"You're bullshitting me."

"I wouldn't bullshit about something like this. It was a Hail Mary that landed. It's a real good deal, if you want it. You take the plea and walk away in a few weeks a free man. No strings, provided you're okay with their terms. As your attorney, if you want to avoid the very good chance you'll receive a lengthy sentence, I'd advise you to take it."

"What could they possibly want from me?"

Doug smiled and reached down for his briefcase. He dropped it onto the table with a thud, snapped it open, and pulled out a large manilla envelope. He slid it over to his client. In small block letters on the front of the packet were the words:

Project: Tempus Servivit.

"It's Latin," Doug said. "These guys seem to have a real hard-on for the pretentious, if you know what I'm saying."

"What does it mean?"

"Time served," the attorney told him.

"So... what does that mean?"

"The way I understand it, they basically want you to take part in a study."

"I don't follow."

"Five more minutes, counselor," a guard called out from the other side of the bars.

"Yeah, yeah," Doug replied before turning back to Ellis, who was leafing through the packet. "They don't give many details in there, at least not any you or I can understand. It's all scientific jargon, but it sounds like they're conducting drug trials—you take this stuff, stick around the hospital a while, and then you're done."

"That easy, huh?"

The lawyer shrugged. "Seems to be."

"How do I know this shit they're giving to me is safe? I don't want to grow a third nipple or have my dick fall off."

Doug reached over and flipped through the packet. He settled on a page and pointed to a particular section of text. "Look at this, right here. Read it. It says that the treatment, *Timeserve*, is in the final stages of development and that it's been successfully tested on many subjects already. *Human subjects*, it says, with no adverse effects."

"Yeah, but what does it do?"

"According to this, nothing that isn't part of the natural human process, it says."

"You weren't kidding about the details being vague, were you?"

"Hell yes, they're vague! But they're offering to let you walk on a manslaughter rap. You gotta take some things on faith for that kind of forgiveness." He gave Ellis a hard look. "You owe a debt, my friend, and the state wants that debt paid. If it's this *Timeserve* thing, what's it matter? They obviously don't think you're a menace, or they wouldn't release you afterwards. Just be grateful and don't question it too much. They're offering you a way out, Ellis. At this point, no one else is going to." Doug pushed himself back from the table and got up. "Take a look at the paperwork, read it over, glean whatever you can from it. They're not expecting you to go into this blind. They want to meet with you and explain the whole thing themselves, all the details that aren't here," he said. "What's it gonna hurt to listen to them? Take a ride up to Bazemore Institute. At least you'll get out of this cell for a day."

"Bazemore Institute?" Ellis said. "Never heard of it."

"It's not the kind of place that advertises itself. They like their anonymity. It's outside the city, up in Westchester. It's some beautiful country, very scenic, you'll love it. Get into some normal clothes, go for a drive, you'll feel more like yourself," he said. "Hey, just listen to what they have to say. Let them explain it all to you." He gave a laugh. "And then come back here and tell me what it is because I'm curious as hell," he said. "If you like what they're selling, sign the papers and we'll do it. Ellis, I'm just your lawyer, it's my job to give you options. This seems like a pretty damn good one."

Ellis Pritchard thought about it. "What if it's a weird psychological experiment or something?"

"Listen to me, prison life is a weird psychological experiment, and not a good one. Especially for guys like you. Whatever this *Timeserve* thing is, it's better than getting put away," he said. "Go up there, see what they have to say. I can set it up for you tomorrow."

Ellis eyed the lawyer as the guard approached. "Do it."

*

The next morning one of the guards brought Ellis a dress shirt, shoes, and a brand-new, navy blue suit to wear. They took him in the prisoner transport van up route 9 past Yonkers, followed the river through Tarrytown and Sleepy Hollow into the hilly, bucolic landscape of the Hudson Valley, with greens that hit Ellis so hard he could practically feel them. Doug was right, this place was beautiful. The whole trip took maybe an hour and Ellis was certain he'd never been this far up Westchester County before. The valley was a big place, after all.

The van's tires crunched over the stone path leading to Bazemore's sixteen-foot-high, chain link fence. It had a helix of razor-wire laid on its side across the topmost portion and was dotted with security cameras at each post. The driver announced himself to the small electronic box attached to a pole outside the gate and the van was buzzed in to the grounds of Bazemore Institute.

From the outside, the windowless structure gave off such an inviolable air that it very well could've passed for a prison, as well as being completely antithetical to its organic surroundings, like a concrete tumor reaching up out of the lush, emerald meadow. This slate-gray fortress with the smooth, steep walls seemed to burst forth from the earth and extend forever upwards; a castle of neo-modernist design, all right angles and sharp-edged corners with, at least it seemed to Ellis, no visible openings. A dirty, square egg nestled on a bed of grass.

Ellis was dropped off at what he could only assume was the front of this enigmatic edifice before the van pulled off down the stone pathway toward the gate. An entry immediately presented itself when a door-shaped portion of the building slid up from ground level and a female figure stepped out to greet him.

"Come inside, Mr. Pritchard, we've been awaiting your arrival. Allow me to introduce myself, my name is Dr. Stam, one of the lead researchers on the *Timeserve* project," the comely middle-aged woman said. She appeared extremely well-put-together to Ellis: Curly, auburn, shoulder-length hair. High cheekbones and a pleasing face. Black-rimmed glasses. Slender yet muscular calves that extended beneath her standard white lab coat to a pair of high-heeled vinyl taupe shoes. "Follow me, please," she said, and she strolled through the opening. Ellis did as he was instructed when the sliding door reemerged above his head, dropped, and sealed itself shut behind him with a resounding thud. "We mustn't forget this." Dr. Stam guided the man to an archway with the outline of a large handprint depressed into one of its sides. "Remove all metal from your person and press your hand to the mark if you would." Ellis placed his hand inside the depression and felt pain pricks immediately over his fingers. But when he tried to pull away, the hand wouldn't budge, as if it were glued to the arch. "Give it a few seconds, you'll feel a bit of discomfort but it's nothing to worry about." A moment later his hand was free. He pulled it away and checked it. "Just taking some samples, getting some preliminary info," the doctor told him. "Blood, tissue, prints, that sort of thing. And as you can see your wounds have already been sealed with a temporary adhesive that will dissolve by itself within a day or two." She winked. "There's little surprises around every corner, but nothing dangerous. Don't be alarmed."

"I'm guessing this isn't any regular metal detector either?" Ellis asked while his eyes scanned the curvature with some reticence.

"Ding, ding, that's correct, Mr. Pritchard. This machine does a whole lot more," she said. "But it does operate as a keen detector of metals as well. Step right through and you'll see."

Ellis stepped through its frame and the arch immediately began to sizzle with electronic activity. Dr. Stam closely watched a large screen that was wired to the apparatus. "Try it again, but this time empty your pockets, please."

Ellis buried both hands into his front pant pockets and then padded his back ones. "I'm not carrying anything."

"Check them again," the woman politely said.

When Ellis unbuttoned and reached into his back left pocket, he found, tucked into a crevice between the seams, a wadded-up chewing gum wrapper. Ellis pulled out the lint-covered, aluminum paper ball and dropped it into a small trash container Dr. Stam held out for him. "This thing is pretty thorough, huh?"

"You have no idea," Stam told him as she put down the trashcan and returned to the screen. "In addition to your wayward gum wrapper you also have a screw in one of the tarsal bones of your right foot, the navicular—newer, from the looks of it, probably due to your recent accident—and they must've given you a new shirt to wear today because you left a pin in the shoulder." Ellis fingered the cotton-weave fabric until he located it.

"That's pretty amazing," he said. "What else does it do?"

"Let's just say you can cancel your next physical. We probably found out more about your biological makeup in the last sixty seconds than is accumulated in all the medical files you've ever had. In fact, I can tell you that the gum from the wrapper in your pocket was from a stick of *Wrigley's Spearmint*," she said. Ellis's jaw drooped and his lips parted slightly until the doctor burst out with a laugh. "Just kidding, it doesn't tell us all that." Stam directed him to the elevators. "But if we wanted it to, it would," she said. "In all seriousness, we're working on some stuff here you wouldn't believe. Let's go upstairs and meet Dr. Tamarov, the mind that's heading up this whole project, shall we?"

The elevator doors swooshed open and the pair stepped inside. The woman swiped her badge, entered a number code, identified herself, "Stam, Alexandria. H Floor." and the elevator started its ascent.

"Alexandra, that's a beautiful name."

"*Alexandr-eee-a*," she said.

"Oh, Alexandria. That's beautiful, too."

She offered Ellis a half-smile. "Why, thank you."

The elevator doors split open and a harsh light flooded in to meet them. Two muscular men dressed in pristine, form-fitting white uniforms approached the doors. "These staff members will escort you to Dr. T's office. He'll be expecting you," she said. "Welcome to Bazemore, Mr. Pritchard, we're so glad you decided to take part in our study."

"Well, I haven't actually decided on anything yet."

"My apologies, I understand," she said. "Once you learn more about what we're doing here, I'm sure you'll feel more at ease."

"I'm hoping so, too," he said. "All this has me very curious. I've got a lot of questions for your Doctor…"

"Tamarov," she repeated. "A brilliant man."

"Yes, I'm dying to hear what your Dr. Tamarov has to say."

"All will be revealed," she told him.

The orderlies led Ellis through the series of winding, mostly selfsame corridors of H Floor, a surreal, labyrinthine area of Bazemore decorated completely in cerulean tile. There was no noise, no signs of life aside from the scuffling of the two men's shoes and the clopping of Ellis's wingtips. When the trio finally reached a set of automatic double-doors that opened slowly in front of them on their approach, Ellis felt a sense of relief to see that they'd entered a wing of the facility that had some activity. There, staff in uniform—a stream-lined version of basic hospital garb—walked the floor purposefully, through and from a collection of draped rooms that emitted the familiar beeps and boops of medical equipment. The men passed all of these rooms, though; they made their way down a solitary hallway ending at a single door, Dr. Tamarov's door. One of the men softly rapped his knuckles against it and a moment later the door swung open.

A slender, clean-cut man with an angular face and a head of wavy, light blonde receding hair, probably in his late-fifties, Ellis thought, stood in the doorway. "Thank you, gentlemen, I'll take it from here," he told the men. He had an unassuming gaze and a gentle demeanor. With a nod from the physician, they returned to the teeming section of H floor. "Won't you come in, Mr. Pritchard, we've been expecting you. My name is Dr. Tamarov and I suspect you have more than a few questions for me."

"You got that right," Ellis said. "I need to know a lot more about this *Timeserve* thing if you want me to join up."

"Oh, of course, you must know everything if you're to make an informed decision." Tamarov slipped into the leather chair behind his desk and Ellis took the other. "Absolutely you should know exactly what it is you're signing up for. It's completely your choice whether you undergo the treatment."

"*Treatment*, you say? Does that mean it's like a form of rehabilitation?" The doctor said flatly, "It's a punitive treatment."

"Punitive, eh? Is it painful?" Ellis asked. "Because it sounds painful."

"I assure you it's not," Tamarov said. "At least not in any unnatural way. It will satisfy the punitive aspects of your sentence without any undue pain or distress. We're not here to torture you, Mr. Pritchard, quite the contrary. We're trying to do away with cruel and unusual punishment in all its forms. It's been my life's work developing a system of punishment that's more civilized, as well as more efficient, than the current one we have in use. Prison overcrowding in this country is rampant and the population continues to explode. I'm sure you're aware of that."

"If you say so."

Tamarov grinned. "Yes, well, we're looking to find a better way of dealing with people like yourself. Not serial criminals, but people who've made mistakes, poor decisions for whatever reason, but that don't show a propensity for recidivism. Those found guilty of lesser offenses as well, but perhaps couldn't afford better counsel and find themselves becoming a statistic in the machinery of our immense penal system. There's a host of good reasons why *Timeserve* would be more fitting than having these people thrown in jail. We're hoping that after the medical trials here at Bazemore are concluded, our little alternate punishment is adopted, albeit probably slowly at first, but eventually making its way nationwide once the benefits become obvious."

"Alright Doc, I'm hooked. What is this *Timeserve*? What do I have to do to get it?"

"You don't have to *do* anything, Mr. Pritchard. We do all the work while you stay with us here, tend to your every need. In a few weeks, you're released, a free man."

Ellis leaned in. "Go on."

"Of course, allow me to explain it. We were tasked with solving the problem of how to keep otherwise law-abiding citizens, like yourself, as well as small-timers from being locked up at the rates we're currently incarcerating them," he said. "But still having them serve their time. The public wouldn't have it any other way." He took out a lozenge and popped it into his mouth. "Anyway, if we solve that problem, we solve prison overcrowding overnight. Did you know that it costs this state well over a half-million dollars annually to care for just one inmate?"

Ellis widened his eyes exaggeratedly. "Are you sure that's accurate?"

"Quite sure, Mr. Pritchard. It's actually closer to six-hundred K a year, that's over $1,500 per day, for every single inmate, and the cost is constantly rising. It's an untenable situation and the lawmakers know it."

"That's insane! And I'm supposed to pay for that with my taxes? Why not bring back the death penalty for some of them? The worst ones, I mean."

Tamarov adjusted his glasses. "Setting aside the ethical questions associated with executing prisoners, the cost, on average, actually ends up being more to put someone to death than housing and caring for them indefinitely. It's a double-edged sword."

"The hell with the ethical questions, just line 'em up against the wall and shoot them. How much does a bullet cost?" Ellis said. "Murderers don't deserve to live."

"But isn't that exactly what the prosecution is calling you, Mr. Pritchard?"

"Hey, I'm no murderer," Ellis said through a clenched jaw. "It was an accident. There's a difference."

Tamarov raised his hand. "Of course there is, that's my point. We're trying to avoid sending people like you to jail. You have no prior record of any kind, you're clearly the victim of circumstance."

"Damn straight."

"Now that doesn't mean you're incapable of committing a heinous act, but what it *does* mean is that if there were another way to mete out justice, perhaps with a lighter hand, that would be preferable to throwing you in with a bunch of lifers. If there were some way to keep you from doing hard time, any amount of it, well... I mean, people like you are so much more valuable to society living out your lives productively, outside those prison walls."

"Exactly, so why throw me in jail at all?"

"As I said, the public demands criminals be punished in some form or fashion. What politician is going to run on a platform of being soft on crime? No, the convicted must pay a debt to society, and what is the standard form of payment?"

"Putting them away," Ellis said. "Doing time."

Tamarov nodded slowly. "Yes, time. Time usually spent in prison. For you maybe fifteen or twenty years, maybe only ten, or somewhere in between. I don't really know for certain, that's not my area of expertise. But it is *time* that must be the payment."

"How are you going to do that? Have me serve time *without* serving any time?" Ellis asked with a shrewd edge to his voice. "I'm all ears."

"Instead of you serving time... we take it from you."

"I'm afraid you lost me, Doc."

"It's simple really. We take time away from you—*your* time, from your own life—just as if you'd served it behind bars," he told Ellis. "I'm a geneticist, Mr. Pritchard. My purview is the very DNA that makes up every cell in your body. What if I told you that we've developed, at that cellular level, a procedure that would allow us to alter someone's DNA makeup, to prematurely age a human being? We can now take months and years from a person's life artificially to allow them to serve out their sentence without costing the taxpayers a dime. Well, maybe it'll cost them a few dimes, but nowhere near what it's costing them now, I can assure you of that. It's becoming a very popular topic of discussion in the back rooms at Albany right now and, if all goes well, the idea could even have allies down in Washington," he said. "There's more than a few sets of eyes on us at the moment, but I'm confident in the science."

Ellis's eyes narrowed. "How's this gonna work exactly, with me, I mean?"

"Well," Tamarov told the man. "Within a few weeks we'll have you aged-up to satisfy your sentencing, or at least a sentencing commensurate with a conviction of this kind. We chose you specifically because you're the perfect candidate. One who can be reintegrated into society, albeit in another area of the country. You'll blend back in nicely—you're not a maniac, you're just a normal guy who caught a bad break."

"Thank you!" Ellis threw his hands into the air. "That's what I've been trying to tell everyone all along. It isn't fair, what's happening to me, the way they were crucifying me for one goddamn mistake."

Tamarov stepped out from behind his desk and perched himself on its corner. "We don't want single bad moments to tarnish otherwise worthwhile lives. That's what *Timeserve* is here to do—save people like you," he said. "You're not cut out for the penitentiary and I, for one, say thank God for it. You're too civilized to survive in a horrid place like that and we don't want you to even have to try. We want you to go back to a life of buying houses and cars and taking trips, being a happy consumer. Not someone forced to live off the teat of the people. That's not you."

"It sure as hell isn't."

"Some people belong in prison, but you're not one of them, Mr. Pritchard."

"You can call me Ellis."

"Alright then, Ellis, let me spell it out for you: the prosecution wants its conviction, the family wants their pound of flesh, and the politicians want to save the voters money. And you, you just want to be free again. *Timeserve* might be the solution to everyone's problems."

While Dr. Tamarov spoke, Ellis slowly allowed the idea to sink into his brain.

No jail time. No living with killers and rapists. No having regret shoved down my throat every day, or anything else shoved down my throat for that matter. What am I risking? A few aches and pains? A few gray hairs? Fuck it, I'll take some supplements, find a good chiropractor.

"How many years would I have to give up?"

Tamarov pulled a folder from off his desktop, flipped it open, and perused the contents. "Let's assume you'd get a reduced sentence for having a clean record before the accident. It's also fair to assume you'd be a model inmate during your incarceration, you could have your sentence lessened even further for good behavior. And we'll even throw in a little bonus time off for taking part in the study."

"So how many years are we talking after all that?"

"Seven," Tamarov said. "How's that sound? You'll have to submit to being medically-aged seven full years. You're thirty-four right now, which means in about a month's time you will be, for all intents and purposes, a forty-one-year-old man, and you'll walk out of this facility into a new life. How about it?"

Ellis tried to stifle a smile that was threatening to break through his otherwise stoic facial expression. "I've got one question for you and I want you to be totally honest with me, Doctor T."

Tamarov crossed his arms and nodded. "Shoot."

"Is it safe?"

The doctor's lips stretched into a wide grin. "Ellis, it's perfectly safe," he said. "One hundred percent. It's all mine. We've rigorously tested it, first on animals and now, here at Bazemore, we have ongoing, human trials." Tamarov's voice got excited. "You can even meet some of the people who've undergone the treatment. But we need data, lots and lots of data, case profiles to prop up and show those at the highest levels of government. They need to see that this will all work, that it can be a viable option for them to use. I know the science on *Timeserve* is sound, I just need a larger sample size to convince the ones that make the real decisions."

"And the family of that lady I hit? They won't ever find out about me? They're sick, vindictive fucks. They'll make a huge stink if they know I'm walking around on the streets. They want me locked up, or worse."

The doctor shook his head vigorously and waved his hands in the air. "No, no, no, the public will never know about what we're doing with you. No one will. As I said, you'll be relocated to the west coast, given a new identity, much like a witness protection program. If they can keep people hidden from the mafia, I think we can keep you safe from a bunch of people who won't even think to look for you," the doctor told him. "You'll accept the DA's bogus plea deal and as far as anyone knows Ellis Pritchard will be doing his time at a state penitentiary. Then, at a time we deem appropriate, it will be released that you met a violent end while serving out your sentence. Do you really think Jeffrey Dahmer was killed by another inmate in prison?"

"You guys let Dahmer out?"

"Hell no, that guy was nuts! But he died of natural causes, in here, helping us test *Timeserve*," Tamarov said. "Anyway, that should satisfy any bloodlust the victim's family might have and allow you to get a fresh start somewhere far from here. You have no immediate family so you can make a clean break from your current life."

"You don't think anyone will recognize me?"

"On the other side of the country? I know New Yorkers like to think the world is obsessed with them but I can assure you it's not. People are too busy living their own lives to notice a slightly older version of you moving in next door to them."

Ellis was quiet for a long moment. "I'm not ashamed, y'know. I can't live the rest of my life feeling like I'm an awful person. It was dumb luck. Wrong place at the wrong time. I was perfectly fine to drive, it wasn't the booze. I hardly had any. That damn lady was the one not being careful, she wasn't watching where she was going. I took my eyes off the road for a minute, man... and she was right there."

"I get it," Tamarov said. "I'm not here to pass judgment, Ellis. My personal feelings about your case aren't important anyway. I'm conducting a study, that's all. That's as close as I'll get, and, frankly, that's as close as I want to get. Trust me, we've got a few patients here who've done some questionable things to land in my lap, but I can't be too picky about it, too sanctimonious. I'm a scientist... and a good candidate is a good candidate. I need them and they need me," he said. His eyes locked on to Ellis's. "We need each other. *Timeserve* is too important to me—I've worked too hard on it to let the little things get in the way."

"How long do I have to decide?" Ellis asked.

"Not long, I'm afraid. Your trial *is* winding down and, as you might imagine, there are plenty of others who would jump at the chance to take your place. If you leave here today, I'm afraid I can't guarantee this offer. But, if you decide to stay with us, I can have a nice soft bed made up for you tonight and you can begin your treatments within the next twenty-four to thirty-six hours. The accommodations here are like a five-star hotel and your every need will be met while you're under my care. I think you'll find it quite nice."

Ellis stroked his chin and stared at the doctorates hanging on the wall behind Tamarov. "I like a down pillow when I sleep," he said. "And a snack before bed."

*

The next morning Ellis was subjected to an array of diagnostic testing that mapped every cell cluster and capillary in his body; blood was tested, drained, treated, and reintroduced into his system, in fact every fluid and solid they could safely extract from him seemed to be fair game. He underwent an interior-body cleanse, was given a series of super-nutrient plasma IVs, his room was infused with a precise blend of oxygenated air and scrubbed of all microbes. Once he was washed, sanitized, and dressed in a hospital-issue gown he was escorted to a clean-room where Doctors Tamarov and Stam were waiting for him.

"You remember Dr. Stam, I assume?" Tamarov asked the man, extending a hand in the direction of his colleague.

"Yeah, we met yesterday."

"Nice to see you again, Mr. Pritchard," the woman said. "I'm glad you decided to stay with us."

"My pleasure."

"Dr. Stam has been a part of the *Timeserve* project since its inception," Tamorov said. "She's been an invaluable part of the team, and I wouldn't think of conducting trials without her input."

"Beauty *and* brains, huh?"

"Uh... yes, certainly." Tamarov offered the woman a demure smirk and directed the patient to sit on the examination table. "Dr. Stam is one of the premier minds in the field of genetics and she was actually the one who brought your case to my attention."

Ellis turned to the woman. "I'm flattered, Doctor Stam. I guess I owe you a debt of gratitude."

"Your participation is all the thanks I require," she told him. "We need people like you *almost* as much as you need us."

Tamarov broke in, "Now then, Mr. Pritchard."

"Ellis. Call me Ellis, remember? Both of you, please, you can call me by my first name."

"Yes, of course, I'd forgotten." Tamarov turned to Stam. "He would like to be addressed as Ellis."

"Not a problem at all," she said.

Tamarov turned his attention back to the patient. "Yes, where was I... ah, the trials. The trials will consist of three separate doses of *Timeserve* administered one week apart."

"What's in it?"

"It's.. a complex mixture," he said. "A chemical cocktail that will eventually alter your genetic makeup, causing every cell in your body to age more rapidly than they normally would. Have you heard of progeria?"

Ellis paused. "Can't say that I have."

"It's a rapid aging condition caused by a defect in the lamin A gene. That gene is in charge of creating the protein that keeps the nucleus of cells together."

"I see," Ellis said slowly.

Dr. Stam stepped in. "Basically, this defect causes the gene to start creating an abnormal version of the protein and, ultimately, the cell becomes unstable and premature aging occurs. That was the jumping-off point for our research on *Timeserve*."

"It's an odd affliction in that it's rarely passed down through families like most other conditions," Tamarov said. "It just seems to be a chance occurrence in those unlucky enough to be born with it. But like Dr. Stam said, studying it led to the breakthroughs we've made here at Bazemore."

The two doctors exchanged bright glances and Stam took her turn talking. "And now that we understand enough about this syndrome we can harness its effects, wield them almost at will. Perhaps someday we'll be able to reverse the aging process as well. The possibilities for this research are limitless."

Tamarov stopped her. "That's still quite aways off though," he said. He then took out a digital camera and started taking pictures of Ellis's head and neck. "We have to document all the changes that may occur with you in detail, before-and-after shots."

"I get it," Ellis said. "Take whatever pictures you want."

He handed the camera to Dr. Stam. "Doctor, if you would, please." She took it from Tamarov and continued to snap shots of the patient. "We were having some issues finding a viable real-world application for our research before we stumbled onto *Timeserve* as a possible punitive measure. One with upsides for everyone involved. Have I told you how much it costs to house and care for-"

"Yes, you gave me all the numbers already," Ellis said. "What's exactly going to happen to me?"

"As I was saying, the treatment will be administered in a series of three injections, roughly a week apart. Each one will quicken the aging process a little more until you've aged the approximately seven years you were sentenced with, give or take a few days. Science is inexact by nature I'm afraid."

"And just like that I'm magically seven years older?"

"It's not magic, but it'll seem like it. Even though you've only spent thirty-four years on this earth, your body will look and act as if you'd aged naturally for forty-one. Now what that will look like, we can't say exactly, it's dependent on your family genetics. A good predictor of how you'll age is to look at your parents, who I understand were healthy before their deaths, in an automobile accident if I remember correctly?"

"That's right," Ellis said.

Dr. Stam had Ellis lift his arms and she took photographs from every angle. "Would you remove your gown, please," she told him.

Ellis paused, then stripped off the garment, handing it to her.

"Thank you," she said. "We have noticed that artificial aging seems to be less taxing on the body. The quick-aging process, just skipping ahead years, doesn't allow for the excesses of life to take their toll," she said. "The effects of unhealthy habits—drinking, smoking, drug use, diet, stress, inactivity—that tend to ravage people's bodies aren't evident with *Timeserve*. It's like a *clean* aging, if there is such a thing. Like the difference between city miles and highway miles on a car. You're putting on seven years, but they're highway years."

"Wow." Ellis shrugged. "Is there a downside to all this? When do I get the bad news?"

"Let's not lose sight of the fact that you're erasing seven years from your life," Tamarov said. "We're actively shortening your lifespan by roughly one-eleventh. That's significant. That's the downside, the debt to be paid. Someone will always need to shoulder the blame, even in the case of accidents," he said. "It's hard for people to process the loss of a loved one without assigning blame somewhere. When there's another person involved, well, it's just easier for them. It isn't a random act of God or happenstance." Tamarov pointed his finger at Ellis. "Their grief is a loaded gun and, without you, they'd have nothing to fire it at." He dropped his hand. "I imagine it'll take the public some getting-used-to to accept this form of punishment, but that's another problem for another time... and another person. That's not why you're here. You're here to help us test it."

"And then what, exactly?"

"I told you, and then Ellis Pritchard is no longer. He dies in prison, and you start a new chapter."

Ellis hopped from the table. "When do we get started?"

Tamarov clapped his hands together. "Love the enthusiasm, Mr. Pritch-, I mean, Ellis. I'll meet with the team today to go over the results of your testing and if all goes as I expect, we can give you the first dose tomorrow morning."

Ellis's gaze lingered on Dr. Stam, who was now taking pictures of his lower body. "It's a date."

*

The doctors encouraged Ellis to get eight to ten hours of deep sleep before the next day's procedure. To insure this, they had the nurses administer him a sedative, which he happily took. It was the most restful night he'd had since before the accident. He didn't know if it was the sedative or being out of that cell but, either way, he didn't care. He was just happy to get a peaceful sleep again. When he awoke the next morning, the room was alive with staff and there was all manner of equipment surrounding his bed.

"Brought the whole hospital in for this, did ya?"

"You're kind of a big deal right now." Dr. Stam's voice reached his ears over the murmur of activity that filled the room. "The new kid always gets the most attention."

"I'm honored."

Dr. Tamarov could be heard even before he strolled into the tumult of the preparations. "The sun is shining. What a glorious morning to start a trial!"

"I'll have to take your word for it, Doc. I haven't seen the sun since I got here. What do you people have against windows?"

"Nothing at all, we have plenty of windows." He tapped the glass covering the far wall. "Retractable panels in every room, no expense was spared in the construction of Bazemore. We just like to choose when to allow Mother Nature's rays in. Sunlight can have an effect on our test subjects and we like to have control over as many variables as we can. Our work here is important, and it demands we consider everything when we're running a trial."

"Welp, I'm ready when you are," Ellis told him. "I've had so many scans I've lost count, and so many needles poked into me that I feel like a pin cushion."

Tamarov laughed heartily. "We need to get as much data on you as possible, make sure you're viable, and get you as ready as you can be for treatment. We need plenty of baselines too, before-and-afters are important, remember?"

"I guess I understand."

"We don't want to rush anything, Ellis, and there's no need for it anyway. We have time to get it right."

"And after three of these shots I'm done? I'm out of here?"

Tamarov spoke to the man evenly and slowly. "A week between infusions, close monitoring with some restrictions, and after the final dose, within a few days, we should be able to release you and then it's, *'Go west, young man.'* After that, we'll simply have you check in to our facility out there for blood draws and scans and the like. We need to see how your body's doing. Every week at first, then stretch it out to monthly appointments for a while. Pretty soon, we'll barely be an inconvenience to you. You can stop in every year, just like you would for a regular physical, and the rest of your time is your own," he said. "We don't have much in terms of longitudinal data with *Timeserve* so we need to track as much of it as we can. After the first two or three years we'll be little more than a minor nuisance in your life."

"That seems fair," Ellis said as one of the nurses swabbed his arm with alcohol. "Whereabouts on the west coast do you plan to send me anyway?"

"Just outside of Portland, that's where the facility is. Beautiful place, you'll love it there. They're farther north than we are here but the weather's a lot nicer. You won't have to worry about snow anymore."

"I'm good with that."

"We got you a gorgeous house, a good job with nice pay. We don't want a bunch of stressors to skew any of our data on you. I dare say you'll be better off there than you ever were here in New York."

"Seems that way," Ellis said. "I don't know how to thank you for everything you're doing."

"No need, it's like Dr. Stam told you, your participation in our little experiment is payment enough."

Ellis felt there was an earnestness in the doctor's eyes. "Well, thanks nonetheless."

"Now," Tamarov said, motioning to Ellis's arm, "If you wouldn't mind, I like to administer each dose of *Timeserve* myself."

Ellis stretched his arm taut and presented it to the physician. Dr. Stam appeared from in between a sea of white uniforms. She held out the hypodermic needle and syringe to Dr. Tamarov. The milky solution churning within it seemed an unusual ichor, equal parts repulsive and mesmerizing to Ellis, a pus-like plasma, chalcedonic in appearance and swirling with an iridescent sheen. Stam raised the syringe and pressed her thumb to the plunger to remove any air from the chamber. The excitement was palpable among the gathered staff. Tamarov gave a few deep breaths, bunched up the flesh on the back of Ellis's upper arm, stuck the patient with the needle, and flushed in the contents. He held a cotton ball soaked with antiseptic to the spot of the puncture for a few seconds and massaged the bump that had formed beneath Ellis's skin. A nurse then stepped forth and applied a bandage.

Ellis felt the lump. "Is that normal?"

"Completely," Tamarov said. "It'll take some time for the solution to fully absorb into your tissue and bloodstream. You won't feel even the hint of a protrusion on your arm by tomorrow."

"So that's it?"

"That's it."

"It wasn't too bad, considering how it looked."

Tamarov smiled. "Never said it would be. That's one down, two to go," the doctor said. "But now comes your part. It's imperative for the next day or two that you get plenty of rest, take your fluids, stay calm, and just generally follow the directions of the staff that's in charge of caring for you. They're getting their orders directly from myself and Dr. Stam, so they know exactly what you need."

"You're not staying?"

"Oh, you'll see plenty of me, whenever I'm here at Bazemore. But I'm all over the place these days," he said. "I never get to just stick around and watch the fruits of all my labors unfold, I'm afraid, the price I pay for being in demand. I'll admit it was exciting at first, but my place is at Bazemore, not traveling the country to meet with an endless stream of politicians and giving seminars until I lose my voice."

"And Dr. Stam, will she be here?"

Tamarov looked over his shoulder to his colleague. "Not all the time, but more than I will," he continued to massage the knot of liquid under Ellis's bandage. "We'll keep you hooked up here for the time being, just until we can be sure your body accepted the treatment without any issues. I don't expect there'll be any, but it pays to be safe. Just behave normally, as you might if you were relaxing at home. Watch some TV, listen to music, read a book, surf the net if you want. Then later we'll get you on your feet and you can explore the facility a bit. I think you'll find plenty to occupy you here."

"Sounds like a little slice of heaven to me."

"I'm sure it does," Tamarov said. He clasped his hands together. "Okay, enough of my yammering, we'll get out of your hair and let you rest now." He signaled to the medical staff and the room began to empty. "Call the nurse if you need something, or you're feeling anything out of the ordinary."

"Thanks, Doc, I will. You don't mind if I call you Doc, do you?"

"Not at all," he said. "I'll check in with you during the week. Otherwise, you're in good hands with Dr. Stam here and the rest of the staff." He glanced down at his wristwatch. "I should get going. I'll see you again shortly." Tamarov turned and rushed from the room. Only Dr. Stam remained.

"And what should I call you?" Ellis asked.

"Dr. Stam is fine," she told him.

Ellis spent the entirety of that day attached to tubes and wires that plugged into devices that sometimes plugged into other devices that plugged into the walls that fed Tamarov's team second-to-second feedback on his health. The idea of staying in bed all day that had seemed so enticing to Ellis that morning had grown tiresome by day's end. He was fine but he would have been lying if he said he didn't feel *something* on that first day of his treatment. Something inside him that was different. A roiling in his gut that he had a hard time describing (and he did try to describe it to them, as he was asked). He wouldn't say it was necessarily an ill-feeling, more like a motion within him, of activity beneath his skin, like bugs scurrying under sheets.

That night he dreamt. He dreamt of his bright, new life. A life where people weren't angry with him, where he wasn't a target. A life where no one knew him yet. Hadn't made up their minds about him. He dreamed of his big new house; his cushy new job with great benefits and a fat pension; his cool new friends and attractive new sexual partners. And a small part of him, tucked away in the dark background of his mind, a part of him he would never let anyone else see or he would ever give voice to, that secret part of himself might've even been a little happy for the accident. That small, awful part that he kept hidden and, only in dreams, was allowed to hold sway over his thoughts, that part might've even dared to believe that shattering a woman with his car might have actually been the best thing that ever could've happened to him.

Ellis woke.

He opened his eyes and did a little morning pandiculation to assess his body's condition.

Feel okay, same as every morning. Might even be better than most. After a few minutes of rocking and stretching he was convinced. *If there's a problem, one of these machines will pick it up and they'll tell me. Either that or one of these ten-thousand tests they run on me will. They'll probably know how I feel before I do.*

He reached for the buzzer to ask if he could have some breakfast. The one thing he did notice about himself is that he was parched and thoroughly famished. He pressed the button and as he was speaking to someone in the nurse's station, he noticed the two men who brought him in three days prior standing on either side of his door, still in their white pants with matching belts and form-fitting shirts stretched over torsos swollen with muscle.

"Hey!" Ellis called out. One of the men twisted his body around the doorframe to face the patient. "Who are you guys anyway?"

"Hospital staff," the man answered in a low voice.

"What kind of staff? You don't look like nurses, and you sure as hell don't look like doctors," Ellis said.

The other man turned around. "What do we look like to you?"

"I don't know, maybe bouncers on The Love Boat or something."

One of the men stifled his first instinct of a reply, instead simply saying, "We're here to make sure nothing goes wrong, Mr. Pritchard."

The other added, "You're an expensive piece of research now." The first man slapped the other's arm in admonishment when young Nurse Jeannie split between them with her rolling cart and entered the room.

"How are we feeling this morning?"

"Right as rain, I think. Just really hungry, thirsty too."

"That's perfectly normal after a treatment," she said. "Your body's hard at work right now so it figures you'd have an appetite. I'll change your IV and get some more fluid into your system. Wouldn't want you to get dehydrated on my shift." She wheeled the cart close to the man's bed. "I brought you breakfast. Try and have as much of it as you can."

"Thanks, but how did you know-"

"It's a variety of traditional breakfast foods." She raised the lid off a steaming plate of scrambled eggs, hash browns, some meat that looked like sausage but probably wasn't, wheat toast, a fruit plate of blueberries, bananas, strawberries and a few others Ellis didn't recognize, two strangely-colored pancakes, a bowl of oatmeal, and several beverages. "They're all infused with whatever your particular metabolism requires. All your meals will be designed specifically for you, with your nutritional needs in mind. I'm sure you'll find it to your liking," she said. "Be sure to take these supplements too." She pointed to a set of six pills beside the plate. "We have to keep you in the right balance. The doctors have thought of everything when it comes to your health."

"And here I thought I was being punished. I may walk out of here seven years older but in better shape," Ellis said before he downed a large glass of flavored vitamin water and shoved a forkful of nutrient-rich, faux-sausage in his mouth.

"Let me just check your vitals and I'll be on my way," Nurse Jeannie told him.

"Take your time," he said with a smile. "I don't mind one bit."

"I'm sure they've got a busy day lined up for you. Scans and imaging and all of it."

Ellis sighed. "Oh, I'm sure you're right about that, Nurse."

"Don't worry, I'm sure you'll be up and out of bed in no time. Hang in there, sir."

Ellis didn't like being called 'sir' by someone young and pretty but he thought he ought to get used to it. If he was old enough that these twenty-something girls thought to call him 'sir' now, they'd definitely be looking at him differently after this was all over. But he was too ravenous to argue, or even hit on her. From just outside the room another familiar female voice could be heard. Dr. Stam sauntered in.

"Up and anxious I see." She scrolled through an electronic chart she removed from beside the bed and studied the myriad humming and bleeping devices Ellis was connected to. "I understand you responded well all through yesterday and last night, that's good." She studied the chart in her hands several seconds longer. "Everything looks okay here," she said and returned it to the hook. She examined his arm where the injection had been given. "Are you feeling any differently than yesterday, before the treatment? Or would you say you're about the same?"

"The same, more or less. I honestly can't tell. Should I be able to?"

"Not necessarily, at least not at this point. We'll test you continuously over the next week to see if the fundamental changes to your physiology that we're looking for have started, but they may not manifest themselves outwardly for some time, everyone reacts differently."

"Do you think it'll start hurting?" he asked.

"Remember, Ellis, *Timeserve* isn't designed to inflict pain, per se, it's just meant to age you. That's your sentence, the removal of time from your body's life, not for you to feel some preordained level of discomfort. That seems unnecessary and, frankly, a little masochistic—it's the old way of thinking. We're trying to do away with that," she said. "Now don't get me wrong, it may be a little uncomfortable for you at your new age. There's no question that the aging process is not a pleasurable one for most people. I certainly don't get out of bed feeling the same way I did when I was twenty, or even when I was forty for that matter, which wasn't that long ago. Seven years will take some toll on you, I'm sure. But what that will look like, we have no way of knowing. As I said, it's different for different people. I would say in your case, no news is good news at this stage. We're only talking seven years so I would think even after the procedure is complete, you'll still feel like yourself," she told him. "More or less."

"I did have some really vivid dreams last night," Ellis said. "Can't remember exactly what they were about, but I know they were strong."

"The mind is a powerful engine," she said. "That may not be the last of them."

Ellis continued to eat his breakfast. "When do you figure I can get up and look around this place?"

"Take it easy today," she said. "We've got your next couple days pretty jammed. Soon enough though."

"Whatever you say."

*

True to their word, the doctors had Ellis spend much of the ensuing days holed up in his room resting amidst a constant parade of nurses checking monitors, conducting interviews with him, assessing every detail of his physical and mental state, getting more rest, taking copious samples of blood and tissue, visiting the radiology unit, and getting even more rest, with sporadic visits from Dr. Stam and, later, one from Dr. Tamarov on the day of his second injection. In the days following that second shot, Ellis still felt no discernible change in his body, just a growing anxiousness to move. Tamarov's team, confident the man's treatment was going exactly as planned, felt it safe to remove him from the around-the-clock, electronic monitoring Ellis had been receiving in place of hourly check-ins from the nursing staff and the same pair of husky orderlies to keep watch in the hallway in front of his door. They further promised Ellis that the following day he would be allowed to leave his room and take advantage of the numerous amenities that Bazemore had to offer. That night, finally untethered from the equipment that had kept him hostage for more than a week, Ellis could wait no longer. With only one of the sentries on late-night duty, and chatting up Nurse Jeannie at the station down the hall, Ellis decided to sneak out and wander the floor.

Hell, I'm their star experiment, their million dollar—maybe even **billion***—dollar guinea pig. What's the worst they're gonna do if they catch me? Not too much I bet. If I can get past the not-so-watchful eye of Mister Horny Whitepants out there, I should be good.*

He crept out his door and disappeared stealthily around the corner. It felt wonderful to get his legs under him and actually walk again. The physical tests they had him performing were very much the *'follow my finger with your eyes'* and *'let's check your reflexes'* variety. Basic stuff.

But he was past all that now. Two of the three treatments were over. He was ready to go. A man on the move.

He loved how quiet the halls were. Loved the absence of all the unnatural sounds that had inhabited his ears since he arrived. All that technology. He loved hearing only the slap of his feet against the tiled floor, and nothing else. He turned corner after corner, passing endless one-square-foot, baby blue wall tiles, utterly lost, but not caring in the slightest. Doors swung open for him on his command, with nothing more than the push of a pad, and then shut behind him. He made sure to peek through the tiny window housed in the center of each double-door before triggering it though, just to be certain he didn't run into anyone he shouldn't. Anyone that might get him in trouble. Nearly every pathway on the floor was deserted at this hour and, therefore,

305

open to him; he marveled at the sheer immensity of the place. He padded down one hall and as he passed a darkened room, the door swung open suddenly and a feminine figure in a nurse's uniform hastily exited, startling him. It was evident by her reaction that he did the same to her. She removed her mask to take a deep breath, revealing an angelic face. Ellis wondered to himself if Bazemore only hired the youngest and prettiest nurses to their staff.

"Oh, I'm sorry," he said. "I didn't mean to scare you."

Once the shock had worn off, she stared him down. "You're Ellis Pritchard, aren't you? I know about you," she said. "Still running ladies over, I see." There was an acid in her tone and she quickly apologized. "I shouldn't have said that, it was uncalled for."

"Inappropriate too," Ellis told her.

"I'm really sorry."

"But I like inappropriate," he told her. "It means you're being honest."

"You should probably get back to your room, sir. I don't think you should be out of bed this late."

"You might be right. Mind showing me the way back? I have no idea where I am."

The girl was hesitant at first, but Ellis persisted.

"Alright, I'll walk you back," she said.

Ellis followed close behind the young woman, who was keeping a brisk pace. "What's your name, I don't think I've seen you before?"

"Cindy," she said. "You can call me Cindy. Come on now, hurry. Wouldn't want you getting thrown out of the program for this."

"Thanks for not turning me in. I was going a little stir crazy in that room. I needed to stretch my legs and since they said I'd have the chance soon, I got a little antsy and jumped the gun. I probably should've waited."

"I'm sure you'll get the chance to look around."

"I sure hope so, and call me Ellis, would ya? I'm not that old, at least not yet," he said. There was an awkward silence as they meandered back through the hallways. Ellis struggled to keep pace with the nurse. "I'm not looking forward to getting back, I can tell you that. I can't stand being cooped up."

"It's lucky you're here then. Imagine how you'd feel if you went to jail."

"Yeah, I guess I shouldn't complain." They walked on in silence through several more corridors. "It's hard to believe I'm gonna be back in the world in a couple more weeks, maybe with a few more wrinkles."

"Hard to believe," she said in a monotone and lifeless voice.

They passed a large painted mural hanging on the wall: some kind of drip-drip modern art, color-spattered Jackson Pollock thing that Ellis couldn't appreciate at all, but that he found familiar-looking nonetheless. The farther they walked on, in fact, the more and more familiar the surroundings started to seem to him. He knew it was only a matter of time before he was back at his room again.

"I get the feeling you don't like me much, do you, Cindy?"

"Sure I do," she said, as listlessly as before. "What's not to like?"

"You strike me as the kind of person who doesn't pull any punches," he said. "What do you think about this *Timeserve*? Be honest with me."

She stopped, huffed out a breath, and turned to face the man. "It's groundbreaking science, obviously."

"Obviously," Ellis said. "But what do you think about the concept, as a substitute for prison? Talk to me."

She hesitated a moment. "You have to admit this *punishment*—if you want to call it that—feels a little…"

"What? A little what?"

"Neat," she said. "If you want my opinion, it all feels too easy."

"But they're taking seven years off my life, isn't that the punishment? Taking my time, rather than me *doing* time, on the state's dime?"

"Stop it, I know all the philosophical mumbo-jumbo around selling it, but it comes down to money, like everything else. *Timeserve* saves everybody money, but my gut tells me you, and people like you, would be getting off a little too easy," she said. "No offense, I mean, I'm sure you're a real swell guy and all, probably not the monster they say you are on TV, but I can't help the way all this feels to me. Where's the satisfaction for the families? How do they move on like you get to?"

How do they move on?

"I don't make the rules," he said. He could feel his hands starting to clench. "It was a fucking accident, that's all it was. I didn't mean for it to happen, that's why they're called accidents for Christ's sake! I looked away for a second—not even a second—and she's right on top of me. I don't know where she came from but there she was, and I hit her. It's just dumb luck, that's all! If even one thing changes that night none of this happens," he said. "If I don't work late, if it's not raining and I can see better and the roads aren't slick, if that car next to me doesn't lay on the horn at that instant and pull my attention away, if any one of those things doesn't happen, she's still alive.

I didn't do anything wrong. I'm not a bad person. I follow the rules. Don't believe that nonsense you hear in the media about me texting or having the radio cranked, that's not the reason it happened. It was cosmically shitty timing, that's all it was. It could have happened to anyone, and I don't think people in my same circumstance deserve to go to jail. I just don't, okay? I'm sure she made a hundred decisions that day that got her to *that* particular crosswalk at *that* exact time. No one asks what she might have been doing wrong when I hit her. You know why? Because she's the victim, so she can't be wrong. She can't be guilty of anything. I have to be the guilty one. I'm a victim too—a victim of the same dumb luck, of all things." Cindy motioned desperately for him to keep his voice down and he strained to speak under his breath. "It was over for her instantly." He snapped his fingers. "Just like that. She didn't suffer, so why is it so damned important that I need to? Let my punishment match the crime. Why should I have to pay for so long?" he whispered.

"Because everyone pays," she said. She peeked around the corner. "Now shut up and move, I'd hate to see you miss your last treatment."

"Aye, aye, Nurse Ratched."

She spun around and got her face close to his. "Hey, you want honesty, don't get all mad when someone gives it to you," she said. "I don't know how people like you will ever feel any real guilt without having to stare at those bars. You need some regret, Mr. Pritchard. And that takes time... hard time." She started down the hallway again. "Now, if they had some kind of shot that aged you *and* made you feel guilty, that'd be something I could get behind. If you're not gonna serve time in a state prison, you should at least have to serve time in your own. That's how I see it."

"No offense," Ellis said, following closely behind her. "But I'm glad you're not in charge."

Cindy stopped short of the next corridor. "I think you can find your way back from here. Left down there, the next turn take a right, go through the set of doors and you'll see your wing off to the side."

"I don't know why you're helping me? It really doesn't sound like you want to, but thanks anyway."

"I do it because I'm not like you. I actually care about people," she said. "Now get back to your room and stop sneaking around."

*

"You sure you calculated those years right, Doc?" Ellis asked.

Tamarov continued examining Ellis's eyes with the ophthalmoscope. "Been doing this doctor thing a little while, Ellis, pretty sure we figured the dosage correctly," he said. He lowered the light and looked at his patient. "You really don't feel any different today?" he asked. "No aches, no pains, blurred vision, nothing at all?"

"Maybe I'm just one of those people who age gracefully," Ellis said with a smirk. "Is that a problem?"

"No, not at all, just a little unexpected. Your workups show that the *Timeserve* is having a measurable effect on your cells. You *have* aged, physiologically. I suppose it just hasn't manifested itself outwardly yet. It may not for some time, who knows? We're learning here, too." Dr. Tamarov's face held a sullen, far-off look.

"Don't get all morose on me, Doc. Maybe tomorrow I'll surprise you with a gray hair or two."

"What? Oh, I get it." Tamarov gave a single half-hearted chuckle. "I'm not disappointed, I promise. I'm only curious. This whole process fascinates me, as you can well imagine, and sometimes baffles me."

"Hey, what do you say you finally let me out of this room like you promised so I can see the rest of this place?"

Tamarov thought for a moment. "Sure, I think it's safe for you to get out for a bit, do some exercise and get your mind right before the final treatment. I can give you the tour right now if you'd like."

"I would, very much."

The doctor took Ellis around Bazemore, introducing him to all the staff and fellow patients alike that they encountered. He showed him to the workout rooms packed with state-of-the-art, anti-grav gym equipment; the sauna, spa, and therapy pods; the meditation center; the arts and media wing; the virtual viewing bulbs; the café and courtyard; the whole facility that was open to him. Ellis wandered H floor some days, watched the staff at work keeping an eye out to avoid Nurse Cindy at all costs, or spoke to the other patients in the *Timeserve* study. The Monday before his final injection he saw an elderly man in the commons area of the floor reading a magazine. Ellis sat down beside him.

"How you doin', I'm Ellis."

"Name's Ray," the man said.

"They got you here for *Timeserve*, too?"

"Yeah," he said. "How much longer you got?"

"Last dose coming up," Ellis told him.

"Well, you still looking pretty good."

"They only aged me seven years so... I'm not much different." Ellis lowered his eyes. "How much time they serve you with, if you don't mind me asking?"

Ray rubbed at the short, silvery stubble spread over his cheeks. "Forty years," he said. "A few weeks ago, I was a twenty-six-year-old man. Now look at me."

"Jesus Christ," Ellis blurted. "What did you do to get-"

"*That* I do mind you asking about," Ray told him. "It's not something I'm real proud of."

Ellis was silent. The sight of this young man trapped inside an old person's skin suit was sobering to him. Ellis viewed it like a costume you couldn't take off.

"What's it like?" he finally asked the man. "To go from twenty-six to this in a matter of weeks?"

"I'm still processing it, to be honest, but it makes you think, man. It makes you realize just how short the time you got left really is, locked up or not. It makes you hurry things up and get to whatever the hell it was you thought you were going to do with your life."

"What if you don't know what you want?"

"I can tell you this, I got busy figuring it out."

Ellis paused in thought. "It was a good thing then?"

Ray gave a scoff. "Ain't nothing good about losing half your life for some stupid shit you did. It just sharpens your focus, is all."

"It's better than jail though, right?"

Ray laughed. "Damned if I know, man, but if I was stuck in some cell for forty years at least I got forty years to be, to figure it out. It might be a shit forty but it's my shit forty—I get to live it out. I mean, when you send someone to the joint what's the essence of that punishment? They ain't paying nobody back, not in any tangible way. They ain't getting rehabilitated. It's just a lot of sitting around, thinking, and waiting. A lot of sitting and aging. You ask me, the punishment's in the aging itself, losing whatever years you got left."

"Not about going to prison? The monotony of it? Losing your freedom? That's not the real punishment?" Ellis asked.

"What's life, man? It's all monotony. Freedom's just an illusion. We may not have bars on our windows but we're all prisoners. Get up, go to work doing the same exact thing at the same exact time every day, come home and sit on the couch staring at the same faces and the same walls every night. Maybe take a walk outside when you can. Go to bed and do it all over the next day. That's basically what they do in the joint, too.

We stick around these little jails we build, that we're paying for ourselves. We keep 'em clean and dress 'em up but they're still prison cells, no different, just nicer. And the nicer they are, the harder they are to recognize. It's the same shit. We're all doing time no matter where we're doing it. Doing the time ain't the punishment, man," he said. "Losing the time is."

Ellis shook his head. "When you put it that way it's hard to argue with."

"Damn straight it's hard to argue with, because I'm right," Ray said. "Ask yourself, if doing the time was the real punishment wouldn't it be better to let people sit and rot until the day they die rather than killing them? You'd want 'em to suffer, right?" He exhaled a long breath. "But we end them altogether, why is that? Because they did something so terrible that we had to take away whatever time they had left all at once. Take it down to nothing. People fight to stay off death row even though they know they'll spend the rest of their lives locked up, because the proposition of some kind of life is better than the proposition of none at all."

"Sounds like, if you had to choose again, you'd serve out your sentence."

"I don't know," Ray said with a glum chuckle. "I'm just talking. Ask me today and I'd say fuck this *Timeserve* shit, lock me up. But I ain't doing a bid right now," he said. "Put me inside for a dime or two and I might be begging for that shot." He shook his head, hapless. "Ellis, I got no answers for you."

*

A few more, mostly enjoyable, days passed with Ellis taking advantage of Bazemore's amenities, the medical staff constantly monitoring his condition.

He was in better spirits as the clock wound down to his last treatment.

*Now **this** I could get used to,* he thought.

"The DNA came back with a few fluctuations, some changes we'd anticipated," Dr. Stam told him.

"What does that mean?"

"It means that the tests are consistently showing us that you're aging up as we'd hoped. Your final injection tomorrow should continue that trend for another three or four days and, after we keep an eye on you a bit longer, you're finished. You're done." She delivered the news with supreme satisfaction.

"You've been very thorough. I'll give you that."

"Would you have wanted it any other way?" she asked.

"Suppose not," he said. "I'm happy it's coming to an end though, all of it."

"You haven't gotten rid of us completely, remember, not yet," she said. "You'll be coming in plenty once you get to Oregon. We need to know of any long-term effects from *Timeserve*. I don't anticipate it, but science can be unpredictable." She peeled off her latex gloves and threw them into the metal trash bucket. "Still experiencing only minor symptoms?"

"I feel fine. Maybe a little harder getting out of bed in the morning but nothing I won't get used to."

"That's nice to hear. Putting on almost a decade can slow some people down. Others, not a dent. You must have good genes, Ellis. *Timeserve* seems to agree with you. Believe me, it's not that way for everyone who gets it."

"I guess I'm just lucky."

"Maybe so."

"Tell me again, when exactly am I getting out of here?"

"Let's play it by ear after we see how you respond to this last shot."

"Do I have a choice?"

"Not really," she said. "I'm sure you understand by now."

"Yeah, yeah... Hey, I saw photos of the house you guys are putting me in, makes my old place in the city look like a dump. The job seems like a sweet gig, too."

"I know it pays significantly more than your previous job," she said. "We want you to be content, Ellis. We don't want a bunch of new stressors undoing all the work we've put into your treatment."

"I feel like a real V.I.P.," Ellis told her. "And you'll still check me out head-to-toe, just to make sure there's nothing weird going on inside me?"

Dr. Stam smiled at the man. "I think it's safe to say you'll be the most looked-after individual in the entire United States for a while. I promise we won't allow anything to sneak up on you."

"Let's get this last one done and over with then—I can't wait. Through this whole thing, I've never felt better. Maybe it's all the supplements and sleep, maybe it's just where my head's at," he said. "I read this article in your library the other day that was all about how your body absorbs foods differently based on your state of mind. Like, for instance, if you're eating some ultra sugary dessert and you feel really guilty about it, it actually does more harm to your body than if you just ate it and enjoyed the whole experience. Maybe that's how it works with *Timeserve* too. I'm in a good headspace about it so it's not affecting me as strongly as it would if I was worrying like crazy.

"Interesting idea," Stam said, nodding her head. "I wouldn't rule it out completely, definitely bears looking into further." She slapped him on the top of his thigh and pointed her finger at him. "Perhaps you missed your calling, Ellis. You could've been quite a scientist."

*

The next morning Dr. Tamarov and Dr. Stam arrived at Ellis's room earlier than before.

"I hear you're anxious for your last blast of *Timeserve?*" Tamarov asked.

"You heard right. As nice as this place you got here is, Doc, I'd love to actually have a life again."

"Ask and you shall receive." The doctor unsheathed the needle for the last time and once again injected the pearly solution into Ellis's arm. The man closed his eyes and imagined it flowing through him, filling him, carrying his sentence to every fleshy extremity of his body. He took it in openly, freely, welcoming it into his tissue like mother's milk. A type of baptism. An absolution. He slept long and well that night. For Ellis Pritchard, it was over. The nightmare was finally finished.

Ellis woke.

He was thirsty, which was nothing new, and with the slightest headache at the base of his skull. He got out of bed and looked outside his door. There was the frenetic movement of hospital staff like ivory mice, scurrying and tending to the patients for whom he assumed there were all sorts of strange experiments going on. He waited and they quickly disappeared through doorways and around walls just as rodents would, leaving the walkways empty.

That's better.

He made his way immediately to Bazemore's café. Once he got there, he guzzled three glasses of juice before filling a fourth to take with him to his seat along with a tray of breakfast. He took a bit more than he normally would knowing this would probably be one of the last times he'd have his meals prepared for him, outside of patronizing a restaurant.

He went to the pool to do some laps because, when would he ever have a heated, indoor pool at his disposal again?

Maybe I should ask them to have one put in the new house, for my mental well-being?

Shit, they might go for it.

Mid-lap he heard his name called over the intercoms. They wanted him at Tamarov's office.

Great, another check in.

Ellis toweled off, changed into dry clothes, and returned to H floor. There, in his office, he found Tamarov seated at his desk, thumbing through some paperwork.

"Ellis, have a seat." Tamarov shoved the papers into a folder and swiveled his chair to face the man. "You know the drill, what's new?"

"Nothing much. I feel fine. A little tired maybe, dehydrated this morning, same ole, but fine. Had a headache earlier that seems to have gone away."

"Fantastic," he said. "All the same we'll have you go in for testing. Stick around the room today if you don't mind."

"Doc, how much longer do you figure-"

"Ellis, I know what you're going to say. I know you want to get out of here and I'm just as anxious to get you to Portland, but we have to be certain your body can handle these treatments. We need to make sure it behaves correctly."

"What do you mean?"

"I mean that we have to be sure that the *Timeserve* worked on you. It wouldn't be much of a punishment if you weren't actually aging the way we intended you to."

"I thought you said I *was* showing signs of aging?"

"You are, you are. We need it to continue to the point where it reaches your seven-year sentence. You weren't nearly there after the second shot. Hopefully when this last one kicks in your body will respond accordingly and level off at that seven-year mark, give or take."

"What are you telling me? There's a chance the treatment didn't take?"

"There's always that possibility," Tamarov said with a little hesitation.

"What then? Am I going back to prison?"

"No, of course not, that road's no longer an option for us. It just means we'd have to try again until we get it right."

"So, I could be stuck here for God-knows-how-long?"

Tamarov put his hands up and a few words stammered from his mouth. "I'm not going to tell you it couldn't happen," he said. "Anything's on the table but, listen to me Ellis, we've got data, I'm talking hard evidence, that you have aged significantly since the treatments started. Have some faith, we're on the right path."

Ellis scoffed.

"I thought you liked it here?" Tamarov said.

"That's not the question, Doc. Your place is top notch, I just don't want to spend the rest of my life being studied like an animal. You can understand that, right?"

"That's ridiculous. You're not going to spend the rest of your life here, Ellis. Sit tight, let us work, keep doing what you're doing. We have no reason to believe *Timeserve* won't work the way it should with you." Tamarov stepped out from behind the desk, latched onto Ellis's arm, and led him to the door. "You're doing everything we ask. This'll all be over sooner than you think, I'm sure. Trust me."

He opened the door to let his patient out.

"Okay, you're the boss, Doc."

Ellis returned to his room. He felt somewhat rundown now. He figured the after effects of his last treatment and his early morning swim, combined with the worrisome exchange he had with Tamarov, had taken a toll on both his body and his psyche. He always felt a little off the day after a flu shot, why would this be any different? *Good idea to get some rest.* He laid on his bed and allowed his mind room to wander.

Don't get antsy now, it's almost over. Play their game—you know how this works. Gotta throw them a bone now and then, give them something to put in their charts. They want to see their little treatment at work. You don't have to lie to them, just exaggerate a bit. No harm in that.

Ellis woke.

Nurse Jeannie was in the room with him, restocking the cabinets with supplies. "How's my favorite patient today?" she asked. "I hope I wasn't making too much noise."

Ellis feigned a groan. "Back's bothering me, arthritis maybe, I don't know."

Jeannie reached for the touchpad by the bed and started recording his symptoms. "Anything else?" she said attentively.

"I think I noticed a little more gray than usual by my temples, right in here." He fingered the strands of hair on either side of his head. "I guess that's par for the course though, huh?"

The nurse examined his scalp with great interest. "Uh-huh," she muttered, then tapped again at the pad. "Is that it?"

"Yup, that's it, just a little creakier in general today than I was yesterday," he said. "I'll call you if I notice any other changes." He thought he'd begin his ruse with a few simple, vague details. He didn't want to make it seem too obvious.

Christ, these people are so easy to manipulate! You just have to know what they want from you and then give it to them—been at that my whole life. I'm so good at getting into character that I think my body even believes what I'm saying, like a psychosomatic thing... unreal.

"I'll bring this to the doctors," she said. "They'll be very interested to read it." She observed Ellis closely. "You do look tired, Mr. Pritchard, I think I see it in you now. You seem older."

A quiet smile grew on his face. "Definitely," he said.

"I'll be right back. We'll get some more samples from you."

"Whatever you need," he said.

Nurses came back within the hour to not only take blood and tissue samples, but perform a whole new set of diagnostics. Dr. Stam showed up later that afternoon with another team of nurses who immediately woke Ellis from a nap and ran through the same tests again. "They tell me you've been getting some stronger reactions to the treatment?"

"That's right. I'm sure feeling those extra years now," Ellis told her. He was groggy from his nap but decided that this would be a good opportunity to sit up and fake a dizzy spell. He placed his hands on the mattress to bluff steadying himself.

"Take it easy," Stam said. "You're not as young as you used to be."

"Yeah," he said. "Gotta remember that part." Still groggy, he tried to shake out the cobwebs from his skull but no matter how hard he tried, his eyesight remained blurred and he could barely make out the doctor's voice. "I guess it's kind of hitting me all at once," he said.

"There will be an adjustment period for you, Ellis. Every person who's ever lived has had time to get used to the aging process gradually. It's a luxury I'm afraid you're not going to be afforded. It'll be a shock at first, but give it a few days, this is why we insist on keeping you here so long after the treatment ends."

Ellis ran his thumb and forefinger over the ridges of his eyes. "This is different."

Stam's brow furrowed. "Different than this morning?"

Ellis closed his eyes and let out a labored breath. "I might have, uh, misrepresented my symptoms a little this morning."

"Misrepresented?"

"Lied," he said. "But just a little. I did feel something, but not this."

"Why would you do that?"

"I didn't want you and Dr. T to think your treatment wasn't working," he said. "And I wanted to get out of here. I thought if I played up the effects a smidge, or even invented a few, I might be able to get discharged sooner."

Stam sighed loudly. "Mr. Pritchard, it's absolutely imperative that you be honest with us at all times, otherwise the data we gather from you is meaningless, it's that important. You may have already jeopardized this trial."

"It was only this morning, I swear."

"Then the lightheadedness I just witnessed was genuine?"

"Well, no, not that part. I was still acting then."

"Mr. Pritchard, you clearly told me-"

"I know what I said!"

The room fell silent. Dr. Stam took a step back and pulled one of the nurses close to her. She whispered something in her ear and the nurse quickly disappeared into the hallway. One of the other nurses pressed a red, triangular button on the wall and huddled with the rest of the team on the opposite side of the room.

"I'm sorry, okay, I screwed up. I made up the part about being dizzy, but everything after that point was the God's honest truth."

Stam took a step toward the bed with her palms raised. "Ellis, look at it from my point-of-view. How can I believe what you're telling me right now is the truth if you just admitted you were lying about your symptoms a minute ago?"

"You're right, Doctor, you're right, I don't know what I was thinking. It was stupid of me to try to fool you like that. It's just that you guys said I would feel these effects and when I didn't, I got scared. It won't happen again— AAAHHH!!!" A shard of pain lodged in Ellis's brain. He clutched the sides of his head in agony.

The two large orderlies arrived at the room and Stam motioned them towards the bed. They immediately strapped Ellis's hands and legs down and the team went to work on him. Within minutes he was fully sedated.

"Do a full workup on him and we'll see where we're at," Stam told the team. "You may not be telling me the truth, Mr. Pritchard, but the numbers don't lie."

*

In his artificial sleep Ellis Pritchard dreamt uneasy dreams. Dreams inscrutable. Dreams of viscous, flowing energies foreign to him, both microscopic and cosmic at the same time. Dreams of life, of systems linking and working in unison, of organisms swarming with activity like a million angry anthills. Slowly these pictures in his mind shrank and shrank until nothing remained but the dark behind his slumbering eyelids.

Ellis woke.

The pain in his head was gone. So, too, were his shackles. It was quiet, peaceful. He rolled onto his side and found that the space between his shoulder blades was on fire with ache. He rolled his shoulders to stretch out the muscles when he heard the loud popping of the vertebrae in his neck, a sound like crinkling paper. He swiveled his head until the awful ratcheting subsided and finally stopped altogether. He slowly raised himself up and swung his legs to step off the bed when he realized that it was not only his spine that was stiff and pained, it was his entire body. All the muscles seemed to house some ache; the joints in his knees, hips, wrists, fingers, and toes throbbed with it as well. He stepped off the bed with difficulty and stood on the cool hospital floor.

I have to piss.

He shuffled to the darkened bathroom and relieved himself, with some effort, when he heard the sounds of movement from outside the door. There was a knock. "Mr. Pritchard, are you alright?" a woman's voice asked tentatively. As he slowly pulled the door open, Nurse Jeannie was standing in front of him with a smile on her face that melted away when she caught sight of Ellis. She withdrew instinctively before, as if remembering her station, she lunged forward to take hold of the man's arm.

"Let's get you back into bed," she said.

Her startled reaction, likewise, threw the man himself.

What did she see?

He looked around him in the bathroom, frantic, while the gentle tug of the nurse led him away from…

The mirror.

There was something in the mirror. Something caught his eye. Something ghostly.

He pulled back against her grip and saw in that mirror the sight of himself. His hair, previously squirrel brown, was now a pale and lifeless yellow, like straw. And at every root were shafts of dull silver, thin and unruly, as if another man's head was overtaking his own. The flesh of his face sagged: his cheeks, under his eyes, and all around his mouth. He lifted his hands to touch it, to press his fingers into its putty-like appearance. It was like a mask to him.

The reflection was dreamlike, fuzzy-edged and out-of-focus. He blinked furiously in an attempt to clear his vision, to rid it of this hideous visage and restore it to normality. But it would not clear. *Dear God, why won't it go away?* The nurse's pull finally overtook him and he left that horrific image behind in the bathroom mirror, though it would remain seared into his psyche. But there was more still: He felt fundamentally weaker. Compromised. Vulnerable. Not only in body, but even in mind and spirit. He could feel it. He shambled back to bed with the nurse's help.

"Where's Dr. Tamarov? I want to see him."

"He's at a conference in Toronto," Nurse Jeannie said. "He left a couple days ago."

"Get him back. I need Tamarov."

"I'll find the physician on duty, hold on," she told him before she rushed from the room.

A young man arrived within seconds followed by a nurse. He was part of Tamarov's medical team, Ellis knew that. He recognized the man's face watching in the background whenever Tamarov held court. "Stay calm, let me get a look at you," he said.

"Something's not right!"

"Just breathe," the doctor said as he eased Ellis's body down onto the mattress. "Nurse, let's get some more help in here please, and call Dr. Stam."

He turned his attention back to Ellis. "I can imagine how much of a shock this must be to you."

"No, you cannot imagine," Ellis told him forcefully.

"We'll run some tests and figure out what happened."

"No more tests!"

The doctor prepped a sedative and administered it to Ellis. "Try to relax now. You're in good hands. Dr. Stam is in the building and Dr. Tamarov's flight was delayed, but he'll be arriving from the airport shortly."

"I want it back," Ellis said, already woozy from the sedative. "I want my time back."

*

That night was not night at all. Ellis was day-sleeping, tranquilized into a dreamless, formless void. He was roused by the voice of Dr. Stam and he opened his eyes to the hazy image of her face backed by several other staff members.

"Wake up, Ellis. Are you with us? Wake up."

Ellis droned a barely conscious, "Mmm-hmm." Stam was speaking to him, at least that's what he thought. Her lips were moving, but Ellis could barely perceive the words she was saying. It was all a muffled fog of sounds, as if she were underwater. He shook his head then tapped his right ear. The doctor placed two small nodules into the man's ears, then she hung a device around her neck and turned it on.

"Can you hear me better?" she asked.

Ellis nodded and told her that he could but even his own words were distant. Still, the sound of her voice ringing clearly in his ears eased him.

"What's happening to me?"

Dr. Stam paused a moment as if to gather her myriad thoughts and figure out the best way to relay them to her patient. "We've gone over everything, Ellis." She paused again. "It appears that the last dose of *Timeserve* you received, obviously, affected your body adversely," she said. "It's aged you much more than we planned."

"How much more?"

"Thirty-nine or forty, maybe forty-one more years," she said. Ellis winced as he raised himself up in the bed. "Don't move, we'll make you comfortable. Are you in pain right now?" Ellis nodded. "We'll give you something for that," she said. "And we're monitoring all your major systems until we figure out something we can do to help you."

Ellis forced a dry swallow down his throat. "How could you miss the mark by that much? I don't understand."

"I don't have any good answers for you. All I can tell you is that we're working as hard as we can to-"

"Fix it."

"Yes, we're working-"

"*Fix it!*"

She turned her gaze to the rest of the team and then back to Ellis.

"We can't," she said.

Ellis's body began to jitter. "I can't stay like this," he said. "I can't stay this age. I was supposed to have more time, much more time."

"I know you were," she said. She took his hand. "Ellis, you don't understand. You're not staying like this."

"What do you mean?"

Her face was the dourest he'd ever seen it. "I mean... the process hasn't stopped yet," she told him. "You're *still* aging."

"How do you know?"

Dr. Stam reached over to the tray beside the bed to pick up a large hand mirror. She held it in front of the man's face. Ellis could see that his scalp was now dotted with nothing more than wisps of stringy hair. Much of it on the topmost portion of his head had fallen out and littered the pillow behind him. The skin was flaking and mottled with so many liver spots that his scalp resembled a snakeskin. His face was a collection of deep troughs made of flesh—loose, corrugated skin with crisscrossing wrinkle lines like a crumpled roadmap, the draperies of time and age. His eyes, made into dead white gems from cataracts; these cloudy opals set perfectly within a blanket of derma.

Ellis slapped the mirror away. "How old am I?"

Dr. Stam's face was strained. "We don't know," she told him. "But we're trying to stop it, or slow it down."

"Where's Tamarov?"

"On his way," she said.

"He should be here." Ellis elbowed the soft mattress repeatedly. "Where's that nurse now? I want her to see me like this. I want to ask her if she still thinks I'm getting off easy."

"Who told you that?"

"One of the night nurses, what's her name? Cindy."

"Don't worry, we'll take care of that," she said. "In the meantime, just try to relax until Dr. Tamarov arrives. They're waiting for him at the airport now." Stam motioned the head nurse to follow her into the hallway. "Do you know who he's talking about?"

"He could be showing some signs of early-onset dementia," she told Stam. "We've never had anyone by that name on staff here."

The doctor clasped her fingers together into a tight ball and brought it to her lips. "I see... let me know if he loses any further lucidity. I'll be waiting for word on Tamarov's helicopter."

"Yes, Doctor."

*

Hours passed before Tamarov touched down on Bazemore's helipad. The doctor stepped off and was promptly escorted through the access stairwell where he was met by his team.

"Can someone please talk to me!" Tamarov stomped down the hallway leading to his office surrounded by several of his inner circle. "I go away for a day or two and all hell breaks loose with one of the test subjects? How did this happen?"

Dr. Stam, in her heels, struggled to keep pace with the older doctor. "Everything was normal until yesterday when he started showing signs of abnormally accelerated aging."

"It came out of nowhere," another chimed in. "It shouldn't have happened."

"And yet, it did," Tamarov said. They all arrived at his door and the doctor dismissed the rest of his staff, all except Dr. Stam. They entered the office and Tamarov slammed the door behind him.

"We tested the hell out of this thing, Marjorie. It works, we know it does, so what went wrong with this guy at the last minute?"

She lowered her eyes and wagged her head, "I have no idea."

"I oversaw the whole process. I did everything, *we* did everything right. I'm sure of it."

She put her arm around the man. "We did, Lionel."

"I gave him all three shots myself," he said. Then his eyes lit up. "You don't think someone got to the *Timeserve*, altered it? Senator-What's-His-Name would do anything to kill this project. Do you think sabotage is-"

"New science is unpredictable, you know that," she said. She placed her hands firmly on his shoulders and looked him dead in the eyes. "We pick up the pieces and we start again, that's all. Try to figure out what went wrong this time and we move forward. That's how this works."

Tamarov was silent. In thought. Then…

"Let me see him."

The two doctors arrived at Ellis's door.

"There must be something we can do for him," Tamarov said before entering the room.

"I think you should see him yourself."

The doctors opened the door to Ellis's room and a sea of pristine, downy white uniforms parted to allow them through to the patient, as if they were walking through a cloud. Tamarov approached the bedside and pulled back the sheet. There, curled into a fetal ball, lay the body of Ellis Pritchard. Bones poked out of the tawny, leathery sack that his skin had become. It was shriveled and as delicate-looking in places as vellum.

The desiccated body, filled with deep grooves and depressions where there had once been healthy tissue, was now devoid of all musculature, had lost its hair and, instead of a man, resembled the mummified remains of some long dead creature. His enlarged cranium sat precariously on a too-tiny neck that could no longer support its weight and the body gave off an unmistakably stale, pungent smell—a longing for imminent decay. Tamarov leaned over and placed his hand on Ellis.

"I'm sorry," he told the man. "I failed you."

Ellis's eyes moved to the doctor's face. He parted his lips and began to speak, though his voice was barely above a whisper. Tamarov bent over to listen.

"I... can... feel it all... slipping away..." Ellis said. "Soon there will be... nothing of me... left."

Ellis Pritchard closed his eyes.

This time, he did not wake.

Tamarov stood up straight and left the room. Dr. Stam followed close behind and as they separated themselves from the rest of the staff Stam touched the doctor's elbow, stopping him. "You're not a failure, Lionel. This was an anomaly, it happens." She grabbed his arm and turned him round to face her. "It was dumb luck, nothing more. Just dumb luck."

*

Two doctors stood in a darkened room enveloped by advanced medical gadgetry. At its center was a clear, anti-incubation tank with an unconscious infant encapsulated inside.

"There's still a lot of brain activity," the first doctor observed.

"That's normal," the other said while his gloved hands fidgeted with the floating virtual controller. "He's probably just dreaming."

The first doctor gawked through the glass at the encased child. "What do you think a person being de-aged dreams about?" she asked. "I wonder what's going on in our little Ellis's mind?"

"Beats me," the male doctor said while adjusting the precise chemical environment inside the tank. "Just keep winding the clock all the way back on him and hope that next time he lives his life he doesn't end up making the same stupid mistakes he made this time."

She craned her neck to glare at him. "A little harsh, don't you think?"

"What? I don't think I'm being harsh at all," he said. "We could be letting these poor bastards sit in jail their whole lives, or kill them straight-off." He made a throat-cutting gesture with his hand that drew a begrudging smirk out of his colleague. "Now that's just barbaric, I can't believe we ever did that kind of thing."

"Yeah, at least nowadays we give people a second chance. I think everyone deserves that. We all make dumb mistakes sometimes." She crouched down beside the tank to get face-to-face with the tiny figure inside. "Still, I wonder what weird dreams are playing out in that head of his right now."

"Probably dreaming about growing up again," he said. "When I was a kid, I couldn't wait to be older."

IF YOU ENJOYED THIS BOOK...

Please leave a review on Goodreads, Amazon, Google, wherever you choose, and please share a comment on your social media platforms and tell your fellow readers, if you are comfortable doing so. Getting books in front of readers is an ever-increasing challenge as technology makes it easier to get something out there.

This book took the author years to write, and another year working with me to publish this version. So, please, tell the booksellers at your favorite bookstores, follow the author via his website (**www.cdelguercio.com**) and social media, and please let Phase 5 know what you thought of his collection at **www.phase5publishing.com**.

And please do the same for all the books you enjoy, especially those by independent publishers and authors, who often have trouble getting the attention of readers. Every sale and exposure is appreciated by them. Vote in book awards contests if you can, buy directly from authors when you can, and appreciate the dedication and courage it takes to finish a book and put it out there. Thank you, on behalf of Christopher L. DelGuercio, Phase 5, and all the indies out there. Be well and share the joy of a good book.

About the Author, Christopher L. DelGuercio

Christopher L. DelGuercio is a writer, teacher, editor, and lecturer from Syracuse, New York. He does this with the endless encouragement and understanding of his wife, Kathleen, as well as his son, Gabriel, and Shih Tzu, Jasper. He writes when it's quiet, in a farseeing place where he can stretch out and let his mojo rise. Mr. DelGuercio is a lifelong Central New Yorker and graduate of The State University of New York at Oswego.

A creator and purveyor of speculative fiction for nearly a quarter-century, he began his writing career seated alone at a tiny desk in Liverpool, New York. Now he writes, seated alone, at a tiny desk in Clay, New York. In between there were stops at tiny desks in Watertown, New York; Cicero, New York; Baldwinsville, New York; and Fulton, New York. A lot of places, a lot of desks… and a lot of writing.

In the realm of storytelling, he is a lover of all that is weird and wonderful, sublimely surreal, a fan of the fanciful and the phantasmagoric. If the tale is preternatural or mysterious or astonishing in nature, if it's well-written and blows your hair back, chances are good he can get into it.

Mr. DelGuercio has authored many long and short stories alike, including the CNY Book-of-the-Year nominated novella, Eden Succeeding. His particular brand of "fantastic fiction" has appeared in print and on the internet for over fifteen years in many magazines, e-zines, serializations, anthologies, and podcasts. He's published many yarns since 2007, even more than contained in this collection, and produced many more recently, culminating in the publication of *An Unsettled Score*, which brings together twenty of his best past and present tales into one magnum opus.

In addition to his years of writing, DelGuercio has served as editor for multiple novels from up-and-coming local authors, served as a fiction writing instructor at the YMCA's Downtown Writers Center since 2009 (where he also co-founded the Young Authors Academy), and has given numerous presentations on the writing process at CNY-area high schools. He is currently the faculty advisor for the Liverpool Literary Society.

He can be contacted through his website, www.cdelguercio.com.

Other Publications

"I Am Tellis Moore" (short story), *Forbidden Speculation* (print anthology), December 2007

"The Mythic Pixecide" (short story), *Chaos Theory: Tales Askew* (podcast), Spring/Summer Edition 2007

"Everyone's Got Problems" (short story), *Tabloid Purposes IV: Something Macabre This Way Comes* (print anthology), 2007

"The Mythic Pixecide" (short story), *Quantum Muse* (webzine), January 2007

Other Books by Phase 5 Publishing

Sheleasoun: Book I of Beneath the Echoes of Memory by Brandy Wayne
    A light fantasy adventure novel
    Classification: Fantasy/Teen Fantasy
    Appropriate for Teens and Adults, some older children

Nerve Zero by Justin Robinson
    A zero-g noir novel
    Classification: Science Fiction
    Appropriate for adults

Dissent: Book I of The Nexus by Thomas Olbert
    A science fiction novel
    Classification: Science Fiction
    Appropriate for adults

Agents of Paradise by Christopher A. Miller
    A science fiction novel
    Classification: Science Fiction
    Appropriate for Teens and adults

Short Fictions, Volume 1
    An anthology of science fiction and fantasy short stories by Allen Wold, Sergey Gerasimov, Michelle Herndon, K.R. Gentile, Nanna P. Vej, James McCarthy and Arnold Cassell.
    Classification: Science Fiction and Fantasy
    Appropriate for mature children, teens and adults

3 Tales of Horror
    An anthology of horror novellas, which were also published separately: *The Solution* by Rick McQuiston; ...*The Colour of Time* by K.R. Gentile; and *Eden Succeeding* by Christopher L. Delguercio
    Classification: Horror
    Appropriate for adults